# THREE'S COMPANY

*Also by Alfred Duggan and available in the NEL series :*

KNIGHT WITH ARMOUR
THE LADY FOR RANSOM
COUNT BOHEMOND
FOUNDING FATHERS
ELEPHANTS AND CASTLES
WINTER QUARTERS
THE CUNNING OF THE DOVE

# Three's Company

ALFRED DUGGAN

NEW ENGLISH LIBRARY
TIMES MIRROR

First published in 1958 by Faber and Faber Ltd.
© Alfred Leo Duggan, 1958

*

FIRST NEL PAPERBACK EDITION NOVEMBER 1974

*

NEL Books are published by
New English Library Limited from Barnard's Inn, Holborn, London E.C.1.
Made and printed in Great Britain by Hunt Barnard Printing Ltd., Aylesbury, Bucks.

45002012 6

# CONTENTS

# PROLOGUE
## 78 B.C.

Never before had Rome seen such a funeral. The head of the procession reached the Forum before the corpse on its towering bier had left the house. By themselves, the veterans who marched before their dead leader made an army great enough to overawe the City. But they marched unarmed, in the decent grey togas of mourning; for their old general, though retired, had nevertheless died master of Rome; and the sensible constitution he had established would endure after his death. Behind the great army of veterans came the pontiffs, grouped in their colleges before the images of the great gods who cared for the welfare of Rome; even the gods wore mourning. After the pontiffs the Vestals rode in their sacred chariots. At the rear of the religious procession marched in solitary state the Pontifex Maximus, controller of the Luck of Rome.

Then came the magistrates of the City. First the young quaestors, dignified in their official togas. Next the two curule aediles, their consecrated chairs, decked with numinous ivory, carried before them. Then the praetors, whose attendants also carried ivory chairs; before each praetor marched two lictors, displaying the fasces, the bundles of rods with an axe in the midst, which were the sign that these magistrates had power to flog or kill.

Behind the praetors marched nearly every Senator in Rome, more than two hundred of them. Not quite all of them were there; for this great procession was a political demonstration as well as a display of public grief. For all that the dead man had been supreme in Rome for many years, he still had political opponents in the Senate.

The tall bier, surrounded by professional mourners and the images of the gens Cornelia, could already be seen in the distance when the supreme embodiment of official sorrow defiled into the Forum. Behind twelve lictors walked this year's holder of the military and civil authority of the republic, Quintus Lutatius Catulus the Consul. He wore the grey toga of mourning, even now veiling his head as though he were in the act of serving the gods; for he was to offer sacrifice to the genius of the dead man as soon as the pyre was lit.

'Where's father?' young Marcus Aemilius Lepidus called into the ear of his pedagogue, in a kind of shouted whisper. He must shout to be heard above the frenzied cheering of the crowd; but he had enough common sense, even at twelve years of age, not to broadcast that question among the bystanders.

'Father ought to be there,' he continued, 'beside old Catulus. He's just as grand as the other Consul, even if his name comes second in the proclamations because he didn't get quite so many votes. He told me so himself, when I asked him. The republic and the City are ruled by two Consuls equal in power. Have those Senators put another slight upon father? Do you think that if I shouted "Up the Lepidi" there are enough of our clients within hearing to start a riot?'

'Be quiet, young master, for your own sake as well as for mine. We ought not to be here at all, as you know very well. If it comes out that we stood in this crowd you will be beaten and I might be turned adrift.'

'We came only to see the show, because never before has there been anything so wonderful. When the bier passes I shall shout for joy, because the old brute's dead at last. They may think I am cheering *him*, but you and I will know different. All the same, something must have happened to father. He went out this morning with his lictors, and we all took it for granted he was going to the funeral.'

'Be easy, young master. Nothing has happened to your father. Here we are on the edge of the Forum, with citizens all round us. If one of the Consuls had been mixed up in a brawl the news would be here in a flash.'

The news was already travelling through the Forum, but because it was not very important news it did not travel very quickly.

'Have you heard about Lepidus the Consul?' A pompous merchant two rows before them in the crowd had turned round to spread information among his fellow-citizens. 'He was outside the house as the procession started. He wore full insignia, and had all his lictors with him, so they thought he was waiting to take his place among the mourners. Instead he tried to prohibit the whole show! He told them such extravagant display was against the law, *his* law. No one took any notice, so the silly demagogue called up his lictors and went home again. It's a shame that *he* should be burned with only one Consul to honour his ashes.'

8

'It's a shame that *he* should be mourned by even one Consul. We are free citizens of a free city.' That was the voice of an angry old man at the back of the crowd.

'Shut up, grandpa. There may be others here who agree with you, but any soothsayer will tell you that it brings bad luck to speak evil of *him* while his veterans march through the Forum.' That was an anonymous voice.

'Here come the incense, and the images,' shouted the peda-gogue, anxious to end this threatening political exchange. 'Mercy me, what a lot of images! Can anyone tell me, who was the Cornelius who was twice Consul, triumphed as praetor, *and* won the civic crown?'

Several bystanders volunteered different identifications, and the dangerous moment passed.

This was the part of the procession which, by infringing the sumptuary laws, had incurred the vain prohibition of the Consul. There were more than two hundred litters full of vastly expensive spices and Arabian incense, and two life-size figures, of a Consul and his lictor, made entirely of this incense; these would be burned on the pyre. There were more hired mourners and musi-cians than had ever been assembled before in the history of the City. There was a golden casket for the ashes, covered with a gauzy veil of purple.

There were also images in great numbers. But the law could say nothing to this, for they were the deathmasks of eminent deceased Cornelians, and it was the right of their descendant to have them carried at his funeral. Behind each bust walked a masked actor, clad in the official insignia of the dead ancestor. Every citizen could read the stereotyped marks of distinction which denoted the officers and honours once held by the living man.

Finally there staggered by the towering bier. On it lay, in his full official robes, Lucius Cornelius Sulla, Triumphator, Consul, Dictator, honoured by the Senate with the agnomen of Felix, in all but name monarch of Rome.

There would be speeches before the torch was applied to the pyre and all this magnificence went up in smoke. But speeches in praise of Sulla did not interest young Marcus Lepidus, whose house was in opposition to the ruling faction. With his peda-gogue he slipped away unnoticed, to return to the family man-sion where an angry Consul was saying what he thought of Dictators who broke their own laws.

In the autumn of the same year young Marcus idled away an afternoon staring at the rain from the portico of a country villa.

9

He ought to have been in Rome, enjoying the envy of his school-fellows and the casual notoriety in the street that was the due of the Consul's son. Instead, just because his father was at odds with the Senate, he had been packed off to waste half this precious year in the country. Such grandeur would never come again. There had been statesmen who held the Consulship more than once, but he knew in his heart that Father was not great enough for that. Here it was November, and in January he would be no more than the son of the wealthy patrician Aemilius Lepidus. It was a shocking waste of golden months.

His mother's despondency added to the gloom. Women were faint-hearted by nature, and she had the excuse that her father had been killed in civil war. Or rather, he had been murdered by those beastly Optimates, after he had surrendered on the promise of a fair trial. At the time he had been a tribune, one of the consecrated protectors of the people whose persons should never be harmed; but that only went to show what Optimates were like. All the same, that was a long time ago, twenty years and more. Since then the murderous proscriptions of the tyrant Sulla had brought peace and order, even at the cost of freedom and justice. Everyone agreed that there could never be another proscription; the memory of that terrible time of slaughter was burned into the heart of every citizen. Equally there could never be another civil war; remembering the stories of their fathers, the soldiers would refuse to fight fellow-Romans.

Grandfather Saturninus had met his fate thirteen years before Marcus was born, but some of the older servants still had stories to tell of him. At school they taught you that he had been a wicked man, who wanted to cancel all debts and free every slave, and in general undo the work of civilisation; and that was the general opinion of the gentry. Even Mother did not seem proud of her father's political programme. But he had heard her maintain that if his revolution had succeeded grandfather Saturninus would have made himself tyrant of Rome, and that it had very nearly succeeded. She seemed to imply that to fall fighting for such a splendid prize was evidence of a noble spirit.

The feud had begun with the murder of Tiberius Gracchus, more than fifty years ago. (That crime had been committed by Optimates. They had shed first blood. They were the aggressors.) Even a boy studying modern history at school could not keep track of all the changes and chances of political life since then; the sudden *coups*, the murders, the open wars and the secret assassinations. But since the death of Gracchus the struggle had continued, between wicked oligarchical Optimates and noble freedom-loving Populars. It would still be going on when he,

Marcus, was grown up; and he must play his part in it.

But the struggle would now be waged constitutionally, in the Forum. There would be no more wars, never a second proscription. Sulla had seen to that, by his overwhelming victory in the field and the bloody repression that followed it. Therefore an earnest young Popular must learn the technical details of law and ritual, and the art of rhetoric; so that in due time he might stand for public office, win his election, and during his magistracy further the Popular cause. Marcus worked hard at his lessons, for Nature had not granted him a quick wit.

It was a pity that he had been born too late, when all the fighting was over (in spite of Mother's fears). Never again would a hero risk his head to free the people, or to make himself tyrant of Rome. Life was dull, and this rain would not stop before sunset. Time passed slowly. . . .

Then brother Scipio rode up out of the mist to announce that the civil wars had begun all over again, and that the Popular army was led by his father. Hastily Marcus adjusted his ideas.

Until six years ago brother Scipio had been brother Gnaeus, heir to all the wealth and influence of the Aemilii Lepidi. Now he was no longer in law a brother, not even a kinsman; for he had been legally adopted into the gens Cornelia, to be heir to the even greater wealth and influence of the Cornelii Scipiones. About the same time brother Lucius had become brother Paullus, in law still a distant kinsman; for he had taken over the heritage of the extinct Aemilii Paulli. So he was still an Aemilius, though no longer a brother. Marcus, the third son, six years younger than Scipio and four years younger than Paullus, found himself legally an only son and heir to his father.

But of course, when it comes to fighting, blood is thicker than the legal tie of adoption. Marcus Aemilius Lepidus the Consul was gathering an army in Etruria, intending to march on Rome and overthrow the Optimate government; Gnaeus Scipio had slipped out of the City to join his standard. He had turned aside on his journey to convey the Consul's instructions to his family.

He sat back in a comfortable chair in the warmest room in the house, sipping hot wine while a servant massaged his thighs. He looked surprisingly adult, nearer twenty-eight than eighteen, dandling his long sword which lent him confidence to give orders to his own mother.

'You understand, madam? You are not to leave this villa on any excuse, not even if you see soldiers foraging in the valley below. If the soldiers are Populars they will respect you, if they are Optimates they may not notice you so long as you keep quiet. You will stay until your husband sends for you. You will keep

11

with you your son Marcus, who is too young for war. You will offer hospitality, should he require it, to your kinsman Lucius Paullus. You will also offer hospitality to the lady Junia, daughter of Decimus Silanus, who is now on her way here. Her stepfather intends to join the Popular party, and wishes to place her in a quiet refuge until the war is over. Furthermore, it has been decided that when she reaches a sufficient age she shall marry your son Marcus. Treat her as a betrothed daughter of the house. Those are the orders of your husband.'

'But surely I can come fighting with you, Scipio,' said Marcus at once. 'I can ride, and throw a javelin; though that sword would be too heavy for me.'

Even this tactful reference to his brother's strength was of no avail.

'You will stay with your mother, young Marcus. You have heard your father's orders.'

'Is Junia pretty?' asked the lady Appuleia, who took little interest in masculine politics. Men were always banging one another with swords for absurdly inadequate reasons. 'Her mother, Servilia, is beautiful and charming and clever. Flighty too, or so they say. Will Junia do us credit?'

'I have never seen her. But she brings a good dowry, and her stepfather's influence is valuable. She's a plebeian, unfortunately, but of very good family all the same. Arrange the wedding as soon as possible, for fear Brutus should change his mind. You hear, Marcus? You will be the last patrician Lepidus, so you must make the most of it. You can be a pontiff, if you are chosen; your sons will be plebeians.'

That was the kind of remark you expected from an elder brother, especially an elder brother who had deserted the family altar to better himself. Marcus took consolation from the knowledge that a match between patrician and plebeian could be only a civil contract, capable of dissolution whenever the husband asked for it; the only lifelong indissoluble tie was the religious marriage between two patricians. When he was grown up and his own master he could send this Junia packing if he did not like her.

Then, to his great mortification, Marcus was sent out of the room while his mother and his ex-brother discussed money. It was his mother who ordered him to leave, and he guessed the reason. Scipio would be asking for all the ready cash, plate, and jewels that could be found at short notice, for legionaries in rebellion demanded very high pay; and his mother would be trying to keep as much as she could, for she hated to see wasted on politics money that might have been spent rationally on fashion-

12

able splendour. He was the heir, the senior male in the household; and of course he wanted to help his father. The lady Appuleia was unwilling to confront two adversaries at once.

Presently brother Scipio came out to the portico, in a thundering bad temper. He had collected only one mule-load of silver; though there must have been more in the villa. As he mounted his sleek warhorse he waved good-bye to Marcus. But Marcus was angry that his brother had left him under the care of the women, as though he were an infant not yet weaned; besides, the warhorse, and the long cavalry sword, were more interesting objects of contemplation than his brother's face, which he knew well. He answered unsmiling, with a perfunctory wave of the hand.

He never again saw brother Scipio, or his father. The improvised revolt was a failure from the start. Scipio was killed in the decisive engagement, fought in the Campus Martius at the very gate of Rome; and his father died, an outlaw and a public enemy, in Sardinia, worn out with the unfamiliar toil of collecting ships to carry the wreck of his army to the rebel Sertorius in Spain. There were whispers that grief at the indifference of his wife had hastened his end, and certainly the lady Appuleia greeted widowhood with stoic resignation. Thanks to her stubborn foresight the Aemilii Lepidi were still wealthy. As soon as conventional mourning was over she went back to the great family mansion in Rome.

# I

## THE PRAETOR CHOOSES A SIDE
### 49 B.C.

On this wintry day the City was full of rumours. The streets were crammed with the wagons of refugees from Picenum, which blocked the way of other refugees leaving Rome for the south. In this public commotion all outside the walls sought refuge in Rome, all the inhabitants sought hiding-places in the country. Throughout the morning the Forum had been crowded, as citizens waited to see if a magistrate would summon a public meeting; by midday they were drifting about the alleys, too restless to go home, gathering into crowds and shouting the catchwords of their parties. Though it was a working day, only slaves were at work; hardly a shop had been reopened since the public holiday for the Ides of January.

Nevertheless, on a working day the praetors must preside in their lawcourts. On the 16th of January they were still new to the duties they had taken up at the beginning of the month, still full of zeal to display their knowledge of law and the equity of their minds. Marcus Aemilius Lepidus, urban praetor, presided over the most important civil court in Rome; it would be shameful if he declined to sit merely because the City was disturbed. An hour after sunrise he had taken his seat in his official ivory chair; there he remained, muffled in an ample toga against the wintry wind which swept through the open portico, until an hour after midday. The custom of the ancestors demanded this display of public duty, and anyway there was nothing else he could do until the situation was a little more clear. But the only causes brought before him were two undefended suits for small debts, and for two hours he sat there with no business to occupy him. No one was going to open an important or intricate case when in a few days there might be no law in Rome, or indeed anywhere else in the civilised world.

All the same, it was very pleasant to be sitting in the curule chair, Lepidus the praetor, third magistrate in the most powerful City on earth. What made it all the more gratifying was that he

15

had won this great position by his own merit. Of course it would be very odd if the head of the Aemilii Lepidi were passed over for public office; but his father had died a public enemy, an outlaw in arms against his City. That had taken some living down. Yet respectable manners, noble birth, and genuine ability will always be recognised, in the face of every handicap. Here he was, praetor at the age of 40; soon there would be another Lepidus Consul, and when he died his image would take its proper place at the end of the long line of Lepidan Consuls which filled the shelf behind the family altar.

An hour after midday the court might fittingly adjourn. He stood to intone the ritual prayer, carefully pronouncing the obsolete words in the archaic patrician mode. For several centuries the gods had endured with patience the ignorant gabblings of plebeian magistrates, but it was just as well to remind them from time to time that the welfare of Rome was in the hands of the gens Aemilia, who knew how they should be placated. He took three measured paces to the right of his chair, the lucky side, and saluted with a formal gesture the spirit of fair-dealing which dwelled in the hallowed ivory; the spirit whose presence he could feel as he sat, rising through his buttocks to inspire his mind with equity. Then he stood as still as a statue while a servant adjusted his toga into the correct folds for walking; his clerks formed up behind him and the two lictors of a praetor took their places six feet ahead, their fasces sloped over their shoulders. At a snap of his fingers the procession moved off; not in the military quick-step affected by sloppy young magistrates straight out of the army, but in the slow swinging stride appropriate to a ruler who had been entrusted with a share of the divine favour which guards Rome. Even now it gave him a thrill to see the lictors going before him; though that was no more than his due, as head of the house of Lepidus.

He went first to inquire whether the Senate were still in session. Three years ago rioting Clodians had burned down the Senate House (what was the world coming to!) and the City since then had been so disturbed that no one had repaired it; the Senate met in any handy temple or public building that was big enough, but most often in the vestibule of the Theatre of Pompeius. He tried that first, and was told to his annoyance that the Fathers had met there earlier in the day, and had already adjourned; they should have waited until the urban praetor had closed his court. Even in these exciting times he would look undignified if he loitered in the Forum to hear the news; so there was nothing for it but to go home. If the Senators had reached any important decision they would of course send a messenger to inform him.

Still in silence and with measured tread the little procession marched to the Aemilian mansion. Its doors stood open, and the lictors swept straight in; to stand at attention while the praetor, as head of the house, poured wine before the statue of the presiding Lar. The custom of his ancestors laid down that Lepidus should sacrifice to his Lar twice a day, at dawn and noon; but ancestral custom also decreed that the urban praetor should hold court until the first hour of the afternoon. Marcus would not dream of slighting the gods by sending an underling to sacrifice while he was absent on duty; it was better to keep the Lar waiting, and then apologise for the delay. He was proud of the apology he had composed, in terms so archaic that King Numa would have understood them.

Then the lictors melted away towards the kitchen. They were free men and citizens, who had walked before many other praetors and next January would walk before his successor. On parade they had an air, but once they had been stood down it was best to get them quickly out of the way before they became cheeky. The clerks were his own clients, most of them freedmen who had once been his slaves; they took a more ceremonious farewell, bending the knee to kiss his hand. A valet advanced to remove the official toga, and with a shrug of the shoulders and a sagging of the neck Aemilius the praetor became Marcus Lepidus the eminent patrician, at leisure in his own house.

He told the servants that he would dine alone with his lady, and as soon as possible. After his valet had sponged his face and hands he went through the hall to the drawing-room beyond, where the lady Junia sat with her maids, dozing over her embroidery. As her husband entered she rose and sketched the gesture of kissing his hand; but of course he interrupted to embrace her, as he had done at every meeting since they were married. Good manners demanded that she should offer him this reverence, but good manners demanded equally that he should refuse it.

The lady Juna was five years younger than her lord, and remarkably good-looking. But then Marcus Lepidus was also handsome in a heavy way, with regular features, a straight back, wide shoulders, and the beginning of a paunch. They had been betrothed in childhood at the command of their parents, to cement a political alliance; but neither had ever fallen passionately in love with anyone else, and long years of partnership and probinquity had brought affection. They were pleased to be alone together, with half the day before them.

'What's the news?' asked Junia. Of course she did; every

woman was asking that as her man came home, all over the City.

'Nothing definite, my dear,' Marcus answered. 'Caesar has taken Ariminum. He still marches south with his single legion. Ahenobarbus is levying recruits in Picenum. At any hour now we ought to hear of the first engagement, but so far there seems to have been no contact.'

'That was what they were saying at dawn. News of battle travels fast. If they had fought yesterday we should have heard. Perhaps after all someone will fix up a compromise. Did anyone make a proposal for peace in the Senate?'

'I don't know how the debate went in the Senate. They had already adjourned when my court rose. On my way home I called to inquire, and all I could find out was the bare fact of adjournment.'

'Then no one had a reasonable proposal. If there was a hope of peace someone would tell the urban praetor, even if he had to interrupt when you were giving judgement. Today was our last chance; tomorrow the swords will be drawn. Little Marcus will be eight next birthday. Can you remember Sulla's proscription? Would they hunt down an eight-year-old?'

'In Sulla's time they did. Any blood-feuds grow fiercer with the years. But why should anyone want to proscribe *my* son? I have been elected praetor with the support of the Optimates who control the City; my father died for the Popular cause. Three years ago I defied the Clodian gangs, and that ought to earn me the gratitude of every respectable householder in Rome. We are not committed to either faction. And, when all's said and done, I *am* Amilius Lepidus.'

'That won't help little Marcus. When once the fighting has started ties of kinship are forgotten. Look at Caesar himself. I've often heard him tell how when Sulla ruled the City he had to go into hiding, for all that his mother was an Aurelia, kin to Sulla's most eminent supporters. Poor Caesar! I saw a lot of him when I was a child, and he was always so gay and amiable; it was exciting just to be in the same room with him. I suppose I shall never see him again. A public enemy, marching with one legion against Pompeius and all the might of Rome! I hope he gets himself killed in battle, so that we can remember him as a gallant warrior. It's horrible to think that he may be executed as a traitor, or more likely die of hardship in some squalid barbarian refuge.'

'My eldest brother fell in his first battle, in the Campus Martius out there. A swordpoint in the throat, a gentleman's death. He may have been a Scipio by adoption, but he charged like a Lepidus.'

18

Marcus was always touchy when anyone referred, even obliquely, to his father's end. He knew that every Optimate remembered the old Consul as a desperate rebel and public enemy, while to every Popular he was a half-hearted leader who had despaired too soon. It was difficult to defend his memory from such opposite reproaches.

'But the weary round of bloodshed and vengeance may not begin again, my dear,' he went on. 'You talk as though Caesar were a foolhardy daredevil. He's not. In Gaul he may have conquered savages, as any civilised army can beat savages; at heart he's a wily politician, more at home in the Forum than on the battlefield. It's ten years since I met him, or since anyone else met him either; I mean met him properly, at a dinner-party or in his place in the Senate. But he can't suddenly have changed his entire nature, even in the frosts of Gaul. He wouldn't be marching through Picenum at the head of a solitary legion unless he had some private contact with Pompeius. In a few days the two of them will meet quietly, bring in some solid statesman to make a third in place of Crassus, and publish their terms of peace. Then we shall have a competent administration, strong enough to keep the mob in order.'

'Let's hope you are right, my dear,' said Junia soothingly. She knew that when her husband was explaining high politics in terms simple enough for the female understanding anything except instant agreement exasperated him beyond all bearing. 'It's time someone kept the mob in order. I can hear them hooting outside at this very minute. I suppose they have recognised some unpopular magistrate.'

Marcus smiled briefly in appreciation of the pun. The mob usually shouted for the Populars, and most Optimates were at present very unpopular indeed. 'Then you no longer fear for little Marcus?' he went on in a kindly tone. 'All Rome remembers the proscriptions. Such horrors can never be done again. We magistrates are busy every day, and we work to make the world safe for Marcus and his schoolfellows. That's enough of politics. I hear the butler coming to announce dinner.'

The butler entered the drawing-room; but instead of standing by the door to announce that dinner was served he came right up and leaned over his master, murmuring confidentially to the top of his head. 'A gentleman has called to see you, my lord, on most urgent and private business. He will not give his name, and he was carried into the hall in a curtained litter. His litter-bearers are those who usually carry Pompeius Maximus.'

'We must postpone dinner, my dear. A praetor's time belongs to the City. Hylas, have the gentleman carried in his litter right

19

into my private office. Tell him I shall be there as soon as I have put on my toga. Let's see. Have we a footman who doesn't understand Latin? Anyway, get one of the barbarian servants to bring in a bowl of wine, and put a guard on the office door. If this gentleman wants his interview to be private we shall show him that the Aemilian mansion can offer him privacy.'

'That's just how I would expect old Pompeius to arrange a secret meeting; to come here in broad daylight, in the most famous litter in Rome,' Junia muttered to herself as her husband bustled out. She spoke too low to be overheard. A praetor's work seemed to be very boring, and it would be a shame to spoil her husband's pleasure in this intrigue.

Half an hour later Marcus was back, his eyes popping with excitement.

'You were quite right, my dear,' were his first words; and Junia knew that he must be very excited indeed. 'Yes, you were right. Civil war has come again. The proscription of Sulla was very terrible, but then at least the foes of Rome were themselves Romans. Now we face war to the knife, war without quarter. The City lies defenceless before a barbarian army. Sack and bloodshed, rape and pillage, our shrines profaned, the tombs of our ancestors rifled, the Gauls once more in the Forum!'

'Merciful gods, will he make a speech at me? They banged so much rhetoric into his head when he was a child that now when he's excited he can't tell a straightforward story,' thought Junia. While her husband stood, his arm thrust out, drawing breath for another outburst of lamentation, she cut in with a sharp question.

'What did Pompeius tell you? And what are you, the urban praetor, going to do about it?'

'I'm sorry. I got carried away. But what Pompeius had to say was really very startling. By the way, how did you know it was Pompeius? He came secretly, in a closed litter. Never mind. The great Pompeius honours my roof, and I can't boast about it to my friends. Just my luck. Well, this is what he told me. He has no regular troops in Italy except the two legions passing through from Gaul for the Parthian war. Those legions have just left Caesar's command, and they can't be trusted to fight against him. Of course no one expected Caesar to march in January; Pompeius was counting on another three months to train his recruits. Those recruits are coming in very willingly. At this very minute Ahenobarbus has thirty cohorts of them in Picenum. But so far they aren't even organised into legions; they must be drilled before they can stand in the line of battle. So there's nothing for it, and this is the terrible news, but for the whole

20

government to leave Rome. Pompeius himself goes to Capua tomorrow; the magistrates and Senators, with their families, follow on the next day. We have thirty-six hours to pack our plate and money, and your jewels. Of course it will be impossible to hire wagons, with all Rome in flight. We must abandon the furniture and most of our clothes, as plunder for the Caesarians.'

'Why should the Caesarians plunder it? They can't take tripods and dinner tables with them on campaign.'

'They will plunder because they are Caesarians, extreme Populars, the dregs of the City. Caesar won't try to control them. In Gaul he has shown himself utterly merciless. He has wiped out whole tribes of barbarians, men, women, and children. He boasted about it in his letters to the Senate.'

'That isn't the Caesar I remember in mother's boudoir. Among savages he may have been a savage, in Rome he will behave like a Roman. But wait a minute, Marcus. Who has ordered you to leave?'

'Pompeius himself. Gnaeus Pompeius Maximus. I told you.'

'This is January, Marcus. Since the beginning of the year you have been urban praetor.'

'Yes, yes, I know. . . . Oh, I see what you mean.' The last words were spoken low, as Marcus sat down in a comfortable chair to think.

Pompeius was a very great man. Three years ago he had been for a few months sole Consul, an office unknown to the constitution but a public recognition of the fact that he was the greatest man in the City. All the same, by the letter of the law Pompeius was merely a Consular, a Senator who had in the past held the Consulship. That gave him no right to issue orders to magistrates.

'Certainly he ordered me to leave, he was not just giving advice,' Marcus went on. 'But the Senate has commissioned him to preserve the peace in Italy, and they have voted the Ultimate Decree. Anyway, whatever the legal position, he has the power of the sword.'

'The Ultimate Decree!' said Junia with explosive scorn. 'What did your father, or mine, think of the Ultimate Decree? How did your grandfather value it, Saturninus the tribune who was murdered by sacrilegious Optimates? Every true Roman who has studied the laws knows that the Senate has no power to declare martial law without the assent of the people. . . . And if Pompeius truly had the power of the sword he would not be getting ready to scuttle out of Rome before a blow has been struck.'

'Pompeius can kill me this evening, if I defy him. His troops outside the City are only undrilled recruits, but there are no

21

other soldiers within a hundred miles of us. Besides, it is still much too early to take a public stand. We just don't know enough about who will win. So far there has been no fighting, and an hour ago I thought the whole thing would be arranged peacefully at another personal consultation between the leaders. Suppose I join Caesar just in time to see the rout of his solitary legion? You know I don't fear death for myself, but it would be the downfall of the house of Aemilius Lepidus. If I obey orders and leave Rome I do only what everyone is doing. Caesar won't hold that against me. Later, when the position is clearer, I can still join the Populars if they seem to stand a chance. I won't destroy my family by taking part in a hopeless escapade.'

Junia admitted to herself that Marcus did not fear death; considering his ancestry and his education it would have been odd if he did. But he was afraid of so many other things, the public opinion of his equals, the hatred of the mob, the displeasure of the gods, poverty, disgrace, insignificance, that in effect he often reasoned like a coward.

'I want Caesar to win. What do you want to happen?' was all her answer.

'I don't know, really. It would be best if Ceasar and Pompeius made another agreement, but I suppose that is crying for the moon. If they must fight it out, well, look at it this way. Every gentleman of good family, nearly the whole of the Senate, practically everyone who has ever dined here or whom you would meet in a drawing-room, they all support Pompeius. Then look at the gang who support Caesar; those Antonius brothers, Curio, Quintus Cassius. I wouldn't trust one of them alone with a virgin or a silver spoon. Of course our good old Popular cause must triumph in the end. The people are stronger than the nobility. But this is not the time for war, perhaps for another proscription. Just because the people must win in the end the nobles will give way gracefully at the last moment. Remember, there was a time when we patricians were the only true citizens of Rome; we made room for your plebeian ancestors, my dear, because the welfare of the City demanded it. And now we live in harmony together.'

'Some plebeian houses are as good as any patricians. Junians have been magistrates for centuries; my son Marcus will be a plebian. But that quarrel was settled three hundred years ago. Let's get back to the point. I want Caesar to win. I gather you want the Populars to win one day; but under another leader, after Caesar has been executed as a public enemy.'

'You are going too fast, my dear. I haven't yet made up my mind. It would be best of all if neither side could overcome the

22

other, so that the war ends in a compromise. But if the time comes when I must declare myself – then I must remember my father. I am bound to the Populars by filial piety and the blood-feud.'

'Very well, then. Now consider what you can do tomorrow. We can go to Capua with Pompeius and the other magistrates. You will be quite safe for the rest of the war. The Optimates also will remember your father; they will not trust you to lead troops against Caesar. When the fighting is finished you will be an ex-praetor, with a seat in the Senate and perhaps a small province to govern for one year. You will never rise higher; you will never be elected Consul. If the constitution survives the war there will be the usual dog-fight, eight ex-praetors scrambling for the two Consulships; but your colleagues will have been commanding armies while you tried civil actions in the praetor's court. You won't have the impudence to stand for election against them. It's more likely that the war will end in a tyranny. Then, whether the tyrant is Pompeius or Caesar, he will have no reason to reward you. Go to Capua, and then retire into private life. You will be rich, and a Senator, and head of the Aemilii Lepidi. But if you want to be Consul you must risk your head, you must join Caesar while his side is still the weaker.'

'I never thought of that, but now you say it I see it is true. The Optimates allowed me to be praetor, I suppose because of my distinguished ancestors. They will never allow my father's son to rise any higher. Yet brother Paullus has just laid down his Consulship, at the end of last month. How do you explain that?'

'Your brother Paullus indeed,' said Junia with a sniff. 'He's no example for an honest gentleman to follow. I've heard you say he only took over the images of the Paulli because they are richer than the Lepidi. A fine Aemilius, to desert his family so. As for his Consulship, no one thinks any the more of him for it. He was elected by the Optimates, because they thought they had him in their pocket. He wasn't even honest enough to stay bought, but took a bigger bribe to act for Caesar. Everyone knows it. Now there's a man who will be very lucky to survive the civil war. Both sides would be happy to proscribe him, as a public nuisance if not a public enemy.'

' "A public nuisance if not a public enemy." A striking phrase, my dear. I shall use it myself, in company where it is bound to be repeated. That will show brother Paullus what we think of him, lording it as Consul while the head of his true family, his father's heir, is no more than praetor-elect. Did I tell you how he snubbed me in the Senate, three months ago? I should like to surpass brother Paullus. To equal him I must one day be Consul.

23

So eventually, when the time is ripe, I shall join Caesar. He will be glad to have me. Look at the gang of cut-throats who support him at present! He ought to make me his second in command.'

Marcus sprang from his chair to stride about the room. 'Marcus Aemilius Lepidus, the champion of the Populars! That's what they used to call my father; one day I shall be even more famous. I would join Caesar today if I could manage it safely. But if I defy Pompeius to his face he will send soldiers to cut off my head, and if I hide in the City everyone will notice at once that the urban praetor has disappeared. The Consuls will confiscate our property, and send lictors to look for me. How can I hide, anyway? Everyone in Rome knows me by sight.'

'Not quite everyone, Marcus dear; though they will when you have done great deeds for Caesar. But I agree that you can't stay behind openly, or ride out towards Ariminum inquiring for Caesar's vanguard. All the same, it will not be too difficult. We shall leave Rome with the other noble fugitives, on the day after tomorrow; we can take our money with us quite openly, for everyone will be doing the same. We start south, with the others. But in the evening we turn aside to visit one of your villas well off the road; then we make the litter-bearers travel all night, first east and then north-east, until we reach Caesar's lines.'

'That's what we'll do. We must take little Marcus with us. That means three big litters at least, probably a fourth for the baggage. They must have strong and trustworthy bearers. I'll tell the steward to parade all the able-bodied servants this evening, and pick out the best of them; even a valuable cook or accountant will carry a litter if he's strong enough.'

'That's splendid, and I'm proud of you. Shall we have dinner soon? It's nearly sunset, and I'm hungry.'

Junia spoke placidly. She had guided her husband into making the bold and sensible decision, which he would never have reached without her prodding; but he would certainly choose the best litter-bearers. He could sum up the capacities of a slave or a workman; his acute though limited brain was at its best in dealing with the practical details of daily life.

*The lady Clodia sat at her dressing-table, chatting with the handsome young man who had called to tell her the news.*

'Do you mean to tell me there isn't a magistrate left in Rome? What a bore! If there are no laws, we can't disobey them. But oughtn't you to be frightened, Lucius darling? My poor brother's gang will look after me. But now any ruffian can knock you down and kill you, just to steal that amusing golden hair-net.'

24

'One magistrate has returned, my sweet: Marcus Aemilius Lepidus the praetor. He left with the rest of them, and then doubled back. He may call himself King of Rome if he wants to, for he is the only lawful magistrate left in the City.'

'You are making this up. Marcus Aemilius Lepidus was Consul thirty years ago. He rebelled against the Senate, was defeated in the Campus Martius, and died soon after. Even I know that. It's in all the books.'

'This is his son, who took office as praetor at the beginning of this month.'

'I've never heard of him, and I know everybody. If you must make up fairy-tales, think of something more amusing.'

# II

## CAESAR AND THE CAESARIANS
### 49 B.C.

Six legions roared through the City; a very shameful sight
within the sacred pomoerium, the hallowed boundary of Rome
within which no loyal citizen should bear arms. The soldiers
appeared to be drunk and out of control, and they were singing
very rude songs. The Thirteenth of course led the parade, the
amazing legion which had invaded Italy alone and unsupported;
the men in the ranks had been on active service for eight years,
without a chance of visiting their homes; now they were masters
of the City, and looked forward to the reward of conquest,
wealth and ease for the rest of their lives. Their songs were really
hair-raising, they did not seem to be in any particular formation,
they staggered and brandished empty wine-flasks. But when they
reached the Capitol detachments ran forward to seize each entry,
and in a twinkling the wall was manned. These men were
veterans who had captured many cities.

Behind the Thirteenth Legion rode their commander, Gaius
Julius Caesar, Pontifex Maximus and public enemy of Rome.
That was undoubtedly his position in constitutional law, as a
wit among his bodyguard repeatedly shouted at the full stretch
of his drill-master's lungs. Like any other conqueror, when he
reached the Capitol he made straight for the treasury, ignoring
the great Temple of Jupiter where generals returning in peace
gave thanks for victory. The City lay nakedly at the mercy of an
invading horde from Gaul, as in the old legends of the two hundred and fifty years ago.

On the barred door of the Aemilian mansion idlers had
scrawled the catchwords of the Popular party: 'Preserve our
Tribunes', 'To the dungheap with the Senate and its Ultimate
Decree'. A large white placard, executed under the direction of
the master of the house, bore more careful lettering: 'Twenty-
nine years ago, from these doors set out the Consul Marcus
Aemilius Lepidus, to wage war on the tyranny established by
Sulla. Romans, respect the dwelling of a hero who died in the

26

struggle for Freedom.' In the hall, below the shelf of ancestral images, sat in his ivory chair the son of the martyred Consul, the present Aemilius Lepidus. He wore the official toga of a praetor, and behind him two freedmen nursed awkwardly home-made bundles of rods; for the genuine professional lictors had of course accompanied the flight of the government.

The roaring of the crowd outside the house was enough to frighten any man of property; but it had been going on since dawn, and so far nothing very terrible had happened. As time passed the praetor recovered his usual self-control. In particular his ivory chair gave him comfort. He knew that it was the only curule chair in Rome occupied by its lawful magistrate. The whole of Rome's Luck, normally dispersed between the two Consuls and the eight praetors, must be concentrated in this throne. As he caressed the carving he felt his hands tingle. Once before he had felt the same thrill, during the terrible riots of three years ago. The street-fighting had made it impossible to hold the annual elections, and when Clodius was killed in a scrimmage there had been no lawfully appointed magistrates to restore order. The Senate, following the procedure devised by the ancestors for such an emergency, had chosen an Interrex to hold supreme power for five days, before he transmitted it to a successor of his own choice. Marcus had been the first Interrex.

His position was not so important as it might have seemed to an outsider, for by ancient custom the first Interrex did nothing at all except transmit his emergency power when his five days were ended; thus Freedom was more secure. But for five days, even though he did nothing with it, the whole of the Luck and Power and Authority of the Senate and People of Rome had been embodied in Marcus. As it happened, to do nothing at all had required great fortitude; for the bereaved Clodians rioted round his house, commanding him to break with precedent and nominate Popular Consuls on his first day of power. The mob looked so dangerous that he sent his wife and child to the country; but he had not given way.

Now he was once more the supreme authority in Rome, and once more a dangerous mob was seeking its prey. But this time the mob was not after his blood in particular; perhaps when these adventures came a second time they were always a little easier.

People were continually banging on the outer door, straggling soldiers looking for an unguarded house to loot, or excited corner-boys who just wanted something to smash. Several times Marcus composed his features and straightened his shoulders, thinking this must be an official summons from the conquering

27

army. But when at last it came it was unmistakable; first the steady tramp of disciplined infantry, then shouted orders and the snap of smart arms-drill. At the first knock the porter opened, and with a sinking of his stomach Marcus saw a dozen tall praetorians march in with swords drawn. Perhaps they were coming to take his head. On the other hand, Caesar needed a bodyguard today, of all days; it was shocking bad manners to bring an armed guard when he came calling on the praetor, but all the same it was more gracious than if he had sent a messenger to summon him.

Yes, there was Caesar himself, darting forward with a grin from behind his hedge of soldiers; there could be no forgetting that smile, even after ten years. It was said that Caesar's smile could charm a bird from a bush, and it had been proved by experiment that no girl could resist it. He was wearing a very curious costume. Merciful gods! The mountebank had come calling in the official robes of the Pontifex Maximus!

Marcus signalled to his amateur lictors to hold their fasces upright, and himself extended his hand in the ritual gesture which signified that the praetor's court was in session. But his wife upset the gravity of this historic interview by dashing out of the drawing-room to hurl herself into Caesar's arms.

Caesar kissed her casually on the forehead, and then picked her up to hold her at arm's-length, as though she were a little girl. 'Hallo, Junia,' he said calmly, 'you look ten years younger than when I saw you last. I hope to have supper with your mother this evening. Where's Tertulla, in Rome or in Capua – and brother Brutus?'

'Cassius took Tertulla to Capua, but I expect she will come back when she knows you are in Rome. Brother Brutus was as stuffy as usual, and said it was his duty to follow the Consuls. You know what he can be like. Oh, it is fun to see you again. By the way, do you know Marcus?'

'Of course I know Marcus. I came to your wedding, though I suppose you were too excited to notice the guests. Besides that, we met often enough in the Senate, and at parties; though it was all of ten years ago. Well, Marcus Lepidus, how does it feel to be sole ruler of Rome? I have a very good reason for asking, you know. By the way, if you really want to introduce ceremony into a reunion of old friends there happens to be a formula of welcome, which should be employed to greet the Pontifex Maximus when he calls uninvited on a fellow-pontiff who is also a patrician and head of his family. It's a very old invocation in the Sabine tongue, with a few Etruscan expressions to make it more difficult. Perhaps it has slipped your memory. I'll let you off this

28

time, though we patricians should foster the ancient customs of our ancestors.'

The worst of it was that Caesar might be telling the truth. He was as famous for accurate knowledge of ancient ritual as for atheism. Marcus felt himself overwhelmed by the unexpected friendliness of this dread conqueror, by his wife's familiarity with the companion of her childhood, by the frivolous chaff of an expert who could beat him in his chosen field of study. The ivory chair was now just a piece of furniture, all its magical comfort gone.

'Now then, Junia darling,' Caesar continued, 'it's splendid to meet old friends, but I really came to talk business. My orderly has a wallet stuffed with papers. Will you show me a handsome table where he can spread them? The table will look even more handsome if you embellish it with a big bowl of good wine. Then, with the praetor's permission, we can dismiss our lictors and bodyguards and lady's maids, and make our plans in private.'

Since Caesar took it for granted that Junia should join in the discussion Marcus did not ask her to go to the drawing-room. There was just room for the three of them in the tiny private office, at the inner end of the hall; and a rank of stolid praetorians kept the household servants out of hearing.

The handsome well-preserved man-about-town seemed to loom larger as he looked Marcus full in the face, his finger tapping a map of Italy. There were lines of anxiety round his mouth, and his voice was deadly serious.

'Pompeius is preparing to fall back on Brundisium,' he began. 'He knows how to handle a rearguard; there's no question of catching him and ending the war at a blow. Once inside the port he might in theory sail west to join his forces in Spain; but his fleet is gathering in the Adriatic and the noble statesmen who impede his staff-officers are mad to get their hands on the money-bags of Asia. We'll assume that when he embarks he sails for Greece. We shall also assume that he's out of Italy within a month at the longest. Once he is safely overseas I must make arrangements for the proper government of Rome, before I march north to deal with his army in Spain. For that I shall need helpers here in the City.'

He broke off to stare once more at his host. 'We shall also assume that you are on my side, Marcus. I know your political beliefs. You are a Popular family tradition, willing to put up with me because I am leader of the Populars. Now Junia is a Caesarian; willing to put up with the Populars because they follow Caesar.'

'And which are you, Caesar?' asked Marcus, greatly daring.

'Oh, a Caesarian, of course. But the Populars won't lose by my leadership. You yourself have broken with Pompeius, merely by coming back to Rome. If you fall into his hands he will chop off your head. So if I lose you also are ruined. But if you take my orders, for in this desperate war I haven't time to advise and persuade, if you take my orders and I win, there is a splendid future for you.'

Marcus did not approve of the tone of this speech, from a public enemy to the urban praetor. But he had known for some days that Caesar must soon occupy the City, and that sooner or later there would be an interview on these lines. He could compose a dignified and appropriate speech on any subject, if he had plenty of time to think it out beforehand. His answer was ready.

'Within a mile of this room fell my eldest brother, fighting for the liberties of the people. My father died for the same cause. If every Roman must choose a side, then I am a Popular. But is there no middle ground, anywhere in the world? Must we all submit to the tyranny of Pompeius, or else draw our swords against him? My brother Paullus left for Capua with the Consuls; so did Junia's half-brother, Marcus Brutus. That shows there are honest men on both sides. Can't you even now negotiate with Pompeius?'

'Not with Pompeius. The old boy has too much sense. He's a very fine soldier, but whenever he negotiates with anyone he gets the worst of the bargain. Do you remember what the Senate did to him when he came back from Asia? He knows that if he negotiates I shall make rings round him; but if he fights he has a chance of winning. I must destroy Pompeius in battle. But that doesn't mean that every Roman must fight in his army or mine. There is room for neutrals. For example, you haven't heard the latest news about your brother Paullus. He left for Capua, certainly; but he never got there. He is hiding somewhere in Campania, waiting to make his peace with the victors. You can do the same, if you like.'

'Pooh, Lucius Paullus,' Junia broke in. 'I suppose you have bribed him again. He's not a nice man. We must do something to save *my* brother. You can't bribe *him* to change sides.'

'I would never offer a bribe to Marcus Junius Brutus,' said Caesar soothingly. 'He's an honest man by trade. In fact he is so busy being honest he has no time to be sensible.'

'But you won't hurt poor brother Brutus, will you?' Junia continued. 'When you have beaten Pompeius you will let him come home and go on being honest in the Forum, where everyone can see him doing it? Then he will live happily until he dies of old age. He will never be dangerous to anyone.'

'Darling Junia, I wouldn't dream of hurting any child of your dear mother. She gave me my start in public life, when I was candidate for quaestor with the bloody memory of uncle Marius like a millstone round my neck. As a matter of fact I don't want to hurt any Roman, not even Pompeius; though I suppose he will fight until I have to kill him. Anyone who is willing to be friendly will be welcome in Rome, at any stage of the war.'

'Is it so certain that you will win?' asked Marcus, nettled to see his wife so familiar with this elderly rake.

'It is. I am as good a soldier as Pompeius, and a great deal luckier. I have conquered Rome in fair fight, and I shall rule in Rome for the rest of my life. Of course I shall be a constitutional ruler, holding some respected magistracy of the republic. I shall need colleagues, and you in particular. The Populars are short of respectable leaders. I'm moderately respectable myself, but I'm sorry to say my legates are not. Mind you, they are all good at their jobs, energetic and faithful and so on. But when I see them assembled at headquarters I wonder that one room can hold so much villainy. There! I don't ask you to fight against your friends. I ask you to govern Rome while I am on campaign, to build a bridge of friendship that will bring honest Senators back to their homes.'

'I consent,' answered Marcus, sitting up in his chair with an expression of noble resolution. 'I shall govern Rome in the name of the people and their liberties, and I do it the more gladly because you, Caesar, have promised that you will show mercy to your enemies.'

'Of course I shall be merciful. I have no enemies. Some of my adversaries will be killed in battle, but none will be executed. The proscriptions ended with Sulla, and they will never come again. That is settled, then. In a few days I must be off to Brundisium. I only visited the City to pick up the money those fools left in the treasury. When Pompeius has embarked I shall come back for a few days, so that the people can elect me to some public office. At present I command my troops as proconsul in Gaul, but that doesn't give me a legal right to post even a sentry in Italy. My next visit will put that right. You are a magistrate, and you can summon an election meeting. Well, I've got a lot to do today. Don't give my escort more than one drink before they leave.'

'But, surely, Caesar, you will lend me some troops? How can I govern Rome if you take the whole army to Brundisium?' The voice of Marcus was reedy with anxiety, and he no longer looked dignified.

'I don't want to quarter troops in Rome if it can be avoided.

It looks bad. I am supposed to be fighting for the liberties of the people, and if I control them with a garrison on the Capitol I shall appear ridiculous. All the same, you must have some kind of military support. Let me see. If the mob gets out of hand you must apply to my legate, Marcus Antonius. He is keeping order in Italy as a whole, and he will have a few cohorts in the neighbourhood. Let everyone know they are near, and can be summoned if need be. Then you won't have to use them. Now that really is all. I must be getting on. By the way, if Antonius tells you that all debts are cancelled, don't you believe a word of it. That's what he would like to happen, but it just isn't so.'

'Good-bye, Caesar. Come back soon. And tell your soldiers to be gentle with my brother. If harm comes to him mother will never speak to you again.' That was Junia, bidding farewell by blowing kisses, in a manner unbecoming to the wife of the urban praetor. Marcus himself bowed with ceremony, and accompanied his guest to the outer porch. The crowd in the street followed after the escort, and at last the Aemilian mansion lay quiet.

Marcus went at once to the bath. It was early in the day to embark on the long and complicated business of bathing; but he thought most clearly while lying relaxed in hot steam, and he must do some clear thinking before he was pushed into making any further important decisions.

As soon as he knew that Caesar was over the Rubicon he had made up his mind to work for the Popular cause; that was why he had eluded Pompeius and returned to Rome. But he had not planned to declare himself a follower of the scandalous and desperate politician; he had expected to conclude an alliance, lending the support of respectability and noble birth to a disreputable faction. Now he was not only a Caesarian; he was pledged to take orders from Marcus Antonius, a notorious rake ten years younger than himself, and, most important of all, one who had never risen higher than quaestor and tribune; therefore one who should take orders from a praetor.

Junia had rushed him into it; it was all her fault. But then, though she was a very good wife and he loved her dearly, the influence of her unconventional childhood still hung about her. Everyone knew that Servilia, her mother, had been Caesar's mistress in the old days. Some gossipmongers said Marcus Brutus was his son, though that was unlikely. At least Junia was the child of her legal father, old Decimus Silanus who had been Consul more than a dozen years ago; that was proved by every feature in her face. The marriage had not lasted very long, few marriages did nowadays; but Servilia had apparently been faithful while it endured. Her other husband, Marcus Brutus, had

32

been the one to wear the horns, even though he risked, and lost, his life for the Popular cause. But Caesar had been in and out of the house, all over the drawing-room and perhaps the bedroom, while Junia was a little girl playing with her dolls. There was a really nasty story that Caesar had consoled himself with Tertulla, the youngest girl, when her mother grew too mature for his taste. Marcus did not believe it, for wickedness has its natural limits. Probably Caesar had heard the unpleasant rumour; it was just like him to go out of his way to inquire after Tertulla, to demonstrate that he was indifferent to gossip.

Junia had grown up in a rackety atmosphere. When she was excited she reverted to the manners of her childhood, which were unfitting in the wife of a patrician and a praetor. He, Marcus, was to blame. He should never have permitted his wife to set the tone of the interview.

Well, he was committed; he must follow where Caesar led. There was a bright side to that, if you looked for it. Caesar was all of ten years his senior, and, after such a riotous youth, unlikely to make old bones. A time would come when the leadership of the Popular party would be vacant; and except for Caesar, who could behave like a gentleman when he chose, there was not a respectable ex-magistrate among the Populars. What could Curio say, or Lucius Antonius, if he was called on to reply to Cicero in the Senate? But Aemilius Lepidus, head of a house that had been noble since records were kept, would always command an attentive hearing.

He concluded happily, as the bath-attendant finished rubbing his legs, that blood tells in the end. Ability is also important, but innate ability was part of the Aemilian birthright.

On this crowded eventful day he had not yet dined, though it was long past noon. Now he ordered dinner at once, and sent to ask the lady Junia to join him. His wife had dined while he was bathing; she came to sit beside his couch, and to volunteer advice. She knew that her husband often left his bath dangerously full of self-confidence, and that unless she implanted the right ideas in his head the wrong ones would take root and burgeon.

'Caesar hasn't changed a bit,' she began as soon as they were alone together. 'He looks older, of course, after that horrid climate in Gaul. His hair is very thin on top. But he's still the Caesar I knew, mother's friend. He used to say that politics are great fun, and well worth fighting over; but not really important, not important enough to call for revenge after victory. I'm glad he still intends to show mercy. We heard such ghastly stories of his massacres in Gaul. Of course the tribes he exterminated were only barbarians. Since he crossed the Rubicon he has treated Romans differently.'

'Naturally. Romans are different. Caesar sees that as clearly as we do. Anyway, this is not the sort of war to make him lose his temper. What's it all about? Those soldiers today sang that they were rescuing the tribunes (among a lot of bawdy nonsense that I couldn't understand). That's Caesar's war-cry; but it's only cant. Curio and Antonius were never in personal danger, though their veto was disregarded when it should have been obeyed. Otherwise the only point in dispute seems to be the validity of the Ultimate Decree. That's matter for a riot in the Forum; but not for a desperate war, with blood-feuds handed down from father to son.'

'This war will decide whether Caesar or Pompeius is to be King of the World. Do you think that worth fighting over?'

'Oh no, my dear. We don't have kings any more. The people would never stand for it. Caesar may be elected Dictator, as Sulla was; or even sole Consul, as Pompeius was quite recently. There are precedents for such appointments. But he's getting on, and presently he will want to retire. When he's gone everything will be as it was before.'

'Nothing will ever be again as it was before Caesar crossed the Rubicon. Don't you understand, Marcus? Elections don't matter now. In future only soldiers with swords will vote. I think Caesar will win; and then he will be King of the World, whatever title he uses. If Pompeius beats him, then Pompeius will rule us. Let it go as it may, there will be only the king and his obedient subjects. But even kings need ministers. As a follower of Caesar you can still be a great man. Unless indeed you propose to try for the throne yourself, and rally the clients of the house of Lepidus to take on both Caesar and Pompeius.'

'That would be absurd. Both Caesar and Pompeius have been Consuls, so they are greater than I. One day I also shall be Consul, and no Roman can rise higher than that.'

'Oh, Marcus, look at things as they are. When Pompeius ordered you to leave Rome he was no longer Consul; yet both Consuls left at his command. No one takes precedence of a Consul; but precedence is not power.'

'There are occasions when the Rex Sacrorum or the Pontifex Maximus take precedence of a Consul. But I see what you mean. Very well, I have agreed to follow Caesar. What more do you want?'

'If you are to get on you must do more than follow him. You must help him without waiting to be asked for help. Marcus Antonius, as tribute, did more than Caesar asked of him; now

34

he commands all the troops in Italy. If you make yourself useful you may surpass Antonius.'

'If I don't surpass Antonius I shall die a very disappointed man. He's a rake and a rogue and so artful with money that he's bound to crash one day. But it's true that as Caesar's legate he wields more power than he deserves, more power than a praetor. Well, if it's the only way to get on I shall throw all my energies into this rather absurd civil war. I'll keep the City loyal to Caesar while he lays siege to Brundisium. I may even arrest a few of his opponents if you are quite sure he will pardon them when he comes back.'

By the middle of March Pompeius had left Italy for Greece, and Caesar was back in Rome. It was seventy days since his one legion had crossed the Rubicon; in that time he had overrun the whole of Italy, enlisting all the Pompeian recruits in his own forces. Marcus had kept the City obedient to its new ruler, but he was very glad when Caesar returned.

The trouble was that no one except Caesar could control his own followers. Curio, the biggest scoundrel of the lot, was busy plundering Sicily; that kept him out of the way. But the three Antonius brothers were always itching to sack temples and confiscate the property of wealthy neutrals. Their soldiers were mostly veterans, thinking only of the snug farms they would soon receive free of charge; they were as eager for loot as their leaders. It was hard to maintain public order with such instruments. Only when Caesar commanded did they obey.

At the beginning of April the victors began the complicated legal process which would give Caesar constitutional authority. For this Marcus was indispensable, since he was the only magistrate in the City empowered to call a meeting of the people. Even then it was not so easy as it seemed; nothing connected with the constitution of the ancestors ever was. At first Marcus proposed to hold new Consular elections, since the Consuls who had assumed office in January must be held to have forfeited their authority when they left Italy without permission. Caesar pointed out with a grin that Marcus was only a praetor, and so could not summon a meeting to deal with the affairs of his superiors, the Consuls. Marcus thought again, and replied that, though in matters of election the powers of a praetor were limited, he could summon the people to vote Yes or No to any law. A Dictator was not elected; he was appointed by a special law, which named him.

Therefore Marcus summoned a meeting; and in due process of law, without any breach of the sacred constitution devised by the ancestors, Gaius Julius Caesar was appointed Dictator of Rome. A group of shady Senators met in an obscure temple to confer the auspices on the new magistrate. This power to discern omens on behalf of the whole City was the very essence of legitimate authority; the Consuls held it by right, but if by flight they had abdicated their powers then the auspices reverted to the Senate and might be granted anew.

By mid-April the lumbering machinery of state was once more in working order, and Rome might be governed by ancestral law. This had come about only because Marcus Aemilius Lepidus had defied Pompeius the tyrant, and at risk of his life preserved the thread of legitimacy.

Caesar, drinking, negotiating, joking, working for eighteen hours a day in the official residence of the Pontifex Maximus which now housed the whole administration of the state, more than once reminded Marcus of the benefit his courage and independence had conferred on every Roman citizen. Caesar was a most stimulating leader. But he never seemed to rest, and he liked to have his chief lieutenants always within call. Often Marcus longed to get away from the raffish atmosphere of party headquarters, which seemed out of place in a house dedicated to the service of the gods.

There was no denying that the atmosphere was raffish. Curio was still absent in Sicily, but the three Antonius brothers brought the reek of the brothel with them whenever they sat down to rip through a pile of reports. They were united in fraternal affection, and for the present loyal to Caesar; but in general they seemed to have no principles at all. The eldest, Marcus, had before the war embarked on a regular political career; the Roman people had elected him to be quaestor, and later tribune; which proved that he stood out slightly from the ruck. Caesar had made him his legate in Italy, so presumably he had some talent as a soldier. But he was seldom sober, and always brazenly seeking bribes. His younger brothers, Lucius and Gaius, had held no public office and seemed to possess no title to consideration; they were as debauched as Marcus, without his facile charm. Yet Caesar doted on the three of them, and they were always at his council table.

At this council the interests of the absent Curio were defended by his wife, the lady Fulvia. It was hard to remember that she had a husband in Sicily, for everyone thought of her as the widow of Clodius the gangster. In his lifetime she had taken lovers innumerable, but after his violent death she had proved a faithful wife; she had harangued the mourners at his funeral until they burned down the Senate House and sacked the mansions of several wealthy Optimates. Now she was always about with the Antonius brothers. Probably one of them was her lover, but it was hard to say which; perhaps all three shared her. She was handsome in a bold masculine fashion, and at party head-quarters Marcus rather enjoyed her company; though of course he did not invite her to the Aemilian mansion.

This business of helping to govern the world as Caesar's minister was exhilarating, if at the same time rather frightening. Sometimes Marcus imagined that he was on the back of a runaway horse, which galloped through very rough country but so far had cleared every obstacle in its path. There was also the interest of witnessing the workings of a successful military campaign, couriers riding in with dispatches and sentries challenging smartly. Best of all was the pleasure of being gracious to nervous Senators and businessmen who had left Rome with Pompeius, and wanted to change sides now that their leader had been driven from Italy. Every day more of these men came in, after go-betweens had inquired about the prospect of a pardon. Marcus had the task of reassuring them; Caesar had chosen him specially for this duty.

'You and I, Lepidus, are the only well-mannered gentlemen in this nest of brigands,' the Dictator said jovially. 'I'm told that even your private life is respectable; so in that particular you surpass me. I haven't time to greet these turncoats. But they are valuable supporters all the same, and must not be frightened back to the Optimate camp. If I asked an Antonius to receive them he would begin by stealing the gold rings from their fingers. Go out and be affable to that sweating windbag in the ante-room. If he's a moneylender tell him he will get his money back one day, or at least the principal without the interest. If he's in debt tell him he will have time to pay, and that his interest will be cancelled. If he's utterly broke say I am working on a scheme for citizens to go bankrupt without being sold into slavery. If he's an honest yeoman farmer remind him that the Populars are the farmer's friend. If he's a speculator point out that there will be masses of confiscated land on the market as soon as Pompeius is beaten. Whoever he is, send him away happy, willing to go back to work and pay taxes to this insolvent administration. You can do it, my dear Marcus; here there is no one else who can.'

The task was important and responsible, and not really dishonest. The Caesarian wing of the Popular party did in fact stand for all these policies, in so far as they could be carried out without inconvenience to Caesarians.

Presently came disturbing news of the war. Curio had invaded Africa, to fight the Optimates who controlled that province. He had been utterly defeated, and himself killed in the rout, though Pollio brought back the survivors of his army to Sicily. The lady

Fulvia was now a widow. While Sicily was held for Caesar Rome would not starve, though already bread was scarce; but Pompeius, gathering a great army at Athens, had under his orders the only organised navy in the Mediterranean, and at any moment his troops might invade Sicily in overwhelming force.

This first Caesarian defeat reminded the little group of politicians on the Palatine that they were not yet masters of the world. Rome was theirs and all Italy, and newly conquered restless Gaul which was rather a liability than an asset. But the veteran army of Pompeius held Spain, that land of mountains and warriors which had been the grave of so many military reputations; and the rival government in Athens controlled the immense resources of the wealthy East. If Pompeius was given time enough he might organise a double attack on Italy from east and west. Rome began to be frightened.

At the end of April Caesar announced that he was leaving for Gaul. 'There's nothing to worry about,' he consoled his nervous counsellors. 'I shall make straight for Spain, over the Pyrenees. That won't take long. It's a good army I must conquer, but they lack a decent general. As soon as I am back here, victorious, I must get ready to leave for Greece; where there is a very good general against me, but he hasn't an army. Poor old Pompeius! If he had sailed west from Brundisium I should really be worried. As things are he hasn't a chance.'

'Who will rule Italy while you and I are conquering Spain?' asked the eldest of the Antonius brothers, with a sudden start of jealousy.

'You and your brothers will stay behind to rule Italy, my dear Marcus. Oh, I know you are soldiers and nothing else. But while I am away I need good soldiers in Italy.'

Lepidus coughed and looked miserable. He often looked miserable when he heard Antonius and Caesar discussing their plans; Antonius was such a scoundrel, and so unfairly Caesar's favourite.

'Do you dislike the idea, Marcus Lepidus?' Caesar continued with a sly grin. 'No, don't bother to explain. I grasp your objection perfectly, even before you have stated it. Of course it would be most unfitting that Aemillius Lepidus, patrician and pontiff and praetor, and forty years of age, should be under the orders of a youth who has never been more than quaestor and tribune. It wouldn't do at all. Besides, we patricians are agreed, aren't we, that Rome can only prosper under the government of a patrician. So this is what we'll do. Marcus Antonius will command all the troops left in Italy. He must, because he knows how to do it and they will obey him. But Rome, the City herself, shall be put under

38

the government of a praefect, as deputy of the Dictator. That's quite legal, isn't it? Of course the praefect will be the senior curule magistrate at present in the City. That's it. Lepidus will be praefect of Rome, and the army that supports him will be commanded by Antonius. But it looks odd to give such a post to a praetor. We'll get a law passed tomorrow, granting Lepidus Consular ornaments. With twelve lictors behind your chair you could rule the earth, eh, Lepidus? And when I get back from Spain we'll pass another law to give you a decent province. You will go there as proconsul, not as propraetor. There! Is everybody satisfied?'

Thus Lepidus could give thanks to the gods for his forty-first birthday in all the glory of consular ornaments. As far as he could find out, not one of his ancestors had attained the highest rank at such an early age. A little of the bloom was rubbed off this splendid promotion when he found out that he was only one of twelve ex-praetors who had been thus honoured by the Dictator. But he could not say that Caesar had broken his word. In any case, he was the only praefect of Rome.

*The lady Clodia lolled in her boudoir, bored as usual.*

*'Tell me, Catullus,' she said, 'who is that man dressed up as an ex-Consul who runs about the City telling us how to behave? He sent a lictor to order me to cancel my midnight sacrifice to Hecate, lest such a ceremony should degenerate into an orgy. I had planned it to begin as an orgy, of course. But I know enough to obey a lictor, and the party is cancelled. All the same, who gave him the right to order me about? And surely he has never been Consul?'*

*'Well, no, he has not yet been Consul. His father was Consul, and so was his elder brother. He is Marcus Aemilius Lepidus. With that name he cannot avoid being Consul one day, unless Jove first strikes him down with a thunderbolt. He's a respectable patrician, and faithful to his wife; but by some accident he got mixed up with Caesar's gang of toughs. Since he's the only honest man in that menagerie they chose him for praefect of Rome. He's quite harmless.'*

*'So he's Caesar's praefect? That's why he has lictors? I see. But why did Caesar choose him? Has he ever done anything?'*

*'Not exactly* done *anything. He's head of the Aemilii Lepidi.'*

*Catullus, you are making this up! Don't tell lies in front of my sparrow; it's a bad example for the bird. As though there were such a thing as a respectable Caesarian! I'll tell you what he is. He's an old wax figure, left over from some funeral. That's just the kind of joke Caesar would enjoy.'*

# III

## LEPIDUS IMPERATOR
### 48–47 B.C.

The army lay strongly encamped, on high ground beside a plentiful spring. The palisade was firm, and the sentinels alert. But Marcus Lepidus the proconsul, commanding this well-found force of two veteran legions, did not feel secure.

The responsibility of supreme command weighed on his spirit. As a youth he had seen three campaigns in the Dalmatian hills; but in those days he had been a military tribune, whose duty was to lead one cohort or two, and to do with them exactly what he had been told to do. He and the other young officers could gossip at the back of headquarters, grumbling at the general's caution and expounding what they would have done in his place; they always had plenty of time to explain their plans, and to push about little pellets of bread to show the right tactical move. Now he was twenty years older, just past his forty-second birthday; and of course he could not make up his mind so quickly as in the old days. Messengers came running in from the outlying picket, bellowing at the top of their lungs that the foe was at hand; and everyone expected the proconsul to rap out orders to his whole force, 6,000 regular foot and as many auxiliaries, as though they were a handy squad in the middle of an empty parade ground. Other generals did it, in fact it was normally assumed that any Roman of good birth could command an army without previous training; but at the start it was undeniably difficult. Perhaps with practice it would become easier. After all, Marcus Antonius had done brilliantly as cavalry commander under Gabinius in Egypt; and look what an oaf he was!

Lepidus peered out from his well-warmed hut at the autumn tints of the Spanish mountains. In the distance he could make out the horizontal line of the walls of Corduba; it was too far off to be seen in detail, but he knew that those walls were strongly manned, and the gates barred. A little to the left, about a mile nearer, he could see the dark square smear of a regular Roman camp; and there also the bristling palisade would be manned and the heavy wooden gates barred. There was no getting away from it. Though today he had halted early, so that his men could dig in by daylight, tomorrow, no matter how he dallied on the march, he must arrive in the middle of a war.

It was a war between disciplined Roman troops, which made it much worse; for in such warfare the commander must give out a stream of tactical orders. He had already discovered that the hopeless, fanatical raids of Iberian insurgents called for no particular action from a proconsul in command of two legions. The barbarians would rush down out of their ambush, more intent on picking up weapons and food from the baggage-train than on killing armed legionaires; scouts would give the alarm and the cohorts would deploy from column of route to meet the charge. If the proconsul sat his horse beside the Eagle of the leading legion, where messengers could find him easily, the centurions would do the rest. During this very march his men had inflicted two sharp little defeats on overbold bands of insurgents. It had been easy to give the command to pursue, and then to halt, which had been the only orders needed. But tomorrow he would have to decide whether to attack with his right, his left, or his centre; whether to send the cavalry charging at the outset or to keep them fresh for the pursuit; what numbers of his men to place in reserve, and when the reserve should come into action. He had read all the Greek books on tactics he could get hold of, and they agreed that battles were won by these decisions; but then they also said that a general ought to recognise the key points in the enemy position, and concentrate on the weakest spot in the hostile line. How did one recognise these things? The steep Iberian ridges looked impregnable all along their smooth faces, and a body of troops in the distance was just a brown line against the grass; how did you see whether the line was nine deep, or ninety? In such practical matters the books were no help at all.

In a gust of bad temper, he made up his mind that if he must fight a battle tomorrow he would form his two legions in a single line. He himself, with the praetorians of the bodyguard, would take post midway between the Eagles; then they would all charge the foe at a smart double. The auxiliaries might make themselves useful wherever they thought best. Either his men would run away; and then he would die gloriously, refusing to flee; or the enemy would run away, and he would be hailed as an intrepid commander. Or perhaps neither side would run. They might fight until everyone was dead. That was nonsense. His mind was wandering.

When you considered the matter carefully, such a blind charge was just what Caesar had led at Pharsalus; and Caesar was acknowledged to be the greatest general in the world. At present Caesar was in Egypt, plundering the temples of that devout land. But at his wonderful defeat of Pompeius, which everyone discussed with such awe, he had done nothing but put his men in line and then wield his own sword very bravely in the front rank. After a suitable delay, in which both sides could prove their courage, the Pompeians had run away. That was all there was to it.

It was a comfort to know that Pompeius Maximus was dead at last, and the Caesarians victorious throughout the world. The Optimates might be rallying in Africa, but they could never make head against the combined resources of Europe and Asia. But why had Caesar given command of a wing at Pharsalus to that young ruffian, Marcus Antonius? Surely, even if the rascal could fight when he was sober, such a public display of confidence in him was unbecoming to a Dictator. The chief point in Caesar's favour was that he had no heirs, neither sons nor nephews. (There was a niece, but she had married a nobody.) His position might be greater than had ever been granted to another Roman, but his pre-eminence must end with his life. He was at least ten years older than Marcus Aemilius Lepidus; in ten years, or fifteen at the outside, there would once again be room at the top for ordinary Romans who had followed the ordinary career, from quaestor to aedile to praetor, with the Consulship as the crown of a well-spent life. But if Caesar was going to make Marcus Antonius his second in command Antonius might become his heir; and Antonius was ten years younger than Lepidus. That would never do. The idea was absurd. Not one of the Antonius brothers was even respectable. His mind was wandering again.

Now about this battle tomorrow . . . would his men fight willingly against fellow-soldiers with whom they had no quarrel, fellow-soldiers who were also fellow-Caesarians? Probably not. But then the enemy also would be half-hearted. As a matter of fact, he still did not know which of the two armies lying on the skyline would be the enemy. The position was complicated.

Last spring Lepidus had laid down his governorship of Rome, to come out, with twelve lictors and consular ornaments, as proconsul in the province of Hither Spain. The province, garrisoned by two legions, was thoroughly Caesarian and loyal. But to the south-west lay the province of Further Spain, and that was in a mess. To begin with the tribes had been pacified by Pompeius, and their chieftains were still Pompeian in sympathy; then Caesar had rashly named as propraetor one of the most unsavoury thugs in the Popular faction, Quintus Cassius Longinus. This Cassius plundered his subjects until they rose against him;

in Spain that was always happening, and the Roman garrison was prepared to cope with it. But in this case Cassius had been so extortionate that even his own troops were sickened by his avarice; the insurgents had been joined by part of the Roman garrison, and Marcellus the quaestor, the personal friend whom Cassius had chosen to keep his accounts for him, had set himself at the head of the rebel army. Marcellus held Corduba for Caesar, the Populars, and the liberties of Spain; Cassius held the neighbouring mountain for Caesar, the Populars, and Cassius Longinus. And in all this confusion Marcus Lepidus had been ordered by the Senate to bring peace to Further Spain!

So here he was, with his two legions, a short day's march from the warring armies. Since Cassius and Marcellus would not combine against him, tomorrow he would be the ally of one and the foe of the other; but he could not guess which would be the enemy. He wished he had Junia in his hut to advise him.

Instead he peered into the hut to ask his secretary whether any news had come in. The secretary was a young Asiatic Greek named Eunomus, a freedman. He had been born free, and educated as a citizen of Miletus; until his family met with misfortune and he was sold to pay his father's arrears of taxation. Except for the slave-dealer, his sole owner had been Lepidus, who had soon freed him. It was possible for a Roman to make friends with a free-born youth who had endured such unmerited disaster. But of course bondage, even for a day, left an indelible stain on the character; Eunomus would never again think with the independent manliness proper to a citizen.

The secretary sat in a corner of the stuffy hut, a portable writing-desk on his knee. At his right stood the official table and chair of the general in command. When messengers came in and saluted the empty chair Eunomus could reach across and pick up the dispatches they laid down; that avoided the social awkwardness of asking a Roman soldier to hand over a letter to a Greek freedman.

The handsome youth looked up with a flash of white teeth. 'Good fortune follows us, my lord,' he said cheerfully. 'A messenger has just arrived from Trebonius. He left him near the Pyrenees. He ought to be entering Spain already.'

'Why should I rejoice that Trebonius is near? I hardly know the man. He's a typical Caesarian rakehell, not the kind of citizen I met often in Rome. They say he did well at the siege of Massilia, though in fact he couldn't take the town until Caesar came back to help him. I don't want another general to share my command. Does he bring an army with him? Why is he coming, anyway?'

'Oh no, my lord, he brings no army. He has been appointed next year's proconsul of Further Spain, and he left Rome a little earlier than usual, to be sure of getting here in good time.'

'Ah, that's why his coming is good news. I understand. Did you send the messenger on to Cassius?'

'Of course, my lord. The news concerns him, and he should be informed.'

It amused the Greek to leave out the essence of any item of news. Lepidus knew his foibles, and when he had followed the working of his subtle mind he felt a glow of satisfaction. He could see it all. The two Caesarian politicians on the hills over there had drifted into the beginning of an armed conflict, because both were obstinate and would not admit themselves in the wrong. Cassius could not be driven from his province by his own quaestor; Marcellus could not ask forgiveness of the superior who had bullied him into revolt. Now Cassius might retire gracefully. His successor was hastening to the province; perhaps a little before his time, but there was nothing very odd in that. Most important of all, if Cassius handed over his charge without making difficulties he might return to Rome with all his baggage, including the plunder he had exacted from the wretched provincials. His honour would be saved, and his money too. On the other hand, if he refused to go peacefully he must now declare war on the whole Caesarian party.

At first Lepidus felt nothing but relief. He would not be compelled to lead his army into battle. Then came a sensation of disappointment. He had brought two legions over all these mountains just to march them back again, without a sword drawn. Surely he ought to do something? After careful thought he discovered there was something he should do.

Eunomus had seen at first glance the way out of the impasse; Lepidus had seen it almost as quickly. But would Cassius see it without prompting? The proconsul of Hither Spain would deserve well of his country if he pointed out to his erring colleague the path of duty. It might be a risky business, but that was all to the good. If he could not win fame as a mighty warrior he would be remembered as a sage counsellor.

'Messenger,' he called, 'warn the officer of the day that tomorrow I shall require a small mounted escort. Better make them Roman troops if he can find enough legionaries who know how to ride. I shall want a herald, too. Choose a smart man who knows the drill about flags of truce. I shall be calling on Romans, not on barbarians, and the ceremonial must be worthy of a proconsul. The party should be ready an hour after sunrise tomorrow.'

He glanced in triumph at his secretary. 'How's that, my boy?' he said with a chuckle. 'Pretty quick off the mark, eh? If I stop a dangerous war merely by a couple of private interviews I ought to get the public thanks of the Senate, and perhaps something more substantial from Caesar.'

'Yes, my lord. It is excellently planned. But, if you will permit a criticism while we are alone, please don't send orders to a military tribune by the mouth of a common legionary. These soldiers have their own etiquette, and they are absurdly touchy.'

'You do right to tell me, Eunomus, and I am grateful. It's so easy to forget the senseless complications of military life. Every legionary is a citizen, and the military tribunes also are citizens. To be a citizen of Rome is to hold the highest rank in the world, apart from the few curule magistrates with the right to inspect omens, such as myself. In the City no citizen is better than another, and any citizen can bear a message to his equal. That's more fitting, more honourable, and more in accordance with the customs of our ancestors, than all this saluting and standing to attention that they have in the army.'

Lepidus felt better after he had delivered this little homily. For a moment the freedman had punctured his self-esteem; but the fellow, though bright and well-educated, was only a foreigner who could not understand the dignity and moral worth of the Roman constitution. All the same, he must be careful in his dealings with these soldiers. Nowadays their opinion mattered, though they seldom bothered to vote in the Forum. An Aemilius could not be expected to drink with them in taverns, or to cap their bawdy anecdotes; the Antonius brothers did, and it made them popular with their men; but they were Antonii.

Lepidus sometimes feared that his troops lacked respect for their commander. He had no experience of leadership in the field, and he could not tell in advance whether he would be good at it when the time came. His men ought to be content with their present service. They were Caesarian veterans, who had earned all the glory a reasonable man should need while following Caesar in Gaul. In this Spanish garrison they were punctually and lavishly paid, well fed and well supplied; he had never harried them with forced marches or compelled them to bivouac under the sky. He was a good man of affairs, whose accounts were always in balance; and with the wealth of the Lepidi behind him he was not tempted to accept bribes from army contractors. Perhaps these men would not respect him as they respected Caesar, until he had led them to a bloody victory. But if they knew when they were well off they must be pleased to be in his army. The unpleasant fear which had come to him a few days ago, that his legions might desert to Cassius if they were offered the plunder of Spain, was only a silly nightmare.

Three days later, riding back from Corduba to his camp, Lepidus decided to get into friendly conversation with his orderly. He wanted to find out what the legionaries were really thinking. The orderly was only a common soldier; but he was an experienced veteran, one of the best type of professional legionary. Quintus Crastinus was a nephew of the famous centurion who had met a hero's death at Pharsalus, but he was without ambition; after ten years' service he was glad to get the comfortable post of orderly to the proconsul. He would sleep in his blankets every night and never go foraging for firewood. His work was responsible, though it could not lead to promotion; in action it was his duty to stand beside his commander and protect him with his shield, since senior officers did not themselves carry shields. With some commanders that might be a very hazardous duty, but Crastinus suspected that the shield-bearer to Marcus Lepidus would probably die of old age.

'Well, my man, do you think the troops will feel cheated of their battle?' began Lepidus, swallowing the slight awkwardness he always felt when conversing with a social inferior. 'If the propraetor had defied us they might have plundered his camp.'

'No, sir, we are all very glad to know it's peace. We are paid to fight, and if there's fighting to be done we'll do it. But we don't like fighting against Romans, even when there is something to fight about. It's dangerous to fence with swordsmen who learned the same parries and thrusts on the same parade ground; not like facing barbarians, when all you have to do is keep in line. And to plunder their camp would feel like stealing from a comrade.'

'Then they won't mind when they see Cassius and his men march away unmolested?' Lepidus persisted. 'There may even be rude gestures as they defile past our camp. If you look at it correctly they have submitted to the lawful authority of the Senate and People of Rome; but this afternoon they were rejoicing as though they had won a victory.'

'That's because they saw themselves trapped, and now they've found a way out. Of course there will be some fingers pointed, in twos I shouldn't wonder. They will be in column of route, free to thumb their noses; we shall be standing at attention. All the same, they will be showing their backs to us, and the men know that. I suppose you knew all along, sir, that if the propraetor had been sticky his men would have deserted to us? What had they to fight for? Their plunder, certainly. But they could have brought it

46

with them when they changed sides. You spoke in Caesar's name, and Caesar's legions won't fight against Caesar. The propraetor must have known that. It's a wonder they followed him against Marcellus, but the quaestor made the mistake of bringing in those Spanish rebels. Then the propraetor's men could kid themselves they were fighting for Rome.'

'So however the interview might go, there would have been no battle after?'

'That's right, sir. No battle. We were quite easy in our minds.'

Lepidus rode on in silence. He had risked his life in a dangerous interview with an armed rebel, and all the time every legionary in Spain had known there was no danger of war. It was disappointing. However, in Rome it would not be known.

His negotiation had been valuable, all the same, Lepidus knew it. Quintus Cassius had been desperate, fearing he might be declared a public enemy; if his army as a whole would not have followed him, he could at least have led into the mountains a very troublesome band of brigands.

Lepidus had talked him over. It was strange that Lepidus could seldom talk to soldiers, or to the citizens assembled in the Forum, without his shyness setting the crowd's nerves on edge and putting public opinion against him; yet when he spoke to an individual, to another nobleman of good position, he could usually carry his point. He was honest enough to recognise that it was a help to be Aemilius Lepidus, for Aemilius Lepidus must carry weight with any nobleman who revered the ways of the ancestors. He did not realise that his manner and his outlook were the very quintessence of the respectable point of view, so that his adversary heard the embodied voice of all the Senate past and present, the images and the ancestors and the rather sententious and sactimonius heroes of old, speaking through this dignified, brave, stupid aristocrat; but in truth that was a powerful reinforcement.

Cassius had agreed to go quietly, on condition he might take back to Rome the enormous sum of money he had wrung from his misgoverned province. Marcellus, after another awkward interview, had agreed to recognise the authority of Trebonius. Marcellus was not a zealous servant of the state. He refused to crucify the rebels who had entered Corduba to join his forces, and instead gave them safe conduct to return to their mountains. That was putting his private honour before the welfare of Rome. Lepidus must in duty report this mistaken clemency to Caesar, and that would be the end of Marcellus's official career. Then Lepidus corrected himself; Marcellus was a Claudius, and there was no keeping down an ambitious and clever member of the gens Claudia. They could survive misdemeanours that would wreck the reputation even of an Aemilius.

Now he was nearing the camp, where the tribunes had called out his legions on parade. He must ride down the line to inspect them, and it would be only humane to tell them that they need not fight after all. Tomorrow they would begin the toilsome march back to the Hither province. Wasn't there a verse about some mythical commander who had marched his men up a hill and then marched them down again? If the troops felt sulky someone in the rear rank would murmur it, and then there would be sniggers. He was not cut out to be a general; the sooner he got back to the Senate and the Forum the better for everyone. Oh well. No use putting it off. Here goes.

'Soldiers! I bring you good news. . . .'

Merciful gods, they were cheering him! The tribunes set the example, and the legate commanding the second legion had thrown his helmet into the air! Now they were shouting his name, all together. 'I told you, sir, that we don't like fighting Romans,' the orderly whispered in his ear. But this was quite unexpected.

It was not his name they were shouting, exactly. They were shouting something much more splendid: 'Marcus Aemilius Lepidus – *Imperator*,' with a great bellow on the final word.

Dizzy with surprise and delight, Lepidus slid off his horse and stumbled into his hut.

Eunomus ran to greet him. 'I've told your steward to begin giving out the wine, my lord,' he said eagerly. 'They tell me it ought to be your gift, from your private store, not the regulation vinegar they get with their rations. There won't be a skin of it left by midnight, but tomorrow we can get the local stuff, which is said to be drinkable. Will you seal a message to the lady Junia as soon as I have scribbled it? She must be informed at once; I can just catch the evening courier. Or would it be better to send the good news by special messenger?'

'What good news?' Lepidus asked vacantly, 'and what's all this about my wine?'

Then the officer of the day stood saluting in the entry.

'Imperator, will you give out the password for tonight?' he asked in the expressionless tone of the soldier on duty.

'I think "Good Fortune" seems appropriate,' Lepidus replied in a weak voice. Now he understood what had befallen him, but he still could not see why it had happened. He had been granted the supreme distinction which could come to a Roman commander; his soldiers, armed and ready for battle, had hailed him Imperator. There had been no collusion, no underhand bribery or distribution of wine in advance; the men had done it of their own free will, in a spontaneous outburst of devotion. He told himself that this was the proudest moment of his life – because it must be. But he could not forget that on this campaign no one had drawn a sword, except to repel the petty raids of brigands.

Eunomus was speaking quietly. 'My lord, I know this was unexpected, and I know also that a general should be hailed as Imperator after bloody battle, while he inspects the heaps of his slain enemies. But the soldiers mean it. They admire you. They know that if once they begin fighting fellow-Caesarians they must pass their lives in unending warfare, and they know also that either Cassius or Marcellus could have cut your throat when in one day you entered two hostile camps to parley. You stopped a war at the risk of your life. They feel for you as though you had held a bridge single-handed to cover their retreat. This great honour has been earned.'

'You need say no more,' answered Lepidus, recovering his gravity. 'Caesar fought the Optimates to put an end to civil war. If Caesar has brought lasting peace there can be no more great victories. Someone must be the first bloodless Imperator, and it happens to be me. Unborn generations of Lepidi will remember it as they honour my image.'

By September of the next year Caesar was back in Rome; and not before he was needed. In the absence of the Dictator no one was willing to take responsibility, and public security declined as the more scoundrelly Caesarians experimented to see how far Marcus Antonius would let them go. Since January there had not even been any true magistrates; Caesar should have endorsed his chosen candidates, but he had been too busy in Egypt and Asia to indicate his wishes. No elections were held, and last year's magistrates continued in office.

Lepidus was still in law proconsul of Hither Spain; but the province was peaceful and his mission had been accomplished. Trebonius ruled undisturbed in Further Spain. Luck had eliminated the disreputable Quintus Cassius. He had withdrawn peacefully, with a free pardon, according to the terms agreed with Lepidus; but the ship bearing his ill-gotten treasure was wrecked, and he had been drowned with his stolen gold. During the summer, while Caesar was conquering the Pontic insurgents, Lepidus turned over his province to a competent legate and returned to Italy.

He did not re-enter Rome, for he knew the law; he had left the City as a proconsul, and if he came within the pomoerium his powers must automatically lapse. He waited quietly in a villa in Picenum, while the private armies of Dolabella and Marcus Antonius fought one another in the Forum, while in Campania Caesarian legions mutinied, while Milo, the veteran mob-leader of the Optimates, launched his aimless insurrection and was killed in a petty skirmish. Rome in those days was no place for a respectable Caesarian, a Lepidus who upheld the liberties of the people but also upheld the right even of the rich to own property.

Then Caesar came. The mutinous troops returned to duty, Dolabella was packed off to comfortable exile, the Antonius brothers stayed within bounds, and magistrates were duly elected. Still Lepidus lingered in Picenum; he was hoping for a Triumph.

If anyone were ill-mannered enough to ask for a Triumph the Senate would vote it down without hesitation; the honour must come unsought. But a magistrate who tarried outside the City, feeding soldiers and lictors at his private expense, reminded the Senators that his claim merited consideration. Lepidus knew that the affair would speedily be brought to Caesar's attention; he would not be kept hanging about, like poor old Cicero.

The matter was quickly settled. Caesar called in person at the villa. Outside Rome the Dictator kept no great state, though of course a man with so many enemies must always have a body-guard; but it was the businesslike bodyguard of a soldier, not the ceremonial escort of an absolute ruler. Lepidus deplored its necessity, but he could not accuse Caesar of unconstitutional pomp.

They talked in a shady portico; just the Dictator and his sec-retary, Lepidus and Eunomus, and Junia with a confidential maid. It was almost like the old days ten years ago, when Caesar had been a gay and rising Senator. But in those days Junia would not have been so free with her endearments. Now anything was permitted to Caesar.

After some gossip about Servilia and Tertulla, a discussion which Lepidus found embarrassing, for it made him feel he was intruding on a family reunion, Caesar came to business. Lepidus was delighted to learn that he was very highly regarded by the government of the republic; all his desires would be gratified even before he had voiced them.

'Of course the new Imperator must enter Rome in Triumph,' Caesar began. 'Have you any trophies or prisoners, my dear Lepidus? It won't be much of a procession without them, you know, even if you did no fighting.'

'I caught some Spanish brigands, and kept them alive in case they might be needed. Trophies are more difficult, but I suppose

I could show pictures of my interviews with Cassius and Marcellus.'

'My dear fellow, you can show a model of the walls of Corduba. Didn't the city yield to your arms? There could be another model of the camp of Cassius. Even if you took no valuable plunder, you must have a few Spanish weapons and curios; if necessary I'll lend you some of my Asiatic spoil. I'm glad you kept some prisoners. I don't like to see harmless slaves strangled as the Triumphator enters the temple of Jupiter; but there must be men killed at that time, to make the gods pay attention to what's going on. Well then, you have everything needful. Tomorrow I shall tell the Senate that they must vote you a Triumph before the end of the month. Now what about the future? I suppose you would like to be Consul, as your ancestors were?'

'Of course I want to be Consul, just as I want a Triumph. I deserve these honours, and they prove me worthy of my family. But, if you will forgive me for saying so, I should like to be honoured by the Senate and People of Rome, not by a decree of the Dictator. If you propose, from your place in the Senate, that the fathers should grant me Triumph, of course they will follow your advice. So that when you said just now that I might have a Triumph, as though it were in your gift, that was just a handy way of saying you would so advise the Senate. The Consulship is different; that is granted by the people. You can speak for the Senate; but I don't like to hear a single man, however great, promising curule magistracies as though they were his private property.'

'Nobly spoken, my gallant husband,' said Junia with a smile. 'But Caesar speaks for the people more truly than he speaks for the Senate. Think how many Senators he had to kill on the battlefield before he was acknowledged as leader of the fathers. The people have backed him ever since he crossed the Rubicon.'

'Junia puts it very well, you know, Lepidus. I am not a tyrant. I hold no office foreign to the constitution; there have been Dictators before me and others will come after. All I propose is that one day you should offer yourself as candidate for the Consulship, and that I should support you. Perhaps it is my vanity that leads me to expect you would then be elected.'

' I want to be Consul one day, and as a loyal Popular I would not stand against a candidate who enjoyed your support. I suppose that comes to much the same thing. Thank you, Caesar.'

'Let's get this settled, now we have started the subject. Next year's Consuls have not been chosen. We postponed the elections because of the disturbed condition of the City.'

'Disturbed conditions is one way of putting it, Caesar my

love,' said Junia. 'The streets were more dangerous than in the heyday of Clodius. Your rapscallions of followers were raping respectable matrons in their own bedrooms.'

'Tut tut, I didn't know things were so bad. The boys must have their fun, and now I'm back I shall keep them in order. Did dear Servilia meet with any exciting adventures?'

'Mother would tell you before she told me, and you know it. But what about this Consulship? Since my husband is too noble to protect his own interests, his faithful wife must look after them.'

'Ah yes, the Consulship. I was thinking of standing once more myself. I have a good following among the people, and a fair hope of success. But I shall be even stronger if I stand in partnership with another strong candidate. The combination of Julius Caesar and Aemilius Lepidus seems to me invincible.'

'Do you mean that next year you will take me as your colleague? That is a greater honour than I deserve,' said Lepidus, forgetful that curule magistracies should not be in the gift of a single man.

'Yes, that is what I mean. Now let's talk seriously. Of course I can be Consul as often as I please. My soldiers will see to it, and if they don't the mob would lynch any opposing candidate. But I want to be chosen ruler of the whole City, not just a faction-leader whose faction happens to hold power. I want to reassure the respectable nobles, and the law-abiding merchants. I'm a patrician myself, descended from the goddess Venus. I don't like feeling that only freedom and sausage-sellers support me, and that every man of honour and education dreads to see me in power. I could have chosen Marcus Antonius as my colleague, or even that scoundrel Dolabella. They are both faithful Caesarians. But then Cicero and the middle classes would take fright, seeing Cinna and Catilina come again. You are my guarantee of respectability. If Aemilius Lepidus is Consul, standing where his ancestors have stood for three hundred years, that proves that Rome has not broken with the past. I am doing you a favour, certainly; but I do it because I need your help.'

'I shall be proud to help you to govern Rome; and together we shall govern Rome worthily.'

'That's true, Junia,' said Caesar. 'There's no call to snigger. On great occasions I'm all for the expression of noble sentiments; it's just my misfortune that my genius always puts flippancies into my mouth instead. With Lepidus as colleague I shall rule more worthily than if I shared power with anyone else. You see, I suffer from bright ideas. If I tell them to the Antonius brothers, or to Pollio or any other of the boys, they encourage me to go

52

ahead and upset all the ways of the ancestors. I need the ballast of an educated patrician like your husband; otherwise when I have finished with the City it will be like any other town in Europe or Asia. I can never remember that some things are part of Rome, and must never be altered.'

'Then my Marcus is the man for you,' Junia answered. 'He doesn't hold with innovation. Do you, darling?'

'Rome has done very well in the past,' said Lepidus stiffly. His sense of tradition was dear to him, and he did not care to hear it mocked. 'While the City continues to prosper I see no reason for any change.'

'Then you are the colleague I need. I'm sorry our Consulship can only last for one year. You should always be beside me to advise me.' Caesar paused, though Junia guessed that every move in this discussion had been planned beforehand.

'Yes,' Caesar continued, 'we must work together even after our year is up. In Africa I must settle with poor Cato, even though he is dear Junia's brother's father-in-law; and when I have a moment to spare there are the Parthians to be conquered. I shall be abroad a lot during the next few years. I had thought of leaving Marcus Antonius in command of Italy; he's a thief, but a loyal thief. Yet he's a young man, who has never held curule office, and a plebeian. It would be better to appoint a patrician and Consular. That's it. As Dictator I can appoint a Master of the Horse to rule Rome as my deputy in my absence. You will be Master of the Horse, Amelius Lepidus. But Antonius must command the troops in Italy outside Rome, because he commanded a wing at Pharsalus and I can't put a public slight on him. Will that suit you?'

In all the glory of purple cloak and golden wreath, Marcus Aemilius Lepidus stood beside the smoking altar of Jupiter the Greatest and Best. At the foot of the stairs his four-horse chariot awaited him, and the people of Rome stood massed to cheer his greatness. This sacred spot was the quintessence of the City; he had been granted the highest honour that could come to a Roman citizen; this actual moment, as he sacrificed to the supreme guardian of Rome, must be the crowning moment of his life. In his youth his teacher of philosophy had advised him to analyse his emotions on great occasions, and he was pleased to recognise that he felt the correct sentiments; no pride, but gratitude and love of the City overflowed his breast. But under the patriotism, lurking below the pride which justifiably came next, was an element of surprise. Here he stood, Triumphator and Imperator and Consul-elect; and he seemed to have done very little to deserve these honours. It proved that, for one of his birth and education, it was quite easy to become a great man.

*The lady Clodia was complaining again, to the young man who sat in her bedroom and quizzed the three maids arranging her hair.*

*'Quintus darling, they had roped off the Sacred Way for a triumphal procession, and I couldn't get near the scent-shop. They ought to warn us before they do these things. Who is being honoured, and why? It can't be Caesar. Isn't he in Africa?'*

*'It's the Triumph of Marcus Aemilius Lepidus Imperator, duly voted by the Senate. But his exploits, my dear, are a well-kept secret. They say he won great victories in Spain. I haven't met anyone who was on the losing side, so perhaps he killed them all. Otherwise, he's just another Caesarian. They like Triumphs.'*

*'Oh, him. He's not a real man. As I told poor Catullus before he turned so horrid, this Lepidus is only a wax figure, left over from a funeral. Come and kiss my ear, before it's covered.'*

# IV

## TYRANNICIDE
### 44 B.C.

In the Aemilian mansion they were preparing for a great dinner.
There would be only nine couches, the minimum for a formal
party, and the kitchen was easily capable of dealing with such a
number. But the host was Master of the Horse, the second
magistrate in Rome; and one of the guests would be the Dictator
himself. Everything must be at the same time easy and splendid.

Lepidus himself supervised the decoration of the dining-room
while Junia had a last word with the cook. Though there was
nothing to worry about, only personal supervision kept servants
up to the mark. In March it was always difficult to get decent
flowers, but the full-blown African roses ought to last until
midnight. Lepidus inspected the ornate centre-piece on the serving table, and passed it as adequate. A massy silver vase rose
from the back of a solid silver elephant, and the sight of his
family badge always reassured him. After all, the Aemilii were
one of the six greater patrician houses, and the elephant had been
granted to them in recognition of eminent services in the Punic
Wars. In the presence of that reminder of his high descent, and
of his present prosperity, it would be absurd to feel nervous.

His wife joined him, pleased with what she had seen in the
kitchen. 'The food will be worthy of us, Marcus,' she said
placidly. 'Caesar never notices what he eats, so I've stuck to roast
peacock for the main course. It's unadventurous, but no one can
fault it. Marcus Antonius is more difficult to please; though
nowadays he has a poor appetite, and I'm not at all surprised.
Decimus Brutus knows about food, but with Caesar at the next
table he'll be so busy making a good impression that he won't be
able to tell octopus from mullet. What a toady that man has
become! The rest don't matter. Just ordinary Caesarians, who
should feel flattered to be received in a respectable house.'

'You will sit with us, my dear, until we have finished eating.
I think young Marcus might be present at the beginning, though
he must leave when the ladies retire. Little Quintus is definitely

55

too young; he would repeat anything he heard. He must dine in the nursery. And I have one piece of bad news for you. Marcus Antonius has sent word that he will be bringing Fulvia. They have been formally betrothed. So afterwards you will be stuck with that harridan in the drawing-room all the time we are drinking.'

'Never mind. Antonius always brings a girl, and it might have been someone even worse. Do you remember Cytheris? They say she used to lie on a couch like a man, and stay drinking with the men until all hours.'

'Never in this house. I wouldn't have it. I didn't wish to distress your feelings by letting you know, but once he actually proposed to bring her here. I put my foot down. As a matter of fact Antonius is behaving rather more discreetly now Caesar is back in Rome.'

'I wish I'd seen him in all his glory,' said Junia with a youthful giggle. 'When you and Caesar were abroad, the story got round that he travelled about Italy in a chariot drawn by lions. Seven litters full of boys and girls followed him, with Cytheris in a litter all to herself.'

'That's the story, certainly. I heard it too. But they may have exaggerated. Cytheris certainly was with him, and it's bad enough that a propraetor should take an actress in his train when he travels on official business. All the same, there must be something in the man, though I can't see it. Caesar seems to be able to get good work out of ruffians, and from all his ruffians he has chosen this Antonius to be his lieutenant.'

'Our dear Caesar is a bit of a ruffian himself, that's why. Is he bringing a girl? I would like to have a chat with the Queen. I have only seen her in public.'

'Calpurnia is not well enough to dine out, so Caesar will come alone. He would never bring a foreign mistress to *this* house. In any case, it's impossible to invite Cleopatra to a formal dinner. She insists on her precedence as Queen of Egypt. You may call on her, if you wish, and talk with her in her boudoir; or she might visit your private apartments, where there is no etiquette. I won't have her in the public rooms; it would make endless difficulties. And for all that she's a genuine Queen you should remember she's a whore also.'

'No, I won't call on the Queen. Her guests are expected to grovel before her, as though they were her subjects. Since she won't call on me until I have called on her, I suppose we shall never meet. A pity. But there are other remarkable sights in Rome.'

'Spoken like a true matron, my dear. In any case, tonight we shall have at our table the ruler of the world. In comparison, Macedonian Queens matter not at all. Well, the butler will only lose his head if we fuss over him any longer. We may as well go and dress for the party. I shall wear a toga. That synthesis affair may look all right on the couch; but it's a sloppy compromise, and Greek into the bargain. Besides, I must stand to receive my guests, and everyone would spot it.'

By the time dessert was on the table Lepidus regretted the formality of his dress, for a toga was never comfortable while its wearer reclined. All his guests had come in the new synthesis, a flowing robe which could be arranged to look like toga and tunic combined; it fastened securely with brooches, instead of being wrapped tightly round the waist. Yet the party itself was a success, and Caesar was behaving most affably.

Of course the great man had begun with a little teasing of his hostess. He inquired why her brother was absent; though he knew very well that Marcus Brutus held him to be a tyrant, and declined any invitation that might compel him to be civil to the Dictator. It was less than a year since he had gone out of his way to marry into the ranks of Caesar's enemies, choosing as his wife Porcia, the daughter of poor old Cato, who was also the widow of Bibulus who had commanded the Pompeian fleet. The match had led to a furious quarrel among the children of Servilia, who herself refused to speak to her disloyal son. A considerate guest would have avoided the topic, but Caesar was always amused by the embarrassment of the respectable.

Decimus Brutus seemed jumpy and short-tempered, drinking too much and too fast, and continually changing the subject of conversation. Lepidus did not know him very well, and guessed that he was merely too anxious to impress his leader at close quarters. Rather surprisingly, the raffish Marcus Antonius saved the situation. He could, after all, be charming when he tried; and tonight he was trying his hardest.

When the ladies had withdrawn there was a political discussion; or rather, Caesar expounded his plans to his subordinates. 'In a few days I start for Parthia,' he said casually. 'I must pay just one formal visit to the Senate, so that the fathers can receive my civil powers and invest me with military authority. Then I join the army in Macedonia and we march on Seleucia as fast as infantry can cover the ground. Even if all goes well it's bound to be a long job, and while I am away the citizens may grow restive. That's why I am leaving Gaul and all the west in hands I can trust. Decimus here has Cisalpine Gaul, with the army nearest to Rome; you, Lepidus, can back him from Narbo, with Plancus and Pollio behind you. If there should be serious

57

trouble you can all get together. The combined armies of the three Gauls and the two Spains should be able to crush any levy my foes can raise in Italy. So mind you keep in touch with one another.'

'What about young Sextus Pompeius?' asked Lepidus. 'They say he's keeping Pollio pretty busy. In a crisis Spain may be unable to spare troops.'

'Then let Sextus Pompeius overrun all Spain, if he must; provided you keep Rome obedient. But young Sextus has no cause and no programme; nothing but a great name and the goodwill of his father's veterans. What he wants is money. If I can't suppress him I shall have to buy him.'

'Rome will be faithful. You can depend on us,' Lepidus answered. 'But any campaign may bring unfortunate incidents. The Parthians will be beaten in the end, but something may happen to you, Caesar. In that case, to whose cause do we keep Rome faithful?'

It was a question no other Caesarian would have dared to ask; but Lepidus was not in the least overawed by a fellow-patrician of ancestry no more distingushed than his own.

'I have thought even of that,' Caesar answered easily. 'My will is deposited with the Vestals. Just for the present it's a confidential document. If you want to know what's in it you must ask the holy ladies. My other papers are safe in the hands of Marcus Antonius. He's not much of a one for reading, and he doesn't know what's in them.'

'There have been bad omens, they tell me,' Lepidus continued. 'There seems to be a curse on these wars with Parthia. Do you remember the terrible portents before poor Crassus set out? They proved true enough.'

'You can't frighten me with omens,' Caesar replied. 'You've heard the story about the sacrifice before I fought at Munda? The ox fled bellowing from the altar, and escaped through the whole army. Of course the diviners pointed out that the gods were rejecting my sacrifice, and that I must retreat at once. Instead we all charged at the double, without any sacrifice offered; and by the end of the day it had been proved that the gods love me more than they love the Pompeians.'

'And you fought all day in the front rank, on foot, without a scratch,' put in Brutus. 'Didn't they bother to throw javelins at you?'

'It wasn't all day, just for half an hour to get the boys into the right frame of mind for the final assault. The Spaniards threw plenty of javelins; but I had a good orderly, and they are rotten shots anyway. It's a mistake to give Roman arms to barbarians;

they don't keep cool enough to use them properly. Don't imagine that I think myself invulnerable, or under the special protection of heaven. I know when I'm in danger, and I never run a risk unless it's worth it. If the common soldiers believe that steel can't harm me, that's all to the good. I myself remain sane.'

'Then you don't put faith in the mysterious prophecy, that only a King of Rome can conquer the Parthians?' asked Brutus.

'I am Pontifex Maximus, and considered pretty good at ritual and divination. I never heard of that prophecy until a few months ago. Let's see, who's the youngest here? Antonius, did you learn it at school?'

Antonius scowled and grunted, while the others smiled. It was generally supposed that he had invented the bogus prophecy.

'All the same, the omens have been bad,' Lepidus persisted. 'Perhaps you ought to go straight to the army in Macedonia. You have no more to do in Rome, except this ceremonial meeting.'

'That's what Calpurnia advises, but I don't agree. Tomorrow's meeting of the Senate may be only a ceremony, but ceremonies are important. I want to fight the Parthians as the duly-accredited commander of the Roman army. Don't let's cross an unnecessary Rubicon.'

'Yes, you don't want to lead another unlawful campaign, and the Senate alone can give you legal authority,' said Brutus. 'Have the omens really been bad?'

'Well, this morning, when I sacrificed as usual on behalf of the Roman people, the diviner told me the dead ox had no heart at all. I answered that in that case it had never been alive. One's no more absurd than the other. Can you imagine a worse omen? I suppose the diviner had been bribed by some stout Optimate, perhaps dear Junia's brother Brutus. If he had not looked so carefully the heart would have been easy to find; it was probably in his bosom when he told me. Anyway, tomorrow I go to the Senate, and the next day I march against the Parthians. So much for omens.'

'What's the use of being forewarned of death if you can't avoid it?' said Antonius. 'Croesus gave an enormous offering to Apollo at Delphi, and Apollo told him he would destroy a great empire. Apollo didn't say the empire was Croesus's own realm of Lydia. Oracles and omens only make fools of us.'

Brutus jumped from his couch and strode jerkily across the room to the nearest chamber-pot. Lepidus frowned. It would be a nuisance if the young man got noisily drunk while the other guests were still sober.

Meanwhile there had begun a general discussion on the subject of the least unpleasant kind of death, a topic well fitted to a decorous dinner-party. Everyone joined in, upholding the theories of his favourite philosophy, except Caesar, who was busy scribbling his initials on a sheaf of papers brought in by a footman. As he scanned the dispatches the Dictator listened with half an ear, and then threw a single sentence over his shoulder. 'The only good death is unexpected – no time to be afraid.'

Silence hung for a moment over the room. It was broken by a ludicrous hiccup from Brutus, who leapt from his couch to vomit into a convenient basin.

That spoiled the evening. One drunken man can make eight sober diners unpleasantly self-conscious. As early as politeness permitted Caesar called for his litter, and once the guest of honour was gone the others hastened to take leave. It was earlier than he had expected when Lepidus entered his wife's boudoir for a final chat.

'Thank heavens they've gone,' Junia greeted him. That Fulvia! We all tried to draw her out about her married life with Clodius the gangster. I am sure she had the most amusing adventures. But she would talk of nothing but the happy day, soon to come, when Marcus Antonius will be ruler of Rome. The insufferable woman believes that her intended has been named Caesar's heir, and that Caesar will die soon. She patronised me in my own drawing-room until I could have scratched her face.'

'I suppose Antonius rules Rome at this moment,' her husband answered mildly. 'He's this year's Consul, and there's nothing higher than that. But Caesar is good for a long time yet; he's only ten years older than I am, not much over fifty. Certainly Antonius hopes to be his heir. He hinted as much this evening, but Caesar wouldn't rise; he gave no definite answer. He has all Rome to choose from; why should he choose one of the Antonius brothers? Anyway, isn't there some incredibly dim great-nephew?'

'There is a great-nephew. Don't you remember? He rode in the Triumph after the Spanish campaign. He's very young, and not quite a gentleman. Caesar's sister made an unfortunate marriage, and her daughter in turn married beneath her. What's the boy's name? Sextus, Septimus, something of the kind. He's not in Rome just now.'

'I remember him. Octavius is the name, not Septimus. A nice-looking youth, and he carried himself well in the Triumph. But I've heard he's an invalid. Caesar will have to find another heir.'

'Well, he has plenty of time to make up his mind.'

Lepidus rose early next morning, in spite of his late night. He wanted to attend the meeting of the Senate. It would be a purely ritual affair, and he could describe in advance everything that would be said and done; but he had a weakness for historic occasions, and this would be something to tell his grandchildren. Before he went to the Senate he must visit his troops; a good commander should inspect his forces every day.

Not long ago it would have been blasphemy and sacrilege to station troops in Rome. All that had been changed when Caesar crossed the Rubicon. Of course the City had no formal garrison; that would be a badge of slavery. But troops marching through Italy now lodged just outside the pomoerium. As proconsul-designate of Narbonese Gaul Lepidus had begun to gather the army he would take to his province; a full legion of recruits was now on the Island of Aesculapius, in the middle of the Tiber. They were quiet, well-behaved boys, and loyal Caesarians; tucked away on their island they were technically outside the City.

Lepidus himself was careful to visit the camp in his toga, with the ornaments that marked him as a Consular. It would have been a shocking breach of etiquette if he had worn armour in the City, even on the way to inspect his troops.

The soldiers, early risers, were already at exercise; throwing javelins at a mark or wheeling by cohorts under the command of their centurions. Lepidus inspected the latrines and kitchens. It was a real inspection, not a formal visit, and he did it every day. The men expected him, and everything was in order; though he was pleased to spot one sack of alleged ration-barley which was more than half chaff and husk. He was not wasting his time in doing so thoroughly the only part of a commander's duty he was fitted to perform; for he had never commanded in battle.

When he had finished his quartermaster's work he paused to watch the drill. In trying to sheathe his sword a young recruit missed the scabbard, so that his weapon fell to the ground. Immediately the centurion stood over him, raining down blows from his cudgel. The boy took it well, holding still with his eyes to the front until granted permission to bend down and retrieve the sword. In an unwonted flash of sympathy Lepidus tried to put himself in the other's place. Even knowing that he had done wrong, could he stand upright to take a beating? No patrician could do that. Seven hundred years of nobility made it as automatic to return a blow as to flinch from a hot ember; if he had been attacked by a lion or an elephant he would have struck back with his bare hands. The recruit was right, of course; such discipline had won Rome's battles. But these professional soldiers were a strange race of men, unlike the ordinary run of citizens.

Crastinus the orderly stood half a pace behind his master,

61

With the freedom of a trusted comrade he now whispered his explanation unasked. 'That boy would defend himself against old Felix the centurion. It isn't the centurion who beats him. It's Caesar, our Imperator. We will take anything from Caesar.'

'But I would not,' thought Lepidus to himself. 'I would return a blow from Caesar's cudgel as swiftly as if it had been struck by a slave. Any Senator would do the same, except for a few jumped-up careerists like Cicero. And Caesar is terribly insolent. One day he may go too far.'

He said a few words to the tribune in command of the parade, then went home to get ready for the meeting of the Senate.

In the vestibule of the Theatre of Pompeius he found a full house, though not a crowded one. More than two hundred Senators had turned up for this formal session, chiefly because it was rumoured that Caesar might make some important pronouncement before he left Rome for the East. The great man was late; it was whispered that he was ill and would not come at all. Then it became known that Decimus Brutus had gone to the Regia, his official residence, to fetch him. The crowded hall waited restlessly.

The Senate could not begin its session until called to order by a Consul. At last a stir in the Forum announced that both Consuls were approaching. As usual, Caesar was attended by a great crowd of petitioners and place-seekers, with Antonius walking humbly behind him as though Rome held only one Consul. Only Caesar entered the vestibule. As far as Lepidus could make out, from his place on the bench reserved for Consulars, someone was talking earnestly to Antonius in the portico outside.

In readiness for the Dictator's speech, the Senators got out their notebooks and arranged the folds of their togas. Suddenly there was the noise of a scuffle. A knot of men had closed round Caesar; they seemed to be beating him with their fists as the centurion had beaten that unlucky recruit. Then Lepidus saw the daggers in their hands.

In less than a minute all was over. More than twenty men passed against Caesar; there was one muffled war-cry, and a few grunts of angry desperation. The group scattered, leaving a flat bloody bundle of clothes at the base of the statue of Pompeius. The murderers blocked the main doorway, waving bloody daggers and shouting for liberty; but there was another narrow door at the far end of the chamber. Lepidus picked up the skirt of his toga and pushed head-downwards through the throng to get clear.

When he reached the Forum it was already deserted. There was not a litter to be seen, or he would have jumped into the nearest and drawn the curtains. Only one thought possessed his mind; the Dictator had been overthrown by armed revolution, and the assassins would turn next on his chief lieutenant, his Master of the Horse. At every stride, as he ran across the empty square, he expected to feel the knife in his spine.

He ran so fast that he outdistanced the terrible news. As he reached the Aemilian mansion the silversmith in the next block was just stirring to put up his shutters. The porter gaped in silent amazement at his dishevelled and frightened master, but his first shout of alarm brought Junia, excited but composed.

While he was pounding down the street he had repeated to himself: 'I am Aemilius Lepidus, Consular, Imperator, Triumphator. There is no shame in fleeing unarmed before armed murderers, but when I reach safety my plan must be ready.' The incantation of his roll of titles had calmed his spirit, as always; and his plan was ready.

He called at once to Junia: 'Caesar is dead, murdered. Rebels are slaughtering the Senate. Fetch Marcus and Quintus, and the box of money from under the bed. Then get over the Tiber at once. Take a few armed slaves as escort. When you are a mile beyond the barriers, and not before, here a carriage. Then gallop as fast as you can to our villa in Picenum. When you reach it write to me at my camp on the Island of Aesculapius. Don't obey any instructions from me unless they are sealed with this signet. Go now.'

Without a word Junia turned on her heel. She never lost her head, and he knew she would obey him. He called next to the frightened butler: 'Fetch Eunomus. I must take him to headquarters. I shall take no one else. Collect all the valuables you can carry and lead the servants out of the City. Join my lady in Picenum as soon as you can. Leave this house empty, and be sure that no door is locked. The mob is certain to come pillaging, but if everything is open they may not burn as well. If you serve me faithfully I shall free you when I come home; if you try to escape I shall hunt you down and crucify you.'

Half an hour later he was trudging through empty streets towards the Tiber, the Greek secretary at his elbow.

Presently Eunomus spoke: 'This is a queer kind of revolution, my lord. Listen. The whole City is quiet. Perhaps everyone is hiding at home, for fear of everybody else; perhaps Caesar's murderers have already been put to death. Anyway, a government is not overthrown in complete silence.'

'I saw Caesar murdered. There were no soldiers near to arrest the murderers. That is why we are hurrying to the camp. This is the first rising since troops have been stationed near the City.

The conspirators will not find it so easy to seize power.'

When they reached the island there was still no noise. The whole City cowered behind barred doors.

The troops were already under arms. They were drawn up in battle order, their shields free of the leather covers which protected them in peacetime, light fighting-swords on their hips instead of the heavier implements used for drill. The tribune in command reported them ready to move off. It was evident that they expected to be led immediately to avenge their dead Imperator.

But no message came from the Forum. Lepidus hesitated to start a bloody battle within the consecrated pomoerium until he had been ordered to do so. He was still wearing his Senatorial toga; when he withdrew to his quarters to change into armour Eunomus slipped in after him.

Crastinus was there also, to fasten his lord's cuirass. As he fumbled with the buckles the old soldier muttered under his breath.

'Caesar murdered, and by a bunch of stuck-up Optimates. We licked them in three continents, one after the other, and spared their lives time and again. This is what you get for showing mercy to an Optimate. Now we must finish them. No quarter. And when we've sacked their houses we shall be rich for life.'

'But, Crastinus,' said Lepidus sadly, 'it wasn't the Optimates who murdered Ceasar. I was there, and I saw it. I saw Cassius among the murderers, and Decimus Brutus. This morning I would have sworn they were loyal Caesarians.

'Never mind who actually struck the blow,' Eunomus put in. 'The crime must have been planned by Optimates. We can kill them all, and sack their houses, before we hunt down the murderers. Don't you understand, my lord? Fortune offers you the greatest prize in the world. There is anarchy in Rome, and you command the only troops near the City. They will obey your orders, but first you must permit them to take vengeance on the Optimates.'

'In Rome there can never be anarchy,' Lepidus answered stoutly. 'The sacred constitution bequeathed to us by our ancestors provides for all contingencies. Caesar is dead, who was both Consul and Dictator. That leaves the other Consul, Antonius. He never entered the Senate House, so I suppose he escaped alive. If not, there are eight praetors. Some of them must be alive and at liberty. It is my duty as proconsul and Imperator to put my troops at the disposal of the senior surviving magistrate. If no magistrate survives the auspices revert to the Senate, and I must await the commands of the fathers.'

'My lord, don't quibble, I beg,' Eunomus continued in great excitement. 'These soldiers will follow you, and there are no other soldiers near. You can be King of the World – today. If there are any magistrates alive I shall see they get killed in the rioting. March straight on the Forum and summon the assembly. Order them to make you Dictator, while your soldiers stand by. But hurry, before some other army marches on the City.'

'I am not a pirate, to make war on my own City. Be quiet, freedman,' Lepidus said sternly. 'Crastinus, ask the senior tribune to come here as soon as convenient.'

Once he was buckled into his armour he gave his order without hesitation. 'Tribune, there has been a terrible murder, and sacrilege also; for the hero they killed was among other things Pontifex Maximus. That does not mean that we must wage war on the City. We are Caesarians, and we grieve. But as loyal Romans we await the orders of our lawful superiors. Post guards on the bridges, and hold this island against all comers. If the streets remain empty send out patrols of steady veterans to find out what is happening in the Forum. I shall wait here, in my headquarters. Let in any messengers, if they come in peace; and send them to me without delay. You may tell the soldiers that the laws of Rome remain in force, and that any plundering or mishandling of citizens will be punished with the utmost rigour.'

After five years in authority he had the habit of issuing orders; they came out with a snap and decision that ensured obedience.

He settled down to wait in his headquarters, reminding himself that sitting still waiting for orders is notoriously nine-tenths of soldiering. Presently, since the City remained silent, he allowed the impatient Eunomus to slip across to the south bank to learn the news. The authorities seemed to have forgotten that there were soldiers just outside the City (which was not surprising; this new departure was not often mentioned). No lictor arrived with orders from a magistrate.

By evening he had dined on ration porridge and bacon, and borrowed some bedding. He would stay with his troops until they received orders of some kind. At sunset his secretary returned, brimming with news and excitement. In the privacy of headquarters he poured out his story.

'For the moment there is no fighting in the City, but neither is there peace. Your soldiers patrol a deserted Forum. Escaped gladiators have plundered the Senate House, otherwise no damage has been done. Caesar is certainly dead; his corpse was carried to the Regia on an open litter. The Senators who murdered him, more than a score of them, have seized the Capitol. But they hold no other ground, and they are surrounded by a mob of armed Populars. Antonius the Consul got away unharmed, but he is afraid to leave his house. Many Senators have fled from the City, but known Optimates dare not appear in the streets. In fact, my lord, there has been a revolution – and it has failed. Though Caesar has been killed, his followers still rule the City.'

'You see, Crastinus?' said Lepidus. 'We are still in control. There is nothing to fight for. I was right to keep my soldiers in camp.'

*That night the lady Clodia whispered to the young man who held her in his arms: 'Is that a swordsman outside the window? For the first time in my life I am afraid. I'm safe with gangsters, but when Senators run amok anyone can get killed. Thank the gods, that man's a legionary. One of Lepidus's men, I suppose. I never thought I would one day feel grateful to the old weather-cock. But, to give him his due, he has kept order in Rome.'*

# V

## PEACE-MAKING
### 44 B.C.

By morning on the 16th of March Lepidus had been in command of his legion, without orders from any superior, for nearly a full day. The habit of responsibility was beginning to govern his mind, and he gave sensible instructions without nervous hesitation.

All round him Rome lay quiet, filled with desperate politicians each afraid to make the first move. The murderers were shut up in the Capitol, whose antique walls might protect them from a Popular mob, but would be no obstacle to trained soldiers. The City held a Consul, who ought to govern it. But Marcus Antonius still cowered behind the barred doors of his mansion, while his slaves, armed with bows and javelins, threatened the street from the upper windows. No proper orders came from the Antonian mansion, though it was reported that the Consul had shouted through a locked door that any soldiers available should patrol the City to prevent pillage.

Lepidus did much more than that. It seemed that he was the only senior official not afraid to take action, and that the life of Rome depended on his common sense. He sent three full cohorts to hold the Forum in force; smaller detachments marched to the octroi-gates on the main roads, which had been barred by their frightened watchmen. The barriers were lowered, and the peasants invited to bring in their produce; there was no point in creating an unnecessary famine because timid watchmen were afraid of Optimate bandits. It would have been much easier if the City had been surrounded by proper walls; troops could have manned them and reassured the citizens. But the wall built by King Servius long ago was rather an ancient monument than a fortification; and anyway it enclosed only half the City. It was the pride of Rome, as of Sparta, that her shrines were defended by swords, not by masonry. However, troops patrolled the octroi-barriers, and small detachments showed themselves in every populous quarter.

After furnishing patrols and sentries, and occupying the Forum, Lepidus had in hand only three cohorts, out of the ten which made up a legion. He kept two, of recruits, as a reserve on the island; and sent the last to picket the approaches to the Capitol. Tribunes and senior centurions kept on begging him to order an assault on that nest of assassins; but even now, when undisputed command had filled his breast with sensations of glory, he shrank from leading his troops to the sack of the most sacred shrine in the City. The murderers were cornered; if all else failed they could be starved into surrender. He explained this to his men, and reminded them that it was the duty of a soldier to defend the citadel of his forefathers, not to destroy it. When the soldiers were quite certain that the investment was complete, and that their Optimate enemies could not steal away in the night, they obediently continued their patrols.

By midday the mob of angry Populars who had been hanging round the approaches to the Capitol had gone home to their dinners, and all Rome lay quiet. As Lepidus inspected his stores (there was flour for three days, and he controlled the barriers; his men would not go hungry) he was told that his presence was requested on both bridges at once.

At the northern bridge he found Junia and the children, in three flashy smart litters. Junia greeted him calmly: 'Here we are, safe and sound. Yesterday we travelled ten miles from the City, and then I heard that all was peaceful. We spent the night at one of the Antonius villas, and when I decided to come back the steward showed me an amazing collection of carriages. I'm afraid it's the place where Marcus keeps his playmates; there were odd-looking boys and girls hanging about, but I kept our Marcus under my eye all the time. I chose the three most sober litters I could find; I wonder who rode in them last summer? Anyway, the steward was most helpful. I gave him a good tip. You ought to pay Antonius for the use of these litter-bearers. Now I shall go home. Let's hope I find some servants. If not, I can borrow a few maids from the neighbours. By the way, have you caught the murderers? I suppose so, or you wouldn't be sitting still, doing nothing.'

'The murderers are where I can catch them. They can't get away. I am doing nothing because no one has given me orders. I am proconsul in Gaul, but that gives me no right to rule in Rome. Antonius must make the next move, and I believe his messenger is now waiting at the other bridge. I am glad you came back, but yesterday it was only common sense to send you away. I shall try to get home for supper, and then we can talk. The house has been guarded, and you will find it unharmed.'

The message from the Consul was laconic. 'You have done well. Continue your patrols. This afternoon there is an assembly of the people, tomorrow a meeting of the Senate.'

Lepidus hastened to change into his toga. There were still no litters in the streets, and with a small bodyguard he walked to the Forum.

The great square was packed with a dense but orderly crowd, and he saw with satisfaction that his three cohorts stood where they could intervene if needed. He looked curiously at the Consul, high on the speaker's platform. Antonius was said to be the most gallant warrior in Rome, but for the last twenty-four hours he had been too frightened to do anything; perhaps to a man who could face hostile swords with fortitude hidden daggers were far more terrifying. Certainly Antonius had been drinking. There were shadows under his eyes, his nose shone red from white cheeks, he looked as though he had just been sick and would be sick again in the next ten minutes. In a hoarse whisper he called the meeting to order, and prepared to speak.

A tribune of the people intervened, calling on the proconsul Marcus Aemilius Lepidus to address the meeting. Tribunes were entitled to upset the agenda of the assembly; in fact their chief constitutional duty was to be a nuisance to the administration. When a tribune commanded any right-minded Roman obeyed. Lepidus climbed on the platform and cleared his throat.

The tribune's intervention was a compliment to his steadfast behaviour in a difficult situation; it was another feather in the cap of Lepidus, Consular, Imperator, Triumphator. He was duly grateful. It was an infernal nuisance, all the same; for he had nothing prepared, and he did not know what line the Consul intended to take.

He began by lamenting the murder of Caesar, and that went down very well. The crowd seemed to be solidly Popular, though he could recognise a few reputed Optimates. Only two days ago he, Lepidus, had walked in this very Forum with the noble Dictator; now Caesar was no more. Consider the mutability of human affairs! Anyone who had undergone a rhetorical training could keep up that kind of thing for hours; but the crowd, expecting something more specific, grew restless. He would have to advise on the punishment of the murderers, and still he did not know the Consul's views. But there was another point he might dwell on: the murder of Caesar had been sacrilege also. He could fill up time with an excursus on the wickedness of shedding the blood of the Pontifex Maximus, with copious reference to past holders of the great office, including his own great-great-grandfather. But when he spoke of his famous ancestor there was an interruption; a small group, standing all together in the crowd, shouted in unison: 'Lepidus Pontifex Maximus!'

Here was something he understood. He was a veteran of the Forum. He looked keenly at the interrupters. They had been hired to shout that day, for only a hired gang would be so single-minded. Here was a standard political gambit; who was behind it?

Respectable middle-of-the-road Senators, he concluded; neither Caesarians nor assassins, but men who wanted concord in the republic. He recognised some of Cicero's hired claque. The meaning of the outcry was obvious. If now he spoke for peace, in due time the Senate would see that he was rewarded with the vacant office of Pontifex Maximus. It seemed a fair deal. He decided to carry out his side of the bargain.

Insensibly his eulogy of Caesar changed into a eulogy of Rome. His friends and fellow-citizens had conquered the world. Why? Because, guided by their sacred constitution, they lived together in concord. Murder must be punished, of course. But the murderers were a small unrepresentative band, not the Optimate party as a whole. The Populars should join with their brethren in the Senate; especially during this crisis, with the Parthians menacing the east, Rome needed concord above all things.

It was not a good speech, and it went on far too long. But a bored assembly is a peaceful assembly. When he concluded the perfunctory applause was quiet and mannerly. Immediately the Consul stood forward in his place.

Marcus Antonius always went down well in the assembly, though in the Senate his levity sometimes jarred on his hearers. He spoke even more strongly in favour of peace. Rome had suffered a great disaster, but without the guiding hand of Caesar concord was necessary as never before. Lepidus noted that he did not threaten even the assassins. Apparently the government had decided that it was no good crying over spilt milk. Luckily his own speech could be made to fit in with this unexpected policy. While Antonius was still speaking he slipped quietly away,

The Aemilian mansion had not been pillaged after all, and most of the servants had returned; only very foolhardy slaves would try to escape from an owner who commanded the only military force near Rome. The butler was there to receive him, and a scratch dinner had been prepared. The boys ate in another room with their pedagogue, while the lady Junia dined alone with her husband.

Lepidus could describe exactly what had passed in the Forum;

this was a world he understood, down to the last whispered hint from a minor gangster to a supernumerary lictor. Junia, though of course she had never heard a speech in the assembly, was also familiar with the strategy of domestic politics. They were agreed on the significance of the meeting.

'After all,' said Junia, summing up when he had finished, 'Caesar was murdered by his own followers. No one would call Cassius and Decimus Brutus Optimates. Of course my silly brother was one of the ringleaders. I see now that he is wicked as well as foolish. Naturally the Popular mob blames the Optimates as a whole; so the more sensible Optimate leaders are now for peace at any price. But why should Antonius the Consul help them to the peace they need? That is the oddest part of the affair.'

'Well, why not?' answered her husband. 'He is Consul, and without a colleague. He cannot rise higher than that. He might have led the mob to the massacre of every noble in Rome, but what would he gain by it? He could hardly keep all the plunder for himself, and if all his social equals were dead there would be no one to dine with him when he feels like giving a party.'

'But Antonius is throwing away his chance of the Dictatorship. He inherited the Caesarian party, without doing any work to get it. Why won't he take his chance?'

'Perhaps he is not so fond of power as you suppose. Caesar was supreme, and he had to work hard every day. Antonius would not like that. Besides, in war there is always the chance that the other side may win. If he makes an alliance with the Optimates he must work with equal colleagues; but he will still be the most important man in the republic, as great as Pompeius Maximus at his greatest. I suppose that is enough to satisfy him.'

'It won't satisfy Fulvia,' said Junia with a laugh. 'She was planning to marry Caesar's second in command; she will be disappointed with a mere Consular, one of a crowd of worthy ex-Consuls. I suppose, by the way, Caesar's fortune goes to Antonius? Or do you think he remembered the dim great-nephew?'

'Antonius will keep any money he can lay his hands on. He's always in low water financially. But I imagine he would rather be the greatest man in a free City, liked by his colleagues and applauded by the mob, than a lonely Dictator, waiting for the end that came to Caesar. You mustn't be too political, my dear. There are other aims in life besides supreme power. For example, this morning I myself might have stormed the Capitol, and assumed a crown beside the statues of the Seven Kings of Rome. My soldiers would have done anything I ordered. Instead, I put my men at the disposal of the Consul. I hope to be remembered as the Aemilius who *could* have made himself tyrant of Rome; I don't want to be remembered as a tyrant indeed.'

'Ah, but you are a man of honour. Antonius does not reason like that. The whole affair puzzles me. After the Senate has met we shall know more. Perhaps the Optimates have offered Antonius something better than he can get from the Populars. Anyway,' she added after a pause, 'I am glad you left that slimy Eunomus in the camp. I can't bear the fellow. I am sure he pestered you to seize the City.'

'Of course he did. He's only a Greek, and a freedman at that. He can't understand a statesman putting liberty above power. He's useful, all the same. I don't trust him, but I admire his brains. I'm afraid he will be back here in a day or two. I must get that legion on the move to Gaul as soon as possible.'

On the next morning, the 17th of March, the Senate met early in a peaceful City. The place of meeting was the temple of Tellus, not the customary Theatre of Pompeius; for the shrine of the earth-god lay in the heart of the Popular quarter, close to the Antonian mansion; while the Theatre was dominated by the Capitol, still garrisoned by armed murderers. Lepidus of course attended the meeting, in the full civil dress of his rank; though at dawn he had found time to go down in armour to visit his soldiers on the island. The camp was quiet and the men orderly. He confined them to quarters, save for the customary patrols; and began to make arrangements for their journey over the Alps.

He came home tired and later for dinner. But Junia, meeting him in the hall, knew from his look of content that some arrangement had been made to preserve the peace. He began giving orders to his valet while he was taking off his toga, and that was another good sign; he was never happy unless he could feel that he was hard at work, managing great affairs.

'Tonight we shall have a little supper for four, and a good one, my dear,' he greeted her. 'See that the cook does his very best. Two couches only, and two chairs, for yourself and another lady. I'll tell you who are our guests when we're alone. This is a political supper, and most confidential. We don't want a mob gathered outside the gate, either to cheer or to boo. After supper you and the other lady must leave us to talk business. But first, where are the boys? I have something to say to them.'

Thirteen-year-old Marcus and six-year-old Quintus lived a life of their own in the recesses of the great mansion. They had a trustworthy pedagogue, and their own staff of valets and footmen. Their father was fond of them, when he remembered their existence. He took trouble over their education, and now and then himself expounded to them the ancestral constitution. But he did not often send for them in the middle of the day. Junia guessed what was to come, and steeled herself to bear it like a Roman matron.

When the grave-eyed children had kissed their father's hand they stood respectfully to hear his commands. Lepidus cleared his throat nervously and began to explain.

'You are Aemilii Lepidi. One day you will have in your keeping the images of our great ancestors. Later your children will take over these images, and yours among them. Boys of your blood are born to serve Rome. Well, it so happens that your service to the City has begun, though you are still too young to bear arms. This evening you will go to the Capitol. You will stay there until your hosts permit you to leave. You will be among gentlemen of good birth, who will treat you as they treat their own sons. But I must tell you frankly that you will be hostages. Someone comes from the Capitol to sup here tonight, and if he does not return in safety your lives are forfeit. Under this roof every guest is safe; but accidents happen, and there is always the chance of a lynching in the street. So if it comes to the worst, remember your ancestors. Don't squeal when you see the swords. I expect we shall meet tomorrow morning; but it would be fitting to take a formal farewell.'

As soon as he was alone with his wife he explained: 'Our guest tonight is your brother Brutus, who has agreed to leave the Capitol on condition his nephews stand hostage for his safe return. He will bring Porcia with him. His visit must be kept a secret, or the mob will stone him in the street. If he gets here and goes back unnoticed our sons will return to us tomorrow.'

'You are head of the household,' said Junia. 'Perhaps there was no other way. I hate to think of my children in that den of assassins; it seems that you, and the Senate, take a more lenient view of them. Can you tell me what the Senate decided today, or is that also a secret?'

'I think we have hit on a peaceful compromise, though it's a very odd one. Briefly, we have decided that Caesar was a legitimate ruler of Rome, and that therefore his acts retain legal force; but that to kill him was also a lawful act, and therefore no one will be prosecuted for his murder.'

'It won't be easy to get an amnesty through the assembly. Why did Antonius accept it? Surely you and he together control the City?'

'We don't control the Senate, as we discovered during the very first speeches. The murderers dared not leave the Capitol; but their friends came to the temple of Tellus, and they were in the majority. I suppose we could have called up my soldiers, and cut the throats of scores of Senators as they sat on their benches. Long ago the Gauls did it. But how could civilised men bring themselves to commit such an atrocity? Merely to say it proves it impossible. The only other way was to carry the Senators with us.'

'Yet these friends of murder agreed that Caesar's acts should stand. That was not very consistent, surely?'

'At first they were all for condemning his memory. They wanted to declare all his acts void, right back to his first Consulship with Bibulus. Then Cicero pointed out that, if these acts were void, there would be no legitimate authority in the City. Caesar made Antonius Consul, he had appointed all the praetors, and, what was the nub of the argument, he had nominated other magistrates in advance, for the next three years at least. Were these appointments also to be voided?'

'Trust a lawyer to see a point of that kind,' said Junia. 'I don't like Cicero. I think he's a cad and a coward. But there's nothing wrong with his intellect.'

'Well, my dear, you see what followed from that? In favour of Caesar's acts were ranged all the present magistrates, and everyone who hopes that among Caesar's papers will be found a note appointing him to some future office. With the faithful Caesarians, that made a clear majority of the house. We agreed that Caesar's past acts shall stand unquestioned, and in addition that any proposal found among his papers shall have the force of law as soon as it is published.'

'Who has these papers?'

'Calpurnia gave them to Antonius. He is sole Consul, and was Caesar's colleague. She could hardly refuse when he asked for them; though I wish she had found a more trustworthy executor.'

'If she had any spirit she would have hidden them under her bed; though I suppose rummaging about in bedrooms is just what Antonius is used to. Or she could have given them to the Vestals. Now your foolish Senate and Calpurnia, between them, have made Antonius ruler of Rome. Don't you see, Marcus? Antonius can produce a bit of paper saying anything at all, giving him the sole right to coin silver, or a title to every farm in Campania, and claim he found it among Caesar's papers. I suppose he has already seized the money stored in the temple of Ops?'

'He has. He claims that as Caesar's colleague he should have it. My darling, you must not think the Senate was hoodwinked. We understood what we were doing. We have given Marcus

Antonius a licence to steal what he wants from the treasury of the republic. But he can take it anyway, by force, so long as the mob looks on him as the Caesarian leader. And we have shown him that life will be more pleasant if he works with the Senate than if he rules as a tyrant. Above all, we have kept the constitution in being. The City is still governed as our ancestors governed it. To achieve that we had to keep the Senate united; and the only way to unite it was to pardon the murderers and at the same time carry out Caesar's plans. I know it doesn't make sense. But it works.'

'Perhaps it will work. You Senators can nod and wink among yourselves, and fix up these little arrangements without giving their ugly names to ugly deeds. But one day the assembly must ratify your terms; and the assembly will be howling for the heads of the murderers.'

'The assembly can vote only on motions brought before it. If no one suggests a prosecution they can't vote for one. And everyone entitled to speak will be in favour of the amnesty.'

'You mean that everyone who matters has been properly looked after? Well, nothing will bring Caesar back to life. . . . We're not forgotten either, if you are to be Pontifex Maximus. I shall preside at the next festival of Bona Dea. I've a good mind not to invite Fulvia. By the way, what do the murderers get out of this? I suppose you had to offer them something to persuade them to leave the Capitol.'

'Your brother is coming here to discuss that very point. We shall offer them something; in fact we shall offer them a lot. There is still an Optimate party; Picenum and Campania are full of dispossessed veterans whose farms have been given to Caesarians. If the murderers flee they can gather an army, and once swords are drawn anything may happen.'

'At least I'm easier in my mind about the children. In such a friendly arrangement hostages will suffer no harm. But it still seems odd to a mere woman, debarred by her sex from hearing your fine speeches in the Senate. I was brought up to believe that a man of honour avenges his friend without counting the cost. The blood-feud used to be a sacred obligation. Here is Caesar dead, and his friends think only of sharing his estate with his enemies.'

'My dear, I was never Caesar's friend. I am a Popular, and I followed him. I admired his statemanlike projects. I gave him what help I could. But he mocked at many things which an Aemilius Lepidus must hold sacred. I mourn him as the father of his country, not as my personal friend.'

'He has friends, mark my words. I am one, of course, and my mother is another. He has true friends among the best families in Rome. But the ones you should beware of are the fifty thousand friends of Caesar who march up and down the provinces with swords on their thighs.'

'Oh, the soldiers liked him, I know. But the soldiers also like Antonius. He can manage the army. That is why we have paid such a high price for his allegiance.'

'Yes, the soldiers like Antonius. They may like him less when this arrangement has been published. But I see that things have gone too far, and there's nothing for it but to fulfil our promises. Supper for my horrible brother, for a start. I hope he has washed Caesar's blood off his hands.'

That intimate little supper was the most agonising social function that Lepidus could remember, though at intimate parties he was often awkward and unhappy. He reclined beside Brutus, much too close to that hairy, beefy, ungainly frame, which to his imagination still reeked of murder. On his right Porcia, as pig-like as her name, gazed on her husband with an expression of simpering adulation; beyond Brutus Junia sat stiffly upright, bristling like an offended cat. The ladies, on their high chairs, talked over the heads of the men, exchanging commonplaces of the kitchen or the nursery. Brutus started at every movement among the servants, as though he would fear assassination for the remainder of his life; he ate greedily and noisily, glad to get away from the scanty rations of the Capitol.

When the ladies had retired Brutus, with a noisy belch, settled himself comfortably and began to boast. Antonius is behaving better than I had expected. I wonder whether the poor creature knows that it is only thanks to my exquisite sense of justice that he is alive today? My friends wished to kill him with his master; I forbade it. So far, Antonius has not attempted to play the tyrant; therefore to kill him would be murder. The killing of Caesar was of course tyrannicide, which is praised as a virtue in all the books. You might let Antonius know as much, if you can do it discreetly. His narrow escape may encourage him in virtue. Now as to the future. If we can spare Antonius we can work with Caesarians of lesser guilt. Antonius is taking Macedonia, the province allotted to Caesar. Decimus Brutus will have Cisalpine Gaul, which was to have gone to Antonius. When you are in the Narbonese he will be your neighbour. He will help you to bring justice to the helpless barbarians of Gaul, so long plundered by Caesarians. We must show the provinces that the righteous laws of Rome rule us now.'

'I hope you will be more lenient in your own next province

76

than you were in Cyprus, my dear brother-in-law,' answered Lepidus, glad to revive an old score. 'Don't lend money to your subjects to enable them to pay your taxes; and if you do lend, charge a lower rate than sixty per cent.'

'If the Cypriots could have borrowed cheaper they would not have come to me. When they owed me money I collected it. That is all that occurred. The law was always on my side. In future also I shall keep the law. Even Caesarians shall have justice. I will do nothing abitrary. The real curse of a tyranny is arbitrary interference with due course of law.' The long bony face took fire as he expounded his favourite topic. 'No one minds very much whether he has a vote; on election day half the citizens don't bother to come down to the Forum. But we all want to know what we may do, and what is forbidden. The laws tells us that, in plain black and white. Caesar used to go about offering advice, as he called it; but if you disregarded his advice you were lucky to get off with exile. He interfered even in our private lives, in *my* private life. He let it be known that he took exception to my marriage with the virtuous daughter of a citizen who had attained curule office. No bride could be more worthy of a Junius Brutus. It was more than I could stomach, so I killed him. Anyway, Caesar was a Popular, and the rule of the majority means the death of personal liberty. I saw that long ago. Though Pompeius had killed my father I fought for him against Caesar, who menaced the freedom of every noble Roman. Caesar thought he could do everything better than anyone else, from augury to ship-building; and he would never leave anyone alone. The mob adored him, because he was brave and a rake. Now perhaps they will recognise the merits of those who are both brave and virtuous.'

'I grant that what you did you did for liberty. Some of your associates had less elevated motives, but we need not go into that. But you should remember that the greatest foe of liberty is war, no matter which side wins. If you wish to keep the peace, I shall help you. But do not perpetually recall your great achievement. Though the voice of Rome, speaking through the Senate, has proclaimed that the killing of Caesar was no murder, let it be forgotten as soon as possible.'

'On the contrary, I shall speak of it continually. The common people must be reminded that they were very nearly enslaved, and that a few brave noblemen preserved their liberty.'

'On that point we disagree. Let us not discuss it further. Soon I shall leave Rome for my province. You I suppose will remain in the City to serve your term as praetor. It is unfortunate that you are bound to exhibit Games; the Caesarian mob will make trouble in the circus.'

'Caesar is dead; soon there will be no more Caesarians. The Populars may continue under the leadership of Antonius; but there is room in the City for differences of political opinion.'

The conversation ceased, and when Lepidus spoke again it was to discuss the finances of the state. He was wasting his time trying to persuade this conceited fool that Caesar had left devoted followers. His tactlessness might well stir up the civil war which could otherwise be averted. There was one consolation; an army led by Marcus Junius Brutus was sure to be beaten.

Presently Brutus went off in his curtained litter, to get back without incident to his refuge on the Capitol. In the morning the hostages were returned, and Antonius rewarded young Marcus Lepidus by betrothing him to his daughter. Such an honour could not be refused with safety, though Lepidus did not relish the prospect that one day the wild blood of the Antonians would be mingled with his own.

Yet Rome did not settle down to peace, though every politician of weight did his best to calm the passions of the mob. Caesar's funeral passed off without the expected riot, save for a few casual lynchings. But the publication of his will made a sensation.

Caesars' chief heir was not Marcus Antonius after all, but the unknown and youthful great-nephew; further, this boy was to be adopted as Caesar's son, and would carry on his name. Some said this must make him leader of the Caesarians, but Lepidus pointed out that a boy who had never held curule office could not lead a party. In this, if in nothing else, Marcus Antonius agreed with him.

During that uneasy summer no one was happy. Antonius was the most important man in Rome, but he was not a Dictator. As Consul, he should have taken the advice of the Senate, and co-operated with his equal colleague, the other Consul.

Unfortunately the other Consul, appointed to fill the vacancy caused by Caesar's murder, was Dolabella; and it was less than two years since his gang had fought the Antonians all over the Forum. The two Consuls were soon at loggerheads, with Antonius encouraging the religious cult of the dead Caesar and Dolabella determined to put it down.

Antonius rarely attended the Senate. He lived splendidly, spending Caesar's treasure as though it had in truth been bequeathed to him; and whenever he or one of his parasites ran short of money some new project found among Caesar's papers justified another source of revenue. Meanwhile a civil war still rumbled in the provinces. It was the old war, between Caesarians and Pompeians, which should have ended after Pharsalus; but it might merge into a new war, between Antonians and Optimates, unless it were settled quickly.

The ending of this Spanish war was so important that the second man in the republic was commissioned to negotiate peace. Hither Spain was added to Narbonese Gaul as the province of the proconsul Lepidus, and both the Optimates and Antonius begged him to see Sextus Pompeius and bring him to terms. He was instructed in two separate interviews, and it amused him to note how different leaders of the state went about the same business.

Cicero called at the mansion of the Pontifex-elect, as was proper between Consulars. He addressed his host by his correct titles of Imperator and Triumphator, and dwelt chiefly on the need for universal concord. If Pepidus would explain to young Sextus that in Rome Pompeians and Optimates and Caesarians were working together without friction the young leader, who could not be bad at heart, would recognise his duty. Nothing was demanded from him but a respectful letter to the Senate; once he had agreed to take orders from the lawful authorities some dignified post would be found for him. Cicero thought that the task would be easy; he took it for granted that Romans of noble birth would follow the path of duty as soon as it had been pointed out to them.

Marcus Antonius sent a message asking the Consular to call, though he was ten years his junior and Lepidus had been Consul when he was no more than quaestor. Lepidus was carried in his litter to the greatest private mansion in Rome, the sumptuous building decorated with the keels of pirate ships which had been built for Pompeius Maximus. Though it was late in the morning, he found the house only half-awake. The Consul received him wearing a tunic but no toga, and obviously suffering from a sick headache. The office was untidy, and not really private; painted boys and young women kept on putting their heads in and backing out with apologies.

But Marcus Antonius was no fool, even when half-drunk. His exposition of the Spanish situation was clearer than Cicero's, and he had a sensible plan to induce Sextus Pompeius to make peace.

'He's a queer youth, by all accounts,' he said easily. 'He got nothing from his famous father except a famous name. He was still a schoolboy when Pharsalus was lost and won; he can't be much more than twenty now. Why the Spaniards follow him I don't know. But they do. Pollio can't suppress him, so we must buy him instead. Luckily I have plenty of money, and the Senate will give him some grand title. He would like a curule magistracy,

I'm told; but we can't have him visiting Rome to stand for election. There is enough trouble between Caesarians and Optimates without rallying the Pompeians as well. Another thing he wants very much, and can't have: this house. Of course it *was* his father's, and in normal times I would hand it back to him. With things as they are I won't. It would look like yielding to pressure, and just now my prestige is important. So there it is.' He paused to drink from a goblet of unmixed wine. 'Sextus Pompeius wants to be praetor; he also wants "The Keels". On both counts you must disappoint him. But you can offer him unlimited money, and any appointment – not an elective office – that it is in the power of the Senate to grant. You should be able to bring him to terms. Oh, and one other thing. Take a look at his soldiers, and try to find out why they follow him. There are some Spaniards who will follow any enemy of Rome, but there can't still be all that Pompeian feeling in the province. Why Sextus Pompeius in particular? I should like to know.'

It was galling to sit there taking instructions from Marcus Antonius, ten years his junior and a notorious libertine. Lepidus reminded himself that the man was Consul of the year, entitled to obedience from all Romans. When the year was out they would both be Consulars, equal in precedence; that would be the time to make clear their relative standing. He agreed to do all he was told.

He was not sorry to leave Rome, on an official mission which gave him a watertight excuse to drop out of City politics. The leaders of both factions might have buried their differences, but their followers refused to drop the age-old feud. Caesar's murderers were never safe from Popular avengers of blood. The instigators of the plot, Cassius, Decimus Brutus, Marcus Brutus, fled from the City in fear of their lives. Decimus Brutus went to govern his province of Cisalpine Gaul; but Marcus Brutus, a praetor, should have remained to preside in his lawcourt. To save his face the Senate invented a post for him in the provinces, something to do with the corn-supply; and a job on the same lines was found to give Cassius an excuse to travel. That was very disgraceful, as showing that the government lacked power to maintain order; but it was better than provoking a civil war by allowing Optimate leaders to be murdered in the Forum.

Young Caesar Octavianus had arrived in Rome, seeking the estate of his great-uncle. Antonius made things as awkward for him as he knew how. He obstructed the passage of the law needed to formalise the posthumous adoption, so that the youth remained in law Caius Octavius Thuricus (though to every good Popular he was Caesar). The boy had a devoted following, espcially among Caesar's veterans, and the Consul's spiteful treatment of him threatened to split the Caesarian party. Lepidus was glad to get away without having to take sides against either the heir or the lieutenant of his old leader.

*The Lady Clodia looked out on the hot June night: 'It's odd to think that it's only three months to the day since Caesar was murdured. I was terribly afraid then, until I saw a legionary on guard outside my door. Aemilius Lepidus sent him specially, and you should have seen how the lady Junia looked me up and down when I called to thank him. She thinks I'm not respectable, and of course she's right. It's odd about Lepidus. On the Ides of March he might have made himself King of Rome; but he was too conventional to try it on. Now he's gone off on some boring mission to the barbarous west, and I don't suppose we shall ever hear of him again. . . . But we waste time. Come closer, my darling.'*

# VI

## THE RANKS FORM
### 44–43 B.C.

Marcus Aemilius Lepidus, Imperator, Triumphator, Proconsul, looked with satisfaction at the smart legionary on guard outside the filthy little Spanish inn. Yesterday there had been sentries outside his lodging; but they had been Spanish rebels, the most terrifying cut-throats he had ever set eyes on. He was grateful, and a little surprised, to be safely back in the loyal portion of his province.

He was so relieved at his escape that he had to talk to someone; even to Eunomus, his only companion. Junia had warned him against making an intimate of the slippery Greek freedman, and usually he followed her advice. But he had left his wife and children in Rome, as did every official posted to a barbarous province; and he was accustomed to discussing the affairs of the day before he went to bed.

'It's all fixed up,' he said cheerfully. 'Young Sextus has agreed to leave Spain. The Senate will appoint him inspector-general of the navy in the west, with the rank of praefect. He can lodge wherever he chooses, except in Rome; and he gets all his father's property except the town-house, which Antonius won't hand over. He would be a fool to refuse these terms, and he's no fool. But I wonder whether he sees that when he is parted from his Spanish brigands he won't matter any more? In Italy he can't gather a band of armed Pompeians. Italians have short memories. To them Pompeius Maximus is a figure in ancient history.'

'Are his followers Pompeians, my lord?' asked Eunomus.

'Some Spanish tribes obey him from loyalty to his father, who showed them mercy when they first submitted to Rome. But that kind of sentimental loyalty will not gather an army, especially an army at war with the rest of the civilised world. There is more behind this rebellion than a young man carrying on the blood-feud to avenge his father.'

'Now then, Eunomus, don't be too clever. You always see something deeper than the obvious, though very often the obvious is all there is to see. These Spanish hillmen would rather plunder than plough; Sextus is a brave, uncouth ruffian who seems fitted by nature to be a leader of brigands. He has been lucky, and I suppose Pollio is not really such a good soldier as Caesar thought. When the boy is back in a law-abiding country he will find that his skill in laying ambuscades has no value. Since for lack of education he can't make a convincing speech to the assembly, he will dwindle into nothing.'

'My lord, did you notice that most of his officers were not Spaniards at all? They were not Roman either. Perhaps all provincials seem the same to you. Those men were Greeks, as I spotted when I heard them trying to talk Latin. I spoke to one of them in Greek. He seemed to know Miletus, and I gathered from the way he listened to my story that he also had been enslaved, for a short time. Born free, enslaved by some catastrophe, then quickly freed. In addition he was devoted to Pompeius. What kind of man satisfies all those conditions?'

'I can't think about men I have never met at dinner, as you know very well. Don't speak in riddles, especially when I am tired. You have had one of your bright ideas again, and you are bursting to impart it. Out with it.'

'Well, my lord, from his age this man's benefactor must have been Pompeius Maximus. Pompeius helped some Spaniards, certainly; but these men are Greek. Now on the whole the great Pompeius was not a friend to Hellas. But once he was remarkably merciful to a fleet manned by Greek sailors, a fleet which he had defeated in battle. When I was a child we all knew the story of how Pompeius solved the pirate problem. He gave land and plough-oxen to the captured pirates, until they were better off than their neighbours who had always lived honestly. The farmers round Miletus were very bitter about it. Don't you see how this fits in? Some pirate captains became the slaves of Pompeius Maximus; and since they were competent leaders, who had come to the top of a competitive calling, probably they quickly earned their freedom. I believe the man I spoke with, Menas his name was, is a pardoned pirate. His seafaring ended more than twenty years ago; but soon he will be on the staff of the inspector-general of the western fleet. Within a few years, unless you watch him closely, young Sextus Pompeius will be King of the Pirates.'

'As usual, Eunomus, you are too subtle,' Lepidus said angrily. 'The young man may have inherited a few superannuated pirates from his father's household. But he is not the man to be a leader, even of pirates. I talked with him, and I can judge. In the first place, he is utterly uneducated; he can't even speak Latin correctly. In the second place, his only asset is his name. If he does 'anything unworthy of a Pompeius he will lose the little importance he now enjoys. Can you see disgruntled Optimates enlisting under a pirate chief? At a time when the Senate is curbing Marcus Antonius, and discouraging young Caesar Octavianus, is it likely that they will allow this Sextus to steal the Roman navy?'

'That is what I fear, my lord. Please remember later what I have foretold today. But it is not fitting that a freedman should dispute with his lord. I hope I am mistaken.'

Lepidus was proud of his successful negotiation, which had not been without its dangers. For the second time he had halted a petty war in Spain, a war which might otherwise have grown into a conflagration of all the Roman world. He was gratified, but not surprised, when the Senate voted him a 'supplication', a public thanksgiving. That was the conventional forerunner of a Triumph, which of course could not be granted until he had laid down the government of his province and returned to Rome.

He passed the autumn in Narbo, a prosperous town which had been for eighty years the capital of a Roman province. The public buildings were adequate weather-proof eyesores, clumsily put together by barbarian workmen to a Roman design; but the official residence of the proconsul was unworthy of Aemilius Lepidus. At the time it was built, before Caesar's conquest of Further Gaul, the Narbonese had been an unimportant province. The planning of the necessary alterations gave him an interesting occupation.

Junia would have planned this new wing better, and he knew it. At first he contemplated asking her to join him. But autumn was the wrong time for a sea voyage, and the alpine passes would be deep in mud. Besides, Junia was too fond of politics to be happy away from the City, and there was the risk that little Quintus might pick up a Gallic accent. He decided to leave his family in Rome until his term of office expired. Junia wrote to him regularly, and her accounts of the complicated intrigues now dividing the Senate enabled him to probe beneath the bald official announcements of what seemed on the face of it a united administration.

He loved his wife, and he had been educated to treat marriage as a binding tie. He did not follow the lax habit of many provincial governors and install a nest of native concubines in his private apartments. But though he slept alone he was not without the society of his equals. A provincial governor was expected to provide for his relations, and there were two of them on his staff. Marcus Junius Silanus was Junia's full brother, son of her father as well as her mother; though he had never been so high in her affections as that oddity her half-brother Marcus Brutus. He was a capable man of business, and a sound but dull speaker; perhaps his speeches would be more interesting when he had finally made up his mind whether he supported the Optimates or the Populars. At present he was so busy seeing the good in both sides that most people considered him a bore. He was chief legate to Lepidus, because he was his brother-in-law; but though influence had got him the post he was competent.

The other kinsman was a more remote connection, a second cousin named Culleo. He was absurdly ignorant of politics, for he wished to make the army his career. He was a fairly senior military tribune, and Lepidus had it in mind to appoint him legate if a vacancy should occur. But though a proconsul appointed his own legates, without ratification from Senate or assembly, the number he might appoint was limited by law. Lepidus had three, one relation and two professional soldiers, which was about the right proportion; he could not increase the number.

One of the other legates was more than a professional soldier; he had a political background, and he happened to be the only fervent Optimate to be found in the army of Gaul. Lepidus had deliberately picked Marcus Juventius Laterensis, precisely because he had been in general a political opponent. It was important to show the world that Caesar's murder had not destroyed the unity of Rome; when it came to holding down conquered Gaul all the survivors of the Ides of March would work together. Besides, Laterensis had held minor office, and had often spoken in the Senate. Though they disagreed politically, he and his commanding officer spoke the same language.

During that first autumn Lepidus was occupied with the government of his province; but once he had got the hang of it he found it really very easy. He ruled both Hither Spain and Narbonese Gaul, which swept round the curving shore of the Mediterranean in a great arc from the Alps to the Ebro. The shore was dotted with walled towns, mostly claiming a Greek foundation; the townsmen, delighted with Roman order and Roman equity, gladly paid tribute. Their private disputes were settled by their elected town-councils.

Even the hill tribes were getting used to paying taxes. Roman soldiers might not be able to catch them on their native mountains, but if they rebelled they knew for certain that their crops would be burned and their children would go hungry. Besides, the Romans showed them how to earn money to satisfy the tax-collectors. They could export corn and olives over smooth roads, free from brigands. The proconsul did not interfere with their private affairs, so long as they appeared outwardly loyal.

After a few months of careful administration he found himself devoting most of his working hours to the training of his army; for it was evident that in spite of the universal desire for peace a great war was in the making. Whatever the Senate might have decreed in that hugger-mugger meeting in the temple of Tellus, public opinion demanded punishment for the murderers of Caesar. Cassius and Marcus Brutus had fled from Italy in fear of their lives. Once they reached Asia they began to levy troops without authority. Dolabella, newly appointed proconsul in Syria, made war on them even while the Senate preached peace; or rather he plundered the cities which had contributed to their war-chest.

Turmoils in Asia need not concern a governor of Narbo, as Lepidus pointed out in one of his letters to Junia. She answered at once, warning him of danger very much nearer his frontier. Her letter began, naturally, with a recital of all recent betrothals, marriages and divorces. This was essential background information, lacking which even an experienced politician could not estimate the strength of parties in the Senate. A paid writer of news-letters could list the marriages and divorces, but only a lady who visited the right boudoirs would know of the betrothals, which were often kept private.

Then she continued: 'I hope your barbarian subjects are quiet, for you must expect war on your southern border. Cisalpine Gaul has got into a tangle which can only be unravelled by the sword. Poor dear Caesar arranged that it should be governed by the faithful Decimus Brutus while he was absent fighting the Parthians. Decimus was one of the first to plunge a dagger into him. Will you believe it when I say he has just taken over his province, with the full approval of the Senate? He has recruited an army from the sons of Sulla's veterans, driven from their ill-gotten farms by Caesar's men. It is not a strong force, I am told; but it is the only army in the world that will fight heart and soul for the Optimate cause.

'Of course Decimus Brutus is the darling of the Optimates, because he used to be a leading Caesarian. They give him anything he asks for lest he change sides again. They won't lift a finger to help Cassius, or my poor Marcus, because they have been faithful Optimates all their lives and will never desert the cause. So while honest Optimates are fighting in Asia, with every man's hand against them, that beastly turncoat gets the province and army nearest the City as the reward of his treachery. That is how Rome is governed today.

'You may be surprised that Optimates can allot provinces and armies, after their leaders have been chased from the City. As a matter of fact the assembly is still Popular. No sooner had Decimus Brutus set off for his province than Marcus Antonius got the people to pass a law, giving *him* Cisalpine Gaul instead of Macedonia which Caesar had promised him. He also wants to be as near the City as possible. In a few days he will march north, with a commission from the Senate and People of Rome, to conquer the Cisalpine province from Brutus, who governs it in virtue of a commission from the Senate and People of Rome. Did you ever hear of such a muddle in your life?

'Perhaps you wonder why I explain at such length. In a straight fight between Optimates and Caesarians your duty would be clear. You would help Antonius, in spite of his reputation, if by your help he could take vengeance on a murderer of Caesar. I must warn you of a dangerous split in our party. Octavius, the dim great-nephew, has made himself universally beloved by paying Caesar's legacies out of his own pocket; for Antonius would not let him touch Caesar's treasure. Where the money came from is a mystery; he must have powerful backers.

'Octavius is a private citizen, who has never held any public office. But as Caesar's heir he has recruited a fine army.

'Now the real point is that this Octavius, who shows his uncouth provincial lack of polish every time he enters a drawing-room, is thrilled to find himself taken up by the aristocracy. I haven't met him, but they tell me that a patronising word from Cicero means more to him than the cheers of the most faithful Caesarians. There is a real danger that he will lead his troops against Antonius; ostensibly as the servant of the Senate, in fact to wrest from him the leadership of our party. So don't take it for granted that in fighting for Antonius you are fighting for the ghost of Caesar. I advise you to stay out of the war, at least until Octavius has declared himself. If he joins Antonius, you can follow them both with a clear conscience; if they fight one another, wait and see which of them proves to be the real leader of the Caesarians.

'Meanwhile my poor Tertulla is wandering with Cassius in Asia, and the best fate my brother Marcus can hope for is exile. Mother is in despair. Never again will she see all her children together; and if they did find themselves under the same roof they would continue the civil war with their bare hands. In my family we take politics seriously. What a pity we could not all choose the same side! At least you have with you my brother Silanus. But he isn't Marcus. All the same, give him my love.'

*

'What is there about Marcus Brutus that makes people love him?' said Lepidus to Silanus, after they had read this letter together. 'Whatever he may plead in justification, his murder of his benefactor was a dirty business. Yet obviously Junia still misses him.'

'I don't know what he has, unless it's his honesty; but he has something. Do you remember, we used to laugh at him for going about the Forum being honest in public, as if that were a life-work for a grown man? But in fact he is honest, even though he makes a fuss about it. How many other honest men are there in the Senate today? If ever I meet Marcus I shall take his head, or he will take mine. The blood-feud lies between us, even though we were born of the same mother. All the same, I wish there were somewhere he could live unmolested. Why doesn't he go into exile among the blameless Ethiopians? If they are really as blameless as Homer says he would pass unnoticed among them.'

'So you are another friend of his. I am not,' said Lepidus grimly. 'My two sons, my only sons, once stood hostage for him. To save his skin he imperilled the continuance of the Aemilii Lepidi. If every other Caesarian pleads for Marcus Brutus, my vote will still go against him.'

Junia's letter was too private to be shown to anyone but her brother, but that evening the proconsul discussed the news in general terms with his legates. The Populars among them were distressed at the prospect of a split in the party. Laterensis, the only Optimate, was dismayed for a different reason.

'This young Octavius who now calls himself Caesar,' he said gloomily, 'his career proves that our constitution is in great danger. Without any legal commission he has gathered a great army. Rome has Consuls, and praetors, a Senate and an assembly of the people. But a man called Caesar, even though he has no right to the name, is more powerful than all the lictors and fasces in the City.'

'You go too fast,' Lepidus replied. 'The republic happens to have hit a bad patch. That's because we have a poor lot of magistrates this year. Look at the Consuls! That rascal Marcus Antonius: Dolabella, who seems to have set up as a brigand in Syria. By spring he will be a public enemy; in the summer his head will decorate a stake. But it's already November. In January new Consuls take office. Hirtius and Pansa are Caesarians, so the mob won't riot; but they are statesmen, not swashbucklers. They will obey the commands of the Senate and People of Rome because they are men of birth and education, in whom such obedience has been bred for many generations. When they hold the auspices the constitution of our ancestors will once more rule the republic.'

88

Silanus looked doubtful. 'Neither of these respected noble-men, I gather, is an experienced soldier. Will they control the legions, who are more Caesarian than any mob?'

'Roman soldiers obey their commanders,' Lepidus answered stoutly. 'By discipline we have conquered the world. Anyway, for more than four hundred years our ancestors lived together in Rome without civil war. Those days must return, for that is the Roman way of life.'

'You know more about politics than I do, Imperator,' Silanus said politely. 'But there were civil wars before I was born, and I expect them to continue after I am dead.'

'I am gathering supplies, and recruiting my legions. But these alarms can't last for ever. The good old days will return.'

Soon news reached Narbo that the war had begun in earnest. Until January Marcus Antonius was Consul, in legal theory commander of every Roman soldier. In his last month of office he led an army against Decimus Brutus, who retired behind the walls of the strong town of Mutina. Antonius was exceeding his powers, for the Senate had not commissioned him to make war on Brutus. But while in office he must be obeyed.

The Alps saved Lepidus from choosing a side. Both Brutus and Antonius appealed for his support, but until the snow was off the passes he could not march. By spring the situation would be clearer.

Before the snow melted another letter came from Junia.

' . . . so he will divorce her, and marry any Claudia available. United, the two families will carry great weight. But for the Aemilii Lepidi the great news is that the Senate has voted you an equestrian statue, to be erected on the Capitol at the public expense. So far as I can discover, none of your ancestors have been so rewarded, not even your grandfather's grandfather, the Marcus Aemilius Lepidus who was twice Consul, Censor, and for many years chief of the Senate. When you die, this honour can be indicated on your image.

'But don't be overcome by pride, my dear husband. Ostensibly this is a reward for your negotiation with Sextus Pompeius. In fact it is the price with which the Optimates hope to buy the army of Narbonese Gaul. They are encouraged in this hope because they have recently bought the most famous Caesarian alive, young Caesar himself (lately Octavius, the dim great-nephew). When the Antonius brothers marched against Mutina they left the City unguarded; it was at once occupied by the quite illegal army young Caesar has raised on his own authority. The Optimates regularised his irregular position by making him propraetor – which is in itself irregular since the boy, who is still too young to vote, has never held the most petty public office. However, he swallowed the bait, and now his army is co-operating with the constitutional forces raised by the new Consuls. Caesar fights for the Optimates! Whichever side you choose, you will be in good company. I think Caesar has been foolhardy. His health is weak, and every diviner foretells that as soon as his usefulness to the Optimates is ended he will succumb to a fatal fever.

'Talking of sudden death, there are now for practical purposes only two Antonius brothers. Caius, the youngest, has been captured by Cassius in Macedonia. When I last heard he was still alive, held I suppose as a hostage in case it should ever come to bargaining. But Caesarians will never bargain with those murderers, so Caius Antonius will never see Rome again. I can't honestly say that his death will be a blow to the Popular cause.

'An item of late news, as the messenger mounts his horse. Word has just come that the Senate has ratified your election as Pontifex Maximus. They could hardly do less. You earned the honour when you saved their necks after the Ides of March. But if it pleases you too much, see above where I mention the equestrian statue. Good-bye.'

There was more in this letter than met the eye. Junia was evidently afraid that he would join the Optimates, in gratitude for the magnificent honours they had granted him. Aemilius Lepidus could not be bought; but he saw the situation differently. Marcus and Lucius Antonius, the two greatest scoundrels in Rome, were about to fight Decimus Brutus, another scoundrel. But Brutus was supported by the legal government of the republic, by the new Consuls who had taken office in January, and by young Caesar, who must be regarded as titular head of the Caesarian party. Perhaps an honest patriot ought to join the side supported by all honest men.

Lepidus called a meeting of his officers, and was astonished at their reaction. Only Laterensis spoke in favour of Brutus and the legal government; the others, and Silanus in particular, saw it all in black and white, without a tinge of grey. Marcus Antonius, who had led a wing at Pharsalus, was carrying on the blood-feud against Decimus Brutus; every honest Caesarian should come to his assistance.

By March the picture had changed. The Caesarian party must be considered irretrievably split. For while the Antonius brothers besieged Decimus Brutus in Mutina, young Caesar Octavianus led his volunteers to join the Consuls in their attack on the Antonians. Silanus summed it up by saying that men who had enlisted under Caesar's heir to avenge Caesar's murder were now marching to the aid of Caesar's chief murderer, besieged by Caesar's favourite lieutenant. A Caesarian and an honest man could join either side without reproach, and no one could blame him if he remained neutral.

Lepidus was delighted to see that duty no longer compelled him to support the Antonius brothers. Perhaps all their friends were about to desert them, and they were finished. But just as he was making up his mind to offer alliance to Caesar Octavianus the situation changed again. Stuck on the wrong side of the Alps, he could not catch up with events in Rome.

This time the change was caused by the unexpected intervention of Caesarian politicians of the second rank, Plancus, governor of Further Gaul, and Pollio, governor of Further Spain; men who in normal times would not have presumed to offer advice to Marcus Antonius or Aemilius Lepidus. They wrote circular letters, suggesting a peace conference; and since messengers from Further Gaul and Further Spain must pass through Narbo to reach Rome, their messages soon became known at headquarters.

Eunomus was most excited. He was sure that his talent for intrigue would speedily make his patron the greatest man in Rome. He pointed out that Lepidus also should suggest a peace conference; if he did not, one might be held without him.

Lepidus therefore wrote a public dispatch to the Senate, suggesting that Antonius might have grievances which would excuse his conduct; at least, before the fighting spread, these grievances should be investigated. The dispatch was a long document; for anyone with a sound rhetorical training could use a great many words to make the point that peace is better than civil war.

The answer was an insufferably patronising letter from Cicero; who ordered Lepidus, in very few words, to take no further part in a project which did not commend itself to the Senate, or to the people, or indeed to any honest Roman. He might have been a patron writing to his client, and this was Tullius of Arpinum addressing Lepidus of Rome!

By now the spring was well advanced, and the Alpine passes open. But Lepidus dared not move towards besieged Mutina. He had never commanded in a serious campaign, and he was surrounded by famous generals. Just beyond his southern frontier the Antonius brothers were engaged with Decimus Brutus, Pollio hovered to the south-west, and Plancus to the north. Pollio was reputed to be a faithful Caesarian, though if young Caesar attacked Marcus Antonius no one could tell which Caesarian leader would enjoy his support; Plancus, though he had served the dead Dictator, was an unprincipled careerist who would fight for the most generous paymaster. If Lepidus should advance into Cisalpine Gaul these two chieftains might combine to attack his rear. He dared not move until one side or the other had been victorious in the fighting round Mutina.

He very nearly found himself committed against his will. Without orders, his legate and brother-in-law Silanus one morning harangued the troops to persuade them to join Antonius. Luckily the cohorts considered themselves very well off in Narbo, and no soldier was anxious to face an unnecessary crossing of the Alps. When he found that his men would not follow him Silanus rode off alone, deserting his commander on active service. Marcus Antonius gave him command of a full legion.

Lepidus wrote bitterly to Junia that the children of Servilia seemed bent on self-destruction; Marcus Brutus led the Optimates in Asia, and now Silanus had joined the outlawed wing of the Caesarians. However the war went, one of them must be on the losing side.

Junia's answer was slow in coming, for Cisalpine Gaul was full of warring armies. When it arrived it contained important news. She omitted the usual political gossip, and after a formal greeting plunged straight into this new disaster.

'I have just come back from the most terrible funeral in the long history of the City. Never before, not even in the year of Cannae, have both Consuls been burned at the same pyre during their term of office. The whole City watched their bodies carried to the burning. Afterwards there were no riots, for the sorrow is genuine; the toughest gangsters were in tears. It is said that the undertakers and the actors who impersonate the ancestors refused payment for their services. I gather that the Consuls were not killed in the same action; first one was wounded mortally; and on the day he died the other was killed outright. What makes it even more odd was that they were not killed in a rout. On the contrary, their armies were victorious.

'This alters the whole situation, and you must move carefully. Hirtius and Pansa, though Caesarians, were faithful servants of the Senate. Now the Senate has no obedient general, except Decimus Brutus in Mutina. In the absence of other magistrates the City is ruled by the urban praetor; the constitution of our ancestors provides for all emergencies. But the loyal army outside Mutina has gone over to young Caesar. The troops were ordered to obey the senior magistrate in Cisalpine Gaul, who is Decimus Brutus; they refused to follow a murderer of Caesar.

'One unexpected result of all this is that the fighting round Mutina has come to an end. The Antonius brothers were beaten;

they are now in full retreat, presumably on the way to your province. Young Caesar has not pursued them, in spite of the Senate's orders. Instead he is leading his men towards the City. At present he holds the rank of propraetor, but after his soldiers have occupied the Forum he can give himself any rank he chooses. The boy is the most dangerous politician in Rome. But the first adversary you will have to fight will I suppose be Marcus Antonius. He is a very good soldier. Be as cautious as you can.

'By the way, while watching the funeral I heard a very odd remark. My litter was jammed against another most splendid litter. The crowd was so great that neither of us could move, even when I discovered that my neighbour was that awful Clodia, the woman they tell so many stories about. Perhaps she is more to be pitied than blamed; I think she is a little astray in her wits. As the procession defiled before us (neither Consul was very well born, but in a double funeral their combined ancestors made a respectable show) Clodia called across to me: 'Please, lady Junia, which is Aemilius Lepidus? I have often heard about him, but I've never met him.' Of course I pretended not to hear. I wouldn't speak to that woman in public. Does she think I am a widow? Even so, how could your image be in the procession, since neither of the dead Consuls was an Aemilius? A strange affair.

'It is most unfortunate that my brother Silanus distinguished himself in the fighting at Mutina. It is said that he was responsible for the death of one Consul, I forget which. So we can't hush up his desertion of his lawful commander. All the Antonians have been declared public enemies. When they are captured it will be difficult to get a pardon for Silanus.

'Our Quintus is a queer little character. When I got back from the funeral he asked me . . . '

Lepidus immediately published in orders the shocking news of the death of both Consuls. The army of Narbonnese Gaul was saddened and impressed, but Crastinus the orderly was also wounded in his professional pride.

'You see, my lord,' he explained that evening, 'it may sometimes be the duty of a commander to fight on in a lost battle until he is killed. But for a commander to be killed while his men are winning can be nothing but bad management. I suppose these noble Consuls disregarded the advice of their orderlies. When I hold your shield, sir, you must stand where I tell you; then this army will not suffer such an unfortunate accident. It's a bad business, and a reflection on the praetorian cohorts who should have been guarding them.

'But it's always a pity,' he went on, 'when a noble commander, new to war, wants to impress veterans with his courage. It doesn't encourage the troops, not a bit, sir. When you're getting set for a straightforward attack, the kind of thing that's all in the day's work and that you won't boast about afterwards, there's nothing more annoying than to have some highborn gentleman wave his sword and exhort you to die gloriously. Of course there must be a speech before battle. It's only good manners, like putting an extra shine on the helmet that will be dinted by evening. But our great Caesar usually told us nothing except that we were bound to win easily. He never told us to die gloriously. Come to think of it, sometimes he told us to go home and leave the fighting to our betters. That stuck-up Tenth Legion! They never got a dirty fatigue. Caesar didn't draw his sword until he was going to use it. I remember one time, though. A young tribune told us the eyes of Rome were upon us. At the end of the day we had stormed a Gallic fort with the loss of two men, and the boys had been so rough with the women and children that Caesar hushed up the whole affair and Rome never heard of it. But that tribune was never allowed to forget it.'

He sighed. 'Now two Consuls go and do the same thing. How long is it since both Consuls were killed in one siege? Not since the taking of Veii, I shouldn't wonder.'

'No Consul was killed at the siege of Veii, though an ancestor of mine was wounded. These Consuls were not killed in one battle. One was wounded first. I understand they both died on the same day.'

'A shameful business, all the same, sir. I hope someone remembered to hang their orderlies. Culpable incompetence I call it.'

'It was a terrible catastrophe, but no one has been blamed. Gallant leaders must risk their lives.'

'Not when they are winning, sir. But you will understand more after you have seen a battle. What happened to young Caesar? He is safe, I hope?'

'Quite safe, I believe; and now commanding all the troops near Mutina. But he is not pursuing the Antonians. It looks as though the war will come our way.'

Letters arrived from the Senate, to say that the Antonians were crossing the Alps. Lepidus and Plancus were ordered to attack them. Lepidus marched eastward, for to ignore the Senate's command would be a declaration of open revolt. But still he had not made up his mind. He summoned a council of war.

His officers, themselves Caesarians, laid stress on the appeal of Marcus Antonius to the common soldiers. Laterensis alone maintained that his colleagues underrated the pull of lawful authority.

'Our soldiers are Romans,' he said in the course of an eloquent speech. 'For five hundred years they and their ancestors have obeyed the Consuls, the Senate, and the laws. If they are ordered to attack, they will be attacking an army which has already met defeat, vanquished by the heir of their old leader. Of course they are reluctant to draw their swords in civil war. I hope the same may be said of every gentleman at this council. If the Antonius brothers can be persuaded to seek refuge in exile, that will be the best outcome of this march. I can assure our noble Imperator that his army will obey him, as every Roman army has obeyed its lawful superior. You will agree, gentlemen, that I know my soldiers. I mix with them daily, and they regard me as a father.'

Laterensis, the only Senator among the officers, was also the only one of them trained in public speaking. In reply gruff veterans grunted and shrugged their shoulders; but to Lepidus, himself a trained orator, a lucid speech carried more conviction than the most heart-felt grunt. He decided to attack the Antonians as soon as those public enemies crossed the border of his province.

He led his army eastward to the left bank of the Rhône. He marched slowly, for he wished to keep his men well supplied; but he sent on his kinsman, the legate Culleo, with a light detachment to seize the Alpine passes. Approaching the foothills he received a shock which made him halt. Lucius Antonius was advancing westward at the head of the hostile cavalry; as soon as Culleo made contact he and his whole detachment went over to these public enemies of the Roman people.

At once Lepidus halted. Behind the little river Argenteus he fortified a strong camp. There he waited for Plancus to join him as promised; though a promise from Plancus was not the foundation on which a prudent leader would build a plan of campaign. But if he remained where he was Antonius would be compelled to attack, and surely his army would fight in defence of its own camp. He filled in the time of waiting by writing once more to Cicero. He pointed out that he was a faithful servant of the Senate; but was there any chance of a peaceful settlement?

He had reason to fear the impending war. Marcus Antonius was a famous soldier; the young veteran who had recently killed both Consuls was almost certain to get the better of a commander ten years his senior who had never seen a campaign. If he sat still in camp until reinforcements arrived his army would be much stronger than the enemy. But would it still be his army? Plancus was a pliant adventurer, who in dangerous times avoided decisive action. But Pollio was forceful, the intimate of the dead Dictator and the most beloved of the lesser Caesarians; the troops might desert their legitimate commander to follow his orders.

There was an obvious alternative: he might join Antonius. You might say that he was already linked to him by kinship, though the betrothal of young Marcus to Antonia was only a tentative step that might never end in marriage. But if he joined a public enemy of Rome he would himself become a public enemy; and then Junia and the children, living quietly in the Aemilian mansion, would be at the mercy of his foes.

To join Antonius would be fatal to his family; to fight Antonius would probably be fatal to his army. He ordered his men to deepen the ditch of his camp, and to fix extra stakes in the palisade; then he sat down to wait for something to turn up.

It was a spacious camp, for it held seven legions, the field-army of southern Gaul and eastern Spain; and it contained as many opinions as were to be found in Rome. Not long ago Antonius had commanded the Tenth Legion, and every man in it was fervently Antonian; but in other formations Laterensis had a following, and he had now come out openly as the agent of the Optimates. As in every Roman army, the cavalry were foreign mercenaries, in this case Gallic nobles. Their touchy barbarian honour ensured that they would not go over to the enemies of Rome; but they did not understand the civil dissensions of their new masters, and in their eyes any Roman commander was as good as another. During the campaign of Mutina Antonius had preserved his cavalry intact, and in horse he was stronger than Lepidus. The rumour that he offered rich bounties to every mounted recruit made some Gauls desert to seek him among the Alps; then Plancus, at last marching south, offered even larger bounties, and more Gauls deserted to this third party. It looked as though Lepidus would be left without cavalry; for he would not offer bounties to his own men, to pay them extra for doing what they had undertaken to do.

Behind the Antonius brothers Decimus Brutus toiled grimly at the head of a starving and threadbare force. But Brutus knew himself to be weaker than Antonius; he dared not attack until his adversary was already engaged with one of the provincial armies.

Lepidus wrote, urgently, to the Senate, to Cicero, to Pollio, to Plancus, to Decimus Brutus. He longed for someone to give him orders. But he was now one of the leading men in the republic, and everyone waited for him to use his own initiative.

\*

One morning towards the end of May he was roused from sleep to receive an excited scout. The man was one of the few remaining Gauls; his excitement, and his awe at speaking directly to the Imperator, made his Latin even less intelligible than was usual with these barbarians. But his message was clear, and it had long been expected. A great army, hungry and battered but strong in cavalry, was less than ten miles from the camp; by midday it would reach the river.

Trumpets pealed the stand-to as Lepidus hurriedly got into his armour, noting with annoyance that his waistline had increased until the moulded bronze corselet was extremely uncomfortable. There was no time for breakfast, no time even for the private libation to the genius of the gens Aemilia with which he had begun every day since he was old enough to hold a wine-cup. But he was Pontifex Maximus. He must perform the customary public sacrifice, to beseech the favour of Jupiter in this dangerous crisis. The fools of quartermasters tried to fob him off with a scrawny ox, and valuable time was wasted while they hunted through the ration-herd for a genuine bull; the animal they produced at last was horribly thin, and no bigger than a ram. Then in his haste he upset the barley-meal, and when at last the victim was dead and disembowelled its liver looked like nothing he had ever seen before. But the recognised bad omens were as absent as the good ones; he could proclaim to his army, without actually telling a lie, that the gods were not displeased with them.

Outside headquarters a zealous groom clutched the bridle of the showiest and most unmanageable war-horse in Gaul. Lepidus could ride well enough if he was put to it, but he did not choose to risk a toss before the eyes of his assembled army. He told the man to go away, and himself strolled on foot to the river-bank. His camp blocked the only bridge for many miles, and the enemy were not likely to ford a swift deep stream in the face of his skirmishers. Today there would probably be no fighting.

Every disciplined fighting-man was at his post, but a commander-in-chief attracts idlers as honey attracts flies. Soon a heterogeneous collection of hangers-on stood round him, discussing the situation and waiting to volunteer advice.

Crastinus was there, of course, because in action his post was beside the Imperator. Laterensis had turned up, ostensibly to receive final orders. Another legate was back with him, one Caius Furnius; in theory he was travelling back to Plancus from Rome, whither he had been sent with dispatches; but he had lingered in camp for several days, and it was easy to see that he was waiting to inform his own commander as soon as Lepidus took action. Besides these there were the mounted orderlies who forwarded routine dispatches, and the young Roman knights, beginning their military service, who would carry urgent orders in the danger of a general action. Altogether, it was a group of more than a score.

Eastwards across the river the country showed tangled and broken; it was hard to get a clear view of the road. But the approaching army disdained concealment. Soon Crastinus muttered in his lord's ear: 'Mounted patrol north of the road, mounted patrol south. There's the point of the vanguard, on the road itself. That's a little bit reckless, but their supports are close behind. Considering that this is the end of a long retreat I should say those cavalry are in very good order.'

The dark blobs of horsemen, with a cloud of dust above them, were unmistakable even to Roman nobles little experienced in campaigning. Laterensis mutttered through clenched teeth: 'Public enemies of Rome, men who fight to steal away our liberty! Here they come, in full retreat! And we are ready for them! This will be a day of glory, which my grandchildren will remember.'

'*Are* you ready for them?' asked Furnius, turning to glance back at the palisade. 'I don't see the battle flag.'

Reminded of his duty, the tribune of the praetorian cohort saluted and addressed his Imperator. 'Sir, have you any orders for my signallers? They are standing by with the red flag. Shall the Eagles be removed from their shrine?'

'Not yet,' said Lepidus shortly. 'I must see more of the enemy before I can give definite orders.'

The Eagles, sacred images as well as standards, were normally housed in the shrine of Mars beside headquarters. Not many proconsuls could sacrifice to as many as seven Eagles, and Lepidus felt a glow of pride whenever he worshipped them. To hand them over to the Aquilifers would be to tell his men that he expected battle before sunset. To hoist the red flag was an even more urgent signal. When they saw it the troops must remove the coverings from their armour, and parade in fighting order without haversacks or blankets. The same signal warned non-combatant followers to look to their own safety; it would send off every sutler and wine-seller by the westward road. The legionaries would be subjected to all the hardships of active service; if no fighting followed they would be very angry.

Lepidus could feel Time hastening over his head; when he glanced up at the sun it seemed to move visibly through the sky. He must issue orders, and very soon; but he still had no idea of the right order to give.

If he advanced to the attack he was sure to be beaten. The slayer of two Consuls would out-manoeuvre him; he might kill him with his own sword, as they said he had killed Ahenobarbus at Pharsalus. Yet to attack, to catch the enemy in column of route as they debouched from the pass, was the advice given by every handbook of tactics. If he retreated without even testing the strength of the foe he would be shamed before all his army. Perhaps if he waited, praying very hard to the genius of the gens Amilia, inspiration would enter his mind and tell him what to do.

His staff would not allow him to seek inspiration in peace. Laterensis was badgering him, there was no other word for it. The man had composed what he thought a good eve-of-battle speech, and wanted to run through it as a try-out in the presence of the Imperator. 'Great issues hang on our courage,' he began with practised fluency. 'Our brethren in Rome gallantly overthrew the tyrant. Before us stands the successor of that tyrant, and all his vile gang. He has been chased from Italy, but our subjects the Gauls lie at his mercy. They look to us for succour. If we prove craven, the legions of Pollio and Plancus will lose heart; they may even despair of liberty, and throw in their lot with those plunderers. Remember, behind Antonius marches our liberator, Decimus Brutus. He endured the hardships of a bitter siege, gallantly withstanding the hosts of tyranny that your children might be born free men. See, beyond the river, those Eagles! Since lawlessly they crossed the Rubicon they have drunk, time and again, the blood of free Romans! Let us charge and overthrow them, with Liberty as our war-cry!'

The young knights looked uncomfortable, but discipline forbade them to silence a legate. Furnius, of equal rank in another army, was not thus inhibited. 'Hold your tongue, sir,' he snapped. 'You do not command a legion of Optimate Senators. All your men are Caesarians, and the veterans among them were at the crossing of the Rubicon. If you continue in that strain they will first cut your throat and then go over to Antonius.'

Crastinus lightened the tension with a little technical comment. 'Yes, here come three Eagles, breasting the rise together. Those must be the three fresh legions of Ventidius Bassus. They didn't fight at Mutina, so they will be up to strength. But the men in the ranks are veterans, so I've been told. Yes, veterans, and good ones. A very pretty piece of marching. But look, over there to the right. Two more Eagles, and some of the men march bare-headed, without javelins. They have seen hard fighting. There are a lot of them for only two legions. Did our gallant Marcus lose an Eagle? It's not like him. I would expect him to be killed before he would yield an Eagle in fair fight.'

'That's no way for your orderly to talk of a public enemy, sir,' said Laterensis. 'My good man, the rebels did not lose an Eagle in the field, though they were defeated. But the gallant Consuls scattered two of their legions. I suppose stragglers from the beaten cohorts now march with the Eagles that remain.'

'They are Roman soldiers. Some of them fought with me in the conquest of Gaul,' Furnius murmured. 'Men like that rally to their standards even in defeat; and I for one am proud to see it.'

'It is indeed pitiable to see gallant Roman soldiers misled into waging war on their own City,' said the Imperator. 'Perhaps there may still be a way to peace. Nothing but the ambition of one man stands between us and universal concord. When Marcus Antonius sees that further retreat is barred by my faithful army he may admit that his cause is hopeless.'

There was a murmur of agreement from all save Laterensis, who snorted. But now Lepidus saw his way clear. He had spoken without thinking, saying merely the obvious soothing thing. But that was notoriously how a supernatural adviser put the right idea into the head of a faithful worshipper; the genius of the gens Aemilia had shown him how to deal with this awkward situation.

'Attention, gentlemen,' he said clearly. 'These are my orders for today, to be carried to every cohort with the utmost speed. The army will remain prepared for action. Alternate cohorts will man the palisade while their comrades eat or rest. Every soldier will be fully armed at all times; but we shall not draw out in line of battle. Sentries will be posted on the river-bank; they will fall back on the palisade if the Antonians advance. The utmost vigilance and readiness is imperative. No man may leave the ranks without permission, which will be granted only for necessary fatigues. Now, are there any questions?'

'Have you further instructions?' Laterensis asked sulkily.

'No, but as you seem puzzled I shall explain my intention. I wish to avoid battle, at least for the next ten days. When the proconsul Lucius Munatius Plancus has joined us we shall be greatly superior to the Antonians; before that it would be folly to risk a general action. I go further. If the troops remain firm in their ranks there may *never* be a battle. The Antonians will see that their struggle is hopeless, and some peaceful arrangement will prevent a shocking effusion of Roman blood. Therefore there must be no provocation; while the army before us refrains from attack our men must not molest their pickets. On our good conduct depends the peace of the Roman world. I shall demand the strictest discipline.'

'Then we may not attack these public enemies of Rome, even

if they come within range of our javelins?' asked Laterensis. 'I want to be quite sure, sir, that I understand you; for these are unusual orders in the thick of a civil war.'

'You have understood my orders, legate, and you will carry them out in every particular. One thing you seem to have mis-understood. We are not in the thick of a civil war. We are trying to preserve a menaced peace.'

Knight and couriers galloped off to spread the orders of their Imperator through his seven legions. Laterensis saluted with exaggerated precision, as though on a ceremonial parade. Furnius permitted himself a low whistle of surprise as he hurried off to his hut, to pass the news to his own commander as quickly as he could get it on paper. The group dispersed, leaving the Imperator alone with his orderly.

'I'm glad we don't fight today, my lord,' Crastinus said quietly. 'Each day's delay is another day of life for thousands of good Caesarians. By the way, if we have to attack after all you should put the Tenth in the centre of the front line, with the praetorian cohorts behind them. Perhaps you can get them to charge if they see sharp swords in their rear.'

'Silence, Crastinus. I must think,' answered Lepidus.

As he walked back to headquarters he had plenty to think about. Furnius had been surprised at his decision, which meant that as soon as Plancus heard of it he would be surprised also. He might even interrupt his march and leave his colleague un-supported, with fierce Antonians prowling round his palisade. Laterensis, of course, was angry and disappointed. Tonight he would write to his Optimate friends in Rome, and when they learned the news there would be an outcry in the Senate. They might even send lictors to confiscate the Aemilian mansion, though of course the lives of Junia and his sons would be in no danger. Noble Romans did not revenge themselves on helpless women and children, even in a bitter civil war. All that he had discounted. He had known his decision would be unpopular. But anything was better than taking the offensive against Antonius, unsupported.

Now in addition his orderly warned him not to trust his best legion. Of course the Tenth were Caesarian, as he was a Caesarian himself; in the west there were no anti-Caesarian soldiers, save the ragged stragglers who followed Decimus Brutus. But the chief of the Caesarian faction, young Caesar Octavianus himself, had recently made war on the Antonians. That showed that it was reasonable to fight them. How could he drive this argument into the thick heads of his veterans?

If his men were wavering in their allegiance, how was he to

101

win back their loyalty? When faced with a threat of mutiny, the ancestors always answered with extreme severity. He ought to decimate that untrustworthy legion, compelling the men to draw lots so that he could execute one in ten. But common sense told him that the surviving nine-tenths would not love him any better afterwards. He was an old-fashioned nobleman, who expected unquestioning obedience from the lower orders; but he was also an experienced politician, and when a politician encounters hostility his instinct tells him to offer a bribe. Could he invent an excuse to give the Tenth Legion a bounty? Out of public funds, naturally, not from his own purse. That was no good. He could not think of a convincing reason, and he would have to make the same payment to every soldier in his command.

Very well. There was nothing to be done. He would do nothing. Presently Antonius must attack, and he would make the best defence he could; or Antonius would march away, and his troubles would be over; or Plancus would arrive and share the responsibility.

He ventured one remark, just to show his orderly that he was not completely stunned by the prospect of action. 'Thank you for your hint. I shall keep the Tenth from any contact with that other army.' (He must avoid calling the Antonians the enemy; there was no telling how the future would turn out.)

'Beg pardon, my lord, but that's the wrong way to go about it,' answered Crastinus. 'You should invent an excuse to get them out of camp, and tempt the Antonians to fight them. If the others attack them first they will do well enough. It's just that they may be a bit slow if they are asked to do the attacking.'

Really, this common soldier seemed to delight in snubbing his commanding officer. Lepidus did not speak again until he had reached headquarters.

Inside the hut Eunomus jumped up from behind his desk of ration boxes to tell his patron the news. Lepidus was fresh from the outposts, and Eunomus never stirred from his cushioned chair; but the freedman always heard the news first. Lepidus was accustomed to this, and nowadays took it calmly.

'They want to negotiate, my lord. A pity they left it so late. They have scared our sutlers clean back to Narbo. They could have sent envoys when they were twenty miles off, instead of waiting until they reached the river. They haven't actually sent envoys, I understand. But they are building huts without making any kind of defence round their camp. That shows they must intend to parley.'

'No, they have sent no envoys. That I would know as soon as you, my Eunomus,' said Lepidus mildly. 'What's all this about their building an unfortified camp? They were at least a mile away when I last saw them.'

'Marcus Antonius moves fast, my lord. His vanguard marched right up to the river-bank, where the bridge used to stand; then they fell out to light cooking-fires, under the javelins of our pickets. They take it for granted that our men won't harm them. The cavalry are watering their horses where the river flows past our palisade. That shows their general will send envoys, doesn't it?'

'Probably, but it's no reason why I should receive them. If Antonius genuinely wants peace he can negotiate from a distance, as you said just now. To picnic like that in front of my troops is rank bad manners. It must be intended to make me look foolish, and I won't have it. Messenger, send a general order throughout the camp. No envoys to be admitted, on any pretext; not even Antonius himself, if he comes unarmed and waving an olive-branch. If someone approaches, the nearest sentry is to cast three javelins: the first over his head, the second into the ground at his feet, the third slap through his belly. He may count ten between each cast. That is an order. Repeat it, to show you understand it.'

'There,' he said cheerfully, as the messenger hurried out, 'that will show them I can make up my mind, even when ill-mannered ruffians try to bounce me into a decision without allowing me time to think. I refuse to be hurried, into making peace or into making war. What I do today may effect the lives of our grand-children. I must have leisure to decide.'

He dismissed even his secretary, and told the sentry that he was not to be disturbed by anyone. Alone, he paced the floor of his hut, balancing pros and cons in his mind.

Only once before had he taken an important decision, when he disobeyed Pompeius to throw in his lot with Caesar; and then Junia had advised him. On every other occasion respectability had been his only guide, and it had been enough. Respectability had made him a praetor in the good old days when no one had heard of the little river Rubicon; respectability had made him Master of the Horse to a Dictator, respectability had made him proconsul of Narbonese Gaul and Hither Spain. Now no course of action was respectable. It was no use asking what his ancestors would have done. His ancestors would have fought Antonius, and beaten him; if he fought, he knew he would be defeated.

Since he could decide nothing, he would do nothing. Until Plancus arrived he would sit out a siege; a strange kind of siege in which the besiegers foraged under his palisade and built their unfortified camp within range of his javelins. All the same, unless his men guarded the camp with the utmost vigilance he would be lost. After he had eaten a little biscuit, for at midday he was still fasting, he set out to walk round the rampart.

His soldiers were cheerful enough, gazing keenly over the palisade with their javelins handy. But every officer he met was worried. As soon as the Antonians arrived there had been a few desertions; though these were counter-balanced by the appearance of a few deserters from Antonius. It was not an organised movement. As far as he could sort it out, legionairies with relations or close friends among Culleo's men had gone to visit them, and veteran Antonians who had once served with the Tenth had come over to see their old comrades. Meanwhile the troops of both sides were beginning to exchange shouted gossip, and he saw with dismay that the Antonians were gathering material to repair the broken bridge. By tomorrow the two armies would be playing dice across the palisade unless he did something to remind them that they belonged to separate, perhaps hostile, forces.

When a quartermaster sought him out with a tale of a valuable convoy on the way, he had an inspiration. Hurrying back to headquarters, he sat down to draft detailed orders in his own handwriting.

Proud of his scheme, he explained its beauties to Eunomus while the secretary made out fair copies. 'I shall need three copies of this order, each certified by my personal signet. One is of course for the officer who must carry it out, the second will go on the headquarters file, the third is to be kept under lock and key with the pay-sheets and the tax-receipts. You see, Eunomus, any action I take during the next few days is sure to be the subject of an inquiry by a committee of Senators. I can't please everybody; by the end of the month either the Optimates or the Caesarians will be trying to put me in the wrong. I think it will be the Caesarians, for this order must bring on a skirmish. Yet on the face of it my action is purely a matter of routine; no Senator who has commanded troops of his own can find fault with it. Here is this convoy of biscuit and bacon, bought from the taxes of Narbonese Gaul. At this time of year the drivers prefer to travel by night, to spare their oxen the heat of midday; so the wagons are due to reach camp about dawn tomorrow. Only a furlong away are the Antonians; neither friends nor enemies so far, but known to be hungry and penniless. If their patrols encounter the convoy they will try to steal it. Duty demands that I protect my men's supplies. Therefore at sunset I send out four cohorts to meet the wagons. There, it's all in the order. That doesn't look as though I were deliberately bringing on a skirmish, does it?'

'No, my lord, it does not. This is a prudent precaution; no Senator can blame you for it. Why are you so sure the Antonians will attack the convoy, when it is guarded by four cohorts?'

'Ah, that's where my cunning comes in; and the best of it is that nothing appears on the records. It so happens that the legion next on the roster to furnish a detachment is the Tenth. So four cohorts of the Tenth will be detailed for the job. But four cohorts is too large a command for a military tribune. I ought to send a legate. Again I consult the roster, and I find that the legate due for the next expedition is Laterensis. Now do you see?'

'I understand completely, my lord. Shall I fake the roster to correspond with your orders? That would be prudent, in case the committee of inquiry impound your papers. A very pretty scheme indeed, if you will accept my humble congratulations. The veterans of the Tenth may be Antonian at heart; but, no matter what their political opinions, they will resist strangers who attack them in the dark to make off with their breakfast.'

'And even if the Antonians allow the convoy to pass unmolested, Laterensis will seek out their patrols and bring on a skirmish unprovoked.' His patron completed the explanation with a chuckle.

'Then you have decided to make war on the Antonians, my lord? Will you throw in your lot with the Optimates?'

'No, and I have not decided to make war on Antonius. Yet he should know that I am capable of making war on him. Then perhaps we can arrange reasonable terms of peace.'

'A difficult task, my lord. But you have seven strong legions against his three newly raised ones and the battered survivors of Mutina. So long as you control your men, he must listen to you. It all turns on that. They tell me that at midday the last of the Gallic horse deserted. No one knows whether they went to seek bounties from Plancus or Antonius.'

Lepidus went out without another word. He had expounded his clever stratagem to Eunomus, and the freedman, forgetting the respect due to his patron, had let it be seen that he considered the scheme too difficult to be accomplished. Of course his soldiers would be loyal to their Eagles! He was Imperator and Triumphator; Caesar had honoured him with the Mastership of the Horse. The men must be impressed with the greatness of their commander. Besides, they ought to be proud that they followed Aemilius Lepidus, bearer of one of the greatest historic names of Rome.

On the parade ground he ran into Laterensis, who was delighted to learn his orders for the evening. There was a brave man and a competent soldier! What a pity that he was a bigoted

Optimate; otherwise he would have been the ideal second in command.

The uneasy day wore on. Half the army manned the palisade, while the other half got on with the unending domestic work of a standing camp. That meant that no one was at leisure. There was all the boredom of a siege without the stimulus of danger. Meanwhile the Antonians frolicked just beyond javelin-range. Their cavalry, grazing the troophorses in the narrow meadow over the river, shouted in Gallic to the Lepidan camp-followers. The legionaries watched anxiously as their girls exchanged incomprehensible badinage with swaggering barbarian cavaliers who had been at the killing of two Roman Consuls; such heroes must prove dangerous rivals. The Antonian foot attempted to repair the bridge, desisting only when javelins whizzed past their ears, deliberately aimed to miss. Then, with the skill of veterans long in the field, they made a narrow footbridge a little way upstream.

By late afternoon there was a steady trickle of traffic across this bridge, though all the travellers appeared to be female. Laterensis, in great agitation, reported that some of these women were Roman soldiers, even officers, in disguise. He begged the Imperator to order a sortie; he volunteered to lead it himself, and to hew down the bridge or die in the attempt. Lepidus could not be persuaded to alter his plan. He had made up his mind to wait for night, when in the confusion of a skirmish at close quarters his men must fight their antagonists or be struck down unresisting; he explained that if he engaged by daylight his men might fraternise with the enemy before a blow had been struck.

That was the excuse he gave to Laterensis. In truth he would not change his plan because he would not begin an unpleasant task any earlier than he had intended. He had braced himself to bring on a clash about midnight; until then he might rest and calm his nerves. He felt about his legate's eagerness as a criminal might feel who, prepared to die at dawn, sees the executioner come for him at sunset. It seemed unfair.

By evening the tension had affected his health. For the first time in his life (but then it was also the first time he had camped in an Alpine meadow in May) he was attacked by hay fever. His eyes watered until he could hardly see, his voice became a croak incapable of shouting orders. There was nothing for it but to go to bed, with a jug of hot wine by his pillow. On this eventful night he had intended to lie down in his armour; in his present condition such a hardship would be absurd. He undressed completely; because he felt feverish he put on a clean cool linen nightshirt.

He was dozing fitfully when Laterensis came to take leave. It seemed to Lepidus that the self-righteous young man disturbed him only to have another opportunity of boasting before a congenial listener; his excuse was that he wanted to run through his orders once more, to make sure that he understood his commander's intentions. These were plain enough, and admitted of no misunderstanding. He was to bring on a clash in the dark, and make sure that his men killed at least one Antonian. Who was victorious in the skirmish did not matter in the least; in fact it might be useful, as likely to anger the troops, if the Antonians got away with the convoy. But by sunrise there must be shed blood between the wavering Tenth Legion and their old comrades outside the palisade.

At last the pompous young bore saluted and withdrew. Sneezing himself into exhaustion, the Imperator fell asleep. It seemed only a few moments later when he was awakened by his orderly.

'My lord, get up at once,' Crastinus cried. 'The Imperator Marcus Antonius will be here in a minute. It would be a discourtesy if he found you sleeping.'

'Eh? What's that? Marcus Antonius? What's he doing in my camp?' Lepidus answered in alarm, and fell again to sneezing.

'My lord, he comes as a friend. Please listen to me. He will be here in a moment, and you must understand. When the legate Laterensis marched those cohorts of the Tenth to the south gate the dirty dogs up and mutinied. They opened the gate, and hewed a breach in the palisade as well. Then they invited the Antonians to come in, and of course the brave Marcus was first to accept the invitation. He is now strolling through the camp, all unarmed and unguarded. He would have been here before me, but the men waylaid him on the parade ground, clamouring for a speech. Please, my lord, get out of bed.'

'Where's Laterensis?' asked Lepidus sleepily. In this picture there seemed no place for the stubborn young Optimate.

'One of the mutineers put a sack over his head, and they had a bit of fun with him. Then he went off alone to his hut, and the rumour is that he has fallen on his sword; but I haven't seen the body. Please hurry, my lord.'

'Very well,' said Lepidus, at last fully awake. 'Tell them in Rome that I met my fate without flinching. Before my body is burned get someone who understands the business to make a good death-mask. After all these generations it would be shameful to leave a gap among the Aemilian images.'

'What's all this about death and funerals?' asked a jolly voice from the door. 'This isn't a wake, it's a joyful reunion of old comrades. Come on, Aemilius Lepidus. Surely you remember

107

me? Is there wine in that jug, or have you been drinking melted snow like me? It's very lowering to the spirits, I can tell you. But now peace reigns, and we can celebrate.'

It was Marcus Antonius, though Lepidus had to look twice before he recognised him. The broken nose and confident, ingratiating smile were there as usual, but the general effect was new. Instead of scarlet cheeks, mottled with purple veins, his complexion was now a healthy brown; his throat was firm and muscular; the flabby jowl had gone, though a short beard hid the jaw; his hair hung raggedly on his shoulders, instead of lying in artificial ringlets. Presumably hair and beard had been permitted to grow in sign of mourning, ever since the defeat outside Mutina. But the biggest change was in his figure. Now he was slender, save where muscles bulged on thigh and arm; and he walked with a swagger of controlled energy. This was not the bloated and petulant lover of Cytheris who had scandalised respectable Senators in Rome. This was Antonius the dashing captain of horse, the leader who could trudge through Alpine snowdrifts or gallop over the sands of Egypt.

Lepidus tried to pull in his own belly. 'Antonius,' he said firmly. 'I suppose peace reigns, since you have stolen my soldiers. Now finish what you have begun. Will you take my head here and now, or will you grant me time to settle my affairs before I open my veins in private?'

'You are still asleep and dreaming, old boy,' and the smile flashed even wider. 'Why should I harm the father-in-law of my darling daughter? By the way, what a filthy cold you have. The Gallic climate doesn't suit you. We must do something for that. Can't have my daughter's father-in-law sneezing his head off in the provinces. Let's go back to Rome and enjoy ourselves. That's what I came to see you about. Of course I have not stolen your soldiers. Why should I? I have some quite good ones of my own. You are still Imperator of seven faithful legions, and I command only three and a bit. So, though we are both Consulars, you rank before me. But now that our men have made friends we ought to act in concert. Let's get back over the Alps as fast as we can, and scare the wits out of those fat Senators who are sitting on the keys of the treasury.'

'You mean we are friends and allies?'

'Yes, yes, of course. Our men insist on being friends, so if we want to go on leading them we must be friends also. It was a silly war, anyway. What were you doing, you, Caesar's old Master of the Horse, to help that murderer Decimus against Caesar's old comrades? I know, old boy; you were bullied into it. Well, now I have freed you, and you can follow your true inclinations. If we Caesarians stick together we can rule the world; and we can have a very jolly time while we rule it.'

Lepidus was overcome with relief. A minute ago he had been expecting death, forcing himself to meet it with dignity. Now this really charming man (and a first-rate soldier too) was offering to make him joint ruler of the world. Antonius would do the fighting, which was so frightening when your men awaited orders on the battlefield; while an educated Senator and patrician kept the republic in the ways of the ancestors, the ways that had made Rome great. What a splendid prospect, and how gratifying that this mere soldier had recognised the innate capacity of Aemilius Lepidus! But there were still obstacles in the way.

'What about Plancus and Pollio?' he inquired. 'For that matter, what about Decimus Brutus and young Caesar Octavianus? Must we fight all their legions before we rule in Rome?'

'Really! Plancus and Pollio! Do you think they will object? They are sound Caesarians, and friends of ours. Of course they will join us as soon as they hear of our alliance. Young Octavianus is more of a problem. We may have to move over a bit to make room for him. But he's only a boy. Give him a splendid title and plenty of money, and he'll leave the hard work to us. Poor old Brutus doesn't matter any more. By the end of the month his soldiers will be under our Eagles. I have offered a reward for his head, and quite soon I shall have to stump up. It's not a thing I do gladly; I'm all for clemency. But the actual murderers of Caesar cannot be permitted to die of old age.'

'Yes, the actual murderers deserve execution. Even the other Brutus, my brother-in-law, can't come back to Rome as though nothing has happened. But I expect he will die in battle, or kill himself. He's not a man to ask for quarter. I suppose we must soon march into Asia to deal with him?'

'*I* shall march, when we are ready. You leave all that sort of thing to me. Your job will be to rule Rome. You did it very well when Caesar was in Spain, and it will come easier the second time. Anyway, it doesn't matter if you do it badly. Don't you see, old boy? We are our own masters. We can do as we please. There isn't even Caesar to give us orders.'

'Our own masters, and masters of Rome! Well, why not? There are a lot of improvements I can make in the City, and I shall enjoy doing it.'

'That's the spirit! It's settled, then. Not worth going to bed again, as late as this. It's ten days since I tasted wine, and I'm due to get drunk. But before we send for the wine-skins you ought to show yourself to the troops, to prove that our interview passed off in a friendly way. No, don't bother to dress. Just go out and say a few words as you are. This isn't the Senate; they won't call you to order for not wearing a toga.'

*The lady Clodia leaned from her litter, her hand squeezing the shoulder of her handsome escort. 'Isn't this fun?' she said happily. 'There will be the most glorious crash in a moment, and with any luck one of those clumsy workmen will be caught underneath. I adore destruction. Since my brother died there hasn't been half enough of it.'*

*'You can't expect the Senate to compete with Clodius in mere destruction. Look, there it goes. I'm afraid the workman skipped clear at the last instant. Never mind, there's a splendid cloud of dust, and I think they have split the marble slabs of the pavement.'*

*'Poor bronze horse! How silly he looks, still prancing gallantly as he lies on his side. Who is the hero riding him? He seems on the chubby side. But I suppose if the Senate pulls down his statue he isn't a hero any longer.'*

*'The fat man riding it? Yesterday he was Marcus Aemilius Lepidus, Imperator, Triumphator, Consular. Now he is merely one Lepidus, a public enemy with a price on his head. The Senate put up the statue in gratitude, when he brought Sextus Pompeius over to them. Now he has joined Antonius; so of course the statue must come down.'*

*'How odd. They should put up another statue, showing him capering in his nightshirt while Antonius captures his camp single-handed. Still, he guarded my house on the night of Caesar's murder. Now I know who it is, I'm sorry the statue was destroyed.'*

*'Don't worry, my sweet. It will be back again before the year's out. Marcus Antonius is marching on Rome. Only little Caesar Octavianus stands between him and his goal. When the child has been beaten Antonius will rule us; and then of course his friends can have as many statues as they want.'*

*'Good. I hope Antonius makes himself Censor. He's just the man for the job. When the Caesarians occupy the City you must take me to see the statues of Brutus and Cassius overthrown. I can identify those heroes, you see. But then Brutus on a horse is unmistakable. Such a seat, such graceful carriage of the elbows! I suppose that is the old Roman manner of riding, one of the sacred customs of the ancestors.'*

# VII

## THREE TO RESTORE THE REPUBLIC
### 43 B.C.

Northwards the flat plain of the Po stretched to the horizon;
only at sunrise was it possible to make out the dim line of the
Alpine foothills. Southward, beyond the little river Lavinus, the
ground was more broken; ridges and steep sudden valleys led up
to the confusion of the Apennines, and among those wooded
crests a great army could be hidden. But the low sun of November shone from a cloudless sky, as though Jove himself was
eager to offer a good omen; and Lepidus, as he peered across the
stream, knew that a twinkle from helm or polished corselet would
give early warning even to his eyes, untrained in tactical appreciation. He could see no troops but the small bodyguard whose
presence had been stipulated in the preliminary negotiations. So
far there had been no treachery; he turned to signal the reassuring news to his own forces.

Approaching the river he had felt his nerves crawl. But as he
looked behind him his courage revived. The army drawn up on
the north bank need fear no foe. Never, in all the seven hundred
years since Rome was founded, had such a mighty force marched
behind the Eagles. Besides his own seven legions there were six
legions of Antonians, and these were reinforced by the field-
armies of the most warlike provinces in the west, men led by
Plancus from Further Gaul and Pollio from Further Spain. As
Antonius had prophesied, those governors had rallied to the
Caesarian cause as soon as Lepidus had shown them their duty.
Save where the ambiguous and unpredictable Sextus Pompeius
sat in disaffected Massilia, all the fighting Celtic west, the best
recruiting-ground in the world, obeyed the Caesarians. Far off
in Smyrna another great army was mustering, equipped by
eastern gold and recruited from faint-hearted Asiatics. Presently
there would come a clash, though the issue could be hardly in
doubt. But today his business was with the levies of turbulent
Italy: street-corner loafers underfed on the corn-dole, or surly
veterans regretting their stolen farms in Picenum. Even if the boy

had been flattered until he lost his head, his troops could not face in the field the disciplined, war-hardened cohorts of Antonius and Pollio.

Looking back, Lepidus could make out the encampment of his own seven legions. Even at this distance their huts showed better built and better aligned than the ramshackle bivouac of the slacker Plancus, or the flimsy shelters of improvident Antonians. Yes, his seven legions were the flower of the army, as brave and well-trained as their comrades and more efficiently administered. There was an advantage in being led by an industrious, conscientious man of business, too wealthy and too honourable to be tempted by the bribes of contractors. Yes, there was an advantage, and his men admitted it.

During the summer there had been times of anxiety. His gallant foolish veterans were impressed by the panache of those swaggering Antonius brothers; it seemed that they might desert their commander to follow the plundering Eagles of Mutina. Marcus Antonius had behaved really very well, though his brother Lucius was not quite so dependable. Marcus had gone out of his way to treat Lepidus with all the deference due to a general of greater seniority. Of course the position was irregular. At thirty-eight Marcus was Consular and Imperator; in normal times no Senator could attain the Consulate until his forty-third year at the earliest. By good behaviour the young man proved that Caesar's undeserved favour had not so far turned his head.

As the army gathered strength, a magnet for every Caesarian warrior in the west, Lepidus had felt himself more and more out of his element. That Pollio, always making doubtful jokes on serious subjects, that Plancus, openly out to plunder his fellow-citizens, were not the colleagues with whom an Aemilius Lepidus normally took counsel. They were so sure of themselves whenever it looked like fighting, and so shockingly ignorant of the protocol of negotiation with the Senate. They were capable of writing to the Senate and People of Rome, as though those two elements made up the whole republic. He, Lepidus, had politely shown them their mistake, addressing his own manifesto to the praetors, the tribunes, the Senate, the People, *and* the Plebs. The praetors, of course, were in place of the two Consuls, killed in action. But the separate addition of the Plebs reminded the ignorant that not long ago patricians alone had been reckoned among the Roman People; those other houses, even the gens Antonia, even the gens Junia, were immigrant foreigners lately granted the citizenship, not true children of Numa.

He had seen things that shocked him, as they marched over the Alps from the Narbonese to Cisalpine Gaul. This habit of levying contributions from friendly townships, or permitting the men to pillage unpunished; it was bad for discipline, and not in accordance with the custom of the ancestors. The generals excused any fault except cowardice in the field, because this was civil war and the men must be kept in a good humour. Worse than that, the generals themselves plundered.

They made a mock of religion, offering sacrifice only when their men needed fresh meat. The Pontifex Maximus did what he could by example, but even his own followers thought his careful daily ritual merely a personal eccentricity, not an essential safeguard against the enmity of the gods. At least he had prevailed on them to allow the spirit of Decimus Brutus to rest in peace. Lucius Antonius had wanted to set the wretched man's head on a spear and use it as a standard. As he explained, it had been bought most expensively from the Gallic chieftain who had murdered his guest; a trophy which had cost so much silver should be used until it fell to pieces, not wastefully burned even before it began to stink.

When Lepidus replied that the head, the seat of intelligence, was the most important part of a corpse, and that the spirit could not rest until it was properly disposed of, they had all been delighted to learn that Brutus would still be miserable, even in the next world. It was not until he pointed out that the ghost of a corpse denied burial was especially malignant, and that it haunted in particular the remnants of the dishonoured body, that Lucius hastily agreed to burn the unlucky relic. To think that Roman magistrates were prepared to go into battle behind the head of another Roman magistrate as standard! These people were more barbarous than Scythians! A world ruled by them would be a nasty place.

An Imperator who had never seen a battlefield was at a disadvantage in the counsels of these bloodthirsty ruffians. But with every step nearer Rome their resolution failed and his influence increased. To give them their due, they were not planning to sack the City and carry back the plunder to Gaul; they wanted to reign in a peaceful world, if possible with the assent of the Optimates in the Senate. But they had no idea of how to go about persuading the Optimates to surrender. Since not one of them could draft a dispatch which might be read with propriety in the Senate, they must follow the advice of this dignified, conventional nobleman, who could talk as an equal with any other old-fashioned aristocrat.

There was another element in his growing self-assurance. He knew that these men trusted him, and that they did not trust one another. In this last they were right. How could Plancus, for example, trust Pollio or the Antonius brothers? They accepted him because he had an army at his back; but they did not like him or admire him, and if they caught him alone, without his bodyguard, they were quite capable of selling him for a slave. (It was odd to recall that Ventidius Bassus, commander of three legions and legate to Marcus Antonius, had been a slave in Rome. Of course the fellow was of decent Italian birth, and had been captured as a child during Sulla's conquest of the Italian rebels. But whenever he dined with him Lepidus realized anew that politics had brought him into very queer company.) Aemilius Lepidus was known to be a man of his word, born to such greatness that he had never needed to intrigue, and to such wealth that he had never been tempted to steal.

For the tricky negotiation about to begin disinterested honesty was indispensable. Little Caesar Octavianus had at last been persuaded to meet Marcus Antonius face to face. Of course he feared assassination. The conditions laid down for the interview proved that both parties trusted Lepidus, and that they trusted no one else.

The place chosen for the conference was an island in the river Lavinius, and each party was to bring a bodyguard of not more than three hundred men; these could be counted as they defiled across the two temporary bridges, one leading from each bank. That was a customary method of arranging an interview between rival generals in time of truce, but it had one obvious weakness: what was to prevent one party or the other laying an ambush on the wooded islet the night before? The objection had been hard to overcome, and at one time it had seemed that the meeting would never take place. Now it had been agreed that Aemilius Lepidus should search the island before either general arrived. When he had signalled that he could find no ambush the two principals, the leader of the Caesarian army and the boy who claimed to be Caesar's heir, would trust their lives to his honour.

As far as he could make out from the north bank, young Caesar seemed to be playing the game. His camp was in plain view, some distance back from the stream. Only the three hundred praetorians were ranged near the narrow footbridge. They stood in close order, easy to count.

In any case, why should Caesar meditate treachery? If he killed Marcus Antonius his brother Lucius, or Pollio, or Plancus, would take over command of the great army of the west. That great army, more than eighty thousand men, was the real rival of Octavianus and the Caesarian idlers of the Forum. Treason could not destroy such a powerful force, and in regular battle it

114

must defeat the untried levies of Italy. Young Caesar had every-thing to gain by an agreement. In these degenerate days, when only the sword held power, Antonius had been generous in offering to treat with him. The boy had assets, of course. The assembly would ratify anything he suggested, and so far he had kept on good terms with the Optimates in the Senate; he could guarantee the Caesarians a peaceful accession to power. But Antonius might prefer victory after a brisk civil war. That would give him greater scope as a ruler.

Lepidus wondered what he ought to do if he discovered an Antonian ambush waiting for Octavianus. It was just possible that a plot had been concocted to rob him of his honour, and at the same time make away with Caesar's inconvenient heir. If he found such an ambush, he decided, he would unmask it; though both Marcus and Lucius had treated him very fairly. But it was most unlikely. The Antonius brothers were too forthright in their wickedness to stoop to secret murder, and in any case if they wished to eliminate Octavianus they could do it in open battle. Any assassins who might lurk on the island would be Optimate allies of young Caesar.

Squaring his shoulders, Lepidus turned to his orderly. 'Come on, Crastinus. Let's cross the bridge and get it over. Remember that if we meet treachery our first duty is to give the alarm. The assassins will leap on me, but they may not attack you. In that case don't try to rescue me. I shall face death like a patrician. Instead you must run away to warn the army.'

Crastinus saluted. Odd, he thought, how these gentlemen can't get a noble death-scene out of their minds. If a man has his throat cut in a scuffle, his neighbours are always too busy to notice whether he screams for mercy or fights back; afterwards you tell his widow that he died like a hero, while his drinking-companions take it for granted that his last act was to wet him-self. It doesn't matter. Inside the head of every real soldier is a little genius who tells him unmistakably when the time has come to prefer death to dishonour. Until then death is the supreme evil, to be postponed as long as possible. If an ambush is hidden on the island they won't be seeking my blood in particular; with luck, I may get away.

The muddy little island was deserted. As Lepidus poked his sword into the reeds he wondered whether the watching legions saw him as a dutiful commander or as a fussy little man. But it was important, at this crisis in the affairs of the republic, to keep on good terms with the Antonius brothers. He did exactly what he had been told to do.

In less than an hour he could signal that all was safe. As he splashed through the mud towards the northern bridge Marcus Antonius dismounted and prepared to pick his way across the narrow planks. On the bridge itself there was barely room to pass. Antonius motioned him to halt.

'My dear Lepidus, surely you won't desert me now, after all the care you have taken to safeguard my life? Come on, my dear fellow. You won't leave me to talk to young Octavianus by myself? I am only a licentious soldier, one of the most licentious soldiers Rome has ever seen. I don't know how to address a student straight from finishing-school, a well-brought-up young man who has heard all the right lectures and read all the right books. Besides, I shan't feel safe, alone with the scoundrel who led his troops to help Decimus Brutus, the murderer of his adoptive father. He might stab me in the back, and then tell the world that the divine genius of old Caesar supernaturally impelled the dagger.'

Lepidus stared in surprise. He had taken it for granted that Antonius alone would speak for the Caesarian army, as young Caesar would speak for the politicians of the City. Then he saw that the invitation was natural enough. Twice he had been formally thanked by the Senate for his conduct of delicate negotiations. He was Pontifex Maximus, strong to bind with solemn oaths. Most of all, he was an honest Roman nobleman, who could arbitrate fairly between hot-headed young warriors who might forget their manners in the stress of bargaining.

'If you need a third to see fair play, Antonius, of course I shall be glad to come with you. I'm not an experienced general, you know. Don't expect me to see the strategic implications of an armistice until you explain it to me.'

'I don't need a general. I'm pretty good at that sort of thing myself. I need a Senator with legal and administrative experience, someone who knows the finances of the state and will see that in any division of provinces I am not left penniless, someone who can put a decent face on an ugly bargain. In fact I need *you*, and I will accept no substitute.'

As they entered the narrow path through the reeds Antonius stood aside to make way for the Pontifex Maximus. Without a thought Lepidus went first; it would have seemed odd and discourteous if the younger man had preceded him. Then realisation of his position struck him with its full force.

On this little island two men were meeting to divide the civilised world; and one of them had invited, nay, pressed him to make a third. Of course he was worthy of the responsibility; if the world needed a ruler then Marcus Aemilius Lepidus was the man for the task. But it was remarkable that his talents should be so generally recognised, without any special exertion on his part. If he betrayed surprise his dignity would be lessened; he must appear to take for granted any honour bestowed on him. Above all, he must not seem shocked at the cynical expedients of these realist politicians. They might expect him to be shocked; his toughness would surprise them.

In a little clearing of the dank scrub they found Caesar Octavianus, seated in a curule chair. Lepidus had been told that the boy was as handsome as his famous great-uncle, and he was disappointed in his appearance. Young Caesar was not ugly, but he looked mean – in this military environment the word would be 'scruffy'. His features were regular. But his grey eyes, set deep, darted suspicion in every direction; his cheeks were pallidly unhealthy, and his chin veiled by an untidy reddish growth, too straggling to be called a beard; he was short and awkwardly built, and there seemed to be no muscle under his skin; he needed a haircut as badly as he needed a shave.

It would not be pleasant to talk business with such an uncouth young man; and the curule chair was vaguely another annoyance. These ivory seats were proper to grave middle-aged magistrates, not to sly young men. Then Lepidus recalled that the boy, still in his twentieth year, had appointed himself Consul-designate, threatening the Senators with the drawn swords of his soldiers until they complied with his unconstitutional command. Certainly the republic was in need of saving when children scarcely of age to vote, children who had never held junior office, were elevated to the highest rank.

Antonius greeted his rival with a careless wave of the hand; and seemed prepared to talk standing with a seated adversary. Lepidus put that right, clapping his hands to summon a guardsman. Soon two leather chairs were ranged beside the ivory throne. Though weather-beaten and shabby, they were something greater than curule thrones; each bore stamped on its worn leather the laurelled eagle of an Imperator. That distinction, the gift of faithful soldiers, was something to which the sickly youth could not lay claim. That was as it should be; Lepidus and Antonius, Consulars, took precedence of a Consul-designate who had not yet been granted the auspices.

Octavianus politely smiled a greeting. Until all were seated he did not speak, but it was evident that his quick little eyes had noticed the indifference of Antonius to matters of etiquette, and Lepidus's insistence that they should not be neglected. When at last he spoke his language was cultured, and his voice that of the trained orator.

'It is good of you to come, Pontifex Maximus. I had expected

117

the Imperator Antonius to visit me alone; but three heads are better than two, when grave matters are to be discussed.'

'Don't bother with titles, Octavianus,' Antonius interrupted brusquely. 'We bestow them on ourselves, and they don't mean a thing. You are Caius and I am Marcus. Now let's get to business.'

'My dear Marcus, that may be good enough for young fellows like us,' the boy replied with a grave smile. 'But in deference to his years and authority the Pontifex should be at least Aemilius Lepidus throughout our discussions. And, pardon me, titles *are* important. That my name is Caesar is perhaps the most important thing about me. In fact I seldom answer to any other name. You may, if you wish, call me Caius in private; but when anyone speaks of me as Octavianus I know him to be an enemy.'

'Very well, Caesar, since that is how you like it. Then I am Antonius, and he is Lepidus. Those are tolerably famous names, in the City and the world. . . . Now I take it you don't intend to fight me, or you wouldn't be here. So I suppose your band will join my army.'

'My army will co-operate with yours, certainly. I don't think it would be accurate to describe me as an Antonian recruit. I am willing to be your ally.'

'Ah, now we are getting down to it. You propose an equal alliance between Antonius, leader of eighty thousand men and the most famous general now alive; and Caesar, a Consul-designate who has held no office, twenty years of age, leader of a group of Italian ploughboys?'

'I propose that Caesar the younger, heir to Caesar the Dictator, should join forces with Antonius, his only rival for the leadership of the Caesarian party. Together we can rule the world. If we fight, we may destroy one another, and the Optimates will reap the benefit. Now don't fly into a passion. If your men will fight mine they are bound to win; but are you certain they will fight for you against me? It's only a year since your best legions came over to me at Brundisium. I was called Caesar then; it is still my name.'

'Tchah, why didn't my father name me Alexander? By your argument I would now have conquered the world.'

'It's true, all the same,' put in Lepidus, venturing to speak for the first time. 'My Tenth Legion won't fight against Caesar. Unless of course Caesar continues his unnatural alliance with the Optimates who murdered his father. But that is out of the question. No gentlemen would behave so.'

'Do you hear, Antonius? That is the voice of the ancestors, calling us to the sacred duty of revenge. Come now. While we

118

stick together no one can oppose us. But you and I alone are sure to quarrel. Why not bring in Lepidus to make a third? He knows how we ought to behave, and he is not afraid to tell us.'

The shaggy young man could produce an attractive smile, and his manner to the Pontifex Maximus was a masterly blend of respect for religion and deference to age. Lepidus felt his soul expand.

'My men will follow wherever I lead,' Antonius said crossly. 'If you doubt it, young Caesar, just meddle with my outposts. All the same, I should be a fool to quarrel with you, while Cassius and Brutus wait in Smyrna to give us both a good stand-up fight. But before we march east together there are enemies in Rome to be cleared out of the way.'

'I concur,' the young man answered. 'We must set Rome to rights and we must vanquish the murderers of my father. But you have not answered my other suggestion. You and I alone cannot rule the world. If we did not quarrel of our own accord our followers would egg us on to civil war; and when two men disagree they must fight or call in an arbiter. But in a college of three equal rulers two could outvote the third, and disagreements could be resolved peacefully. We need a third opinion to keep the balance. Since I am going out of my way to meet you in everything, I suggest that the third ruler shall be your old friend and colleague, Marcus Aemilius Lepidus. He is personally unknown to me. There is no tie between us. But his son is betrothed to your daughter. There, can I make a fairer offer than that?'

'Well, why not?' said Antonius with a cheerful grin. 'I had rather looked forward to fighting you, Caesar. I like fighting, I suppose because it's the only thing I'm any good at. But if we are to stay friends we need a third to keep the peace, and there is no one more worthy than my gallant Lepidus. What do you say, Marcus? Are you willing to take on the job?'

A little nettled at this familiarity, Lepidus answered as formally as though addressing the Senate. 'I am ever willing to serve the republic, as is fitting in a son of my ancestors. You offer a heavy burden, but I have supported burdens as heavy. While I was Consul the City took no harm. I have ruled all Italy single-handed, as Master of the Horse to a Dictator on campaign. Having survived such tasks I feel myself capable of ruling, and all the more easily with two equal colleagues to help me.'

'There, Caesar, you see? Our friend was ruling the world while you were learning your rhetoric. As he implies so delicately, his career has been more distinguished than mine; and of course very much more distinguised than yours.' Antonius spoke with a smile that was almost a leer.

Lepidus felt obscurely that his companions might in some way be making fun of him. But he knew by experience that he could not answer irony in kind; dignity was his best defence.

'We three are Consulars,' he said stoutly. 'That should make us equal in rank; save that as Pontifex Maximus I am supreme in all matters of religion. Antonius has greater experience in war, and I admit it; as Caesar has greater influence with the voters in the assembly. Yet I know myself worthy to be one of the three rulers of Rome, if three are needed.'

'Then that is decided,' young Caesar struck in quickly. 'I think it is enough to decide in one day. We three will fill the position once held by my father and Pompeius and the unfortunate Licinius Crassus. But we shall not rule as an unofficial caucus of party-leaders. We must get our position regularised by law, a proper law passed in due form by Senate and assembly. Tomorrow we can settle the terms of this law, and discuss how we shall divide our responsibilities. I suggest that we now go back to our armies, and tell the soldiers that peace is assured. Let us meet here again tomorrow, with clerks to record our decisions. And I suggest that we remain encamped by this river, meeting every day, until we have agreed on a complete programme for the better government of the world. Thus we shall present waverers with an accomplished fact, and there will be no opposition when we march on the City.'

'I would enjoy a little opposition, and so would my soldiers. If we encounter no enemies it looks as though we shall be driven to plunder our friends,' said Antonius with a sigh. 'All the same, your plan is a good one. Back to the camp, Lepidus. Caesar, will you sup with me tonight? No? How very sensible. I'm an honest man myself, but some faithful praetorian might be tempted to cut your throat.'

Once again he made way for the Pontifex Maximus to precede him on the narrow path; but when they reached open ground the two Consulars walked arm-in-arm, equal colleagues and familiar friends.

Refusing a pressing invitation from Antonius, Lepidus supped alone in his headquarters. He then sent for Eunomus, to discuss with his secretary the proposals he should lay before the meeting next morning. The Greek was a stimulating companion. His deft flattery always increased his patron's self-confidence. But tonight Lepidus needed no encouragement; he was already intoxicated by gratified ambition.

'I never once asked for anything,' he repeated. 'Caesar offered, without prompting; and when it was put to him Antonius agreed without demur, though I am sure that when he set out for the

120

island the idea had not entered his head. Surely that is public recognition of my innate ability? What is it Aristotle says about the Magnanimous Man? That he is worthy of a great position, and knows himself to be worthy of it? Just so do I feel myself to be worthy of ruling Rome. I am not conceited. It is very remarkable, in its way, that my talents have been thus recognised although I have done nothing outstanding. Antonius is a skilful soldier, Caesar controls the assembly of the people; both have a host of loving supporters. I have none of these advantages. My soldiers like me, I suppose; but I am not extravagantly popular. I was elected Consul, but only on Caesar's recommendation. Yet when two very powerful men agree to divide the world between them, they spontaneously ask me to be the third, the arbiter of their quarrels.'

'My lord, of course you are not conceited. What you have just said proves your innate modesty. Lucky Rome, where such merit can be found, and where such merit is recognised! If the citizens of Miletus had been equally far-sighted they would have remembered to bribe the tax-collectors, and I would never have been sold into slavery.'

To himself Eunomus reflected that a question had been settled which had long puzzled him. Luck was the prime mover of the universe, not intelligence or courage. Well, if he himself had met with undeserved misfortune, he was now private secretary to the luckiest member of the human race; there might be a future in that.

'Now, Eunomus, what shall I propose tomorrow? We are going to parcel out our responsibilities, each assuming the task for which he is best fitted. I want to come to the meeting with my mind made up. It's time I took the initiative and gave advice unasked. Today the others did all the talking, and I merely agreed when they sought my opinion.'

'No more of that, my lord. If you always agree you will not remain equal with your colleagues, and if you disagree they might combine against you. You must make proposals of your own. Yet you should propose what will please Antonius and Caesar; they will admire your wisdom the more. Now let me see. There are two main tasks to be undertaken. Someone must lead an army against Brutus and Cassius, someone must rule Rome.'

'I don't want to fight Brutus if I can avoid it. He is my wife's half-brother, and I should feel scruples about killing him.'

'Besides, Cassius is a very fine soldier,' Eunomus could not help answering, though it was the merest common sense to keep his patron in a good humour. 'I think it would be prudent to leave the rough work of butchery to Antonius, who delights in it and does it well. Tomorrow you must propose that Marcus Antonius shall lead the great army of revenge. Offer him the pick of your legions; if you don't they will desert you to follow his Eagles anyway, and by offering you lay him under an obligation. That is the obvious move, and they will be expecting it. Your second proposal is rather more subtle, and I must explain what lies behind it. You should suggest that young Caesar Octavianus rules in Rome, while you govern the barbarian west.'

'Eh, what's that? I don't like it. If I do that I renounce my equal rank.'

'My lord, Caesar will not accept, though your offer lays him also under an obligation. Consider. In the field Caesar has never done anything, except guard his own camp while two Consuls died gallantly outside Mutina. His only power lies in the devotion of his soldiers, and so far he has done nothing to earn it. He dare not allow Antonius to win more glory. He will insist on marching with him to the east. But someone must rule the City. Therefore both your colleagues will beg you to stay behind and govern Rome, while they make war in Asia. No one will be surprised if only one of them returns. But even if they don't quarrel they will come back, after several years, to find you chief of the Senate and leader of the assembly. You will allot the farms to veterans, you will control the treasury. You will be very powerful.'

'That's a clever move, and I would never have thought of it. But then I am only a simple, bluff Roman.'

Thanks to this prompting, at next day's meeting Lepidus had everything his own way. It soon became apparent that his colleagues thought only of the war against the Optimates; Antonius offered to lead the expedition, and Caesar insisted on sharing the burden. Neither was anxious to wear a toga in Rome while his rival marched in armour at the head of the legions. Both combined to press the task on Lepidus; he was able to accept what he wanted, with the air of one conferring a favour.

The other principal topic of discussion was the legal foundation of the new régime. Young Caesar showed a grasp of the niceties of constitutional law remarkable in one of his tender years. He was firm that they must not break the law; instead, the law must be altered. He had a draft ready, a bill setting up *tres viri reipublicae constituendae*, three men to restore the state; their commission would run for five years from next January, but of course it could be renewed later. With affairs in such confusion, five years was far enough to plan ahead. The ordinary magistracies would continue, under the supervision of the Triumvirs. Caesar offered to resign his promised Consulship, since he would be out of Italy for most of the year; instead Lepidus was again to be Consul, with Caesar's insignificant cousin Quintus Pedius as colleague. To cement the alliance more firmly, the young bachelor offered to marry any female connection of Antonius; but since Marcus Lepidus the younger was already betrothed to the only unmarried daughter, he had to be content with Clodia, daughter of Fulvia and Clodius and now step-daughter of Antonius. As Antonius remarked cheerfully to Lepidus, walking back to camp from this second meeting, the boy could not have been more eager to keep on good terms with his elders if he had been a client. Accidentally, he had come by a powerful name; among experienced politicians he was out of his class.

At the third day's meeting Lepidus revised this opinion. There was more in young Caesar than met the eye. Perhaps he still lacked the ability to make broad plans, as was natural in one of his youth; but once the plans have been sketched by his elders he had a good administrative mind for filling in the details.

By this time the Triumvirs had settled into a routine, as though it was quite natural to govern the world from a swampy islet, under a sweeping November sky. They met in a weatherproof hut, with comfortable office-chairs for the principals and desks for the secretaries. A field-kitchen provided hot food and mulled wine; and a crowd of civilian servants and clerks had replaced the grim bodyguards of the first day. This was planned to be the last meeting before they marched to take over the government of Rome. The agenda was short and simple: what was to be the fate of their Optimate adversaries?

When they were comfortably settled Antonius called on Lepidus to speak first. Nobody had appointed Antonius chairman, but he normally took charge of any meeting at which he was present; his character was forceful and his self-confidence unbounded. Young Caesar hung back in the presence of his elders, and Lepidus was slow to collect his thoughts.

On this matter he had made up his mind. Besides, he had run through his speech the night before, with Eunomus for audience. He spoke briefly, anxious to impress these rivals with his speed in making a definite decision.

'The murderers of Caesar must be killed. They are guilty of the death of a fellow-citizen, of sacrilege in that they laid hands on the Pontifex Maximus, of disturbing a session of the Senate; all capital crimes. Luckily they are now in arms against us; I suppose most of them will be killed in battle, or will kill themselves to avoid capture. Perhaps none of them will be taken alive, especially if we announce beforehand that they cannot hope for quarter. That would be the happiest solution. Since the bad old days of Sulla no Roman has been executed for a political offience. If we execute even the most guilty we will shock many citizens, and perhaps lose votes in the assembly. As to the other Optimates, political opponents who have not stained their hands with murder – well, we are Caesarians. Our great leader pardoned any Roman who was willing to submit.'

'That's all very fine and large,' said Antonius. 'I'm for clemency myself, and for drinking with pardoned adversaries until they become my friends. But Lepidus has forgotten one very important point. I must have a lot of money as soon as I reach Rome. My soldiers are devoted to me; one reason for their devotion is that they expect me to make them rich. Unless we plunder the Optimates I don't see where we shall find money; though perhaps we don't have to kill them after we have robbed them.'

'Yes, we must,' said young Caesar decisively. 'If you steal a man's property you make him into a dangerous enemy. That was Sulla's mistake, to confiscate land for his veterans and leave the original farmers alive. All Italy has been filled with dispossessed countrymen, or their grandsons, ever since. I found them useful to fill my legions, but they will join anyone who attacks the established order. Every enemy of society, from Catalina to Milo, has raised an armed band in Picenum or Etruria. I have a plan to settle these men in colonies overseas, but we must not add to their number.'

'And our Optimate enemies are not rustic farmers. They are experienced magistrates, accustomed to command in war,' said Lepidus, before he had thought out the implications of this remark. As realisation came to him he continued: 'Oh dear, I hope that doesn't mean we must kill them. Perhaps Antonius can find his money in some other way.'

'Not in the quantities he will need,' said Caesar with a thin smile. 'Quite a lot of money was stored in the temple of Ops, the savings of my lamented father during a lifetime of service to the republic. It barely sufficed Antonius for one year.'

'There was a crisis, my dear son-in-law-to-be,' Antonius said hastily. 'There was the assembly to be bribed, and the expense of a splendid funeral. That is not my normal scale of expenditure. All the same,' he added with a grin. 'I like to know there is money behind me, and I must provide for fierce and greedy swordsmen. Rather than go hungry, the legions will take his wealth even from a proved Caesarian. Must we sell our ancestral lands to provide bounties for our own veterans? One other point. Twice Caesar pardoned Marcus Brutus, and Cassius at least once. Did such clemency prove a sound policy?'

'No one proposes to pardon the murders,' exclaimed Lepidus,

'Oh, I see what you mean. We must not pardon men who will murder us afterwards.'

'Gentlemen,' said young Caesar formally, 'we must follow one of two paths. Either we offer forgiveness to every adversary who did not wield a dagger on the Ides of March, or we must make such a clearance of our enemies that not one is left to carry on the feud. It would be fatal to show ourselves ruthless, and then to draw back halfway. It must be all or nothing. I myself favour clemency; but I am willing to be persuaded.'

'Let us call things by their true names,' Antonius said impatiently. 'I want to take all the money of a lot of rich men, and I shall feel more secure if I kill them when I rob them. Besides, in the history-books confiscation of the goods of convicted felons looks much better than plain theft.'

'But that means a proscription,' Lepidus wailed in dismay. 'You young men grew up in security. I can remember Sulla's reign of terror. The citizens will never forgive us for bringing back the proscription, and it's a foul business anyway. It always gets out of hand, with subordinates making away with their private enemies, and informers inventing evidence for the sake of the reward. We seek special powers to reform the state, not to murder the most eminent of our fellow-citizens; and half the Optimate leaders are related to me by blood or marriage. It's bad enough that I must make war on my brother-in-law, Brutus, and my wife's brother-in-law, Cassius Longinus. Must I also hunt down every other nobleman who has been considered worthy to marry into the gens Aemilia?'

'Alliances of blood and marriage are very good things in their way,' Antonius answered coolly. 'They help a young man at the outset of his career. But when you have come a certain distance you must ignore them. For example, your Marcus Brutus fought for Pompeius, though years before Pompeius had murdered his father. You may be sure Brutus has never done anything that seemed to him wrong.'

'If you alone are governed by family affection, you will be handicapped in dealing with your equals,' added Caesar. 'I suppose you want to save your brother Paullus. Do you know that he was the Senator who moved that you be declared a public enemy when you joined Antonius? I was in Rome at the time, and I heard him.'

Both stared together at Lepidus, willing him to consent to the massacre. He was conscious of their gaze, Antonius amused and quizzical, Caesar stern and speculative. It came to him anew that he had nothing in common with these men. They were utterly rapacious, bound by no scruple, determined to get to the top; he was a God-fearing patrician, anxious to walk in the honourable ways of the ancestors. But they had chosen him to be their equal colleague. He was offered power, greater power than any Aemilius had held in the past. Besides, the City had changed since his boyhood. These were representatives of the younger generation, men who looked clear-eyed at the beastliness of the modern world, to pick their way in safety past its pitfalls. He must not show himself a stuffy old fogy. To cure the distempers of the modern republic, modern surgery was needed.

'Very well,' he said with a sigh. 'I vote, with Antonius, for a new proscription.'

'That makes us two to one, Caesar. By the terms of our compact you are bound to accept the decision of the majority.'

'I agree, with a heavy heart,' said Caesar. 'You have convinced me that no other course is open to us. On one point, however, I am determined. Rome can stand *one* more proscription; it must be the last, within the lifetime of the youngest of us. If ever we repeat it, all confidence will vanish. Therefore . . . ' he paused, and Antonius completed the sentence for him.

'Therefore we must finish the banquet without any leftovers, eh, my Caesar? We must be ruthless, even to our nearest and dearest? That goes without saying. In addition we must take care not to overlook the dangerous but obscure, since this dose of medicine cannot be repeated.'

'I would go further,' said Caesar. 'We think of the Optimates as our only foes. We should bear in mind that Caesarians can be dangerous also. Anyone whom we cannot trust absolutely must be eliminated, even though he fought gallantly from the Rubicon right up to Munda. Most of my father's murderers were discontented Caesarians. Let there be no exceptions. We each of us can think of at least one prominent opponent whom it would be pleasant to spare. For example, I like Cicero as a man, and in the past he has helped me. But once we begin making exceptions we shall find something to be said in favour of everyone; and then our reign of terror will never get started.'

'No mercy for Cicero,' Antonius said firmly. 'He was very rude to my dear Fulvia. I have promised her his head.'

'My brother must die, I see that,' put in Lepidus, determined to show himself a clear-sighted realistic tyrant, like the men in the Greek history-books. He must prove his fitness for supreme power. This was not the code of the ancestors; but then none of his ancestors had been offered a place in a Triumvirate.

'Gallantly spoken, old boy,' said Antonius, slapping him on the back. 'Just to prove that I also am selfless when the welfare of the republic demands it, I contribute the head of my uncle,

Lucius Caesar. He's a kinsman of yours too, young Caesar, isn't he? So perhaps he can stand in addition for your sacrifice of family feeling to the common cause.'

Caesar bared his teeth in a smile which showed almost insolently that he was not amused. 'Cicero is my contribution, and worth more than any of yours. Incidentally, I gave him my word of honour that he would be safe; so I sacrifice something more precious than family feeling.'

'Ah well, our country must come first. Cicero goes, and all his house with him. He's not really rich, for a Consular; but if you add in his brother and his nephews the Tullians will contribute something to my pay-chest.' That was Antonius, of course.

'What about your allies, Antonius?' asked the unsmiling boy. 'I mean Plancus and Pollio. We mustn't give them the chance to desert us, in pious horror at our bloody deeds. They are rogues, out only for what they can get; but we should commit them to our side, if we can.'

'Them? Nothing easier. Plancus envies his brother Plotius, who is a little bit too rich. He will be pleased to see that head on a pole, and when he has put it there the other side won't have him even if he tries to join them. Pollio is slightly more honest, though not enough to hurt. But he quarrelled with his father-in-law about his wife's dowry. I think a quarrel with Pollio ought to have fatal consequences, don't you? We can find other victims, until all the prominent army-leaders are committed to our cause.'

'Then all is settled, in principle. But the arrests must be planned with care. I suggest we got into that this afternoon. Let no one leave the island until our orders have been written and sealed. I am thinking especially of our secretaries, who are as venal as all freedmen of that class.' Caesar looked round with a thin-lipped smirk, and the waiting secretaries wilted under his eye.

'That's right,' said Antonius. 'We must put a guard on both bridges. Shall I make out an order? I am senior officer.'

'You are the most famous general, but Lepidus is senior officer. He was Consul and Imperator under my father, when you were propraetor and I was learning my book. Besides, my soldiers might not like to take orders from you, who were recently my rival. Lepidus, will you tell the sentries on my bridge, the southern one, that no one is to pass until I cross it myself? And give the same order, if you agree, to your men on the northern bridge?'

'Of course I will, Caesar. Glad to be of service.' Then he thought guiltily that he had given quite the wrong answer; he was Caesar's equal, and must guard his precedence.

That name Caesar was the root of the trouble. The young man had very little right to it (though if he was not truly Caesar's son Caesar had chosen him to be his heir); yet it was almost impossible to call a man Caesar and treat him as an equal. Junia had spoken truly when she said, nearly seven years ago, that nothing would be the same after the crossing of the Rubicon.

The sentries on both bridges saluted respectfully when he gave them their orders. The instant obedience he now commanded from legionaires even of other armies was most gratifying. But he had business of his own, for his brain was working with a speed that surprised him. As he had expected, he found his orderly chatting with the guard-commander by the northern bridge. He called the man aside and spoke to him quietly, careful not to be overheard.

'Crastinus, we have decided, the three of us, that my brother Aemilius Paullus is a danger to the republic. He is to be killed without trial, by a detail of soldiers sent for the purpose. He is not the only Senator whose fate has been decided, but the others do not concern you. Your duty lies with him alone. Take this signet of mine, and with it seal your own orders. Draft them as you please. You will take to Rome a dozen picked men, starting at first light tomorrow. You may requisition on the road for your needs. When you reach the City you will seek out my brother, and deal with him.'

He paused, looking steadily into the veteran's eye. 'In this signet I trust you with my whole authority. When you stand before my brother you stand in my place. You know your duty. I am confident you will perform it.'

The man stared back, disciplined but assured. 'Imperator, I shall carry out your will. When my task is done I shall report to the lady Junia, and await your arrival in Rome.'

There had been a slight but unmistakable emphasis on the word 'will', where 'command' was the routine formula. Lepidus knew he had been understood. It was ironical that one of the three rulers of the world dared not tell his orderly in plain words what he desired to have done in his name.

When he returned to the meeting he found young Caesar scribbling in a notebook with his own hand. The boy had an orderly mind, and an amazing memory. He had lived in Rome for less than eighteen months, and his manners were evidence that he had been bred in the more rustic parts of Italy; but he could remember every public figure in both parties, his kinsmen, his wealth, and in which quarter of the City he resided. Relentlessly the list of death proceeded; when Antonius contributed a

128

name it had usually been set down already.

For nearly four hours the grim enumeration continued. Lepidus could not fix his mind on the concrete particulars; it kept on reverting to his own situation.

'Here I am, Aemilius Lepidus, patrician, Consular, Pontifex Maximus, a nobleman of ancient lineage, who for all the forty-seven years of my life have walked in the ways of the ancestors; and I sit unprotesting while the companions of my boyhood are condemned to death untried. I ought to jump up and cut Caesar's throat here and now, before he can carry his bloody plans into effect. But then his bodyguard would torture me to death, and my friends would be killed all the same. In this ruin my own house will continue; my first duty to the ancestors is to ensure its continuance. One day young Marcus will be Aemilius Lepidus in place of his father. That comes first. Perhaps every great statesman does as I am doing; for I am certainly a great statesman. No Lepidus before me attained such authority. That's it,' he comforted himself. 'All great men do these things, and later the historians hush it up. I must not betray my anguish of spirit. The others would despise me.'

At length Caesar paused, gathering up his papers. 'That's all the Senators, I think. We shall have to eliminate some knights as well, but we can consider them later. We need not go lower than knights. Most of the common people are stout Caesarians, and they are too poor to be worth robbing.'

'How many names have you?' asked Antonius.

'About three hundred, more or less, I should say.'

'But that's more than half the Senate!' cried Lepidus.

'More than half the Senate are our enemies. That's why the Optimates have a majority there,' answered Caesar with another of his bleak grins. 'We can replace them with our own nominees, faithful Caesarians who will vote for our decrees. Incidentally, that's a nice bit of patronage. In the provinces there are wealthy citizens who will pay heavily for a seat in the Senate.'

'Ah, money, we can never ignore it,' said Antonius, rubbing his hands. 'But, my dear fellow, I don't want to throw cold water on your plans, yet have you considered how Rome will take this news? All these Senators have clients and tenants. They may hold the City against us, rather than die like beasts at a sacrifice. There are such a lot of them, if they should combine.'

'That had occurred to me,' Caesar sounded annoyed. 'I have a plan to avoid the danger. That miserable cousin of mine, Pedius, is Consul in Rome. He will do whatever I command, but there is no need to take him into our confidence. We shall send him a list of seventeen names, the names of our most dangerous enemies. We shall let him know there are a few more names to come, but not how many. If we do it little by little our enemies will be destroyed before they have a chance to combine.'

'I see. No list bears more than a score of names, but lists keep on coming out. Is that how Sulla managed it? It seems sensible.' Antonius spoke calmly.

'I am sorry to learn that so many of my old friends deserve death,' put in Lepidus. 'Can't we spare their lives and send them into exile? It seems an awful lot of heads to be taken, just to make three men feel safe.'

'It is not to make three men feel safe,' Caesar said hotly. 'We shall never feel safe, anyway. That is one of the penalties of power. No, this proscription serves a greater end than our convenience. If we carry it out thoroughly we shall put an end to these everlasting civil wars. Do you realise that they have continued for ninety years, ever since Tiberius Gracchus was murdered by the Optimates?'

'No more civil wars. That will seem strange,' muttered Antonius. 'Unless of course at some future date the Triumvirs should fall out among themselves.'

'When I examined the liver after this morning's sacrifice I saw that today would be peaceful. Whether there will be peace tomorrow is still hidden from me,' snapped Caesar.

'Gentlemen, friends and allies, we have just taken a most desperate resolution,' Lepidus bleated. 'This is no time for comrades to be threatening one another.'

'I do not threaten the saviour of Mutina,' Antonius said haughtily. 'I have seen real war, and plenty of it. They tell me that Caesar is overcome by his distressing but punctual fever whenever he sees the red flag hoisted. He was standing gallantly on guard before his camp while I slew the two Consuls who did his fighting for him.'

'What you say is true, Antonius. My health is weak, and I have never commanded in a great battle. Had you, when you were twenty years old? If I have given offence, I apologise. I suggest that we end this conference now, and march in company to Rome. We have been dealing with a most unpleasant business, which is now behind us for ever. Of course our nerves have been strained, and we are very near to quarrelling. It is time to part while we remain friends.'

'Yes, Antonius, it is time we went to our quarters. There is no ground for a quarrel, but we have been shut up together too long.'

'Very well, Lepidus. You are right, as usual. And you too, Caesar: I have never before stuck to one piece of business for four hours, in all my misspent life. It has made me irritable. Caesar, as Consul-designate you command in Italy. If tonight you send me your marching-orders my legions will conform to your movements.'

The handsome warrior swept out of the hut; he could be heard whistling as he trudged towards the bridge.

Lepidus turned anxiously to his young colleague. 'Antonius was gracious to leave you to arrange the order of march. I hope you will take it as an apology. It shows that he really wants to be friendly. When we arrive in Rome we must work together.'

'I harbour no resentment against Antonius,' young Caesar answered. 'He acts after his kind, which some philosophers hold to be the essence of virtue. Anyway, he doesn't matter. The soldiers like him, and he can charge like a bull. But he's neither a good general nor a sound statesman. If he makes a nuisance of himself I can deal with him.'

'How wonderful to be named Caesar!' said Lepidus, without a trace of irony. 'I envy your self-confidence. But after plotting the murder of three hundred Senators we shall have to stick together.'

*At last the lady Clodia was taking an interest in politics.*

*'You see, Publius, my niece is to marry this young Caesar, who was made Consul before he was of age to vote. So I shall be well in with the new government, even though Fulvia doesn't like me. How odd that poor dear Lepidus, a figure of fun for the last five years, should be one of the rulers of the City. What are they thinking in the Senate?'*

*'The Caesarians are delighted, naturally. The Optimates are afraid. Do you believe soothsayers?'*

*'I don't believe anything. I am a Claudia. But I like to know what the soothsayers are prophesying. Sometimes they give me the most delicious thrills of foreboding. What has that to do with the Senate? Don't tell me the magistrates have come to believe in their own omens?'*

*'Not as bad as that. But the helpless Optimates are longing to know the worst. Some of them sent to Etruria to fetch the oldest and wisest of the genuine Etruscan augurs. The old man came to Rome, and all day he watched his birds. At evening he told what he had learned. "The Kings return to Rome," he said. "You will all be enslaved by them. I won't." Then he fell dead.'*

*'That's a nasty story. Let's forget it. Lepidus, at least, can't frighten me. All the same, you might put me in some out-of-the-way country villa until things are quiet again.'*

*With a shiver, the lady Clodia reached for the wine-bowl.*

131

# VIII

## ORDER REIGNS
### 42–41 B.C.

The procession was everything it should be. There were seven
legions of soldiers, every man in high spirits at the prospect of a
feast when he had done his duty by marching along the Sacred
Way. There were captives in herds, and wagons piled high with
sacks of money and strange works of barbarian art. There was
the sacred chariot, drawn by four white horses and escorted by
the priests of Mars. There was a hecatomb of white bulls, each
one of the hundred led by a handsome young camillus, a youth
from one of the ancient families of Rome. The path was strewn
with laurel. From the open doors of their temples the gods,
wreathed in flowers, beamed approval of this joyous occasion.

Yet as he stood in the famous chariot, robed in purple, crowned
with laurel, so splendid and glorious and lucky that a slave
behind him must continually whisper that he was a mortal man
and not a deity, Lepidus felt that something was missing. He
was not experiencing the pleasure he had anticipated. Perhaps
that was because nothing is ever quite so exciting when it is done
for the second time, and he was already a Triumphator. Perhaps
it was because he knew, everyone knew, that the ceremony was
an empty sham. The soldiers' glittering shields had never been
scarred by hostile javelins, the captives were common brigands
or runaway slaves, the trophies were plunder stolen from defenceless subjects of Rome. No, that could not be the only reason.
He had known for more than a year that his Triumph would be
a sham. But the Senate had decreed a public thanksgiving in
gratitude for the treaty he had concluded with Sextus Pompeius;
a public thanksgiving implies a Triumph when next the hero
enters the City. Even though he had never in his life won a battle
he was lawfully entitled to this honour. All was as he had expected, in the days when he governed Narbonese Gaul and
looked forward with such pleasure to this wonderful occasion.
After all, the exploit which had earned a Triumph was soon forgotten; but that he was Triumphator iterum, had enjoyed two

separate Triumphs, would be indicated on his image when it was placed on the ancestral shelf. It would also be set down in the official records of the City, engraved on bronze to be preserved until the end of time.

No, something he had expected was lacking. Why was the procession so flat? At last he understood. It was because the streets were nearly empty. A Triumph should fill the Forum and the approaches to the Capitol with a cheerful crowd of sightseers, proud to share in the glory of Roman arms and awaiting the largesse of the victorious general. Today the few knots of spectators cheered loudly. But there were stretches of empty roadway; many houses were hung with the myrtle of mourning instead of the laurel of victory.

Strangest of all was the silence. Had there ever before been a Triumph, in all the seven hundred years of the City, in which the chief sound was the shuffle of marching feet? He passed a group of shabby loafers, who cheered with the perfunctory unanimity that betrayed the hired claque, and an underpaid claque at that; a furlong beyond stood a few more spectators, genuine Caesarians who joked with the soldiers in the ranks. Between them lay a zone of complete silence. Not only cheering was absent, but the usual sounds of a crowded and busy metropolis. Was there no one in Rome today to cry olives for sale, or to quarrel with a neighbour at a public fountain?

Lepidus had kept the rules laid down by the ancestors. Nowadays some victorious commanders slipped into the City unofficially to make sure that all was in order for the Triumph. But a Triumph should mark the return of the victorious army; in theory every man in the procession was seeing his home for the first time since he vanquished the foe. In obedience to protocol, the Pontifex Maximus had remained outside the City until today, the 31st of December, the day before he assumed the Consulship for the coming year. He had heard rumours of the dismay in the City, for whatever happened in Rome was discussed all over Italy; but the reality was more daunting than he had expected.

At the Capitol priests were waiting to receive him, and a handful of Senators; barely enough of them to represent the Senate as a whole, though at this point he must return his imperium to the fathers, in recognition of the fact that he had victoriously fulfilled all their commands. Until tomorrow he would be a private citizen, open to prosecution for misdeeds committed during his term of office; that is, if anyone should dare to prosecute the commander of seven legions of rejoicing veterans. He duly offered his sacrifice to Jupiter the Greatest and Best, standing in

133

an attitude of dignified reverence while the hecatomb of bulls were slaughtered, in a din of bellowing and a stench of blood and excrement. Perhaps the ancestors had been right to sacrifice a single victim; these modern large-scale offerings made the Capitol more like a butcher's shop than a dwelling-place of the gods. Yet Homer spoke of hecatombs, and grandfather Aeneas must have been familiar with them. The trouble is that we have a great many ancestors, who did not all follow the same customs.

The sacrifice was the culmination of the Triumph. As he came down from the Capitol Lepidus had accomplished completely his duty to the republic, and received all the thanks due to him. But of course he must remain with his soldiers while they marched to the Campus Martius for their feast of victory. Soldiers nowadays were very important personages, and their commander in particular must take great care to be civil to them. At last, by mid-afternoon, he had seen them seated at their banquet; as a private citizen he was free to go home to his family.

It was nearly two years since he had seen his wife and children; for a time he had wondered whether he would ever see them again. In the old tradition of civil war women and children were not harmed; but each new outbreak of the traditional blood-feud was more savage than the last. When Lepidus was outlawed for his alliance with Antonius Cicero had proposed to kill Junia and the boys; even Aemilius Paullus, blinded by jealousy of his successful brother, had spoken in favour of the murder of his nephews. Oddly enough, they had been saved by the intercession of Brutus, writing from his camp in Asia. That strange young man was genuinely fond of his half-sister, and, for an assassin, eccentrically averse to bloodshed.

Lepidus did not blame himself for hazarding the life of Junia and risking the extinction of his line. He had joined Antonius because no other course was open to him, and he had not looked for such savagery from decent Optimate gentlemen. But if Junia chose to hold it against him she could make his home-coming very unpleasant.

When he entered the Aemilian mansion he saw at once that his fears had been unfounded. His reception was worthy of a returning Triumphator. The doorposts were wreathed with laurel, and the footmen gaily garlanded. Two elderly gardeners, inexpensive labourers whose working lives were nearly over, capered in the Phrygian caps of emancipation; the liberation of slaves was a pious method of rejoicing, and Junia had done it sensibly, with an eye to economy. At the head of the assembled servants and freedmen his wife and sons stood to greet him in the hall.

As usual, he found nothing to say to Marcus and Quintus.

They were good boys, and their father was a great man; what was there for them to talk about? They kissed his hand, and he patted them on the head; in his baggage he had presents suited to their years. After a word of welcome they withdrew to their own apartments.

The lady Junia greeted her lord with solemnity. After he had venerated the images she handed him the wine and stood beside him as he poured it to the Lar. With her own hands she took off the purple robe and wreath of laurel, which must be preserved with other relics of Aemilian greatness. Taking from a footman a tray of wine and cakes, she herself served him with the first food he ate in his own house after long absence. Throughout her eyes were cast down, and she spoke nothing save ceremonious greetings. In the last two years she had lost all trace of girlish frivolity; she was all Roman matron.

Though he prolonged it as much as possible, even the ceremonial welcome of a returning paterfamilias must end at last. The time came when he was alone with his wife, in her pleasant little boudoir.

In Spain and Narbo, even more when in camp with his legions, he used to think with longing of the comfort and peace of his wife's apartments. Once he was back he would take up the old life where he had put it down. But in fact he was not the man who had left her after Caesar's murder. He had faced responsibility, he had commanded seven legions, he had become one of the three rulers of the Roman world.

Nor was she the Junia he had left. In Caesar's company she had reverted to the witty scatterbrained frivolity of her childhood, though even then she was a mature matron. The two years since the murder of the Dictator had brought deadly peril and nerveracking anxiety. There was a grim set to her mouth and a stiffness in her backbone which showed that she had long been afraid, and determined not to show her fear. These two middle-aged aristocrats, sitting together in the little room, were strangers; even though for many years they had been partners in the unending adventure of marriage.

He had been afraid that she would fall on his neck and weep, reproaching him for selfishly endangering the lives of his family. But there was no softness in this new Junia. She sat appraising her husband with level eyes, more like a brisk aunt who wonders whether the small boy entrusted to her care is as beastly as the neighbours say than like an obedient housewife receiving one of the three rulers of the world.

Neither would be the first to step back into the old shared intimacy of thought and discussion. Clearing his throat, Lepidus prepared to launch into a full account of the affair in the Argenteus. Junia cut him short, and herself began to speak. He realised with dismay that he had earned the contempt and dislike of his wife; but not because he had gambled with her life to save his own. His offence was something graver, something that would lie between them, even in the marriage-bed, until they should come to die.

'Well, Marcus,' she said coolly, 'this is your first visit to Rome for a long time. I expect you noticed the state of the City, even in the middle of your Triumph; though you should have been thinking of nothing but your gratitude to Jupiter. Rome lies in abject terror, terror of your doings, and the doings of your horrible associates. I suppose you know what has been done in your name, by soldiers who claimed to be obeying your orders?'

'Do you mean my brother Paullus? I thought Crastinus would understand. By the way, I expected to find Crastinus waiting for me. Have you seen him?'

'Crastinus has been here. He took today off, I suppose to get drunk with his comrades after the Triumph. I don't know whether he carried out your orders or bungled them; but Paullus is now on his way to Miletus. Once across the Adriatic he is under the protection of my brother Brutus; so there's no harm in telling you his destination.'

'That was what I intended, of course. I was forced to condemn him, but I wanted him to escape.'

'I'm glad to hear it. But who forced you? I thought you were a Triumvir, one of the three heroes who will set the republic to rights.'

'The others forced me, naturally. We set up a government of three men so that in case of disagreement two could bind the third.'

'I see. And then of course, as soon as you had come to your wicked decisions, you began to cheat one another. You condemned Paullus, meaning all the time to save him. In the same way Antonius condemned his uncle. Lucius Caesar took refuge with his sister Julia. They say she went openly to Antonius and told him to his face that if his uncle Lucius was to lose his head, she also must be condemned for the crime of concealing him. Even Marcus Antonius shrank from executing his own mother. So both Paullus and Lucius Caesar are safe. The only one of you who seems to have carried out his bond in full is young Octavianus; Cicero had no mercy.'

'Quite right too. He wanted to murder you.'

'I dare say. But Aemilius must not sink to the level of Tullius.'

'The Dictator pardoned his enemies again and again, until in

136

the end they murdered him. With that example before us we dare
not show mercy. At the outset young Caesar was against the proscription; though once we had persuaded him he was uncom-
monly apt at arranging the practical details. By the way, try not
to call him Octavianus. The law has made him Caius Julius
Caesar, and he likes to be known by those names.'

'It's disgusting that those famous names should be disgraced
by a bloody-minded young puppy. But I suppose I must be care-
full, or he will take my head. There's no mercy in him. Though
he must be moderately clever, to make you think *he* was reluctant to begin a proscription. Can't you see that is was his idea
from the start? I know you, Marcus. You would never propose
such horrors. Marcus Antonius is ruthless enough, and not afraid
of a pile of corpses; but all he wants is money. If the boy hadn't
led you both by the nose you would have been content to steal
the wealth of these men, allowing them to escape into exile.'

'I tell you, Junia, we had to do it. The civil wars have lasted
too long. Do you realise that it's more than ninety years since
Gracchus was murdered by the Optimates? Since then the fighting has never really ceased.'

'You didn't think of that argument by yourself. Starting ten
thousand blood-feuds isn't the way to end a civil war, though
Octavianus may think it is. Even if you had to kill some Optimates, and I grant you there were blood-feuds in plenty to give
you an excuse, need you have gone about it in such a ghastly
way?'

'Sulla started it, and he was Optimate enough. Now they are
getting a taste of their own medicine. It's not pretty, but what's
so ghastly about it? No one has been tortured, or put to death
with ignomy. Just a clean stroke of the sword, which a true
Roman should meet with fortitude.'

'Fortitude! A clean stroke of the sword! But I forget, you
have not been in Rome. I suppose you don't know the way your
orders have been carried out. Your soldiers have made it plain
that only the sword rules. The constitution of our ancestors! The
times I've heard you declaim about it! Well, it's gone – gone, and
you've smashed it. Tribunes used to be sacrosanct, especially to
us Populars. So the first man they killed was the tribune Salvius.
He was giving a supper-party when a squad of soldiers marched
in. Without a word spoken the centurion went up to him as he
lay on his couch, caught him by the hair to get his neck into
position, and took his head. Then he told the guests it seemed a
pity to break up such a good party, and that they might carry on
drinking. For the next hour he stayed in the dining-room, watching those terrified people drinking wine, with the headless trunk

of their host on the first couch. He showed his warrant, sealed by all the Triumvirs. Your instructions?'

'Of course not, Junia. What do you think I am? Salvius was a dangerous man, and rightly proscribed. I remember Caesar saying that he must be one of the first to go, so that our enemies would see that even the tribunate would not protect them. But none of us thought to affront common decency in this manner. What was the Consul thinking of to allow it?'

'You forget. The Consul died of shock when he heard of it. Oh, I know it's down in the records that Quintus Pedius died of a sudden fever. But it was shock and remorse that killed him, as all Rome knows. He was an ordinary decent nobody, who had the bad luck to be born great-nephew of a famous statesman; not a man in the same class as you mighty Triumvirs. I except he's happier dead.'

'I didn't know. You must believe me when I say I didn't know. Mind you, we have to get rid of our enemies, or die ourselves as Caesar died. The proscription is necessary. But in future things will be done with more decency. And when this last, necessary purge is over Rome will be at peace for evermore.'

'Can you control your men? Do you command them, or do they command you? This is civil war; if you rebuke them they may change sides. I think the soldiers have come to hate every honourable citizen who does not carry a sword, everything decent and dignified. Otherwise why should they go out of their way to kill a praetor as he sits in judgement? They could have caught poor Minucius at home; no one resists them. But they had to come while his court was in session. He saw them coming, and jumped off the bench to hide among the crowd. When they caught him they cut his head off, and left it propped in his curule chair. That's what has been done with your signet as warrant. Is it the kind of thing you approve? If not, how will you stop it?'

Lepidus took a deep breath, preparing to exercise his authority as paterfamilias. Then he saw that Junia had right on her side, and decided instead to persuade her.

'My dear, this is, as you say, a ghastly business. I didn't like it when it was first suggested, and I had no idea it would be carried out with such a beastly mockery of everything a good citizen should reverence. But it's there. We are too late to stop it. If you insist, we can flee into exile. We might, I suppose, join Brutus; though I think Cassius would take my head. But there is another side to it. At present Rome is ruled by three men. One of these tyrants is a swashbuckling captain of horse, little better than a brigand. Another is a cold-blooded youth from the provinces, who sees nothing of the glory of our ancient constitution, nothing of the respect due to our ancient families. I am the third. Will Antonius and Caesar rule better without me? May it not be my duty to remain in the great position to which Fortune has called me, to limit the damage caused by the atrocities of my colleagues?'

'I'm glad to know, Marcus, that you are as horrified as I am. I never believed you would approve what has been done. You are right, I suppose. We can't draw back. You must continue as Triumvir, trying to introduce a little justice, even a little mercy, into the conduct of affairs. Rome is governed by tyrants, as you say. At least the tyranny of an educated patrician will be more tolerable than a partnership between a rake and a lout.'

'Then you forgive me? We are friends again?'

'We shall always be friends. We married for life, not until the weather changes. You are head of the household, and what you do cannot be questioned by your wife. Be as merciful as you can, and remember your dignity. There is no more any of us can do, with Rome in her present plight.'

Certainly there was nothing more that her poor husband could do. What had induced even the frivolous Marcus Antonius to make him a Triumvir? Probably a misplaced sense of humour. However, he must hold on to his position, or lose his head; this government would not accept a peaceful resignation.

'I suppose there was a time when I could have made a stand,' Lepidus continued in a puzzled tone. 'But I don't know when it was. What has come over the City? In our fathers' days freemen would not have submitted to the rule of an Antonius.'

'We submitted to Caesar, who was something more than a man. Once freedom has been lost it is very hard to regain it. I suppose our children will submit to any rascal who can persuade the soldiers to follow him.'

'I didn't expect that from you, Junia the Caesarian. But you are right on all counts. Not only have we lost our liberty, we must recognise formally that Caesar was more than a man. Tomorrow I meet my colleagues to trace the foundations of a temple in which he will be worshipped as a god.'

'How disgusting. It puts Rome on a level with the mongrel Greek-Asiatic cities, where they deify the retiring town clerk instead of giving him a silver casket.'

'Disgusting, perhaps; but not very serious. Of the three of us, Antonius is a scoffer, the boy doesn't count, and I, though I worship the great gods with due reverence, disbelieve in the divinity of Caesar. It's nothing but a form; unless indeed Antonius plans to embezzle the endowments of the new temple.'

139

'Just now we can't make things better. Perhaps, if they leave you to rule Rome while they fight my brother, you can restore a little decency. At least they will take their unruly soldiers with them. Oh, Marcus, let's forget politics for a little. It's nearly two years since we were alone together.'

On the next day Lepidus met his colleagues for the first time since they had occupied Rome. The ceremony of tracing the foundations was carried out with great splendour. A golden ploughshare turned the sacred furrow, and young Caesar displayed a knowledge of ritual remarkable in one so young. For what it was worth, he appeared to believe in the divinity of his great-uncle; his face was rapt in an expression of devotion, and the birds from whose flight he drew his augury were visible to other onlookers. Antonius winked at the crowd, as though to say he was wasting his time and knew it. The Pontifex Maximus went through the motions correctly, for any religious observance must be duly performed or the gods will be angered; but he found it impossible to think of Caesar the Dictator as an immortal. That knot of struggling figures by the statue of Pompeius had not been engaged in forwarding another deity to Olympus.

Afterwards they dined in private at 'The Keels', the great house built by Pompeius Maximus to display his naval trophies, since Pharsalus the booty of Antonius. There was too much to eat, and a great deal to much to drink. The wine was barely watered, and at every toast the host pressed his guests to drain bumpers.

Marcus Antonius was no longer the weatherbeaten campaigner of the Argenteus. The elaborate dressing of his hair emphasised the red blotches of his cheeks, and his neck seemed as broad as his shoulders. During the olives and anchovies he reclined morose and silent; but wine revived his spirits, and he was presently in a state of high excitement. To Lepidus he seemed all attitude, with no reality behind it. Such a man must always strut before an audience, to cover the emptiness of his spirit. This afternoon he was posing, even to this audience of two colleagues who knew him thoroughly; and the pose he had chosen was that of the devil-may-care captain of horse.

'The place we consecrated was the actual spot where the old boy's body was burned,' he said cheerfully, rubbing his hands. 'No one else can ever be burned there, and no one will speak another funeral oration where I did. Probably the best speech I ever made in my life; I roused the mob, and yet controlled it. You were there, Lepidus; you must have heard me. Not bad for a rude soldier, what, to make the most famous speech on a famous occasion? If I'd had time to learn rhetoric I could have answered Cicero to his face, even in the Senate. But I had other things to do; and anyway, where is Cicero?'

'Dead and buried, I suppose. But not soon to be forgotten,' said young Caesar gloomily.

'Dead, my boy; but not buried. Do you remember, Lepidus? Once you told me that we mustn't use the head of Decimus Brutus as a trophy, because if we did his spirit would never find rest? Well, I'm not afraid of Cicero's spirit.' He clapped his hands to summon a servant. 'Under this cover you will find his head. It's twenty-five days old, and getting pretty ripe. I kept it back specially for this dinner; tomorrow it will be stuck up in the Forum. Look, that's what we'll all come to, unless our friends burn us before the maggots get to work. It doesn't look the best brain in Rome, does it?'

'The mouth is very ragged,' said young Caesar coolly. 'I hope you didn't torture him. You promised me he would be killed cleanly with the sword.'

'He was killed with the sword all right. Stuck his neck out like a little gentleman when he saw there was no escape. Probably the first time in his life he behaved like a gentleman; but anyone will die well when he knows the writing-fellows are going to record his last moments. No, that mess round the lips is my Fulvia's handiwork. I had promised her this head; that's why I couldn't show mercy. When she saw it the thing was quite fresh and lifelike. The little dear got all excited. She scrabbled away at the tongue that had insulted her, hammer and tongs with hair-pins and eyebrow-tweezers.'

Lepidus hid his face in his wine-cup. He tried to fix his thoughts on the Absolute, as recommended by the philosophers; but he could not shut out the dispassionate voice of young Caesar.

'We've all had a good look at it, and I for one don't want to see it again. Stick it up in the Forum with the heads of the other proscribed. When it's been there long enough for everyone to know that Cicero's dead I shall myself give it decent burial. What's under that second cover? The head of another of Fulvia's detractors?'

'That thing? No, that's still Cicero. A little joke my dear wife put me up to. As you remember, Cicero couldn't talk without waving his hands; I've heard it said that if he were handcuffed he wouldn't be able to speak. Fulvia had 'em cut off, to go with the head.'

'I see. Quite witty in its way, if that sort of joke appeals to you. It will take some explaining to the crowd in the Forum.'

At last Lepidus had thought of a remark that might turn the gruesome conversation. 'You say he stretched out his neck at the last? Didn't he offer any resistance? He was a Consular, he even styled himself Imperator on the strength of some skirmish with Cilician brigands. Consulars do not often die so meekly.'

'Of course he hadn't the guts to fight. He hadn't even the guts to run away on his own feet. He was in a litter when my men caught him. At that he might have got away, if one of his own freemen hadn't told them where to find him.'

'That's downright shameful,' said Lepidus, glad to express some of the disgust which filled his breast. 'I don't know which is worse: that a Consular should be killed in his toga, when he had plenty of time to pick up a sword; or that a freeman should betray his lord. I hope you did not reward the scoundrel.'

Antonius roared with laughter. 'Philogonus was rewarded all right. I don't like treachery. I handed him over to Pomponia, you know, Quintus Cicero's widow. She has been taking it out of him ever since. Yesterday, I believe, he was still alive; but very mangled, and praying for speedy death.'

'Cicero was our foe. We agreed that he must die.' The carefully modulated voice of Caesar was non-committal. 'But this kind of joke should not be repeated. We still have a little dignity of our own, and we shall lose it if we dismember the corpses of our enemies. We agreed that the vote of two should bind the third. I am sure Lepidus will concur when I vote that the proscription must end as soon as possible.'

'Anything you say, Caesar. We have enough money to be getting on with, and when we have conquered Brutus and Cassius we shall have the plunder of Asia. I don't enjoy killing people, unless like Cicero they have been rude to me. I'm not sorry so many of the proscribed escaped oversea. They couldn't take their money with them, and I have it.'

'That is another subject, which we must discuss seriously when we are sober. It's not a thing to laugh about over the wine. Lepidus, you have met this young Sextus Pompeius, haven't you? He is becoming a much greater nuisance than I had expected. We shall have to take him seriously.'

'He's not so young as all that, Caesar,' Lepidus replied with some pleasure. 'About twelve of fifteen years older than you, I should estimate.'

'Ah, but I am extraordinarily young for my great position. I am the first Roman to hold a curule magistracy as the age of twenty. Do you think I might be under the special protection of a divinity?' The youth spoke without boasting, as though he himself was puzzled by the question.

'There have been strange portents, or so they say. As Pontifex Maximus I am kept informed of unusual omens. But I myself have seen nothing remarkable, either in the flight of birds or in the livers of victims. It is not a subject on which I should care to venture an opinion.'

'You are named Caesar, young man,' said Antonius with a belch. 'Your luck is in your name and nowhere else. Don't lean on it too hard, that's my advice. Keep away from war, and your reputation is safe. If you insist on crossing swords with Cassius, remember that he was fighting Parthians when you were playing with your marbles.'

Caesar's grey eyes flashed. But when he answered his voice remained level and expressionless.

'You are the finest soldier in Rome; in anything connected with war I am content to follow your advice. But really, my dear Antonius, you are serving this wine too strong. My head buzzes and I can't talk serious business. If you have any dancers to entertain us, now is the time to send for them. Otherwise I shall go home and to bed. My doctor advises me to rest in the afternoon.'

After that the dinner followed the usual course of a party at 'The Keels'. The three rulers lay on their couches, drinking steadily, while tumblers and jugglers performed before them. Presently it was supper time, and not worth while moving to another room. When Lepidus staggered to his litter, to be escorted home by torchlight, Antonius was snoring under the table.

In all the novelty of his unconstitutional greatness it had almost slipped his memory that he was once more Consul. His colleague was Ventidius Bassus, the Italian who had once been enslaved (the partnership must have been planned by the whimsical malice of Antonius, who knew how deeply it would irk an Aemilius to appear in the records as colleague to an ex-slave and, worse still, a provincial). As Consul and Pontifex Maximus the opening of the year brought him a mass of ceremonial business, which he must perform single-handed since Bassus was shamefully ignorant of ritual. He was kept hard at work, offering sacrifice, presiding at meetings, invoking the blessing of the gods on this and that; so busy that he hardly had time to notice the slackening of the proscription.

All the same, by the end of January the hunt for heads was over. Money was still needed, to pay the enormous and undisciplined army now encamped in central Italy; the last flicker of the great purge was the confiscation of the dowries of four hundred wealthy ladies, who were graciously permitted to live. By this

143

time nearly every mansion in Rome had been shuttered in sign of mourning; three hundred Senators, and more than two thousand knights, had been proscribed.

Social life of a kind continued. Rome was still the wealthiest city in the world; her wealth, the tribute of defenceless provinces, had merely changed hands. New men, army contractors or Caesarian soldiers, entertained on a great scale; for those who happened to possess money wished to enjoy it. After the lesson of the great proscription only an optimist would expect his estate to descend to his grandchildren.

At any party a Triumvir was a lion, and Lepidus found himself dining out more frequently than in his youth. Antonius was a bothersome guest, drunken and riotous and inclined to break the furniture. Caesar was unwelcome for the opposite reason; his provincial lack of breeding had left him so reserved and shy that at any party he was a wet blanket. It was remarked that Lepidus displayed the gracious formal manners of the good old days, the days when Rome was governed from the boudoirs of highborn ladies. That was odd, he thought. When he was an unknown quaestor his stiff shyness had made him a social failure.

These modern Caesarian parties were strange affairs. In the old days there were two kinds of party; either you took your wife, to meet the well-born wives of other noblemen; or you went alone, and your host provided dancing-girls to entertain you. Now Lepidus never knew whether to bring Junia or not. Whatever the company, and whatever the type of entertainment provided, the wives of some leading Caesarians would be there. But some leading Caesarians, soldiers whose youth had been passed in a provincial garrison, had picked up very odd wives; their presence did not make a party respectable. Often they would be mingled with smart actresses and dashing Greek courtesans, who reclined on couches like men as they conversed with these broad-minded Roman matrons.

All the same, it was rather fun. He would be forty-eight on his next birthday, and he had come to think of himself as middle-aged. Really he was in the prime of life. Reclining between two witty beauties from Alexandria, crowned with roses and drenched with perfume, waited on by deft footmen who had been trained in the service of some now headless Optimate, he enjoyed himself like a young man. The house itself, the cooking, even the servants, would be familiar to him from the old days; only the burly figure of the host, his shoulders scarred by the buckles of his corselet, would strike a strange note. Even if these parties began with decorum, they usually ended in a drunken riot. More and more often Junia stayed at home, as was only fitting; perhaps it

144

was not quite so fitting that the Pontifex Maximus should be present and enjoying himself.

Then he was taken up by Fulvia, the wife of Marcus Antonius. That was curiously exciting. In his youth he had not been a success with women, partly because he was shy, even more from laziness; while Rome was full of harlots the strenuous effort needed to seduce a lady had seemed to him more trouble than it was worth. Now that he was a Triumvir, nearly any lady would yield to him for the asking; perhaps the only exception would be the wife of another Triumvir. If Fulvia was attracted he must be more attractive than he had supposed.

Fulvia was not strictly beautiful, though she would have made a handsome man; her sparkling black eyes and curved nose seemed to demand a helmet above them, instead of a mat of glossy curls. She was short, with fine legs and very small hands and feet; she had a trim waist, and she moved gracefully. It seemed unfair that such a dainty, attractive, energetic figure should be overbalanced by a pair of billowing breasts in front, and large, though well-curved, buttocks at the back. She lived her own life, independent of her husband, and was always saying so; it seemed to keep her very busy.

During the proscription she had been busy taking vengeance on her personal enemies. Now that the executions were over she had become the patron of every Caesarian veteran who wanted a farm; a folded petition always protruded from the deep cleft of her bosom, and it always appeared to deal with some very hard case. If subsequent inquiry showed that the ill-treated veteran had lost his bonus because he had been discharged with ignominy for cowardice in the field, no one was more surprised than Fulvia. He had spoken so well when he approached her; it was hard to believe that a true Caesarian could be guilty of such wickedness.

There were officials who found this lady a formidable bore; it would seem that her husband was one of them. Though Marcus Antonius was devoted to her, he seldom had time to accompany her when she paid afternoon calls or went out to supper. She was always trying to interest some magistrate in her latest deserving case, and it was natural that she should fix on Lepidus, the only Triumvir who was not working day and night to mobilise the great army which would take vengeance on Cassius and Brutus.

She attracted him. Perhaps she was a little too emphatic, too inclined to catch hold of his toga and repeat long case-histories into his ear; but the widow of Clodius the gangster understood the personal side of politics as thoroughly as he did. She had a deep concern for the questions which concerned him: who was to fill the vacancy in the College of Augurs; which score of blameless young men, out of a hundred indistinguishable smooth-faced young men, were worthy to hold the quaestorship; which shady contractor merited the plum of providing marble for the new temple of the Divine Julius. In the old days, before the Rubicon had been crossed, such questions as these were the very stuff of politics, causes for which great men would marry or divorce. Now nearly everyone who talked politics discussed only the strength of rival armies, and the doubtful allegiance of legates of unknown birth.

Junia could not abide Fulvia, and refused to go into company where she might encounter her. She had an excuse which her husband must accept: a woman who had mutilated the head of her dead enemy could not be a respectable Roman matron. In reply, Lepidus pointed out that they lived in a time of change; things were done in the City every day which would have shocked his father. Privately he had an uneasy suspicion that his wife put him on a level with Fulvia; she never spoke of the proscription, but he knew that she had not forgotten it. A sense of guilt made home-life irksome; with Fulvia he could feel superior.

His colleagues were engrossed in planning something that did not concern him, the great campaign to crush the surviving murderers of Caesar. They spent their days studying maps, interviewing sea-captains newly arrived from Asia, discussing boots and mules with breezy over-confident businessmen. He was supposed to govern Rome by himself, without wasting their time which must be devoted to military affairs. The Caesarians were so powerful that this work did not occupy all his energy; long talks with Fulvia were a pleasant distraction.

Only once was he called into a serious conference with his military colleagues, and that was because he happened to have personal knowledge of the obscure but now powerful enemy whom few other Romans had met. One morning young Caesar wrote asking him to call at the Julian mansion. The wording of the message was polite enough, as deferential as was proper from a boy to the Pontifex Maximus; but even the scored wax of the tablets conveyed Caesar's bleak aroma of joyless responsibility. As Lepidus alighted from his litter he felt that in some obscure way he had been neglecting his duty.

In the private office he found Antonius with young Caesar. Besides a confidential secretary to take down their decisions there was only one other man in the room, a boy no older than Caesar himself. There was about this youth a certain craggy ugliness which marked him as a member of the lower classes; Lepidus had an infallible nose for that sort of thing. Caesar had his arm on the boy's shoulder. Ah, so young Caesar, that pattern

146

of all the more tedious virtues, had somewhere picked up a boy-friend.

Without shame, Caesar introduced the boy as though he were a gentleman and an equal. 'May I present my friend Marcus Vipsanius Agrippa, who will command our fleet in Sicilian waters? Agrippa is an old comrade of mine, chosen for me by my deified father. We served together in Spain, and studied together at Apollonia.'

'And he is to command the fleet? Let me congratulate you, young man, on your speedy promotion.'

'Don't be a stick-in-the-mud, Lepidus,' said Antonius in a lazy drawl. 'Agrippa knows as much about naval tactics as I do, and I am the military expert in the partnership. Not one of us can tell the sharp end of a ship from the blunt until it starts to move, and where we're all novices a young novice with his wits about him may pick up the tricks of the trade more quickly than a veteran.'

'Agrippa is my loyal follower,' added Caesar. 'In naval matters my deified father relied on Decimus Brutus.'

'If Antonius and Caesar are satisfied it is not for me to object. You are planning the campaign while I supervise home affairs. But if you are marching into Asia, why do you need a fleet in Sicilian waters?'

'That's where you come in, old boy,' Antonius explained. 'You have negotiated with this terrible pirate who dares to defy the massed legions of the republic. That's Sextus Pompeius, of course. Before we leave for the east we must squash him, or buy him.'

'How curious that you should use those words,' said Lepidus. 'Caesar, your deified father, dined in my house on the last night of his life. The talk turned to the rebellion in Spain, and that's more or less what the Divine Julius said of him.'

'The Senate said it also, more than three years ago, when they sent you to negotiate with him,' Antonius went on. 'For the last five years everyone has said it. Squash him, if you're not too busy; or buy him cheap, because he's notoriously for sale. Well, we go on saying it, and what happens? At the end of the five years Pompeius is stronger than ever.'

'Yes, something must really be done about him, now, before we march,' Caesar said firmly. 'I can't see where he gets his support from, and that's why I want your opinion, Lepidus. He's not an Optimate, because he's not even a gentleman. He isn't working with Cassius and Brutus. Surely there isn't still a Pompeian party, after all these years? If there is, what does it stand for?'

'There's no Pompeian party, of course,' said Lepidus weightily, enjoying his role of elder statesman. 'There never was much of a one, except for the veterans who had defeated Mithradates. They must all be dead, with no successors. All they wanted were free farms, and they got them. When I met Sextus in Spain I asked myself the same question: who supports him and why? A freedman of mine, one of those clever Greek secretaries, found an answer to the problem, and he may be right. He believes that Pompeius Maximus never really crushed the pirates; he just settled them òn farms in the provinces – and they were grateful. Now they have rallied to his son.'

'That's what it is, by thunder,' exclaimed Antonius, banging the table. 'How stupid of those old buffers in the Senate not to see it. They gave the command of their fleet to the King of the Pirates, and now we have him on our doorstep.'

'Surely that appointment lapsed when we took over?' said Lepidus.

'Perhaps. But the news has not reached Sicily,' Caesar answered dryly. 'Pompeius Bithynicus was the Optimate propraetor of Sicily, and our troops did not cross over to dislodge him. It didn't seem worth while, when Sicily must surrender after we have beaten Cassius. Now Bithynicus has come to terms with his cousin Sextus. The Optimate authorities in Africa send them supplies and money. Sextus has made himself ruler of all the western sea. What's very much worse, he is rescuing fugitives from our proscription.'

'He had the nerve to offer twice as much for every man saved as we had put on his head,' said Antonius with a wheezy chuckle. 'That's impudence, perhaps, but amusing impudence all the same. Of course he can draw on the treasury of Africa. How easy it is to be noble when you have plenty of money! I envy him.'

'It's most high-minded, and most amusing,' Caesar said coldly. 'But the object of that unpleasant proscription was to strike terror into our enemies. If half of them get away we look foolish, which is the worst thing that can happen to us. So we must deal with Sextus before we conquer Cassius and Brutus.'

'Well, why not deal with him – literally,' young Agrippa suddenly put in. 'If his fleet is the old federation of the pirates I shan't destroy it in a single campaign. Yet by summer you must be on the march to Asia, unless Cassius is to gather strength for another whole year. The Consul Aemilius Lepidus has negotiated with Sextus in the past, and might reasonably write to him again. If that looks too much like official recognition you could get this Greek freedman to write, ostensibly in his own name. Offer Sextus whatever he wants, provided he will keep quiet for a year. When Cassius has been beaten he will have to surrender without a blow, or fight a war of Sicily against the rest of the world.'

'That's sound advice, Antonius,' said Lepidus eagerly. It seemed to him that any course was better than giving command of the government's only fleet to a boy who was not even a gentleman. 'Africa is held by the Optimates anyway, and we haven't time to conquer it before the great campaign in Asia. Let's leave Sextus to rule Sicily. With any luck he will quarrel with his African supporters. That will make next year's campaign all the easier.'

Caesar looked up with a queer glint in his eye. Lepidus realised that he had been tactless to answer as though the decision lay with Antonius alone. It was a natural mistake. Antonius the soldier led the Caesarian party; the boy, though in theory his equal, was a mascot, called into their counsels because he bore, by unmerited good luck, a famous name.

'We shall do that in the end, if Antonius agrees,' Caesar said quickly. 'But first Agrippa must make some kind of naval demonstration. A show of force will convince Sextus that we are in earnest; and anyway orders have gone out to the fleet at Misenum that Agrippa is coming to take command. A change of plan might make us foolish.'

'We shall look very much more foolish if you, Caesar, send orders in the name of the Triumvirs without first consulting your colleagues,' snapped Antonius.

'You consented,' Caesar answered hotly.

'I didn't know things had gone so far as the issue of written orders. I don't like it. Operational orders should go out only over my signet. What I say casually, especially at supper, should not be conveyed directly to the troops.'

'Indeed, if everything you said at supper was conveyed directly to the troops they would think they served under a very eccentric commander.'

'Gentlemen, if we quarrel Rome will be destroyed,' Lepidus said urgently. He said it, sooner or later, at all these conferences. But at each meeting the outbreak of bad temper seemed to come earlier.

'I apologise, Antonius,' said Caesar with a gentle smile. 'Blame my error on the impetuosity of youth. Agrippa is my friend, and in addition I have a very high opinion of his talents. I wanted to make sure he would have his chance.'

'All right, young man,' Antonius answered carelessly. 'Your friend, your very dear friend, can have his command. What do ships matter, anyway? Rome is governed by soldiers in stout marching-boots.'

'But Rome eats corn that can come only by sea, and pirates in Sicily can prevent it reaching us,' said Lepidus. 'However, this Sextus is after money, I understand. We can give him money until we have leisure to conquer him.'

It was stimulating to talk about conquest in this carefree way, knowing that Antonius would do the necessary fighting.

When Eunomus learned of the plan he took up his task with enthusiasm. He wrote a strictly unofficial letter to Menas, the freedman of Pompeius whom he had met in Spain, now commander of the Sicilian fleet. Menas's answer arrived in a very few days, for hostile squadrons were hovering off the mouth of the Tiber. Menas professed himself delighted at the chance of a peace which would leave his master official ruler of Sicily, and suggested a personal interview to discuss details. After some hesitation, Eunomus went off in a fishing-boat. In three days he was back, with an exciting story to tell.

'My lord, this is a very much bigger thing than anyone here supposes, 'said he, his eyes twinkling with eager cunning. 'Brutus and Cassius haven't a chance against our legions; even so, the Roman world has a fourth ruler. Sicily is a large island, and very fertile. If the Sicilians themselves can't fight, they can support a numerous army. Sextus Pompeius has revived the great confederation of the pirates, and his navy is by far the strongest in the world. He is adding to the legions Bithynicus handed over to him. He has an army and a navy, ample revenues to support them, and a population of civilised and contented subjects. But the most significant fact is that all his principal officers are Greek.'

'I don't see what you are getting at. I've read, of course, that Syracuse was once a great power. So was Athens, long ago, and what does she matter now? I don't want to insult your pride of race, but nowadays a Greek army is a second-rate army.'

'Perhaps, my lord. But Greek sailors remain the best in the world. There has never been a Roman navy, manned by Romans. The fleet which young Caesar is collecting, to provide a salary for his boy-friend, draws its crews from the Greek cities of Campania. But Campanian Greeks, soft merchant traders, are no match for the Greek pirates of Cilicia, once the worthy antagonists of Pompeius Maximus. Even Greek soldiers are not to be despised. Most Greeks dislike Romans, though as a rule they are afraid to show it. A rising of all the Greek subject-cities, with a

150

Greek hero to lead them, would test the strength even of the mighty Triumvirate.'

'Sextus Pompeius is not a Greek hero. He is as Roman as I am.'

'No, my lord. That's what no one in Rome understands. He is the son of a famous Roman, but he himself was brought up by Greeks. Greek is his native tongue, and he speaks Latin like a foreigner. Menas plans to make him a figurehead for all the Greeks, in a rising against the sway of Rome.'

'Do you mean to tell me this movement is led by a freedman?'

'It is led by Menas, my lord. He was once the slave of Pompeius Maximus, but he is not what you think of as a freedman. He is a pirate chieftain.'

'It all sounds very uncivilised and unpleasant. You don't tempt me to join forces with Sextus, which I gather is what you advise.'

'I don't advise that you should join him now, my lord. I advise you not to throw away an advantage which is yours alone, not shared by your colleagues. Sextus fears Rome, and would like an ally who could bring him Roman legions. But he is very much stronger than is generally supposed. When Antonius breaks with Caesar, and that must happen before very long, you will be free to support either side. Then, if you have secretly made terms with Sextus Pompeius, you will yourself be stronger than you seem to be. The next civil war may leave you ruler of the world.'

It was a fascinating dream; but then Eunomus was always propounding these fascinating dreams. Lepidus sometimes wondered whether, since he had already risen so high, he might be destined to rise higher. But to defy his colleagues at present would be absurd. None the less, the plan might be kept in reserve. He answered firmly, to show that the conversation was at an end.

'Keep in touch with Menas, but don't commit me. At present Sextus Pompeius is our foe, though a foe so weak that he may be disregarded. If, later on, I should seek his alliance, he will be glad to help me. You may write again, in your name but not in mine. Tell no one, and of course do not use my signet.'

*The lady Clodia gossiped with the maid who combed her hair.*
*'This has been a terrible winter. Everyone in mourning, and the only parties given by drunken rankers who have stolen the property of dead Optimates. But the summer will be better. All those frightful soldiers will be leaving Rome, and funny old*

*Lepidus will be in control. He may have the brains of a wax-work, but at least he has the manners of a gentleman. Think up a new way of doing my hair; in a few months we shall be gay and smart again.'*

# IX

## PERUSIA
### 41–40 B.C.

In early spring Caesar and Agrippa marched into southern Italy to demonstrate against Sextus Pompeius. Their amateur navy proved no match for experienced pirates, and after a few unlucky skirmishes they patched up a peace. In the meantime Pompeius had added Sardinia and Corsica to his island dominion, so that now he ruled all the western sea between Italy and Spain. But so long as corn-ships could sail freely to Ostia there was no reason why the rulers of Rome should quarrel with the ruler of Sicily.

Then Antonius and Caesar crossed the Adriatic, to begin the great campaign of vengeance. Supreme in Rome, Lepidus could devote himself to the internal affairs of the City.

That was a splendid summer. There was not an opponent to be found, not even a wit to compose satirical epigrams; proscription had silenced that carping malice for ever. A wise ruler, in the prime of life, could give all his time to the intricate ballet of the constitution, telling Consuls, praetors, aediles, quaestors when to enter, when to withdraw, when to exhibit Games to the populace. The City was worthily governed, as the ancestors would have governed it. Lepidus knew his rule gave satisfaction to his loyal subjects; for though he constantly mingled in society he never overheard a single complaint.

His wife's fit of the sulks was the only shadow on his happiness. Junia would not help him in his arduous task, though he would have been glad of her advice. At home she was loyal and discreet, so that the idea of divorce never entered his mind; she was the mother of his sons, part of the furniture of his house. But she took no interest in public affairs, never expressed an opinion, never asked his plans. Of course, politics were to her a depressing subject. Brutus had recently thrown away his last chance of pardon by murdering his prisoner, Caius Antonius. Ostensibly this was a reprisal for the murder of Cicero, but it proved that at last hate had overcome even the honesty of Brutus; Caius had been as raffish as the other Antonius brothers,

153

but he was himself innocent of murder.

Instead of Junia, there was Fulvia. As her husband's representative, that great lady constantly busied herself with tangled questions of appointment and promotion. She knew as much about the management of the assembly as if she had been a man and a voter, and she had at her finger-ends all the details of family alliance and hereditary influence which governed the nomination of unproven young men to be quaestors and military tribunes. As befitted the widow of Clodius the gangster, she was forthright in her dishonesty; a connection with the gens Antonia was the only qualification that weighed with her. On the other hand, as she pointed out, even the most unsuitable magistrates could do no harm when the wise hand of a Triumvir was always ready to correct their mistakes. Lepidus might govern through her nominees as easily as through any other instruments.

He took to calling frequently at 'The Keels' to talk things over with her. She was always ready to see him, listening to his troubles with an anxious sympathy very flattering to a middle-aged nobleman who had never, even in his youth, been a breaker of hearts. She seemed to be glad of his company; the gay young rakes who hung about the place were sent packing as soon as the Pontifex Maximus was announced.

Lepidus began to wonder whether he had made a conquest, even without trying. Everyone who mattered was to be found in Fulvia's boudoir; but even great men like Pollio and Lucius Antonius tactfully made themselves scarce when Aemilius Lepidus dropped in for a private chat with the most influential lady in Rome.

There was plenty to talk about, for Fulvia suspected that her husband's followers were being slighted in the new land-settlement. Her bugbear was Pollio, though she never was rude to him to his face. That made her complaints all the more forceful the moment he had left.

As the summer dragged on, and the campaign against the murderers remained at a standstill, Fulvia's temper grew shorter. Her assumption that Lepidus must side with her husband against his rival, young Caesar, was even more trying.

The July day had been blazing hot, and Lepidus had spent the hottest part of it standing in the sun, seeing that the assembly of the people ratified some urgent decrees of the Senate. There had been no debate, because no one dared to speak against a Triumvir; and most of the formal speeches of commendation had been delivered by underlings. But he had spoken twice, all the same; because he was sufficiently old-fashioned to treat the sovereign

154

people of Rome with a decent show of respect. When he reached the cool boudoir of the lady Fulvia he was longing to forget everything political.

Instead he found Pollio closeted with the lady, and evidently in the middle of an argument; though Caesar's legate almost at once withdrew, from respect for his superior in the government.

Fulvia was lying on a day-bed, in the attitude of a man at the supper-table; because of the heat two maids fanned her, and she was very lightly dressed. Her well-turned legs were exposed above the knee, and though Lepidus tried to keep his eyes on her face he was aware of large breasts peeping over the edge of her tunic. At once she burst into angry speech.

'That mealy-mouthed turncoat wants so steal all the towns of Italy, while better men risk their lives in deadly war. He's so sure of himself he's quite open about it. Guess what he proposes to do next? He wants to confiscate the whole territory of Mantua, to give it free to his jackals.'

'My dear lady,' answered Lepidus with a smile, 'that's what he was appointed to do. Our soldiers have been promised the usual farms that every veteran expects nowadays; and since we have no money to buy in the open market we must confiscate the land of our enemies. It's not a pleasant job, nor a dignified one. I'm glad I'm not doing it myself, as was very nearly my fate. But since it's got to be done it seems to me that our Pollio is the man to do it. His dignity won't be hurt, because he hasn't any; and if he makes a little money out of bribery and blackmail that is only what we expect from a creature such as him.'

'He was told to confiscate the land of Sullen veterans, who had been illegally rewarded for oppressing the Populars. But those men don't form whole communities, and if they do Mantua isn't one of them. I happen to know that several Mantuans are serving in my husband's legions. Most of the others were neutral in politics. Why should they be turned out to make room for the toy soldiers who follow that boy, the boy who is always sick when there is a battle to be fought?'

'It isn't as straightforward as that. You ladies see politics in black and white, when in fact both sides are a dingy grey. If there are Mantuans in our legions we shall have to save their farms; though it will mean breaking promises made to other faithful legionaries. The real trouble is that nowadays soldiering has become a hereditary trade; men no longer fight for a political cause. A lot of Sulla's veterans were settled round Mantua, on land stolen from oppressed Populars. You will agree that they deserve to be dispossessed. That happened a generation ago. Their sons went into the army, because that was the family business. But they enlisted in any legion that happened to be nearest. Some fought for Pompeius; there's no difficulty in dealing with *them*. Others joined Caesar the Dictator, and then followed your Marcus, or young Caesar. That makes their farms a genuine problem. But if land was stolen from the Populars in the first place, it ought to go back to the Populars now we are victorious. You see that?'

'Then why shouldn't it go back to the original Popular owners, or their sons if they are dead? That's another grievance. Thousands of dispossessed farmers look for justice now that their cause is triumphant. Pollio disregards their claims.'

'My dear, those original farmers did not fight for it. Or if they did fight for it they got beaten. That's how Sulla got it in the first place.'

'But, Marcus, land isn't held only by the sword. There are title deeds.'

'Nevertheless, dear lady, all land is held by the sword.' Lepidus was mounted on a favourite hobby. 'We Romans conquered Mantua from the Gauls, after they had conquered it from someone else, the Etruscans most probably. If you look far enough, there are descendents of dozens of previous owners of every piece of land knocking about Italy. Which do you think we should restore?'

'Nonsense,' she said sharply, addressing the Triumvir with a curtness he seldom heard nowadays. 'There is a rightful owner for every square foot of land in the world. It's your duty to find him, and safeguard his title.'

'I didn't know you were a philosopher, my dear. Plato taught that the Ideal is laid up in heaven, so that all we have to do is look for it. In your opinion, I suppose, the Ideal includes an Ideal land-register.'

'Now you are making fun of a mere woman, who had nothing but a miserable feminine education. I don't know about Plato and his Ideals. All I know is that soldiers who follow my Marcus ought to keep their land. They should get that of others into the bargain.'

'That's not the talk of a mere woman. That's the argument of every male politician. "My followers should keep their land and get the land of your followers as well." It's not often put so laconically, but that's all we really talk about in the Senate.'

'Oh dear, I was forgetting. You have come straight from that boring assembly, in all the glare of the Forum. You must be longing for rest, and for a little frivolous chatter. Instead I go on about politics. Forgive me.'

'Well, I did come here to relax; though do you know, my dear,

156

that they call "The Keels" the new Senate House, because every appointment is settled here? In a way, it's even more true now that your Marcus is fighting overseas. He finds it hard to fix his mind on politics. Yours is the more forceful character.'

Fulvia looked at him appraisingly. 'I haven't seen dear Junia for ages,' she said abruptly. 'I hope she is well?'

'She is well enough, I believe. As a matter of fact, I don't see very much of her. There were old friends of hers among the proscribed, and now she regards me as a kind of public executioner.'

'That proscription was a terrible bloodletting. I also lost old friends; but then there was a time when I knew everyone. Yet, like any other bloodletting, it was done because it was necessary. Never reproach yourself because once you put the needs of the City before private affection.'

'That's what I tell Junia. But she doesn't understand me.'

Lepidus was thinking how much more pleasant life would be if he could talk every evening to some lady as understanding as this, a lady who had grasped that a great and turbulent City could not be ruled by kindness alone, and that in civil war it is legitimate to kill your enemies. For a moment he recalled with distaste her treatment of Cicero's head, and then remembered that he had only her husband's words as evidence that she had done anything to it at all. No one would convict a cat of killing a mouse on the unsupported evidence of Marcus Antonius.

Now she spoke gently, with a winning smile. 'Don't think harshly of poor Junia, my dear. And don't despise women in general; some of us can think for ourselves. You are different. You are one of the three rulers of the world. You came to the top in open competition with your equals. There are few in the City, whether male or female, who can enter into your thoughts.'

'Few, my dear Fulvia? There is only one, yourself. We live in an age of iron, and I thought that I alone had strength of character to accomplish the unpleasant things that must be done. In you I have met a worthy helper.'

'Flatterer! But poor dear Clodius used to say the same; so does my darling Marcus when he happens to be at home. I must have some trifling aptitude for politics. All the same, you must be kind to Junia. She is a faithful wife, and a devoted mother. It's just that you have risen beyond the reach of her intellect.'

'I expect that's it. We were married as children, when I was no more than the head of my family. She could not foresee that I would rise to be supreme in the City. If anyone had prophesied it then I wouldn't have believed it myself. Now about this Mantuan business. Of course we shall make an exception for any

157

loyal Antonian, but I hope to persuade you, dear lady, that Pollio is following the sensible course.'

'Don't persuade me, I beg. It's not fitting. You are Triumvir, and your commands must be obeyed without argument. All the same, I made a note of one or two Antonians who are menaced with confiscation. If you move your chair closer we can talk it over in comfort.'

The discussion followed the usual course. Lepidus announced general decisions; Fulvia applauded them, and then asked for exceptions in favour of her own dependants, which were granted without argument.

Lepidus was more conscious than ever of those two mounds of flesh half-revealed by the top of her tunic. She was a very fine woman, as well as an intelligent politician; if she saw him as an attractive man as well as a Triumvir, well, was that absurd?

Their talk was sprinkled with endearments, but that was the fashion and meant nothing in particular. Fulvia had a habit of seizing his wrists to make sure she had his attention, or else with every other word she patted him on the chest. He tried to recall whether she spoke to everyone in the same manner, or whether she touched him because his body pleased her.

When it was time to leave he was still sitting beside her couch. For some hours they had been alone together (maids didn't count). If it became known many people would think the worst. Marcus Antonius had divorced his first wife on flimsier evidence; and then hounded her reputed lover, Dolabella, until he fled the City. But Lepidus had not wronged his colleague, and on the whole he was glad of it. He felt sure he could win Fulvia, if he tried hard enough. But she would be a demanding mistress, and Junia would soon find out. It was more pleasant to sit chatting with this intelligent, loyal comrade, knowing that she would yield if he pressed her, but deliberately refraining from breaking the moral code of the ancestors.

That night they met again at a rowdy supper-party, where dancing-boys made such a racket that rational conversation was impossible. She sat beside his couch, on an ornate chair; again he passed hours with her bosom and legs before his eyes. Pleading a headache, Junia had stayed at home.

By October bulletins were being read to the Senate twice daily, with the latest news of the fighting in Thrace. Forty legions were crowded round the little town of Philippi, digging trenches and assaulting palisades, as two mighty armies tried each to besiege the other after the new fashion of tactics. Presently came word that an accidental collision had developed into a pitched battle;

or rather, into two simultaneous pitched battles, with differing fortune. Brutus had beaten young Caesar; he had broken his line of battle, and barely been repulsed from his camp. But the famous soldier Cassius, pittied against Marcus Antonius, had fallen on his sword when he saw his army dissolve in rout. Looked at as a whole, the result was a draw; two great armies still faced one another, and all was still to be won or lost. That was not how they saw it at 'The Keels'.

When Lepidus looked in to show Fulvia her husband's official dispatch he found her with the two consuls-designate, Plancus and the third Antonius brother, Lucius. All were excited and elated; Fulvia in particular was talking at the top of her voice, too interested in her audience to order them to withdraw and leave her alone with the ruler of Rome.

'The boy has been shown up in his true colours,' she exclaimed in triumph. 'Even Brutus could beat him, Brutus who can't inspect a guard of honour without tripping over his own sword. After this exhibition his soldiers won't stick to him. My Marcus overcame the conquerer of the Parthians, the only commander who came well out of that disgraceful business at Carrhae. I used to hope that he would one day prove himself the best soldier in the world. Now he has done it.'

'He has avenged the Dictator,' Lucius put in. 'Cassius instigated the murder-plot. He has still to avenge poor Caius, who was butchered by Brutus. In my family we stick together, and he won't rest until that's done. Then, I suppose, he will take over all the Caesarian legions, little Caesar will die of his next bout of fever, and Marcus will come home to make himself King of the Romans.'

'Shut up, you fool,' said Plancus roughly. 'That's no way to talk before a Triumvir. Don't you know that the three of them are united in eternal friendship? All the same, Lepidus, there's no denying that Antonius has shown himself a better man than young Caesar. Do you think he will be content to remain his equal?'

'The war isn't finished. Young Caesar may yet win a great vitcory,' Lepidus answered mildly. 'Marcus has been content to remain my equal, though he is a much better soldier than I am. War is not the sole activity of the government.'

He was not annoyed with Lucius Antonius, who had only said openely, in his brother's house, what was known to the whole world as his candid opinion. Plancus had been far more irritating; untimely tact is more offensive than frank insubordination. To put the fellow in his place he continued: 'Rank and title are at best only a rough guide to real power in the republic. When we crossed the Alps Marcus was my leader; at Bononia he made me his equal. Whether I am in fact his equal you may judge for yourselves. In the same way, every year the City is ruled by two Consuls, supreme embodiments of the authority of the republic. Yet in fact some Consuls are more important than others.'

'Listen to that, Lucius,' Fulvia shouted cheerfully. 'The Triumvir has put you both where you belong. You and Plancus may be next year's Consuls, but what do Consuls matter while there are Triumvirs to rule us?'

'That's right,' Lucius shouted back (among themselves the Antonius family always conversed in shouts). 'Of course we don't matter, we humble Consuls. But we are also the faithful servants of good old Marcus, who will soon be tyrant of Rome. You're an Antonian, aren't you, Lepidus? You will help us if little Caesar Octavianus gets uppish?'

'The Triumvirate is united, and all Triumvirs are equal in power,' said Lepidus, now thoroughly nettled. 'This conversation is most unsuitable. My dear lady, I came only to bring your husband's official dispatch. It seems I intrude on a family gathering. I hope so call on you again when you are less occupied.'

Amid stunned silence he stalked to the door. These people might be relations of the greatest soldier in the world; but in Rome, on that day, Lepidus held power of life and death.

He was content with his warning, and took no further action. The next time Fulvia met him she apologised for her brother-in-law's indiscretion, and Lepidus repeated his little sermon on the duty of Triumvirs to stick together. The government remained united.

Other observers had seen the increased importance of Marcus Antonius. Eunomus passed on to his patron a proposal, alleged to have come from Sextus Pompeius though there was nothing to authenticate it: beginning with a blunt suggestion that young Caesar should be killed by poison, and that Pompeius should take over the resulting vacancy in the Triumvirate, it continued with hints, impossible to pin down, that eventually Pompeius would combine with Lepidus to overthrow Antonius. 'And then, I suppose, he will poison *me*,' Lepidus said impatiently. 'Does he think I am a halfwit, to join forces with a pirate who is looking for an accomplice in murder? Little Caesar is no danger to anyone, and I get on well enough with Antonius. Why should I wish to change the Tirumvirate, when I am already as great as any Roman?'

'Caesar the Dictator was greater, my lord, and so for a short time was Pompeius Maximus. At present you are one of three rulers. Sextus proposes to make you one of two. Then of course he will plot against you. But you will be plotting against *him*, and who knows which of you will be victorious? The plan is worth consideration.'

'I won't consider it. If he puts it in writing I shall inform my colleagues, and we shall attack Sicily together. They might doubt my unsupported word; it's so obviously to my interest to make trouble for young Sextus.'

'Young Sextus commands a much greater force than is generally realised, my lord. I hope I have convinced you of that. It is something we should keep to ourselves. Private knowledge is useful in any negotiation.'

'Young Sextus is a pirate, and an enemy of Rome. If you have been bribed to put in a word for him you may keep his money; you have earned it. I remain unimpressed. When the time comes Antonius will sweep him away. What can sailors do against legions?'

'Very well, my lord. The decision is for you. If you combine with Pompeius you may destroy Antonius, and so rule the world. But if you combine with Antonius you must without fail destroy Pompeius, who is the weaker; though afterwards Antonius will still surpass you.'

'I am content with my rank. Antonius may command more legions, but in the records I am set down as his equal. I have risen higher than any of my ancestors.'

It was typical of Eunomus to stake his winnings on another desperate gamble, to win even more if all went well; these Greeks were never satisfied. For a great statesman the game was too hazardous.

Within fifteen days the political situation changed again. News came that, after more siege-operations, Brutus had fought a second pitched battle on the old ground at Philippi. This time he had been defeated, to such effect that he must kill himself to avoid the dishonour of public execution. But, most tiresomely, young Caesar had behaved with the utmost gallantry in the hard-fought battle; with the unfair advantage of his name, he was now equal in popular esteem with Marcus Antonius.

This time Lepidus, hurrying round to 'The Keels' with the official dispatch, found Fulvia alone. She received him in her boudoir, lying on the usual couch, as though their friendship had never been interrupted. It was disappointing that she already knew all about the campaign. Antonius had written to her, including in his letter news he had not bothered to pass on to the Senate.

'My Marcus is a family man,' she said proudly. 'He was anxious to avenge the foul murder of poor Caius; Brutus has avoided punishment by his timely suicide. However, in this letter dear Marcus explains that he captured a fellow called Hortensius, the man whose sword actually killed Caius. So Marcus arranged a pious little ceremony, in which Hortensius was pole-axed on the very tomb of my unfortunate brother-in-law. They made it a proper sacrifice, with wine and barley-meal, and the liver cut out for inspection by a haruspex, as though this Hortensius were a four-legged beast. Don't you think that shows a pretty vein of sentiment?'

'A most impressive display of fraternal affection. But I hope your husband doesn't develop a taste for that kind of thing. He is a man of extremes; if he does it too often he will make himself disliked.'

'It won't happen often. A brother is someone special, after all. Though I need not remind you of that. Your brother may have been proscribed, but the soldiers couldn't catch him. I suppose he will be coming home, now the proscription is over.'

'As a matter of fact, he won't. I wrote to him not long ago, advising him that he could return in safety. His reply was most discourteous, when you remember all I did for him. He wrote that he preferred Miletus to Rome, because over there they don't fight civil wars or murder their own kin. He says it is a cultured city, and he has no intention of leaving it. I suppose I shall never see him again.'

'Oh well, that's all the thanks a great ruler ever gets for his kindness. My Marcus also has a forgiving nature. He writes that he is sending to Rome the ashes of Junius Brutus. They will be delivered to Servilia, for burial in the family tomb. I suppose it's too much to hope that Junia will write to thank him for his reverence. That obstinate wife of yours never has a kind word for my Marcus, though she thinks little Caesar the greatest man in the world. The two of them killed her darling brother between them, but Marcus gets all the blame.'

'My dear lady, you know how things are in my home. I respect my wife; but she goes her way and I go mine.'

'And your way, I hope, will be the way of my dear Marcus. Seriously, when the break comes you must line up on the right side. Marcus is staying behind in the east, where he can raise all the money he needs; he will fix up some kind of working agreement with Sextus Pompeius, who is stronger than most people think. Silly little Caesar Octavianus wants to come back to Italy, to find farms for his veterans. That's the duty of Lucius, as next year's Consul, but Caesar grudges him any authority. When

162

Caesar begins to steal land he will make enemies on all sides. Then we pounce on him together; Marcus from Asia, Pompeius from Sicily, Lucius at the head of the dispossessed farmers of Italy itself. If you give us in addition control of the City we shall be grateful; but even without Rome we can't lose. Will you join us?'

Lepidus sat up with a jerk. On the very day that news came of the ending of the civil war he was being invited to start another. Ought he to arrest this reckless lady? No, he dared not. To arrest his colleague's wife would mean war with Antonius. But she was proposing that he join Antonius in war against Caesar. Was there no hope of peace? Then he recovered his spirits. Dear Fulvia was talking nonsense, not for the first time. If Antonius meditated war he would himself write to his supporters; he would not leave the organisation of a plot to his wife. This must be her own idea. He would persuade her to be sensible.

Fulvia continued to pour out her plans. 'You see what's in Caesar's mind? He wants to control the land-settlement of all Italy, while my Marcus defends Syria from the Parthians. Then Caesar's troops, who didn't do any fighting, will get immense estates; and loyal Antonian veterans will be fobbed off with the promise of some barren rock in the Appenines. A nasty plot, the sort of thing that sly shirker would think up. But the silly boy has forgotten one thing; from next January Italy will be governed by loyal Antonians. The Consuls-designate are my brother-in-law and Plancus, whom Marcus made Imperator. When the war starts we shall have the government in our hands, the treasury and all the prestige of the City. That will count with neutrals – if there are any neutrals. We shall have young Pompeius also, the surprise-packet who is so much stronger than people think.'

Lepidus jumped at this opportunity to stem the flow of words. 'My secretary keeps on telling me that Sextus is stronger than I suppose, and now you repeat it. Very well, I shall faithfully suppose that he is very strong indeed. By this time every politician in Rome must know it. But his father was a failure. Don't count on him too much.'

'His father was a failure, but the youngster is great in his own right. Marcus Lepidus, I offer you supreme power – with my friendship. Don't be false to your destiny.'

As she spoke the lady Fulvia moved restlessly on her couch; her arms opened as though for an embrace, and her tunic at last slipped below her breasts.

Lepidus was left dazed by a sudden flash of comprehension. Fulvia wanted *him*, as her partner in love, as her partner in power. All this talk about the rivalry between Antonius and young Caesar was just a blind, to keep the support of Lucius and Plancus. Here was a challenge to his manhood. He must accept it, or for the rest of his life mourn a lost opportunity.

He sprang from his chair. 'Darling, with ardour I embrace my destiny. Together, you and I will rule the world!'

Before he could gather her in his arms he sat down again, with a thump that jarred his spine. The lady Fulvia had seen many boxing-matches, and her uppercut came from nowhere as she rose to her feet; but he could see her right hand travelling, palm open, to smack his cheek.

Then the assault was finished. She stood over him, hands on hips, shouting hysterically. 'You fat miserable slug. You common hangman, employed to murder noble Romans while your betters do the fighting. You Lepidus. I can't think of a fouler name to call you. Here, Melissa, fetch a looking-glass. Let the oaf see his scraggy neck and wobbling paunch. Did you imagine, you fool, that I would betray my husband for you? I, who am married to Marcus Antonius? Think for a minute, if you can. My Marcus is the bravest man in Rome, and the best looking, and the most ardent in bed – it's known to all the world. And you thought to supplant him! Go away, and never come back. I don't want to see your face again until I see it stuck on a pole, like Cicero's.'

On his way home Lepidus imagined the passers-by could see the red marks of fingers on his cheek, even through the drawn curtains of his litter.

In December young Caesar returned to Italy. His health was poor, but he was urgently needed in the countryside, where farmers threatened with eviction were gathering in menacing bands; they were themselves mostly old soldiers, prickly men to deal with. It was worse when they were harangued by Lucius and Plancus, the Consuls-designate, who explained that the new confiscations were the work of Caesar alone, and that as soon as Marcus Antonius came back he would see justice done.

The City also was restless. From Sicily the cruisers of Sextus Pompeius levied blackmail on the corn-ships, and the price of wheat rose. Marcus Antonius was collecting an enormous tribute from Asia; but he spent money as fast as he gathered it. No funds reached the central government, which must pay off a victorious army with the revenue of Italy alone. Even the most short-sighted could discern another civil war piling up on the horizon.

It broke very suddenly. In the middle of a December night Lepidus was roused from his solitary bed by Eunomus, to be told that Lucius Antonius was marching on Rome.

As soon as he understood the news he asked the question that came first to the mind of any experienced politician: 'Never mind the strength of his army. What's his warcry?'

'Liberty, the republic restored. So I've been told.'

'Then he's too late. The men who would have rallied to that programme were killed in the proscription. He's bound to lose. Anyway, it means alliance with the Optimates, so I can't support him. Do you think I can stay neutral?'

'No, my lord. You command in Rome, and you must defend the City. It's the most maddening piece of rash imprudence. No one knows whether Marcus is behind his brother, and anyway he's a thousand miles away. Nobody warned Sextus Pompeius in advance, so he will wait until he can offer assistance to the victor. All the army commanders in the provinces are equally in the dark. We were just organising a coalition that would have forced Caesar to retire into private life without even making a fight of it. Now they have struck too soon, and their allies are afraid to move.'

'Very well. Since I must choose, I have chosen. Mark that, Eunomus. I am a man of instant decision, twice Imperator, used to war's alarms. Plans come to me in a flash, and I am never dismayed. I shall support young Caesar. Later a time may come when it is my manifest destiny to be sole ruler of the world. Then, let Caesar beware. For the present I shall preserve him.'

As it fell out, this resolution was not put to the test. At the last moment the soldiers of Lucius Antonius refused to march on Rome. Instead they called a peace-conference.

This was an unheard-of development. Every politician must sit down and reconsider his position. In the past legions had deserted their commanders, or changed sides on the battlefield. Never before had soldiers remained loyal to their leader, willing to follow him in anything except civil war – just because there was nothing to fight about. It was as though the pieces on a chess-board had developed minds of their own. From the Rhine to Calabria armies mobilised and baggage-animals were impressed; but nowhere did a legate give the order to march.

For one Antonian there had to be war. Lepidus was surprised in his office by an early visit from Junia. In these days she seldom came to talk with him alone.

'I have news of a dear friend of yours.' Her voice had something of its old gaiety.

'Indeed?' He must not sound too welcoming. That would be unworthy of a paterfamilias. Junia hurried on in her unnoticing way.

'Fulvia has flown to arms. Yes, literally. She is stumping all

165

over Campania hung round with her husband's old swords. What an enormous baldric she'll need to go over that great bust of hers. She's supposed to be inspiring the troops. I got it all from Crastinus.'

Lepidus composed his face to an expression of gravity, which he hoped would mask the confusion of his thoughts. Fulvia's behaviour did not much surprise him, but Junia's did. She seemed positively friendly, and nearly as light-hearted as of old. She had listened to gossip from Crastinus too. Ever since the unfortunate affair of Paullus she had taken a dislike to Crastinus, refusing to speak of him except as 'your tame butcher' or 'the official assassin'; and then only to complain that he hung about the buttery or molested the maids. But he must say something.

'What an extraordinary story.'

'No, Marcus, not so extraordinary for Fulvia, at least not nearly so extraordinary as the rest of it. Crastinus says she is bellowing all over the provinces that you have been plotting the murder of her darling babes!'

'Babes? But Clodia is ready for marriage! Oh, of course, she has two boys by Antonius; not that I've ever seen them. Junia, you surely don't believe that I was planning child-murder?'

'Of course not. I just thought the whole story rather funny. Everyone, even Fulvia, knows you are not cut out to be a baby-killer – or a lady-killer either.'

The lady Junia left the room with an air of satisfaction. Lepidus was left to marvel uneasily at the network of intelligence that enmeshed the boudoirs of Rome.

Young Caesar paid a flying visit to the City, and then was off to raise more troops in the countryside. His manner to Lepidus was distant, in fact barely civil to a Consular old enough to be his father. Caesar's normal manner was stiff and awkward, and now he had many worries. Lepidus regretted that he had been forced into alliance with such an unsympathetic young man; but he consoled himself with the knowledge that at least he had chosen the stronger side.

For now it was war in earnest, and the pitiful remnant of the Optimates rallied to Lucius Antonius. His brother's veterans, anxious for their promised farms, joined him also; and he had the authority to levy troops inherent in his office of Consul. He was soon at the head of six legions, reinforced by a mob of brigands, gladiators, runaway slaves, and other loafers who would rather fight than work. In Italy Caesar had only four legions; but they were the men who had fought at Philippi.

Lepidus was still in control of Rome, with two legions under his orders. It seemed to him, as he bustled about supervising the digging of earthworks, that this was the Argenteus all over again. Once more every Roman soldier was on the march, and once more his headquarters was the goal they strove to reach. Lucius Antonius pushed up from the south, Salvidienus hastened from Gaul to oppose him; on the heels of Salvidienus came Plancus, Ventidius Bassus, and Pollio. These last were loyal adherents of Marcus Antonius, though whether they would obey his brother was uncertain.

In such a situation the obvious tactics for the man at the centre of the knot was to shut himself up on the defensive, waiting for the dust to settle. That was just what Lepidus could not do, for Rome was an unwalled city. Only two courses were open to him; he might offer battle in the field, or he might withdraw northward without fighting.

Caesar sent a message bidding him stand firm; Rome must be held at all costs. Salvidienus would soon arrive to restore the situation. Deputations of frightened Senators begged him to withdraw; if Lucius defeated him outside Rome the City would be sacked by a victorious horde of bandits. Apparently everyone took it for granted that if he fought he would be beaten; indeed the odds were more than three to one against him. But it would have been more tactful of the Senators to conceal their opinion.

Meanwhile, Marcus Antonius, the ostensible cause of the quarrel, was enjoying himself in Alexandria, boating and picnicking with Queen Cleopatra. He sent no orders to his followers; without word from him the provincial commander hesitated to make war on Caesar.

In this dilemma Lepidus decided that if he did nothing he could do nothing wrong. He sat tight. Perhaps Lucius Antonius would be killed by a thunderbolt.

What he wanted was sound advice. If someone would speak to him at length, marshalling his reasons properly and clothing them in correct rhetorical form, he could pick holes in the argument and arrive at a sensible decision; every Senator was trained in that intellectual exercise. Junia was more friendly now, and of course Crastinus eagerly volunteered his counsel. But neither of them would examine matters from the correct point of view.

He wanted to know what would be best for Marcus Aemilius Lepidus. They kept on telling him what would be best for Rome.

At last the crisis was upon him. Late on a blustery December afternoon a young knight galloped through the crowded streets to the Aemilian mansion. Riding was prohibited in the streets of the City, so this in itself was enough to show that the time of decision had arrived. When the courier entered the hall he found the Triumvir struggling into his armour.

'Antonian horse at the Capua gate, sir,' he blurted out as soon as he had saluted. 'They are in contact with our outposts. In the distance we can see one Eagle, though the immediate supports are light infantry, probably gladiators. Our tribune ordered me to inform you without delay.'

'The Capua gate? What force have we there? Three cohorts, isn't it? They are well dug in. Cavalry can't help them, unless they dismount to attack on foot. Very well. I shall come at once, with two cohorts from the reserve. You have identified one Eagle, but we know Antonius has six legions. Your three cohorts must stand fast until the enemy has developed his strength.'

This last bit of professional jargon made Lepidus feel more warlike for saying it. The young knight saluted and rode off.

Crastinus appeared, with his special large shield. A war-horse circled outside the door. There seemed no chance of more delay. In a moment the Triumvir, twice Triumphator, twice Imperator, must assume command in his first action. Crastinus exerted himself to soothe his nervous master.

'Only gladiators, and peacocking cavalry. I'd like to see them charge a regular cohort, dug in. Loose off arrows at long range and then straggle away to plunder the suburbs, that's more their mark. When it comes to the point, the Antonian legionaries won't want to fight. Why should they kill old comrades, just to please the lady Fulvia? I'll bet there is less blood shed today than in one of the old election-riots. You'll see, my lord; no need to hurry. Here, let me buckle that greave properly.'

Her eyes shining, the lady Junia stood before him with a cup of wine. She was taking this crisis seriously, but her husband was annoyed to see that she enjoyed the excitement. 'Off you go, Marcus,' she cried cheerfully. 'Here's a last drink, old wine with no water at all. Father used to say that makes the enemy look smaller. Remember, your brother died gloriously, within a mile of this house. There ought to be an omen in that; as Pontifex Maximus you should know whether it's a good one. What's the phrase? "Come back with your shield, or upon it." Oh, but you can't. No shield for an Imperator. It seems silly to say it to Crastinus.'

There was no escape. Pulling his face in to a resolute frown, Lepidus loosened his sword in its scabbard. 'Thank you, my dear, for your good wishes. You had better drink that wine yourself, or give it to Crastinus. Wine after dinner always makes me drowsy.'

Then there was more galloping in the street, and the great entrance-door was blocked by a horse and rider. It was the young knight again. Without dismounting, he leaned over to call into the echoing hall. 'Sorry, Imperator. Those cohorts at the Capua gate have just gone over to Lucius. My kit's with them, and my servant, and all the ready cash I have in the world; so I can't very well fight against them. I'm just off to join them, but I thought it only decent to give you a start before the Antonians come to arrest you.'

Crastinus began a string of military obscenities, realised he was in the presence of a matron, and fell silent. Lepidus stood dazed, his chief emotion relief that after all he would not have to command troops in action. Junia was the first to recover her wits.

'Ride for it, Marcus, across the river and out to the north. Make for Caesar's army. I shall hide, with the boys. Don't stand gaping. Get mounted.'

It was the Ides of March, the fourth anniversary of the terrible murder. But this scene was more terrible by far. On the hill the ancient city of Perusia flamed to the heavens; in the valley, among the huts of the victorious Caesarians, an altar of turf had been constructed on the parade ground. It was an altar for sacrifice to the Gods Below, as the deep drainage-trench proved, the trench that would soon be filled with blood. Three hundred Roman knights and Senators stood in rank, the victims who would furnish that blood. In the stillness of attention Caesar's praetorian cohorts were drawn up to witness the atrocity. They were veterans, motionless on parade; though some were almost too drunk to stand upright, and others were wounded, in witness that the Perusians had defended their homes.

Young Caesar advanced at the head of a little group. He wore armour, but his head was bare; as he came forward he veiled it with the end of his military cloak. Lepidus, also in the splendid armour of a Consular and Imperator, plucked timidly at his wrist.

'You've given them a good fright,' he whispered. 'Surely you won't go through with it? You allowed Fulvia and Lucius to go free, and these men are not dangerous without Antonian support. They are very small fry, not worth the trouble of killing.'

'But I shall take the trouble to kill them,' Caesar answered. 'Don't mistake me for my deified father, who pardoned his enemies over and over again until at last they murdered him. He may be a god, or he may not. This sacrifice may give pleasure to his spirit, or there may be no spirit of Caesar anywhere. But this I know: these Optimates have disturbed the firm peace we brought to Rome. They deserve no mercy. If I kill them thus, publicly, I strike terror into my remaining enemies.'

'You drive to desperation opponents who might otherwise submit.'

'I do not fear any opponent, anywhere. All must submit to me, or die as these traitors die.' He fixed his colleague with a cold grey eye. 'Whatever his rank, no one is safe from my justice. Which reminds me; I want to see you afterwards, in my office.'

No further word was spoken until Caesar intoned the ritual prayer dedicating this sacrifice to the spirit of his deified father. Then the slaughter began.

All the victims were Roman citizens; they were treated as cattle. Instead of the honourable decapitation which was their privilege, these men were pole-axed; then they were ripped open, and their livers removed for inspection. Their executioners were *victimarii*, the hefty acolytes whose task was the ritual slaughter of oxen, men whose naked torsos accentuated their workman-like, their butcherlike, appearance. Lepidus, watching with fascinated eyes, thought the denial of human dignity even more appalling than Caesar's ruthless cruelty.

There was one thing to be said for it; it was quickly over. In ten minutes the squad of *victimarii* had done their work, and three hundred eviscerated corpses lay on the verge of the reddened trench. A trumpet pealed the merry signal that marked the end of every public sacrifice; the watching cohorts turned smartly to the right and marched off to share in the plunder of Perusia; and Lepidus, queasy and shaken, walked stiffly, on legs that did not quite tremble, to Caesar's private office.

There he found himself alone. A polished shield hung on the wall, and he buried himself in adjusting his baldric, tightening his belt, and smoothing his epaulettes before this mirror. By the time Caesar entered he looked every inch an Imperator.

The boy strolled in casually, dressed only in the padded tunic which protected his ribs from the chafing of the corselet. 'Sorry to keep you waiting,' he said carelessly. 'My armour was splashed with blood, and I want it clean for tomorrow. Sit down, and have a drink. Now then, what shall I do with you?'

'Do you wish to consult with me concerning the welfare of the republic?' asked Lepidus, so angry at the insolence of this tone that fear was driven from his mind.

'I do not. I don't value your advice. Once you had an army, and then you were important. Your soldiers have deserted you, so you don't matter any more.'

Lepidus gobbled, too furious to find words.

'Yes, you are an Imperator without legions, and that's a horrible thing to be,' the insufferable youth continued. 'Your men left you for a better leader. Since I have just defeated that better leader I must be far above you.' His tone changed, as his own anger rose to match his listener's. 'You fool, you utter fool! You couldn't hold the City even against the gladiators and freed slaves who made up the comic army of that other fool, Lucius Antonius! I very nearly had you hauled out to the altar just now, to make the three hundred and first victim. There was nothing to stop me; I could have done it if I chose. But there's an old superstition that it brings bad luck to kill the Pontifex Maximus; certainly my father's murderers have met with ill-fortune. So I held my hand. You are useless alive, but your death might bring me bad luck. What shall I do with you? I ask it again.'

Lepidus felt death very near, and that made everything easier. At once he became the master of himself. His education had left him in doubt about the survival of the spirit; though he feared the ghosts of others he could not picture any kind of future life for himself. But one thing his teachers had impressed on him: that it is the duty of a nobleman to make a good end. For more than forty years he had been preparing for his last hour. He knew what to say.

'Octavius of Velitrae, you may slay Lepidus of Rome, but you cannot make him fear you. My father died for the people; my brother also. I suppose that was about the time your father set up in business as a money-lender; you are too young to remember it. If I too must die for the people, I am ready.'

'My name is not Octavius,' the other answered, 'though indeed I come from Velitrae. The Roman people have made me Caesar.' He paused, and continued more quietly, smiling as though admiration were mingled with amusement. 'But in everything else you are quite right. I can't frighten Aemilius Lepidus, and Rome would be in a bad way if I could. I shall not kill you. All the same, what shall I do with you? Or, if you prefer it, what will you do with the rest of your life? You don't know how to lead an army, and you can't go back to govern Rome as though nothing had happened. Would you like to retire from politics?'

'I shall die a Triumvir, or else a public enemy,' said Lepidus proudly. 'If you strip me of my offices I shall go into rebellion. All Italy is discontented with your rule. Both Antonians and Optimates would rally to my Eagles.'

'They would; and of course that's the trouble. You have been a very great man, though an incapable one. If I leave you to wander at large you will become a focus of revolt. By the way,' he shot out, 'what were you up to, intriguing with Sextus Pompeius? I know all about it. I have agents everywhere. Do you think he would prove a faithful ally, against me or against Marcus Antonius? Do you recall what he did to Bithynicus, his own

171

cousin? Sextus is becoming important. All the Optimate stragglers from Philippi have joined him. He's too important to be second string to a Lepidus, a man who can't hold the Capitol with two legions. He will be *my* ally. I have divorced young Clodia, and I shall marry the lady Scribonia, his aunt. You see? I surpass you in intrigue, as in war.'

He continued in a friendly tone. 'I think that gives us a way out. I want this government to remain an alliance of three men. If I am left alone to face Marcus Antonius we shall be at war within a month. This is what I propose. I am sending an army to mop up the Optimates of Africa. That won't take long. They are the only Optimates left in the world, and they have no allies. After they have been conquered, and not before, I shall make you governor of Africa. You will still be a Triumvir, Imperator, Consular, all the rest of it. The ostensible reason for sending you from Rome to Utica will be, not your incompetence, but the suspicion that you have intrigued with Sextus. Now will you accept that, and continue as a loyal Triumvir? There's no reason why you shouldn't make a success of it. In Africa there will be no fighting, so your army can't desert you; and you have shown that in peacetime you can govern well. Besides, you are Aemilius Lepidus. We need a man of your rank in the government, to demonstrate that all Populars are not money-lenders from Velitrae.' With a charming smile he added: 'After all, your birth imposes on you an obligation to serve the republic. Africa needs sound government, and you can supply it. Besides, by remaining in the Triumvirate you prevent a civil war between myself and Antonius, which might do great harm to the world. Come now, will you accept?'

'If I do, I shall govern without human sacrifice. Perhaps Antonius, who pole-axed Hortensius on the tomb of his brother, and yourself, who sacrifice so piously to your adoptive father, will think me an unworthy colleague.'

'No don't be spiteful. Marcus did it out of genuine family feeling. He believes in the gods, and the next world, and all that sort of thing; and he was truly fond of that scoundrelly brother of his. I don't believe in anything in particular, though I'm all for encouraging the practice of religion as a reinforcement to morality; and I never knew my adoptive father until the last year of his life. I thought it prudent to kill a clutch of rebels, so I used them in a ceremony which will impress the whole world. At the same time I proved that I am not vindictive at heart, by sending off Lucius and Fulvia to join the head of their family. Perhaps Marcus won't thank me for that.'

'Very well. I accept your offer,' said Lepidus, taking the plunge with a rush of words. 'But, mind you, this must be a genuine proconsulship. I must have all Africa, with an adequate army; and in my own province I must be really supreme. If you try to make me your deputy I shall rebel against you. I'm no warrior. I know that. But I can administer a peaceful province; Africa will be the better for my rule. My other stipulation is – no hostages. I want my wife and sons with me in Utica, not living in Rome under open arrest.'

'No hostages, I agree. My dear man, I trust you; and certainly after your last flight from Rome, I do not fear you. So there need be no precautions against treachery.'

*The lady Clodia halted her litter, peering out to read the programme of the forthcoming Games. 'Caesar again,' she said with satisfaction. 'He always shows plenty of lions and elephants. So he should. The common people made him great, and in return he must be generous, But why does he still call himself Triumvir? I thought he ruled the west, and Antonius the east?'*

*'There is a third ruler somewhere,' said the young man in attendance. 'Old Lepidus is the third Triumvir, in some barbarous place, Gaul or Spain or Africa or something.'*

*'Dear me, I thought he was killed in the proscription, like everyone else. Once he did me a good turn. I'm glad he's still alive, even though he doesn't matter any more.'*

# X

## AFRICA
### 37 B.C.

The temple of Jupiter in Utica was not so splendid as that on the Capitol, the central shrine of the Roman People; but it was a fine stately building, worthy of an ancient citizen-colony. Today the forecourt and the Sacred Way leading to it were thronged with citizens in holiday dress. It was not often that the Romans of Africa had an opportunity to witness the sacrifice of a complete hecatomb by the Pontifex Maximus in person, with all the ritual of old Rome.

First there had to be a good many speeches. Every town-councillor must say his piece, even though he were more practised in dictating business communications than in turning graceful compliments. But these speeches could not be omitted; by custom, each orator presented to the governor a bag of gold pieces, in theory sufficient gold to make a crown; and these compulsory free-will offerings were a valuable item of revenue. For three hours Lepidus stood, in full pontificals, while businessmen repeated over and over again the same compliments. Even the new town-council of Carthage had sent a representative; though that modern foundation, the pet of young Caesar in Italy, was perpetually at odds with the official headquarters of the province. Luckily the bulls chosen for sacrifice were well-fed and placid; they stood quietly in the forecourt, though sometimes their bellowing drowned the oratory.

At last the time came for the Pontifex Maximus to sprinkle barley-meal, while the *victimarii* got on with their butchery. All the hundred livers were lined up for inspection, but the Pontifex gave them only a cursory glance before announcing satisfactory omens. How could the omens be anything else, on such an auspicious day? Besides, it was getting on for noon, and in this climate fresh meat must be cooked before sundown. Sacrificial beef was tough and stringy; but it was lucky, and it was free. The poorer citizens would be disappointed if it was not ready by supper-time.

Lepidus was too experienced to exhibit Games in the afternoon, when he must sacrifice in the morning. That would mean at best a stampede from the temple to the amphitheatre, at worst that Jupiter would have no worshippers. The Games would begin at sunrise on the morrow; the afternoon, as was proper, could be devoted to dining and bathing.

He came out into the strong African sun, to walk in procession the short distance to his official residence. An escort of praetorians, tall soldiers in splendid armour, surrounded him with drawn swords; for in the provinces it was fitting that a Roman magistrate should be accompanied by military force. Twenty-four lictors marched ahead, which was perhaps a little ostentatious. But the constitution of the ancestors had laid down no establishment for the attendants of a Triumvir, since the office was a novelty; and it was really only putting his power in the right perspective for him to assume all the majesty of a Dictator.

When he reclined at the dinner-table, clad in a synthesis of specially thin material against the heat of midday, he could congratulate himself that all the intricate ceremonial had gone off without a hitch.

Looking round the table, it was an added satisfaction to see himself as the paterfamilias of a true old Roman household. Only his family were present, as was fitting on such a personal anniversary; but there were enough of them to prove that he was a great man who could protect his relatives. On either side of him his sons reclined: Marcus a youth of seventeen, almost ready to put away his purple-bordered gown and assume the plain white toga of the young citizen; Quintus still a child, but old enough to behave himself when dining with the family.

On three chairs before another small table sat the three ladies. In the centre Junia the matron; on her left her sister, the widow Tertulla, who long ago had left Servilia's gay boudoir to marry the treacherous Cassius; on her right young Antonia, the well-behaved child of fourteen who by next year would be a beautiful woman and the bride of young Marcus. Tertulla had always been the beauty of her handsome family, attractive enough as a child to take the fancy of the great Caesar. She knew herself lucky to be living comfortably in this great household, instead of under police surveillance in Rome; she always did her best to flatter and amuse her brother-in-law and protector. The mere sight of her there, secure and at ease, gave Lepidus a comforting sensation of power.

When the meal began Tertulla took the initiative. The subject was in everyone's thoughts, but they might spend the evening sparing her feelings unless she was the first to broach it. She knew

175

very well that she must sing for her supper, and, being an intelligent woman as well as a pretty one, she did it gracefully.

'Aemilius Lepidus, you must lie there quietly, like a god at a ritual feast, while we pay you due worship. All the rest of you, fill your cups and drink to the renewal of the Triumvirate. Just think of it! We are dining with one of the three greatest men in the whole long history of the City! There was a Triumvirate before, and some of us can remember it. What happened to those Triumvirs? Crassus, defeated and killed by barbarians; Pompeius Maxicus, killed by barbarians while in flight from his fellow-citizens; Caesar, struck down at the summit of his power. This second Triumvirate has stood the test of time. You have given the City five years of peace and prosperity, and still we can't get on without you. Never before has a Triumvirate been renewed. I drink to Aemilius Lepidus, Triumvir *iterum* (again).'

After that handsome declaration the rest could talk freely, without hurting the feelings of a lady whose husband had committed suicide at Philippi. Marcus and Quintus knelt to kiss their father's hand, Junia crowned her husband with a special wreath of roses, and Antonia tactfully proposed the health of young Caesar; whereupon Lepidus himself must give the toast of Marcus Antonius, her father.

'It doesn't seem as long as five years,' said Lepidus, half to himself, 'and it's not quite true that we brought peace to Rome. At the beginning we had to do a lot of fighting, and there are still more legions under arms than when I was a boy. But it's true that our victory brought peace in the end. In Italy there has been no fighting since the fall of Perusia, and here in Africa the last tumult was finished before I took over.'

'It's more nearly six years than five since you joined forces with my father,' said young Antonia. 'I was in hiding at the time, with my horrid step-mother, and I remember well the relief we felt when we heard the good news from the Argenteus. Really, when I think of all the bother my family has caused you, I appreciate how kind it is of you to have me here.'

'Where else could you be, my precious?' Junia said kindly. 'Your father keeps great state in the east, but it isn't a suitable household for a young girl. The lady Octavia, your new step-mother, isn't exactly what you need, is she?'

'My mother means that she isn't quite a lady,' young Marcus said firmly, 'and that is putting it mildly. How could she be a lady? Descended from a long line of money-lenders in Velitrae! Her brother is bad enough, in spite of the noble name he bears. But Octavia never knew the great Dictator, and no one has taught her how to behave in society.'

'It takes all sorts to make a world,' said Tertulla, smiling gently in the cause of peace. 'The lady Octavia is virtuous and sober. Perhaps she isn't smart; some men prefer their *wives* to be dowdy.'

'Yes, Marcus, we don't discuss absent ladies,' his father said ponderously. 'It may be clever to speculate about them, but it isn't good manners. I can remember when the highest praise of a lady was to say that she was unknown to her next-door neighbour. Nowadays no one seems to have any private life.'

'We have a private life, here in Africa,' said Junia, with a contented sigh. 'Utica isn't Rome, but it's a decent old-fashioned town. The citizens behaved most piously at the sacrifice this morning, and now they leave us in peace. If we were in Rome there would be a crowd outside the door, shouting for the Triumvir to come out and make a speech.'

'We are very lucky, Junia darling,' cooed Tertulla. 'When we were young we had all the excitement of politics, the cheering mobs and the fighting on election-day, the great Dictator discussing his plans in mother's boudoir. Now that we are old enough to prefer quiet we live in this charming backwater, where we may decline into old age among customs that were old-fashioned when we were born.'

'Don't talk like the oldest inhabitant,' her sister said sharply. 'The whole family knows that you are younger than me. I don't yet feel old enough to sit in a corner and watch the world go by.'

'In one thing Tertulla is right,' said Lepidus. 'This is a good sound old-fashioned town, and a pleasant place to live in. But I wish it wasn't so far from Rome. Since I never meet my colleagues I have to do everything by letter. This afternoon, on what ought to be a holiday, I must shut myself up with Eunomus to compose an answer to the official decree, and to the letters of congratulation from Caesar and Antonius.'

'You would have prepared your speech of thanks to the Senate, even if you could walk across the street to deliver it in person,' his wife pointed out. 'In the old days you never addressed the Senate without spending at least an afternoon in preparation.'

'In the old days I was trying to persuade the Senate, and sometimes they would vote against me. Now we three rule the City, and no one dares to speak against us. All the same, I like to polish any formal message that is likely to be preserved in the archives. The old patrician style is dying out. When the young men get into a tangle they take refuge in Greek, where you can invent new words as you go along and put them in any order you please. They excuse themselves by saying Cicero began it; so he did, but a man of his eloquence could afford to take liberties.'

'Well, you need not polish your letters to father,' Antonia said cheerfully. 'They tell me he speaks well when he's excited, but he knows absolutely nothing about style. I had a letter from him this morning, to say that uncle Lucius is dead. He forgot to tell me how or why he died, and the whole thing took up only two lines; though it's on the most sumptuous Egyptian paper.'

'Lucius Antonius dead? I hadn't heard it, though of course in a day or two it will be in the official dispatches. I'm sorry for your sake, my dear, if you were fond of him. But I can't really mourn him. Three years ago he did me a great deal of harm.'

There was silence in the dining-room as the Triumvir fell into a reverie.

That afternoon, lying cosily side by side in the privacy of the ladies' bath, Servilia's two daughters discussed the events of the morning. 'Poor dear Marcus,' said Junia with a sigh that turned into a giggle. 'I'm afraid Antonia spoiled his pleasure in these celebrations by bringing up the name of that odious uncle of hers. Marcus can't live unless he has a good opinion of himself, as I expect you have noticed. He tries gallantly to persuade himself that he came out to Africa to govern a continent on behalf of the Roman People, because the work needed doing and there was no one else to do it. As a rule he manages to forget that he was sent here in disgrace. Now, as he composes his letters, he'll be thinking of nothing but how he was chased out of Rome, and trying to discover what he ought to have done to stop his men changing sides. From that he'll go on to plans for recovering his old power. Eunomus encourages every wild scheme. It may take me a month to get him back into a safe routine.'

'I suppose you have always managed his career for him. Do you think he ought to end his days in Utica?'

'I try to manage his career, when it's anything political. I know what other people think of him, and that's the last thing he ever guesses. But when he is in camp with his legions I can't be with him. If you look back, all his mistakes have been made on campaign. If he had marched over the Alps to attack Antonius outside Mutina his men would have followed him. Young Caesar's name would have been enough for the ardent Caesarians, and the others would have bowed to the prestige of the lawful government in the City. Then a loyal army would have made him the most respected Senator in a Senate of free men. He can speak very well, after I have put the right ideas into his head. As to ending his days in Utica, or in this new Colony of Carthage if they ever get it finished, what else can we do? We are *safe* here, among old-fashioned Romans who think along the same lines as my dear old-fashioned husband. What would we do in Italy, in

178

competition with those wolves on their hind legs, Caesar and Antonius? Probably we would end up as human sacrifices, like the Senators who were butchered outside Perusia. Do you know that Lucius betrayed them? He could have held out much longer. When Caesar guaranteed his personal safety he surrendered, and made no terms for his Optimate allies. I hope he had a painful sickness and an agonising death. But Lucius was no worse than the rest of the gang. Yet they dazzle my poor Marcus. Even Fulvia could impress him.'

'Poor Junia, you have a lot to put up with. Of course you must stay in safe Africa. I for one never want to see Rome again. I wouldn't know anybody there, apart from a few heads stuck up in the Forum.'

Meanwhile the Triumvir was conscientiously enduring the afternoon heat of his office, talking over dispatches with Eunomus and drafting his replies.

'I suppose the Triumvirate has in fact been renewed,' he said querulously. 'This proclamation has it in black and white, but there's no mention of a law passed by the assembly, not even a decree of the Senate. I don't see how it can be legally binding. Anyway, our powers expired more than three months ago, on the 1st of January last. Is the proclamation retrospective? If it purports to be, can a proclamation have retrospective effect?'

'Perhaps not, my lord. I am not skilled in the forms of the Roman constitution, which is admitted to be a subject of great intricacy. But is any of this of the slightest importance? You command every soldier in Africa. Caesar commands every soldier in Italy. Antonius commands every soldier in the east. Between you, the Triumvirs commands all the soldiers in the civilised world. When you speak, unarmed Senators and the mob in the assembly must obey your proclamation as though it had the force of law.'

'That's true enough, of course. But I wish Caesar would take a little more trouble. I don't like ruling without a legal sanction, and there's no reason why we should. Caesar sits in Rome, at peace with all his neighbours and with very little to occupy his time. He could get a decree through the Senate and a law through the assembly at the cost of two formal speeches. Then we would be lawful rulers of the City, lawful in the eyes of posterity. Instead, to save himself one day's work, he puts out this unsatisfactory proclamation. I've a good mind to send him a stiff reminder of his duty, instead of congratulations.'

'That would be unwise, my lord. We don't want trouble from Caesar. Though the boy has no military record, he commands a great many legions. If we have to put Africa on a war footing it will interfere with all your plans for development.'

'Oh, very well. I shan't bother to rebuke Caesar. It's only another example of the sloppiness of modern youth, which you meet in every department of government. Nowadays no one does anything thoroughly. You compose my message of congratulation for me, Eunomus. You know the kind of thing to say. Make it flowery and fulsome, in the new Asiatic style. Patrician gravity would be wasted on young Caesar, and he might think I was trying to be offensive. When you have something on paper I shall just skim through it and then put my signet at the bottom. Now what else have we today? Anything more besides routine business? Any other letters about the renewal of the Triumvirate?'

'You ought to congratulate Antonius, my lord. I don't know whether you should also send a notification to Sextus Pompeius. He's not exactly your colleague, but he shares in the government of the Roman world.'

'Marcus Antonius? Of course. I had nearly forgotten him. Stuck out there in the east he seems more like a foreigner than a colleague in the government of the City. Send him a duplicate of the letter to Caesar. He used to be a friend of mine, a close ally, much closer than Caesar. But we have been out of touch for years. I haven't anything in particular that needs saying to him.'

'And Sextus?' the secretary persisted.

'Have it as you wish. Compose a friendly letter to Pompeius. But I must read it carefully before it goes off. He's not exactly a colleague. We found him already there, and recognised his position because for the present he is too strong to be overthrown. He's neither a Triumvir nor a subordinate of the Triumvirate. In fact he's an awkward anomaly. I am a Popular by ancestry and conviction, and I can't bring myself to like any Pompeoius. But for the moment Caesar is friendly with him, and we ought to keep him informed of the state of the republic.'

'My lord, you can't have read the latest dispatches from Italy, or you could not think that friendship still endures. Last year they were firm friends, and Pompeius was granted the province of Achaea. That's Caesar all over, my lord. He can't do a kindness to one man except at the expense of another.'

'Come, come, Caesar is my trusted colleague. Even in the privacy of my office I can't listen to continual abuse of him. Besides, what was so wrong in transferring Achaea from Antonius to Pompeius? It may have been Caesar's suggestion in the first place, but I gather Antonius was perfectly willing.'

'Perhaps, at Misenum, with Pompeius's splendid dinner still sitting on his stomach. But the transfer was bound to cause a quarrel, as Caesar knew from the start. Remember, Achaea is the real Greece, venerated by all true Greeks; and Antonius had been ruling it in the modern Rome fashion.'

'I am a Roman myself, though not perhaps a modern one. What had Antonius done that you consider so shocking?'

'Only collected the taxes for ten years in advance, my lord, until free men had to sell their children to satisfy the publicans. Of course the legions must be paid; that comes first, as every provincial knows. The result was that Pompeius took over a penniless province, and when he asked for tribute the Greeks showed him Antonius's receipt. Pompeius then asked Antonius for the money, as was proper. You can guess the answer he got. As though anyone could make Antonius pay his just debts.'

'I'm sorry to hear it, but there it is. Antonius is a gallant soldier, but he has no money sense at all. It's true about the legions. Their pay must be kept up to date, or the provinces will be pillaged by mutineers. There may be too many soldiers. I wish I could fix up some kind of disarmament by mutual agreement. But the world is still very disturbed, and we have only just emerged from a century of civil war. Of course Caesar won't reduce his army unless Antonius disarms first, and Antonius can't disarm until the Parthians have been conquered. At least my legions here in Africa are no great burden on the taxpayer. Everyone tells me the African provinces have never been more prosperous.'

'That is generally admitted, my lord. But then you are not a blustering soldier, thinking only of the next campaign. You govern a peaceful land as though peace were destined to endure. That's just what can't happen now. Thanks to Caesar, Pompeius has quarrelled with Antonius. When they fight, probably during this coming summer, Caesar will help one against the other; and you, my lord, must decide in advance whether you will help Caesar, or Antonius, or Pompeius.'

'You need not continue, Eunomus. I see at last whither this conversation is leading. You want me to help your favourite, Pompeius, even if it means war against Caesar and Antonius. That's been your hobby-horse for a long time, as I remember. I expected that by now you would have changed your mind. You were for Pompeius because you saw him as a figurehead for Menas, and you saw Menas as leader of all the Greeks. But Menas has gone over to Caesar. As things are, doesn't that make Caesar the Greek hero?'

'Menas has not yet led his ships against Sicily, my lord. Until he does so I shall continue to doubt whether his was a real desertion; he may be playing a double game. But the point is that Pompeius rules a powerful army, besides the strongest navy in the world. Whenever he wishes, he can cut the City's food supply. If you combined with him you could wrest Italy from Caesar.'

'As leader of a Greek rising against the sway of Rome? I am not a renegade, to open a campaign by starving my own City. Anyway, I have no liking for war, and no desire to rule more than I now possess. If Caesar fights Pompeius, I shall keep out of it. Whoever wins, there will be one rogue the less in a misgoverned world. If Caesar fights Antonius, which is far more likely, I shall still keep out of it if I can; though if I can't stay neutral I suppose I must help my old leader, Antonius. What I want is another ten years of peace here in Africa. In ten years' time I shall be ready to hand over to my son, and our rule will be so firmly established that whoever then governs Rome will not dare to upset it. That's why I welcome this renewal of the Triumvirate. It takes me halfway to my goal, and keeps me within the law of the constitution. So write a polite but non-committal dispatch to Pompeius, reminding him that I shall be here, across the water from his southern harbours, for the next five years at least; and don't try to entangle me in any more of your warlike schemes. Do you understand? Now we'll treat the rest of this afternoon as an ordinary working day. Tomorrow, and for five days after, those confounded Games will be wasting all my time. Have you the latest parade-state of my legions? How many recruits have come in this spring, and have we plenty of armour to fit them out?'

'I'm sorry, my lord. Your interests are mine, and I serve you to the best of my ability. I shall plan for peace, if you desire it; and of course I agree that it must be an armed peace. The recruiting figures are most encouraging. We might venture to detach four veteran cohorts, and make them the cadre of another legion.'

Peering at the sheet of rough jottings, Lepidus rubbed his hands. He had come out to Africa with six legions, picked by Caesar as loyal Caesarians. Careful and thrifty administration had filled the military chest, and the sons of local Roman-Africans were eager to embrace a military career that would not take them out of their native province. Now he had ten legions, and his army was increasing.

That evening he supped with his family. Even on this auspicious day there were no guests, and no hired entertainers. It was a good old Roman family meal, with nothing to shock the susceptibilities of the fourteen-year-old Antonia. To amuse them, he told them all about the devious scheme of his freedman; and then Antonia told the inside story of the famous conference at

Misenum, when Achaea had been transferred from her father to Pompeius.

'And did they actually dine with the ferocious pirate-chief? Wasn't that rather imprudent?' asked Lepidus.

'Oh yes, they did, and it was, awfully,' Antonia answered. 'There was lots of eating and drinking, of course, and sailors did acrobatics in the rigging to amuse them, and father said it was all splendid fun until afterwards, when they were going ashore, Pompeius told them that during dinner his captain, that friend of Eunomus, that Menas man, had said wouldn't it be a good idea to sail away with father and Caesar just stuck on the poop. And Pompeius said, yes it would, only it was no good now he had asked because a host can't kidnap his guests, and why hadn't Menas done it without asking him and then he'd have rewarded him, and father said he was so scared he went stone-cold sober, though he couldn't help admiring young Pompeius.'

'I suppose Caesar had ships within call,' said Tertulla. 'He's not a man to trust his life to someone's word of honour. But they might have cut his throat in half a minute, before rescue could arrive. Another chance missed! Men are the clumsiest creatures!'

'Anyone can be murdered at a conference, even though his bodyguard will then cut down the murderer,' said Lepidus. 'We are all at the mercy of any man who will buy revenge with his own life. Yet we must meet in conference or the world would never know peace. I don't like young Pompeius any the better after hearing that story. He was honourable in keeping faith with his guests; but it was un-Roman to boast about it afterwards.'

'He's not a Roman, except by the accident of birth,' said young Marcus. 'I gather he's entirely Greek by upbringing, and thinks of himself as Greek.'

'You have been listening to my secretary. Eunomus is clever; sometimes I think he is too clever by half. But you must not believe everything he tells you,' said his father weightily. The conversation died, and Antonia understood that her new family were not a suitable audience for Antonian funny stories.

That night, as they lay side by side in the great marriage-bed, Junia spoke to her husband for his own good. 'That silly Eunomus has been filling you up with his clever theories about another war to make you ruler of the world. I can guess it, from the tilt of your nose. Now, Marcus, we all know there will be another war quite soon. The City can't put up with endless blackmail from those pirates in Sicily; the corn-ships must sail unmolested. If there isn't a war against Pompeius, it will be because Caesar wants to fight Antonius first. Whatever happens, there will be all manner of changes. But you must keep out of it. We have been beaten once. You were forced to flee from the City with no money, not even a clean tunic; I had to hide the boys in a miserable hovel, and go marketing dressed as a kitchen-maid. We were very lucky to end up here, safe. You rule Africa well, and the Africans like you. It's enough. Don't try for anything greater, or we may lose what we have.'

'I can take care of myself with Eunomus,' he answered indignantly. 'I like to hear him run on, that's all. For years Pompeius has been bribing him to bring me over to the side of the pirates; he can't persuade me, and the money keeps him happy. I am not deceived, I give you my word. I'm no general. My troops deserted me in the battlefield the only time I tried to fight. I won't risk that again. Those terrible fellows in Rome and Asia and Sicily may tear each other's guts out to their heart's content. I shall sit on my bench, conveniently near the arena, and when it's all over I shall honour the victor with a crown of African Olive. No wars for me. If I keep my army up to strength, and never lead it into battle, after a few years I shall be as firmly established here as Hannibal ever was. Then I would like to hand over my government to young Marcus, and myself retire to Rome to perform my duties as Pontifex Maximus.'

'I'm glad to hear it. I always knew you were sensible. It's just that all these legions, with their officers hungering all the time for greater power, are a standing temptation to any ruler. No more wars, and many happy years as Pontifex Maximus! That's all I ask for you.'

The great Games to celebrate the renewal of the Triumvirate began the next morning. They were very good Games, of an old-fashioned kind; but then in Africa it was easy to gather material. Lions were cheap and plentiful, and the garrisons towards the south were always catching black raiders, who fought lions most gallantly. In Africa every malefactor was a stout warrior. There were none of the spiritless petty thieves from the slums whose execution set such a problem to the magistrates of Rome, fellows who just ran away when you put swords in their hands. The combat between an elephant and a band of crocodiles was a failure; the beasts ignored one another, and spent their time trying to escape from the arena. But this was nearly always a disappointing exhibition; though because crocodiles were awkward creatures to transport the crowd always demanded it, as proving that the giver of the Games had taken trouble in his preparations. If no crocodiles had appeared there would have been angry barracking.

All the other turns were straightforward duels between armed men; and not too many going on at once, so that the spectators could appreciate the finer points of the fencing. Lepidus had insisted on that. In Rome ambitious young aediles were always trying to show something different, men striking at random in helms which covered their eyes, or mounted Amazons charging naked swordsmen. Such meretricious displays might win the cheers of a crowd eager for novelty; they were not Games as the ancestors had understood them. The object of this solemn religious rite was to accustom citizens to the sight of wounds and death, so that they themselves might fight more bravely in defence of the City; and to sacrifice a good number of victims for the service of the dead hero in whose honour the Games were given. These particular festivities, naturally, had been dedicated to the Divine Julius, the true founder of the Triumvirate.

As he sat in the president's box, with his family round him, the Triumvir could feel satisfied. The amphitheatre was packed with his loyal, contented, prosperous subjects; the applause from the soldiers' benches showed he was popular with his legions; the dedicatory procession had been a moving and dignified ceremonial; most remarkable and encouraging of all, everything had been paid for in advance and the provincial treasury was still solvent.

His sons watched the fencing critically, never flinching when a broadsword disembowelled a beaten man; the Games were doing them good, teaching them to survey future battlefields without unmanly dismay. The ladies also watched with interest, their behaviour impeccable except that young Antonia was rather too eager to place her bets; the Games would fortify feminine courage also, since at some future date honour might compel these ladies to stab themselves to the heart. It was just as it should be; they were interested, but showed no unhealthy excitement.

It came into his mind that here in Utica the old Roman virtues lingered, virtues that had almost vanished from the City. There was no frenzied rush for wealth, no indecent trafficking in political influence; these Africans, as solidly Popular as in the days when poor Cato fell on his sword, nine years ago, took their politics seriously, debating on liberty and the dignity of the free man. They did not share in the doles and donatives which the mob of the City grabbed so avidly, and since they never journeyed to the Forum they could not sell their votes for hard cash paid in advance. Utica was a fine place, and its townsfolk virtuous.

Perhaps he had been chosen by the gods to preserve all this from contamination, a reservoir of ancestral virtue. He would continue to govern honestly, holding to the ancient ways. He would withdraw as far as possible from the filthy struggle whose harvest was a crop of heads stuck up in the Forum. He would strengthen his army without emptying his treasury; he would allot to settlers of sound Roman blood new areas of fertile land, at present wastefully grazed by barbarian nomads; he would enforce honesty on the tax-gatherers, if by working day and night at his desk such a task might be achieved. At the end of it all his realm would not be as splendid as Caesar's Italy, as wealthy as the Asia of Antonius. But it would be self-supporting, well-armed, populous, and content. While the children of his colleagues rioted magnificently through bankrupt cities his young Marcus would be the warrior-leader of a nation of true Roman husbandmen. Presently the seat of power might move southward over the sea. It was a splendid dream, and there was nothing to prevent it coming true. During the six days of holiday which celebrated the renewal of the Triumvirate it was seldom far from his thoughts.

As soon as the holiday was ended interruptions from the outer world battered at his contentment. The leading corn-merchant of Utica sought an audience, to show him a most disturbing communication from Sextus Pompeius. The merchant was a citizen born, with the impeccably Roman name of Cornelius; but his dusky complexion, and something in the insinuating tone of his voice, suggested that his ancestors had reached Africa in the train of Queen Dido.

'My lord Triumvir,' he began deferentially, 'this province exists because you protect it. Without your fostering care our fields would become once again the pastures of Numidian cattle. You are our refuge. But we need helpers oversea also. Our wealth is in our wheat. We harvest more than we can eat. We must sell it abroad, to buy the products of the outer world.'

'I know, I know,' said Lepidus testily. 'It's the first thing any schoolboy learns about Africa. You must sell your wheat. Well, last year you sold it. What's the new obstacle?'

'Sextus Pompeius, my lord. He blocks the sea-road to Ostia.'

'And has done for the last six years,' Lepidus interrupted impatiently. 'Yet all that time your wheat has gone to the City. I haven't time to listen to oratory. This is my private office, not the town hall. Tell me, in as few words as possible, what is the matter, and what I can do to help you.'

'In two words, my lord. Last year, as for years before, we paid blackmail to Pompeius, and our ships sailed safe. That added to the price of wheat in Rome, but the Romans can afford it. This year Pompeius writes that he is at war with the City, and that no payment can open a way for our ships. If Africa is to live you must come to terms with him, or else overthrow him.'

'I see. It's serious, I grant you. But I don't want to do either of those things. Is there anywhere else you could sell your wheat?'

'There isn't,' said Cornelius, now chatting easily, eager to explain his problem to this sympathetic ruler. 'The south is desert; to the west live the Numidians. They would be glad to eat our grain, but they can't pay for it. To the east is Egypt, a land which also exports grain. We must sell to Rome. There is no other market.'

'If you don't?'

'Then I for one go bankrupt. Other shippers will go bankrupt more slowly, because they deal in other things besides grain. Then the price of wheat will fall; for one winter the poor will fill their bellies and bless you. Next year the farmers won't be able to pay their taxes, the soldiers will go unpaid until they mutiny, and over the whole province civilisation will collapse.'

'Dear me, we can't have that. I'll see what I can do. Perhaps Pompeius is just feeling greedy, and giving you a fright before he puts up his tariff. He's not exactly recognised by the Triumvirate, but I have ways of communicating with him. I shall write today, and let you know as soon as I get his answer.'

'Thank you, my lord. It's really urgent. Last year Rome was very prosperous, with Caesar starting all these new public works. The market looked most promising. So we expanded our business, and we can't wait very long for our money. Of course we would be willing to pay Pompeius a little more. It all goes on to the price of bread in Rome.'

'That's it, I expect. Just a matter of more money. Pompeius has no reason to starve the City, for he can't be hoping to conquer Italy. I shall find out what's the least he is willing to take, and you must raise it among yourselves in any way that suits you.'

When Cornelius had bowed himself out Lepidus rang the bell for Eunomus. 'What's this about Pompeius?' he said as soon as the freedman appeared. 'When he makes a move I generally hear of it before anyone else. Now Cornelius has been complaining that he threatens to blockade the whole of Italy.'

'And I, my lord, have just opened this dispatch from Caesar, asking you to aid him in the invasion of Sicily. It seems that a first-class war has broken out. We shall have to join one side or the other. We can't ignore it.'

'Perhaps we can. What does Caesar ask of me?'

'Nothing specific, just help in general terms. Any troops you can spare, and especially warships with trained crews.'

'We haven't any of those, and without them it isn't safe to

187

send troops. He can't expect help from Africa unless he lends me some of his navy as escort. Give me the dispatch. Does he say anything about sending his own ships?'

'He says Antonius has lent him warships. Look, my lord, he says it twice; once when he's describing the conference with Antonius, and again when he puts down the list of his forces ready for action. That's to remind you that two Triumvirs are in agreement, and that the vote of two binds the third.'

'Antonius won't really help him. Either the ships will never turn up, or they are ships Antonius doesn't need. What an enormous dispatch! It must be as long as the Iliad. Leave it with me. When I have read enough of it to find out what it's about I shall call you again.'

Caesar had indeed written at length, relating all the wrongs Pompeius had ever done to him, describing the comic misadventures of his conference with Antonius at Brundisium, and finally enumerating the forces he was making ready for the campaign. Lepidus read carefully the passages dealing with Antonius, and realised for the first time how near his colleagues had been to civil war. When he read that Antonius had evacuated his camp because the evil omen of a wolf howling outside the gate had dismayed his praetorians, he laughed aloud. What impudence, typical of Antonius! And what a neat way of annoying the cold-blooded young savage who was so busy in public observance of the prohibitions of the ancestral religion!

But outside the barred gates of Brundisium Caesarians and Antonians had very nearly come to open war. That clumsy provocation was also typical of Antonius. It was asking for trouble to march up to a Caesarian garrison in the company of Ahenobarbus the younger, last survivor of the murderers of the Divine Julius. This Ahenobarbus still commanded what had been the Optimate fleet. It was now merely a troublesome squadron of pirates; presumably Antonius wanted to get him into western waters, where he would be a nuisance only to Caesar. If even Antonius was making mistakes, Lepidus must walk carefully.

After further study he came to the conclusion that Antonius genuinely wished Caesar to overcome Pompeius, if it could be done cheaply and easily. There could be no doubt that one hundred and twenty Antonian warships were serving with Agrippa's fleet. That was too large a force to be detached as a blind, though perhaps Antonius, who could draw on the Egyptian navy, was glad to get an expensive burden off his payroll. He would need no ships to conquer the Parthians.

On the other hand, the naval command was still committed to

Caesar's boy-friend, young Agrippa. Menas was attached to him as naval expert. Even so, Caesar might not be in earnest.

Still undecided, Lepidus consulted Eunomus. 'I don't want to fight anybody, anywhere. But if I refuse Caesar's request he may fight *me*. Here is the dispatch, in which Caesar tells me everything. But I don't know what Pompeius is after, and I expect you do. Tell me what he hopes to get out of this unnecessary war, and I shall see my way a little clearer.'

'He hopes to overthrow Caesar, whose adoptive father destroyed Pompeius Maximus.'

'Well, that's straightforward enough. A blood-feud is a very sound reason for war. But it's absurdly optimistic. Pompeius has no support in the City, and Caesar commands all the legions of the west.'

'He doesn't hope to replace Caesar. He wants revenge. That's not so absurd. The City is growing tired of Caesar. There are always politicians who want a change of government, and if there's a really severe famine the gangs will begin to riot.'

'I think I understand. In that case I should prefer to stay neutral. I would like to see Caesar overthrown, for reasons you know very well. But I can't help a mere tyrant of Sicily against the established government of Rome. Unless he plans one day to rule the world Pompeius is useless to me as an ally.'

'Pompeius wants only Caesar's head, my lord. He is a pious son, indifferent to worldly advantage.'

'Very praiseworthy, but not practical politics. Whoever rules in Rome must eventually conquer Sicily. That reminds me. Who is to buy our grain? If Pompeius wants me to stay neutral he must make me an offer. I know that Sicily does not import grain in normal times, but he could give the excuse that he is building up a war reserve.'

'Yes, my lord. I shall see that your proposal reaches him. A very pleasant and profitable way out: stay neutral, and sell to both sides. Africa will be grateful to you.'

Junia did not see things in the same light. In her view, the easiest way to stay out of the war was to send Caesar the contingent he asked for. Her husband need not lead his troops in person; he could send three or four legions under a legate. It would be good training for the men, few of whom had seen active service; and if the war went badly for Caesar they could easily be withdrawn.

For some days Lepidus listened to conflicting advice, Eunomus in the office advocating a neutrality friendly to Pompeius, Junia at home begging him to take part in the war. In the end the question of the African grain crop decided him.

Pompeius would not buy it. He was as short of cash as any other leader of greedy mercenaries. He made vague mention of the benefits of victorious Sicily could confer on Africa, and vague threats of what his invincible navy would do to faint-hearted neutrals; but it was easy to read between the lines of his letters that he was in fact desperately hard-pressed.

Caesar was willing to buy the harvest as it lay in the granaries, and himself to transport it from Utica to Rome; though he did not promise to move it until after the conquest of Sicily. He offered a very small price, in postdated drafts on Roman bankers; but it was enough to stave off insolvency. Rather than see his whole province go bankrupt, Lepidus closed with the offer.

The province was safe until next year. But it followed that the army of Africa must promise to intervene in Sicily. The promise need not be fulfilled at once, for until the seas had been cleared of enemies invasion was impossible. Lepidus, as he pointed out in his letters to Rome, had no fleet of his own; the great navy which Agrippa was training for Caesar must open the way. To this Caesar agreed. But he suggested that Africa needed a navy for home defence; he would send a few ships from his Campanian squadrons, with boat-builders and technical experts of every kind. This promised to be a long war. If everyone worked hard in the winter, by the following year there would be a useful African fleet.

So during that summer the province was not only solvent but booming, as in every harbour the shipwrights worked on new war galleys and transports. Ultimately some taxpayer somewhere would have to pay for them; though whether he would be a plundered Sicilian or a starving Roman was still unsettled. In the meantime Punic financiers, elusive men who lived in the hills and were never at home when the tax-gatherer called, advanced money to buy timber and pay wages.

The army was on a war footing. A drive for recruits brought in men enough to make up sixteen weak legions; and if many of these recruits could not show their certificates of citizenship when they enrolled, they had them, suitably backdated and bearing every sign of age, as soon as they had been fitted out with sword and shield. This was a task at which Eunomus and Crastinus could work in harmony, each appreciating the expertise of the other; Crastinus knew what military documents should look like, and Eunomus enjoyed the fabrication.

Auxiliary horse presented no problem. There were always more Numidians anxious to enlist than any army could pay. When the time came to sail, Lepidus would take into service as many of them as he could afford.

It soon became clear that he would not be sailing this year. Nothing could be done until Caesar had destroyed the Sicilian fleet, and for the present the Sicilian fleet was getting the best of it. Pompeian squadrons cruised off the shores of Italy, and the Caesarians dared not put out from harbour.

During the hottest part of the summer news of a great battle seeped into Utica, in the uncertain manner of all rumours of war. Lepidus had been down to the dockyard, inspecting a newly completed three-banker. The carpenters could have made it a merchantman, or for that matter a barge or a water-mill, and he would have been none the wiser; he had the vaguest idea of what a three-banker should look like. But it was generally understood that craftsmen worked better when the commanding officer visited them, and he was conscientious in doing his duty. As his litter lurched back up the steep shadeless street he noticed that the dockside crowd was discussing some exciting rumour.

These slaves and lowly workmen talked an African language among themselves; he could not understand what they told one another with such unusual noontide animation. Then he saw Cornelius in the entry of a warehouse, and recalled that the grain-dealer was reputed to understand every tongue spoken on the continent. He beckoned, and asked him the news.

'I wish I knew myself,' was the answer. 'Perhaps, lord Triumvir, you don't understand how these things get about in a seaport. Men arrive quietly, men who don't report to the harbour officials. If you spot a stranger he always explains that he's a shipwrecked mariner, just arrived floating on an oar. These men talk, and their talk is soon all over the town. Unfortunately they are ignorant men, smugglers or pirates or fugitives from justice. They don't know themselves the import of their news, and it's impossible to disentangle when you have heard it. At present the whole dockyard is excited because Neptune has manifested himself at Messana in Sicily. Most of these men worship Neptune, naturally. Well, Neptune's home is the sea, and every so often I sacrifice to him by throwing something overboard from one of my ships. If he wants to visit dry land Messana is a handy place for him. But what it all means I don't know.'

'Obviously it means that a great battle has been fought at sea, and that the victor attributes his good fortune to the favour of Neptune,' said Lepidus angrily, annoyed by the suspicion that Cornelius was trifling with him.

'Of course it means that, lord Triumvir. I didn't think that part of it worth mentioning. But we still don't know which side won. Messana now. . . . It's the headquarters of Pompeius. But

191

if Caesar had won it's where he would land, to complete the conquest of Sicily. So it fits either of them.'

The merchant suddenly darted up a side street; he came back holding a naked waif by the slack of his canvas breechclout. 'This man was shouting in Berber that five days ago he saw the son of Neptune, clad in sea-green robes, pouring libations from a golden goblet. He must have come straight from Messana. There's no point in asking him why he left or how he got here. Even under torture he couldn't tell you the truth, because he has never told anyone the truth in all his evil life. But he himself believes that bit about the libation. He was trying to persuade idlers to buy him drinks and listen to his story. So Pompeius won the battle. I wonder where they fought?'

'Ah yes, Pompeius won the battle. This is grave news. I must consult with my advisers,' said Lepidus, completely bewildered, but determined to hold on to his dignity in the presence of this un-Roman Cornelius. He signalled to his bearers to move on, and made them carry him right inside the cool dark hall of the governor's palace.

It was dinner-time, and Junia was waiting to greet him. While a servant poured water over his hands he told his wife the whole story as he had heard it; and wound up by asking whether he ought to punish Cornelius for making game of his ruler.

'Oh no,' Junia answered. 'It was crystal-clear to Cornelius. Even I see how he got there, as soon as I think it over. Poor Cornelius! He has a very quick mind, and since he never learned rhetoric he just blurts out his conclusion, without knowing himself how it came to him. Let me see, it goes something like this: In Messana there have been celebrations in honour of Neptune. In other words, someone gave thanks for a great victory at sea. But Messana is Pompeius's headquarters, so either he sailed home in triumph or Caesar arrived to take over Sicily. But then this smuggler actually saw a man who called himself the son of Neptune, who dressed in Neptune's sea-green robe, who carried on, in short, like one of those silly Greek tyrants who are always pretending to be equal to the gods. Now does that kind of behaviour fit young Caesar? He talks too much about his deified father, who is no more a real god than he was his real father. But Caesar is just as likely to prance naked before the people of Messana as to sacrifice in public in such a get-up. Therefore the man who poured the libation was Pompeius. Therefore Pompeius won the battle. Now do you understand?'

'When you explain I understand everything. It's just that these African minds don't work in the Roman way. So Pompeius has won a great victory. That means no invasion this year. I suppose Caesar will write. When I have his account of the affair I shall know better what I must do.'

Caesar's account was some time on the way, for the pirates were now supreme in the Sicilian sea. When it arrived it put the whole blame on the weather. After an indecisive engagement a storm had sprung up, to shatter Agrippa's squadrons. 'But the storm didn't sink any Pompeian ships, though they were riding the same waves,' Eunomus interpolated, as he read the dispatch. 'All the same, Caesar may be telling the truth. A storm that would be too much for Campanian longshoreman, Agrippa's sailors, wouldn't bother the Cilician pirates who serve Pompeius.'

'Hallo, my lord, just listen to this,' he continued, still reading the dispatch. 'One competent observer, with first-hand knowledge of both navies, thinks Caesar can't win. Menas has deserted all over again, and gone back to his fellow-pirates. Caesar says he did it out of pique, annoyed because he was second-in-command under Agrippa. Certainly that's enough to annoy any experienced pirate, to be under the orders of a twenty-five-year-old landlubber. Of course he was annoyed. But pirates don't desert from the winning side just because they are disappointed of promotion. Menas believes Pompeius can't lose, and he ought to know. That's really very lucky for us. By next spring our fleet will be ready for action. When it sails to Sicily it can help carry the Pompeians to the invasion of Italy.'

'Now will you read what my fellow-Triumvir has written, in his own words, without commentary,' said Lepidus sternly. 'You are only a Greek, and you have been a slave. This time, therefore, I forgive the slight you have put upon my honour.' He looked so grim that Eunomus took fright, and read quietly to the end. He found it wearing to keep constantly in mind that this foolish man, with his slow and undecided mind, happened to possess powers of life and death over every inhabitant of Utica.

From his dispatch, it seemed that Caesar was not yet defeated. Nothing more could be done this summer, and of course in winter no ships could put to sea. But next spring a bigger and better fleet would sail from the Campanian coast, and at the first opportunity the Italian legions would invade Sicily. Caesar ended by begging for co-operation from his colleague. Rome, the City herself, was in great straits, blockaded by pirates. Every true Roman must rally to her assistance.

'And that's just what I'll do,' cried Lepidus, thumping the table. 'Write to Caesar at once. Tell him the African fleet will be ready by next spring, and that it will be at his orders. Offer him an expeditionary force of sixteen legions. I shall lead it myself, subject to his general direction of the war. Make it clear and definite, but be soldierly and brief.'

'And for your own information, Eunomus,' he continued, 'what you write in that letter is the absolute literal truth. I know you have your private contacts with Pompeius. You may write to him once more, to tell him that henceforth your patron is his mortal foe. That must be your last communication with the enemy. If I catch you sending him further news I shall have you killed. You are not a citizen. If I choose, I can crucify you.'

That evening he expounded his new policy to Junia.

'What finally decided me was the news that Menas has gone back to his fellow-pirates. Menas against Pompeius was just a squabble over the blackmail they levy on ships sailing to Ostia; but Menas and Pompeius against Caesar is a war between a foreign foe and our dear City. I don't care who rules in the Capitol; if the Optimates seize power I shall not change my plans. Greeks are trying to starve the Roman People. All Romans must rally to the fatherland.'

'You can't do anything else, I see that,' his wife answered doubtfully. 'But I wish you were not taking all your army, and leading it yourself. You are not a general, my dear husband. Utica and all Africa prosper under your government. Couldn't you send a few legions under a legate? Suppose you are defeated and killed? That would mean the end of all you have built up here.'

'Yes, my dear, that's sound and cautious. If I send Caesar only reinforcements I hazard nothing valuable. But what do I stand to gain? After the conquest of Sicily Caesar will still be a lukewarm colleague, and more powerful than before. But if I come myself with all my force, if I prove myself his true friend and ally, our formal collaboration may develop into a genuine partnership. I have never aspired to be sole ruler of the world. I'm not good enough, and I admit it. Marcus Antonius gave me my chance, and I followed where he led; until Lucius and Fulvia turned on me, and I saw that I had no place among the Antonians. Now Marcus himself has run to seed, parading about those oriental cities dressed up as Mars or Bacchus, perhaps as Cupid if the fancy should take him. He has lost standing among respectable Romans, and yet those eastern Greeks will never accept him as one of themselves. In a year or two Caesar will fight him, and then I shall support Caesar. With Antonius out of the way there will be only two of us at the summit, and no reason why we should not remain colleagues. That's as far as I want to go. But go I must, forward or back. Unless I prove myself Caesar's ally Caesar will one day take from me even this backwater of a province.'

'Very well, if you say so. What a pity there never seems to be a stage in political life where you can sit back and close your career. In the old days a man could be Consul, perhaps Consul more than once, and then live at home with his family until he died of old age. Perhaps my dear Caesar was wrong to cross the Rubicon. Since then, every statesman must go on until he kills himself after defeat, or until his friends grow tired of him and kill him.'

'Perhaps. The world grows worse every year. All the same, as I said just now, I am not chasing supreme power. I may yet be the only statesman of this generation to die peacefully of old age.'

'That's hopeful. But I still think it is running an unnecessary risk to lead your whole army in person. There are so many veteran commanders, and you are not among them.'

'That would be sound advice if I were trying to compete with Antonius. I'm not. In Sicily there will be no veteran commanders. Caesar and his friend Agrippa are young and untried. Pompeius may be a good sailor, unless his freedmen do it all in his name; but he has never commanded in a campaign on land. We start equal, all beginners. At least I have long experience as a quartermaster and trainer of troops. I wouldn't be frightened by the enemy's reputation, as I was frightened of Marcus Antonius while he marched to the Argenteus. I may find that I am a very good general. There is no way to know until I fight a battle.'

'If you are set on going there's no more to be said. After you have won a great victory Caesar must treat you as an equal, so I suppose the risk is worth taking.'

'And this time my soldiers will fight for me. All our troubles began when those three cohorts changed sides at the Capua gate. In a way I can't blame them. Then there was really nothing to fight about; I still don't know what Lucius and Fulvia were after. This time we are the army of Rome, fighting to free our City from famine; and our enemies are foreigners, pirates or Sicilian Greeks. The men will be as keen as if they marched against Hannibal.'

'That is a point in our favour. It makes it all the more important that you should really co-operate with Caesar. I hope you will allow him to plan the campaign. He speaks for the Senate and People af Rome; he's young, but there's nothing derogatory in taking his orders.'

'Caesar is the leader of our party, now that Antonius won't

195

leave the east. I can do nothing without his fleet. He will plan the invasion, and I shall comply with his instructions. That is, at least until we are safely landed in Sicily.'

*The lady Clodia grumbled to her steward, going over the household accounts. 'The cost of living is beyond all bounds, and I can't get ostrich-feathers for any money at all. I've a good mind to leave Rome, to get right away from young Caesar and his misfortunes. The east sounds amusing, but I can't compete with Queen Cleopatra; I would look like a poor relation. Then there's Sicily, of course. But even the Optimate refugees can't stomach the airs of young Sextus; they are coming home as fast as they can. What about Utica? Perhaps Junia would not receive me at first, but once I was good friends with Tertulla; and they say the place is just like Rome nowadays.'*

*'Not Utica this year, my lady, I beg you. The Triumvir Lepidus is gathering his army to fight Pompeius, and Africa is most unsettled.'*

*'Lepidus gathering an army? How ridiculous, at his age. Oh well, until he's been beaten Africa will be dangerous. I shall stay in Rome after all, at least until the next civil war reaches the gates.'*

# XI

## VICTORY
### 36 B.C.

It was the first day of July, the month named in honour of the
Divine Julius, a day propitious for Caesarians; though rather
late in the season to open a campaign. When the Imperator embarked the transports were already clear of the harbour, hoisting
sail and shipping their oars in the open sea; but a squadron of
fast war-galleys manoeuvred smartly in the confined waters of
the port, and marines stood at the salute as the Triumvir's
banner fluttered on the flagship. This banner bore a red lion
against the yellow background of the African desert. Lepidus had
been born under the sign of Leo, and he used this badge, instead
of the ancestral elephant of the Aemilii, to match the Capricorn
of young Caesar and the Bull which had been the device of the
Divine Julius. It was reported that the Pompeian rebels fought
under the golden trident of Neptune. Since every legion in every
Roman army used Jupiter's Eagle as its main standard, these
lesser flags, displayed by each cohort, were needed as identifica-
tion.

Trumpets pealed, at the quayside the lady Junia scattered
incense on a little altar, the crowd cheered, and the Pontifex
Maximus poured a libation. Then the flutes on each quarter-deck
shrilled to mark time for the rowers, and the great invasion of
Sicily was under way. As his flagship passed the end of the mole
Lepidus went down to his cabin, to get rid of the ornamental
corselet which bathed his whole body in sweat.

On a war-galley there was only one cabin. It was revoltingly
hot and stuffy, too near the waterline for portholes; and filled
with the reek of sweating galley-slaves, whose benches, just beyond the leather curtain that served as door, were on the same
level. Lepidus must keep his bedding there, for dignity's sake.
But he knew that if he remained below he would be sea-sick. As
soon as he had changed into a light tunic he went up to breathe
the fresh air of the poop.

It was early, and not yet unbearably hot. Since the poop was

197

the only free space on a crowded galley he found his senior officers already there. As much to pass the time as for any other reason, they were soon conferring in an impromptu council of war.

The sailing-master, Cleonas, began it, coming up to his commander to complain of the weather. 'I told you before, sir. We ought to wait a few days. That sky looks unsettled. There may be no wind now, but I'll eat my sea-boots if we don't get a norther tomorrow.'

Gallus, the senior legate, answered brusquely. 'I never yet met a sailor who was satisfied with the weather. It's always "Wait a few days. Today it looks fine, but a storm may be coming". If we waited for sailors to give the word, no army would ever cross the sea.'

'Cleonas understands the weather, and we don't,' said Lepidus mildly. 'He is right to warn us, though we are right to disregard his warning. Menas and his pirates are more dangerous to us than any storm, and by sailing on the appointed day we make sure they will be too busy to attack us.'

'I suppose they are a danger,' the legate murmured doubtfully. 'I've never fought at sea, but it's hard to grasp what a handful of Greek pirates can do to twelve legions of well-trained Roman foot.'

'They can do anything they choose, if they catch us,' Cleonas said angrily. 'They don't fight with swords, they fight with the beaks of their ships. It's a crazy idea, to arrange the date of sailing months in advance, without making allowance for the weather. Perhaps Pompeius could do it, if he is really the son of Neptune. But Caesar knows nothing of the sea.'

'No one knows anything of the sea,' Gallus answered with equal heat, 'and that goes for sailing-masters as well as Imperators. You creep from headland to headland, running for shelter whenever you see a cloud. If you happen to blunder into the enemy you all charge at random, like a pack of Gallic barbarians, instead of fighting in due order like civilised men. Your silly wargalleys are so crowded with rowers that you can't carry drinking-water for more than six days, and no one can sleep properly unless the ship is drawn up on shore. We'd be better off on decent merchant ships, with water-tight cabins and a smell of grain and leather; instead of curling up on the open deck of this galley, suffocated by the stink of the rowing-slaves.'

Cleonas shrugged his shoulders. 'I'm doing what I can, Imperator. I wasn't allowed to pick the date of sailing, I'm not allowed to choose our course, and here is a sample of the cargo

I am expected to carry. I'll get you to Lilybaeum, or I shall drown with you. That's all I can promise.'

'I didn't choose these things either,' said Lepidus. 'You mustn't mind Gallus. He crossed the Rhine with the Divine Julius, and the Rubicon too. He may not know much about sea-faring, but we shall all be proud of him when we get ashore. You understand why we must sail today, and why we must make for the western corner of Sicily? It's because today that dangerous pirate fleet will be busy at the other end of the island. At this very moment Agrippa will be engaging Menas, while Caesar ferries his army over the straits. The plan is ambitious, but it can't fail if we all keep faith. Perhaps the weather will harm us; we know the enemy can't.'

'Then we are luckier than our allies,' said Cleonas, mollified by his commander's courtesy. 'The gale that's breeding will come from the north, and the mountains of Sicily will shelter us. If three great fleets are manoeuvring north of the island, there won't be room in Neptune's locker for all the sailors drowned today.'

'That's upsetting. Agrippa's men can fight, but in bad weather the pirates are the better sailors,' Lepidus said gloomily. 'I hope Caesar carries out his invasion as promised. Otherwise this army alone will have to take on all the rebels.'

'I'm not worrying over that,' said Gallus. 'We have twelve legions, first-class material, well trained and well equipped. If that freedman of yours was telling the truth when he gave us the Pompeian order of battle the Sicilians have only ten legions in all. Pompeius must know we are going to land in the west, because in a harbour town like Utica you can never keep a military secret. But he must hold back a reserve to defend his main base, Messana. We ought to have a superiority of two to one; and our men are Romans, not Sicilian Greeks.'

'Yes, two to one is comforting odds,' admitted Lepidus. 'But I'm afraid it's not quite so simple as that. We must capture a harbour as soon as we land, or see our fleet sail back to Africa, leaving us cut off. If they hold the strong walls of Lilybaeum we may have trouble turning them out.'

'There are ways into Lilybaeum. I've never been there, but there's no secret about those walls. Our map must be reasonably accurate, even if Pompeius has dug more earthworks. With your permission, Imperator, I'll get the map on deck, and go over the plan of assault once again.'

As they knelt to move leaden blocks about the map Lepidus wished he had Eunomus leaning over his shoulder to whisper his fluent advice. Leaving his secretary behind had been a wrench.

But no one else could be trusted to bring on the four other legions when the empty transports returned to Utica.

That night the sea got up, and by dawn all the ships in the fleet were wallowing most uncomfortably. But as yet there was no wind, and the air was clear; the squadrons could keep formation. Africa was a line of cloud on the southern horizon, and Cape Lilybaeum was not yet in sight to the north. If Menas disregarded the threat from Italy, or divided his fleet, this was where the Sicilian pirates might be expected to pounce. At every masthead a look-out scanned the waves, but until midday no enemy appeared.

Lepidus was munching biscuit and bacon in the cabin (*you* could not call it 'dining'), when the look-out shouted the warning for 'enemy in sight'. In a moment he was on deck, barefoot and wearing only his tunic; but by the time Crastinus arrived with his sword the alarm was over. Those were certainly pirate galleys in the offing, sleek craft very low in the water and much handier than the standard Roman warship. They were painted light blue, without ornament, so as to be hard to discern in the distance; and each flew the blue flag, bearing a golden trident, of Sextus Pompeius the son of Neptune. But there seemed to be only six of them, and they kept well away from the invading fleet. Cleonas said they were signalling with flags to another ship, a mere blob on the northern horizon. They were only scouts, keeping in touch with the invasion.

'If the weather holds we'll get to land without fighting,' said the sailing-master. 'But there's a storm raging now, not far to the north; and if it reaches us we shall be in for a troublesome day. For all their low freeboard, those pirates are handier in a seaway than our broad-bottomed transports; and their crews never feel sea-sick. If we lose formation they will be in among us like wolves in a sheepfold. Oh well, it might be worse. Here I am, on the flagship, with a cargo of heroes to guard me. The Pompeians will go for the store-ships; they want booty, not fighting. Unless they know we are carrying the pay-chest they won't attack the best-armed warship in the fleet.'

He seemed prepared to go on talking for ever, without pausing for an answer. Lepidus left him, to walk along the raised gangway between the rowing-benches until he stood in the prow. If you did not mind getting wet, he realised, this was the most comfortable place in a war-galley. There was a pleasant smell of spray, instead of the sickening stench of unwashed, sweating rowers; and the play of foam round the beak gave an impression of purposeful speed which was lacking on the poop. Best of all, the prow was a narrow platform; there was no room for officers to come and grumble in his ear. In this crowded ship here was the only place where he could be alone.

He had not been alone since he left Utica, yesterday morning. For the first time since setting out on this voyage he had the leisure and the solitude to think. Very soon he was going to command a great army in his first action. If Cleonas was right he might be fighting in an hour or two; certainly he would fight before tomorrow's sunset. Was he frightened at the prospect?

He was nervous, but that was not quite the same thing. He was within a few days of his fifty-fourth birthday, and he could not expect to enjoy the careless equanimity of youth. For a year he had trained with his army; he knew his men were fit and disciplined, and he was accustomed to giving orders without hesitation to large bodies of troops. He had firmly fixed in his mind's eye the most difficult technical accomplishment of the veteran commander; he could look at a stretch of empty ground and calculate without conscious effort exactly how much of it a cohort would fill. He sweated slightly when he remembered the occasion last autumn when he had ordered two legions to defile across one narrow footbridge; that sort of mix-up would not happen again.

He was a Roman of noble birth who for more than thirty years had practised the normal drill of the parade ground. The conquerors of Hannibal and Antiochus had been men of the same stamp. The Roman army was a machine, complicated yet certain in its operation. Such a machine worked all the better if it was managed in the routine fashion of the ancestors; a commander of eccentric genius might puzzle the troops.

There was no need for him to lead a charge in person, unless the battle was going very badly. Crastinus had impressed on him that the proper station for an Imperator was behind the third line of reserves. Centurions fought in the front rank, in a crisis a military tribune might wave his sword and run ahead to encourage his followers; but the supreme commander must stay at the back, where he could take in the whole fight at a glance. That was comforting. Nowadays fast movement in full armour made his heart thump unpleasantly, and he was afraid of tripping head over heels if he ran over rough ground.

It meant that if the army was beaten and the soldiers ran away he would be left behind, to die gallantly where he stood. That was on the whole an advantage. Even to save his life he could not lead a disgraceful retreat. Was he afraid of death? Carefully he examined the question.

He was afraid of pain. Who isn't? Even in imagination the prospect of a wound on the elbow, or in the groin, made him wince; he had seen ugly things in the amphitheatre. But death, unconsciousness merging into extinction, ought not to worry a noble patrician with two fine sons to carry on his line. Perhaps he was not actually afraid; he was only reluctant to terminate his career. Life was very good just now, with his family united and Africa flourishing under an enlightened government. Besides, he was not yet a grandfather. Antonia seemed a sickly girl, for all the notorious potency of her sire. He would be wronging his family if he risked his life before Marcus had achieved paternity.

He stumped back to the poop. He was worrying himself about nothing. Of course life was good, and he was reluctant to leave it. He was not going to leave it for many years to come.

Darkness fell on a heaving sea, but even a landsman could tell that the storm was diminishing. The wind has dropped, and the rowers were getting to the end of their strength; the whole fleet huddled round the lights of the flagship, hardly moving except to the roll of the waves. There was no hurry. They were very near Sicily, and for landing on a hostile shore they needed daylight.

What with sea-sickness and nervous anticipation, Lepidus could not sleep. When they roused him at first light he felt like nothing on earth; but a cup of strong wine settled his stomach, and as they reached the shelter of the land the rolling lessened. By sunrise he was standing on the poop, fully armed, ready to lead even the most desperate attack that would get his feet back on dry land.

High ground to the eastward left the shore in shadow; but the sun caught the rock of Lilybaeum, the ancient Carthaginian fortress which had cost so many Roman lives. The officers, clustering by the rail, gazed at those steep walls crowning the hilltop; but Cleonas, whose eyes never seemed to leave the sky except to glance at the waves, was the first to notice something significant.

'The town's yours, Imperator,' he called cheerfully. 'The Pompeians are not even trying to hold it. Look, the harbour's empty; not so much as a fishing-boat. There may be a garrison in the citadel; that's the business of your flatfooted legionaries. But the waterfront is clear. We can anchor within the mole, and perhaps draw up some of the galleys on the strand. My sailors will sleep tonight. I might put even the rowing-slaves ashore, if I can find a safe lock-up for them.'

'There's a banner on the citadel,' Gallus put in. 'Yes, it's the trident. But the sailing-master is right, they are not holding the lower town. Pompeius himself will be farther east, near Messana, to face Caesar. I wonder who commands for him in the west? If he knows his job he will hold back his main force, to attack while we are in the middle of disembarking. And yet I don't know. There may be no Pompeian army within miles of us. Lilybaeum is our obvious target, but they can't be *certain* we will land here. Their field-force may be miles inland, waiting until the invasion has fully developed. I see signal-flags going on the citadel. That looks as though their high command is a good distance away. What shall we do, Imperator? Keep our legions on shipboard until the cavalry have done a bit of scouting? Or take a chance and get ashore as quick as possible?'

Lepidus answered without hesitation. His orders might be wrong, but it was better to be wrong with decision than to dither before coming to the right conclusion. Besides, in warfare you could never prove that any particular move was wrong, however disastrous its result.

'Get the legions disembarked as soon as possible. They can have the plunder of the town, as a foretaste of what this campaign will bring them. Don't let them make an orgy of it. Have them drawn up in column of route on the eastern road in an hour or so. The cavalry will disembark at the same time, and patrol to the east and south. The praetorian cohort remains under my personal command. As soon as I am on shore I shall myself storm that citadel.'

There, it was out, and now he could not alter it. Perhaps he was foolish to risk his life at the outset of the campaign. Long ago a stray roof-tile killed Pyrrhus of Epirus in just such a pointless skirmish; that would be a squalid end for Aemilius Lepidus the Triumvir. But while leading a charge he could not *look* foolish. Any Roman of good birth could attack a fortified wall; but the disembarkation of twelve legions and five thousand horse was a complicated affair which he could not manage. His legates had been trained for that sort of thing; let them get on with it. But in his excitement he was forgetting an essential preliminary.

'Before fighting begins the gods must be served,' he said gravely. 'As Pontifex Maximus and proconsul I shall sacrifice on behalf of the whole army. There isn't room on this poop to cut up an ox; but I must have some living creature, to inspect its liver. A goose will do. And I shall want three big goblets of wine, for the libations.'

His praetorian cohort crowded the deck to see their commander call down the favour of Heaven on this righteous war, undertaken to relieve Rome from famine. Veiling his head, the Pontifex intoned the ritual invocation as only a patrician, trained from childhood to the task, could pronounce those awesome words. He was unfamiliar with the normal appearance of a fresh goose-liver, but it would be absurd to suppose the omens anything but favourable. He declared them so, and then went on to pour the libations: to Neptune, because they were on his sea; to Jupiter, ruler of gods and men; to Mars, progenitor of the Roman race who had given his children dominion over all the world. Every soldier was familiar with the routine of sacrifice before battle; but to many of these veterans it was a new experience to hear it performed devoutly, by an eloquent speaker who believed in the value of his own ritual. Everyone felt braver when at last the Pontifex Maximus put on his helmet and became once more the Imperator.

A phaselus, a fast scouting-boat, nuzzled alongside the quay, and a patrol of skirmishers dashed ashore. Five banks of oars churned up the water as the great flagship crept stern-first to the harbourside. Then the gangway was down from poop to dry land, and the praetorian cohort disembarked, ready for action.

The praetorians were the bodyguard of the commander; their cohort, double the normal size, was kept at full strength even when the legions were below establishment. As Lepidus set himself to trudge up the steep deserted street to the main gate of the citadel a full six hundred men fell behind him. Picked veterans, they marched composedly, without cheering or excitement. By evening a few of them would be dead, but this was not an especially hazardous operation.

Lepidus walked stoutly uphill, setting a pace that Crastinus could barely equal, burdened as he was with his great shield. All eyes were fixed on the closed gates of the citadel; perhaps the fortress was empty, despite its flaunting banner. Not a head showed above the wall. In shuttered houses a few women screamed and a child was yelling at the top of its voice; Lilybaeum had not been emptied of its civilian inhabitants. So far they had nothing serious to lament; praetorians did not break ranks to plunder while there was an enemy to be fought. The pillage, the rapine, the enslavement of free Sicilians, would come later in the day.

Lepidus was visited by a wild fancy that he was making this assault single-handed; for the women's wailing drowned the thud of marching feet, and his followers kept silence. So strong was the absurd idea that he ventured a glance over his shoulder. It was a lucky move, perhaps inspired by some favouring god; for thus he did not duck like a raw recruit when the first flight of stones came from the engines of the citadel.

The swift, silent, determined advance had surprised the defenders, and most of their missiles flew over the heads of the approaching column. Lepidus heard and felt the wind of one sharp-edged chunk of granite, but it barely stirred the horsehair of his helmet-plume. Crastinus clucked his tongue in reproof of such sloppy marksmanship; then he spoke, through gasps of labouring breath.

'Now then, Imperator, this is far enough. Draw your sword, if you like, and tap the gate with it. That's supposed to encourage the men, though I don't know why. But remember your age. Leave the scaling-ladders to youngsters of forty.'

It did not occur to Lepidus to rebuke his orderly for insolence. They were all in this exciting adventure together, and he felt himself the loving comrade of the hairiest ruffian in the ranks. As he walked he drew his sword. He was looking at the iron-studded gate only a few yards away, seeking a good place to strike it, when suddenly his view was cut off; all he could see was the inside of a shield.

Metal clanged all round him, and Crastinus swore urgently. 'Your sword is in your hand, Imperator. Cut off the head of this javelin. You can reach it easily, and I can't. They must be using those soft-nosed bastards. The point is twisted under the shield-rim, and I can't get it free.' The javelin hung quivering from the edge of the shield, whose leather centre had been ploughed by other missiles.

As Lepidus swung up his sword for the blow a large hand caught him by the back of his corselet. 'Bend over, Imperator,' a voice muttered in his ear, 'or my javelin will carry away those fancy plumes. Now, boys, altogether. Don't give them time to wind their machines.' Again the air was filled with the soft whisper of javelins.

Everywhere men were pushing, and he must stagger to keep his feet. But there was the gate, quite close; and he had not yet struck it with his sword. He knew how that should be done; he must turn his back on the foe, and wave his men on with a sweeping gesture of the left arm. The eager praetorians did not wait for his signal. As he reached the gate the end of a scaling-ladder caught him in the belly; he was swept aside by an urgent rush, and when he looked again the face of the gate was hidden by the wagging rumps of climbing soldiers.

'Halt, Imperator, Stay here,' shouted Crastinus. 'They will hand you the keys of Lilybaeum on a silver platter, if they know where to find you. But you mustn't go through the gate while that confetti is still flying about.'

A javelin, hurtling vertically from the top of the gate-tower, struck sparks from the pavement at his feet.

The orderly pressed on his commander's shoulder, forcing

him to a squatting position. Breathless and shaken after his dash up the steep hill, Lepidus felt his heart hammering with excitement and fatigue. He remained where he was, his back against the stone jamb of the gate, his knees drawn up to his chin. All he could see were the muddy greaves of Crastinus, as the orderly held the great shield over him.

Within the citadel there were confused noises, cries of triumph and cries of mortal anguish. In a surprisingly short time the gate was opened from within. In the entry stood a centurion, his helmet pushed back from his forehead, a bloody sword dangling carelessly from his fingers.

'Imperator, deign to enter your fortress of Lilybaeum,' he said with a smile. 'It's not a bad place in its way. But we can't find the pay-chest, and the garrison drank all their wine, to get up their courage.'

Lying within the gate was a wounded Sicilian. As the Imperator passed he plucked at a dagger. 'Now then, you,' said the centurion, 'the fighting's over. We'll bury you properly, never fear.' Casually he flicked his sword through the other's neckbone, and then stooped to wipe his blade on the mop of sweat-matted hair.

Victorious soldiers pressed round their commander. Then, visibly, the centurion remembered the responsibilities of his rank. Standing to attention, he glared fiercely. 'Lepidus Imperator,' he cried, dipping his sword in salute. Apparently without moving their feet, his men shook themselves into triple rank. 'Lepidus Imperator,' the salute rang out, as the lion banner was hoisted in place of the trident.

Limping happily down the hill, Lepidus felt his heart glow in his breast. 'It's easy,' he thought, 'and not even very frightening once you have begun. I was too busy to be afraid. Crastinus was frightened, though, or so I think. That only proves that I behaved with remarkable courage. I have displayed exemplary dash and determination. That citadel is notoriously one of the strongest fortresses in Sicily. I went straight at it, and overran it in half an hour. There are experienced veteran commanders who would have dug lines of circumvallation, and installed siege-engines, and sat there for three months before venturing an assault. Marcus Antonius could not have been more dashing. Caesar will be impressed when he hears of it. It was fun, but I mustn't do it too often. My life is precious, to Rome and to my family. I shall let the army win the next few battles without me. Only if things go badly will I lead another charge.'

As he rode at the head of his great army towards the eastern uplands he was not quite so happy. It was a pity that Lilybaeum had gone up in flames, so that in after years he would never be able to find the narrow street he had traversed at the head of the storming column. The sale of the captives had been another depressing experience. Until today these wretched men and women had been free burgesses, some of them Roman citizens; they had done nothing worse than pay taxes to Pompeius, and cower in their homes while the armies swept by. He would have preferred to spare them. But when he suggested it every senior officer had clamoured that the idea was quite impracticable. They had found very little treasure in the town, and the troops must not be cheated of their rightful plunder.

He must keep the allegiance of his troops. In this kind of war that was more important than anything else. He would have liked to win fame as the liberator of Sicily; but even if he was remembered by the islanders as a barbarous invader from Africa that was better than to see his army desert to the enemy, as once his army had deserted to Lucius Antonius. Thinking of that terrible betrayal, he rode out of ravaged Lilybaeum with unmoved countenance.

Two days later the Imperator, weary and saddlesore, dismounted with relief at the farmhouse where he was to spend the night. The heat, trying even to troops newly arrived from Africa, was made worse by the stinking haze of smoke which veiled the sunset; in every valley farms and villages were burning, and very often the ricks and granaries as well. The sound military reason for this destruction had been carefully explained to him; a column of smoke informed the main body that their scouts had reached that particular point, and gave notice that no enemy was near. He wished that his men could have used some other method of signalling.

This particular farmhouse stood untouched, only because it had been guarded all day by a detachment of praetorians. At least the Imperator's bodyguard could be trusted to do their work efficiently. Spits turned in the kitchen and a sentry kept watch over half a dozen big clay jars of wine; there was even a bath of sorts, though the room was clouded with wood smoke and steam. Veterans might be skillful at plundering a friendly countryside, but they knew how to keep their commander in a good temper.

Lepidus longed for a bath, to take the stiffness out of thighs unused to riding. But a group of legates and military tribunes was waiting in the courtyard, and he knew that he must discuss the events of the day and issue orders for tomorrow before he could get out of his armour. The agents who kept watch on the morale of his troops had passed on the envious whisper that he was getting too old for active service, an obvious titbit of slander which of course his enemies were spreading through the ranks; he must not do anything to give currency to that spiteful lie. Though he felt old and tired and hungry he straightened his back, greeted his officers with a bright artificial smile, and swung out of the saddle with an energetic sweep of his right leg that made all his weary bones tingle.

'Good evening, gentlemen. What news of the enemy? Do we fight tomorrow?'

'We've picked up quite a bit of news, sir, and important news too,' Gallus answered, speaking for his subordinates. 'Not much concerning the enemy, but something about our allies. It's so important that I think we ought to discuss it in private. If you approve, sir, the maps are spread in the dining-room, and I have rounded up stools enough for all of us.'

'Very well, in the dining-room. With shutters closed and sentries posted, I suppose. Though it seems a pity to go indoors in this weather, just when we can hope for a cool evening breeze.'

Seeing Gallus frown at this unmilitary hankering after fresh air, Lepidus recalled that soldiers never thought of the weather except in terms of mudbound roads and flooded rivers; they hated the open sky, under which so much of their lives was passed, and even in the height of summer liked to make themselves snug in draught-proof cubby-holes. Of course they would want to confer in the dining-room, close to the baking-oven for choice.

As soon as all were seated in the stuffy room Gallus began to expound the large map of Sicily which covered the table. 'I'll begin by showing the position as it is tonight, Imperator. That's for the benefit of tribunes who must return to their commands. They must know where the rest of our forces are camped, or we shall have false alarms all night. Now look, gentlemen. These lead blocks represent our twelve legions. Here we are, nicely closed up, heading across the plateau from Lilybaeum towards Messana. It's very hot, the men have had a tiring day, and there's no enemy in touch with us; so for tonight we shall not concentrate and entrench our camp. Tomorrow, unless the Imperator orders otherwise, we shall march by *this* road to about *this* point. Tomorrow evening we must dig in properly, with palisade and double ditch; for by then hostile legions will be within a day's march of us. Any questions?'

He paused and continued.

'These grains of sand scattered to the east represent our cavalry patrols. They have covered the ground thoroughly, and we can be sure they have left no ambushes undiscovered. All this patch is in our hands, with no enemy present. But late this afternoon our cavalry met some Pompeian horsemen; they were just about to charge when the strangers made it plain they were deserters, not hostile scouts. They are Greek mercenaries, long unpaid, who complain that Pompeius thinks only of his sailors. Had they been Roman citizens I would have held them on a charge of rebellion against the Triumvirs; but Greek mercenaries are entitled to follow any leader for pay. So I merely questioned them and set them free. They tell me there is a Pompeian army of eight or more legions about *here*, where I place this apple. The legate in command is Plinius Rufus, who had a sound military training under old Pompeius Maximus. His men are more or less Roman soldiers, hereditary followers of Pompeius or the last remnant of the Optimates. They are diluted with Sicilian Greeks, and with brigands and runaway slaves from all over the world. But on the whole it's a Roman army, and will fight like one. They are short of cavalry, but they have plenty of food. They may offer battle in a strong position. It's more likely they will retire before us, waiting to attack when we are entangled in the siege of some fortress. Is that clear?

'Pompeius himself is with his fleet, at Messana. He is more of a sailor than a soldier, and unlikely to take command of his army. Messana itself is garrisoned, of course, and so is Panormus in the south; but in general the towns have been left empty of soldiers. They have walls, and the townsfolk can man them if they decide to resist. They are more likely to offer tribute to any army that marches against them. There it is. That is a pretty complete appreciation of the whole theatre of war in this island.' As he sat down Gallus preened himself, like a rhetorician at the end of a lecture.

'But that's not nearly complete,' cried Lepidus. 'You have forgotten the other invasions. On the 1st of July, the day we sailed from Utica, two fleets sailed from Campania. One was led by Caesar in person, the other by his legate Agrippa. Agrippa was to seek out the hostile fleet and destroy it in battle, while Caesar ferried his army over the straits. By now Pompeius may very well be drowned, and Caesar entrenched before Messana. What had the deserters to say about these other armies?'

Gallus bared his teeth in a sardonic grin. For a plain blunt soldier he had brought off a very neat oratorical trick.

'The deserters knew all about those other expeditions. Nevertheless, such is the fame of the army of Africa, they decided to forsake the victorious Eagles of Pempeius. I said I had given a complete picture of the war in Sicily, and I told the truth. Neither of these invasions reached the island. Agrippa found the pirate fleet, as he intended; but in the battle that followed he was completely defeated, and his surviving ships fled back to Campania. Caesar tried to slip across the straits while Agrippa kept the pirates busy. A storm caught his transports, probably the storm that worried our sailing-master. Most of his men were drowned, and the rest felt very frightened. They also fled back to Italy. Caesar and Agrippa are out of the game. You, Imperator, must conquer Sicily alone.'

Only one answer was possible.

'Then that's what we'll do, gentlemen,' said Lepidus at once. 'We shall march against this Plinius, and press him back to Messana. Sooner or later Pompeius must stand and fight, on dry land with the good old Roman broadsword. When he meets us shield to shield his dirty little Greek freedmen won't save him. This army alone has the task of delivering our dear City from famine. An inspiring thought; make it known to the troops.'

'The trouble is,' put in a junior legate, 'that Pompeius still has a navy. When we march into Messana we shall be just in time to see him and all his followers disappearing over the horizon; and, what is really terrible, taking their plunder with them.'

'Messana will always be worth plundering,' Gallus said soothingly. 'They may sail off by the hundred, but thousands must remain behind. If they take the gold and silver, they will leave the wine and corn.'

'If that fleet sails eastward then the grain-ships can reach Ostia and we have done what we left Africa to do,' said Lepidus. 'But in a few days our transports will be nearing Sicily with the four remaining legions. What will become of them if the Pompeians break into the convoy?'

'Soldiering is a dangerous trade,' answered Gallus with a shrug. 'It's astonishing how many soldiers get killed, in spite of all our precautions. We have twelve legions ashore. They ought to be enough.'

'If four legions go to the bottom it will be one of the greatest disasters since Cannae,' Lepidus went on. 'Worst of all, my secretary is crossing with that convoy.'

'If your Eunomus is with the convoy one ship at least will come safely to land,' said Gallus rudely. 'If ever a man was born to be crucified it's that freedman.'

Gallus proved right, though for the next few days Lepidus rode with his army in a very worried frame of mind. On the sixth day Eunomus, weary and travel-stained, rode into the fortified camp where twelve legions lay among the Sicilian uplands. The Imperator had given orders that he was to be brought to headquarters the moment he arrived, whatever the hour of the day or night. It was now shortly after sunset, and he found his patron finishing a solitary supper.

'So you crossed safely after all!' Lepidus cried in delight.

'I crossed, my lord, but not safely,' the freedman answered. 'There were four legions on the transports, and we took it for granted the pirates would be out of action. When we sighted a strange squadron we thought they must be Agrippa's scouts. They turned out to be Pompeians. I've never seen such a shambles in my life. They rammed ship after ship until their beaks couldn't stand any more collisions. They didn't dare board, because of our legionaries. So they came up astern, and broke off the steering oars without actually ramming us. That went on all day, until in the evening the wind got up. Then they drew off, and in the dark we got away from them. In the end the Eagles of two legions got to Lilybaeum, though with heavy loss. The other two legions turned back for Utica. I don't know whether they reached harbour, or whether the pirates drowned them on the following day.'

'That's bad enough, but I had been expecting worse. I now command fourteen legions, and Plinius can bring only eight against me. I suppose you know the rest of the news, that Caesar has failed us? I had a letter from him yesterday, sent round by Sardinia to avoid the pirate cruisers. He says he will try again in a month's time, but he has taken a terrible beating. He must build more ships, and impress crews. And there's no reason to suppose his second attempt will have any better luck.'

Eunomus stared at the Imperator. He had known his patron for many years, but this was a Lepidus he had never met. He was sunburned and fit, and his corselet had bitten calluses into his shoulders. He spoke without hesitation instead of waiting for advice; and he had taken the news of his loss calmly and bravely, instead of tearing his hair and calling for help. The freedman rearranged his ideas; he would not betray his patron to Pompeius, or jockey him into a position where he must line up with the pirates against Caesar. This confident Imperator could destroy the pirate realm with his own forces. Then there would be Caesar, now licking his wounds in Italy; but that bridge could be crossed when they came to it.

'You don't need reinforcements, my lord,' he said cheerfully. 'Your army sees itself as capable of conquering the world. That's what matters, what the troops themselves think of their chances. When you have cleaned up this island we must lay plans for the future. Rome depends on grain from oversea. You have been sending it from Africa; the other source of supply is Sicily. When you rule both lands Caesar, and the Senate, must listen respectfully, or see their people go hungry.'

'I cannot starve my own City; no Aemilius could do such a thing. But in general you are right. Similar ideas had occurred to me. I have no ambition to rule the world single-handed, but in my position there is no sitting still. I must either rise or fall.' Lepidus seemed quite sure he would rise.

Then Eunomus delivered the message with which Junia had charged him, and for a time they spoke of domestic matters; until the officer of the day came in with the final reports from the outposts, and Gallus called to discuss orders for tomorrow.

Sitting on a stool in the corner, Eunomus got out his tablets. In Utica he had been well known to senior officers, and without question he slipped back into his old position of confidential secretary.

The orders for tomorrow were not difficult to draft, though everyone grumbled about the slowness of their victorious advance. Plinius Rufus was the hindrance who held them to a snail's pace. His army was as inferior in quality as in numbers; in particular he had no cavalry who could face the Numidians. But he was a sound, unimaginative, drill-book tactician; and eight legions, even of second-rate troops, were not a force that could be ignored. His men were well disciplined and willing to use the spade. He could not be tempted to come out of his fortified camp, even when weak detachments of foragers were displayed at the foot of his entrenchments. Gallus considered it too risky to attack an unbeaten army behind the stakes of its hilltop palisade; so the only way to dislodge him was by wearisome flank marches. Tomorrow the African legions must toil up more of these steep roadless crests, and perhaps threaten to dig trenches of their own round the Sicilian camp; in the end Plinius would withdraw, behind a well-organised rearguard. A few miles to the eastward they would run into him, dug in again.

'I suppose he is dragging out the campaign until Caesar tries again, and loses another fleet,' said the legate. 'It's odd that Pompeius doesn't invade Italy; there must still be a few Optimates in Campania. Evidently he is determined to keep to the defensive. That's it. He will beat Caesar once more, and then open negotiations. But if when that time comes we are outside the walls of Messana he must treat with us, not with Caesar. Perhaps there is no real hurry. While Pompeius controls the sea we can't starve Messana, and it would take years to breach its walls. Why fight, and get a lot of good men killed, when marching and countermarching will get us there in the end, without bloodshed?'

'I agree,' said the Imperator, with the abrupt decision that was a new feature of his character. 'But we must keep up the pressure. Next month Caesar intends to try again. By then we must be close outside Messana. Meanwhile we might be doing something with the towns in the south of the island. From Syracuse right over to Agrigentum they obey Pompeius, but they are defended only by local volunteers. They must be just about ready to come over to the winning side. My secretary, who is experienced in that kind of thing, will get in touch with the town councils. If by any chance Agrippa should happen to beat Menas, we don't want a Caesarian squadron taking over the south coast.'

'That's right, sir,' Gallus answered. 'When we negotiate what will matter is the area we control, not the amount of fighting we have done. Plinius is very hard to move, and he blocks the road to Messana; but our horse can ride round his southern flank to menace the harbours facing Africa. They will see reason as soon as we threaten to burn their suburbs.'

'That is decided, then,' said Lepidus. 'Send out a strong body of horse tomorrow. Don't let them plunder unless the Sicilians defy them. You can make them respect private property if you try hard enough. They are only ignorant Numidians, too barbarous to say they will mutiny unless they are permitted to pillage.'

Gallus frowned at the thrust. But this Imperator was becoming more than a figurehead. He had been something of a hero ever since the assault on Lilybaeum. He was losing his dependence on professional advice; it was necessary, nowadays, to swallow an occasional rebuke.

'Very good, sir,' he said formally. 'The cavalry will start at sunrise. And I will see that our legionairies stop this wasteful burning of farms. We can say with truth that most of Sicily is on our side, and that they may not behave as though they were ravaging a hostile country.'

Before he went to sleep Lepidus permitted himself the indulgence of a little boasting, with the discreet Eunomus for audience.

'For the last thirty years I have commanded legions. Now, as you may have noticed, I am beginning to command legates as well. I led a gallant charge, you know, as soon as we landed. That gives me standing with the veterans. If I ordered my praetorians to arrest Gallus, it's quite likely they would obey me. Of course I don't propose to do anything of the sort, but it's nice to believe I could if I wanted to.'

'You are a very great man, my lord. In Utica you had rank, wealth, a large army, and extensive dominions. Now you have in addition the prestige of victory. In the whole world you used to be third. The conqueror of Sextus Pompeius will be something more.'

'Perhaps Caesar will be drowned at his next try. But a patriotic Roman must not indulge these dreams. What matters is to defeat Pompeius and deliver the City from famine.'

The future semed as vague, as promising, as exciting, as it had been in the old days, when the Divine Julius sought the help of a young praetor.

*'Have you heard the latest saying about Caesar?' said the lady Clodia to her maid. 'He's got so tired of always being beaten that now he plays dice with himself, left hand against right. That way, some part of him is bound to win.'*

*'Poor Caesar. It is awful, isn't it, my lady? But they say the great Imperator Lepidus will soon bring bread to Rome.'*

*'Oh, him,' answered the lady Clodia with a sniff.*

# XII

## MESSANA
### 36 B.C.

In a full month the campaign had moved only sixty miles to the east. Plinius Rufus and his eight legions still barred the way to Messana, while Lepidus, with fourteen legions, strove to bring him to battle. To the troops on both sides the war had become a routine; Sicilians digging trenches and hanging on to them until they were almost surrounded, Africans marching endlessly over the roadless uplands. Hardly a man had been killed in battle, but heat and forced marches cost both armies many stragglers. When Lepidus dismounted at the usual farmhouse he was doing what he seemed to have been doing ever since he could remember.

This evening there were more officers than usual at head-quarters, and even the cooks looked interested. Of course, they would be expecting news from that other seat of war, incredibly remote though it was only fifty miles away; news of Caesar's second attempt at seaborne invasion. 'Has the message come?' he called to his scoutmaster.

'No, sir, no news yet. But the message will reach us without delay. At every beach fresh horses are waiting, and in case of disaster I have laid signal fires on the cliffs.'

'What do you mean, in case of disaster?' asked the Imperator sharply.

'Well, sir, they might never send a message. They might all be killed, or driven back to Italy. Local fishermen say that if ships are destroyed in the straits wreckage will be thrown up all along the northern shore. If our look-outs don't hear from Caesar, and see wreckage instead, they will assume that the fleet has been sunk. They will light their beacons, and we shall know that we have been left to win this war by ourselves.' The officer smiled proudly, glad that he had been lucky enough to report his in-genious plan to the Imperator in person.

'It's as well to be ready for anything,' said Lepidus condes-cendingly. 'But Caesar has eighteen legions. I can't imagine a force that size being so utterly destroyed that no messenger survives to bring news of disaster.'

'I should add, sir,' the scoutmaster continued, detaining his commander, 'that the enemy has been receiving signals all day. There must be a chain of beacons between Messana and their camp. They were hoisting flags from midday onwards, and now that the light has gone they are continuing with flashes from a lamp. We can't read their code, of course; it's impossible to break a Greek code. But that shows that something important must be happening outside Messana.'

'That's very good work. I shall bear it in mind,' said the Imperator as he hastened into the little room where at last he might recline on a soft couch. His thigh-muscles had become accustomed to riding, but to his bottom practice only made the saddle seem harder.

He preferred to sup alone, treasuring this solitude in which he might think over the events of the day. So long as he was on horseback he was on parade, and must be cheerful, energetic, and affable; apprehensive soldiers were always trying to read omens in the visage of their commander. Lying on his couch, with the supper table at his elbow, he might groan, or curse aloud, without spreading alarm and despondency. In the beginning Gallus had been annoyed, as though it were the right of the senior legate to share the inmost thoughts of his commander; now Gallus had been taught his place, and if he was still disgruntled he did not show it in public. There was only one commander of the army of Africa, and his name was Aemilius Lepidus.

This evening he found it impossible to think consecutively, impossible even to eat with enjoyment; though he was very hungry. He could do nothing but shift restlessly from one buttock to the other, waiting for news.

Events which might decide the future of the world for ages to come were happening less than fifty miles away, and he was as ignorant of them as if they were taking place on the far side of the moon. His scoutmaster worked hard, and on the whole skilfully, but very little information came through the enemy lines. After the opening days of the campaign there had been no more deserters. Eunomus had broken with his correspondents in Messana and Syracuse, obeying the stringent orders of his patron. That freedman could find out anything, by using his own methods; but it was impossible to stop him playing the double agent if he communicated with the enemy at all. When Greek towns in the south gave in their allegiance, as happened nearly every day, the town councillors reported recent movements of Pompeian troops, which Lepidus knew already, thanks to the excellent patrolwork of his Numidian cavalry. But unarmed Greek civilians could tell nothing of the plans of the enemy command in guarded Messana. He was completely in the dark.

All he knew, and that by slow roundabout letters from Italy, was that on the 15th of the month Caesar intended to try another double invasion; his fleet would offer battle to the pirates while the army was ferried over the narrow strait. And this was the evening of the 15th.

It was strange that Pompeius had made no proposals for peace; he must be very confident. Suppose he destroyed young Caesar, what would be his next move? An invasion of Italy, to restore the Optimates? But after the great proscription there were hardly enough Optimates alive to form a Senate, let alone an army. It was more likely that, after killing a Triumvir, he would himself seek the vacant place. He might offer to co-operate with Antonius and Lepidus. But Antonius had lost interest in Roman affairs; he craved the adulation those degenerate Asiatics lavished on their rulers. Such a Triumvirate would in fact be a partnership between Sextus and Lepidus. . . . The idea promised a possibility of good government. Sextus must naturally be the junior partner. If he advanced such a plan he would not find Lepidus implacable.

What was that? A bang on the door? Here was Gallus bursting in, too excited to salute. 'Forgive me for disturbing you, sir, but you must know this without delay. Beacons are blazing for seven miles along the coast. The whole shore must be littered with wreckage. The Italian fleet has gone to the bottom!'

'Very well. I must come out and see for myself. That leaves this army to face Pompeius alone, but we are capable of conquering him. Do you think Plinius knows? Is his camp acknowledging signals from Messana?'

As he peered through the door the centurion of the guard pushed forward a dismounted trooper. 'Courier from the outlying picket, Imperator. He says his news is urgent, and that he must tell it to you in person.'

'Sir, Plinius is preparing to move,' said the cavalryman. 'We noticed his camp-fires burning more brightly than usual, and suspected he might be building them up to leave them burning behind him. When we patrolled forward we found his pickets had withdrawn. Two of our men peered right through his palisade, and saw his legionaries mustering in full armour, with shields uncovered. They are marching off to fight somewhere, sir, but hardly to attack this camp. They are keeping reasonably quiet, but not as quiet as if they were going to try a night surprise.'

'Then some of Caesar's men got ashore. Not very many, or Plinius would not march out to attack them. Enough to give Pompeius a cheap tactical success, not enough to be a threat to him,' said Lepidus, as much surprised as his hearers that this sudden flash of military insight should have come to him.

'Sound the Assembly,' he continued. 'We march at once. This opportunity must not be wasted. With Plinius blocking every defile we have taken a month to gain sixty miles. Now that he moves of his own accord we must make ground to the eastward.'

'Would it be more prudent to wait for daylight?' asked Gallus doubtfully. 'If we follow Plinius in the dark we may blunder into an ambush.'

'We shan't delay, even for an eclipse or an earthquake,' Lepidus answered in high excitement. 'Whatever the weather, we march as soon as the men are mustered. And we shall not follow Plinius. We shall move north to the coast road, and then make straight for Messana.'

'But, Imperator, we are now in touch with the enemy. It is tactically unsound to allow him to march off into the blue. Besides, if we follow on his heels we might overwhelm his rear while he is engaged with the Caesarians.'

'You can't teach me tactics, legate. I have been an Imperator these fifteen years, and I can plan a march as well as the next man. Why should I risk a battle to help the Caesarians, when they have not once done anything to help me? Why should I risk an ambush for the sake of crushing Plinius, when already he dares not meet me in the open field? Don't you see, gentlemen? The way lies open to Messana. Once that is ours the pirate fleet will sail away to plunder in some other sea; and the Pompeian army must either disperse, or, better still, enlist under my Eagles. If we move at once we may win all Sicily without a battle. Send for my horse. Come with me, all of you. I want to see the vanguard under arms in half an hour, and the last of the baggage loaded before midnight.'

He was amazed at his own military qualities. The whole plan had appeared in his mind as soon as he heard that Plinius was on the move. Why, he was a great general, after all! You never know how much you can do until you try. The Divine Julius had shown no soldierly qualities until at the age of forty-two he undertook the government of Gaul; Aemilius Lepidus planned his first campaign at the age of fifty-four. But the spur of action had shown him to be worthy of his ancestors. While Crastinus was still packing him into his corselet his charger arrived; with straps and buckles flapping he scrambled into the saddle, and set off at a brisk gallop to the camp.

His staff followed more sedately, first stuffing their uneaten supper into wallets and saddle-bags. When an Imperator gets these fancies into his head there is no point in arguing. The old boy might even have guessed right, for once in his life; any student of recent politics must recognise that the Aemilii Lepidi had more than their fair share of the favour of the gods.

The troops took fire from the excitement of their leader. Hard marching, heat, the labour of foraging in the wake of well-handled Pompeian rearguards, had made this war unusually exhausting; now, after a month of stalemate, one forced march would lead them to victory. Good old grandpa Lepidus! At Lilybaeum he had shown himself brave as a fighting-cock, for all that he fell over his own feet when he tried to charge. Perhaps there was something in the old buffer, in spite of appearances. He for one, at any rate, was quite sure they had out-guessed the Pompeians. Get armed and fall in! The first cohort on the road will be first into the treasury at Messana! Before midnight the legions were stumbling urgently behind an old gentleman who bounced up and down with impatience in the padded saddle of his war-horse.

Thirty-six hours later long stony miles had drained the excitement from every heart. They had seen the smashed timbers of Caesarian warships, grinding against the northern cliffs; the allies from Italy had failed them again, and they must conquer a horde of ferocious pirates by their own efforts. The walls of Messana looked very strong. So long as the Pompeian fleet was free to import supplies from oversea investment would be a waste of time. There was no way in but by bloody assault. How many attackers would be lying in the breach when that enticing treasury gave up its riches?

Worst of all, they could recognise, crowning a hill two miles to the south, the familiar Eagles of Plinius. His camp still held eight legions, and there was no evidence that they had been weakened by the casualties of a pitched battle. Though their general's inspiration had gained them valuable ground, all the bloodshed of the campaign still lay before them.

Lepidus felt as nonplussed as the meanest of his soldiers. The siege of a fortified town offered even greater opportunities to an inspired commander than a pitched battle in the open field. He knew exactly what he ought to be doing; it was laid down in all the books on tactics. He should examine the wall with the keen eye of the born soldier. Somewhere there would be a weak spot, which the defenders, blinded by custom, could not see; a badly sited tower offering dead ground for the emplacement of scaling-ladders; an unnoticed crack in the curtain-wall; a forgotten postern; a drain; an aqueduct. Hannibal had spent his life spotting these things, and so had the great Scipio.

But if he approached the wall he came within range of Pompeian javelins; then all he could see was the inside of the shield Crastinus held before him. Anyway, every stretch of wall looked alike to him. He himself could not escalade it, or knock it down with any kind of engine he had ever seen; and he could not imagine how someone else could do these things for him.

Perhaps the troops were encouraged when their commander braved the darts of the enemy. A display of daring might be good for their morale and would certainly be good for his own reputation. Conscientiously he continued his inspection of the defences, trying to recall, from the distant year when he had served as curule aedile, the stains which showed that a length of masonry was in a bad condition. He thought he could recall what they looked like; if his memory was correct this wall was in very good repair from end to end.

Once the sun had set there was obviously no point in remaining so close to the foe. He trudged stolidly back to his army. His staff were waiting for him, and as soon as he reached them he gave his orders crisply and decisively, just as though he knew what ought to be done.

'Our camp will lie here; not more than half a mile from the town, facing the north-western angle of the walls. There's a beach not far away. We can communicate with Caesar, if he has ships capable of putting to sea. Plinius may join with the garrison of Messana in a surprise assault, so our camp must be very strongly fortified. We shall draw our supplies from the west. After a day or two we shall get to know these walls, and then we can decide where to build our engines. In the meantime we shall do nothing rash. Now post a strong covering party and get on with entrenching the camp.'

That was enough to set forty thousand men to work. It was amazingly easy to command an army. The only difficult part was telling them what they ought to be doing.

As soon as his quarters were prepared he disarmed and lay down in the steam of an inefficient bath. It was astonishing that these Greeks, in general so clever with their hands, could never get the hang of a real Roman bath. But anything warm would take some of the stiffness out of his bones, overtaxed by a day and a half in the saddle. As usual, the bath stimulated his mind. He felt a longing for company, especially intelligent company; he sent a servant to fetch Eunomus.

The secretary was in a bad temper; at first he would do nothing more than answer direct questions. The forced march had been much more trying to him than to his lord; he had been furnished with a most uncomfortable mule, and a Greek freedman was less hardened to riding than a Roman general. But his real grievance was that since he had reached Sicily he had not been allowed to meddle in politics. Here was a fascinating civil war, in which allies who disliked one another fought against an unprincipled rascal who at any moment might desert his own standard; and Eunomus was forbidden to use his carefully prepared underground channels of communication.

At last his patron seemed to be relenting. It was too much to expect him to countermand his own direct order, but evidently he was hungry for news of the Pompeian camp. After his first questions had been answered briefly, almost curtly, he began to grumble at large.

'It's absurd that I should be groping in the dark like this, especially when my Numidian horse can patrol wherever they like. I don't even know for certain what happened in that naval battle. Caesar lost a lot of ships, for I have seen their wreckage; but the Pompeians may have lost even more. In fact it's possible that Caesar won the battle; though I can't imagine Agrippa beating Menas unless he had a tidal wave to help him. For all I know, on the other hand, Caesar may have been drowned; or Pompeius may be in the middle of making peace with him. I lead a magnificent army, and my men are devoted to my person. But it seems hazardous to risk their lives in a desperate assault when I don't know how I stand in the politics of the City. I wish I had a reliable account of the sea-fight, and in particular reliable news of Caesar. A man who could tell me everything that has passed since Plinius began to receive those signals would get a muleload of silver, and no questions asked.'

'May I hold you to that, my lord?' asked Eunomus eagerly. 'I know you don't like it when I communicate with the enemy, and of course I understand your reasons. It would be wrong if even the appearance of treason could be suspected in one so near your person. I don't want to communicate with the enemy now, or at least to remain in communication with him. But it so happens that I could get in touch with a respectable merchant now resident in Messana. He is a citizen of Ephesus and a cousin of mine. I know how to send word to him. He could be here in your quarters by dawn, and by midday on the road to Utica with any reward you are gracious enough to give him. He will be glad to get out of a besieged town; he is essentially a man of peace. But he is well informed on public affairs. He would know what has happened in Messana, and in all the region that still obeys Pompeius. After he has told his news he goes away to your loyal

Africa, and no one is scandalised.'

'H'm, I suppose you are after your share of the silver,' Lepidus said grudgingly.

'My lord, I am your devoted follower. To put it on the lowest level, one mule-load of silver would not tempt me. If I wanted one I could steal it tonight, and be out of reach by daybreak. I am a man of the world, and I have my contacts everywhere. But as your confidential secretary I am better off than even the wealthiest fugitive from justice. I don't take *bribes*. Respectable men give me *presents* quite openly.'

'That's true. No mule could carry as much money as sticks to your fingers in the ordinary course of a month's business. Anyway, I choose to think you are faithful. I rather fancy myself as a judge of character, and I don't see you deserting an Imperator and Triumvir while he is successful.'

Eunomus stretched his lips into a perfunctory smile. One day he would be revenged on this pompous barbarian; but in the meantime this business would move more quickly when he had admitted that self-interest was his only guide.

'Agathon may keep the whole reward, my lord. He will need it, for he will have to leave his stock-in-trade behind in Messana. But if he gets to Utica with a nest-egg he will quickly be rich again, and I shall have gained a useful friend in Africa. Shall I send for him tonight? I shall need a pass to show to our own pickets, but after that I can easily get a message into the town.'

'Very well. Bring out your spy. But make it clear that he isn't going back again. He may sell me the Pompeian order of battle, I won't have him selling Pompeius a plan of my camp.'

Lepidus dismissed the secretary. You had to talk to these freedmen in a way they could understand; no use treating them as though they were Roman citizens.

It was not yet dawn when he was awakened to interview Eunomus and his chosen agent. Agathon was a fawning elderly Greek, at once flabby and slim, the kind of man Lepidus disliked on sight. He determined to strike the right note at the outset.

'What's your line of business, my man? Or rather, what was it, before you took to the trade of betraying your ruler?'

'Dancing, noble Triumvir, or rather the training of dancers. It's a great shame I had to leave my stock in Messana. My most promising boy had his operation only two days ago; I hope the foreman can manage the dressings. And there were three clever little girls, only half trained, but with talent. But there! When the town is sacked the whole stock will be pulled to bits anyway. You know what soldiers are, my lord. A great pity. I had been

222

buying very well lately. It's always the way in wartime. Parents sell, rather than see their children starve.'

'Enough of that. I don't want to learn your business. Tell me about the sea-fight, and what happened after.'

'Quite so, noble Triumvir. Well, let me see. Perhaps the most important news is that Caesar is missing, believed killed; but I expect you would like me to tell you everything, from the beginning.'

Eunomus gasped with excitement. 'Caesar dead! And Antonius in Syria! My lord, you have only to make peace with Pompeius to become ruler of the world!'

'Don't talk treason,' said Lepidus sharply. 'And don't interrupt. I want to hear everything, from the beginning.'

'Well, the sea-fight now,' Agathon took a deep breath and began to relate a story he had evidently prepared. 'That was the day before yesterday; or rather three days ago, for now it's getting on for dawn. Two separate fleets sailed from Italy to attack us. The warships made for Messana, while a convoy of transports nosed into the narrows. Pompeius also divided his fleet. While he delayed the transports his admirals attacked the galleys. Towards evening Pompeius joined Menas, and the united fleet was more than a match for Agrippa. The Caesarians were checked, though they did not lose many ships. Agrippa put back to Italy, but he still has a navy. All this happened somewhere off Mylae, the rocks where dozens of sea-battles have been fought in the past. It's the obvious place to meet an invasion coming from Italy. The citizens of Messana could see what went on, and the victory of the son of Neptune gave them great encouragement.'

Agathon paused, and when he spoke again it was in the tone of one revealing a secret.

'What became of the other invasion is not generally known. Our ruler issued a proclamation to tell us that the whole Roman army, every man of it, had been drowned in the straits. That does not tally with my information. I like to know what goes on, and I make it my business to find out. The Roman transports suffered heavy loss; but when Pompeius sailed away to fight Agrippa the leading squadron got through. Three legions scrambled ashore before Pompeius could get back from Mylae to chase the others away. At this very moment three Caesarian legions lie near Tauromenium, on the far side of the lava-fields below Etna. They have no transport, no baggage, and very little food; but they have fortified their camp and they will make a fight of it. After he had dealt with Agrippa our son of Neptune led his fleet against them, and Plinius attacked them on the land side. Yet the

223

Caesarians held firm, and there they are. Only three legions, under strength; but veterans of Philippi.'

'That's most important,' said Eunomus, 'especially if Pompeius is trying to keep it secret. You are sure of it?'

'Absolutely certain. Of course Pompeius is afraid of them, or he would not put out official lies about having killed them all. When a ruler starts publishing lying proclamations it's time for a careful businessman to move away.'

'Is that what decided you?' asked Lepidus. 'So far, by your account, the Pompeians appear to be winning. Why are you so certain that Messana will be sacked?'

'Because it is a rich town, and treasure from all over the island has been stored in it for safety,' answered Agathon, too engrossed in his narrative to offer the usual titles of respect. 'Those Caesarians will take a lot of stopping, and they must be hungry for plunder. But even if they are beaten it's quite likely the pirates will sack their own town, and then sail away. Pompeius may win this time, but in the end Rome must rule Sicily. I can smell a sack in the air.'

'I see,' said Lepidus doubtfully. 'That's what comes of hiring pirates to defend you. But so far you have not mentioned Caesar. Why did you say at the beginning that he is missing, believed killed?'

'Because his own men don't know where he is, my lord. Only a few hours ago a servant of mine slipped into the Caesarian camp. I have friends there, of course. The servant was noticed, and taken before Cornificius, the legate in command. The legate asked him for news of Caesar, and presently let him go. In this kind of war everybody uses informers, and the legate was glad to send back a friendly spy into Messana. My man will return to him, of course, with the latest Pompeian news. It's a trade like another; dangerous but well paid.'

'I suppose Caesar's ship was sunk in the battle,' Lepidus muttered to himself. 'Drowning – an undignified, un-Roman death. A man of good birth should never fight except on land.'

'No, my lord, it wasn't quite like that,' said the merchant. 'Caesar was seen alive after the sea-fight. As I told you, only three legions got ashore. Presently Caesar joined them, because his ship was leaking. Then, while they were fighting off the combined assault of Pompeius and Plinius, he left them, hoping to find a boat to take him back to Italy. That was nearly two days ago, and no one has seen him since.'

'Ah, it's likely he killed himself,' said Lepidus. 'Nowadays these young men lose heart very easily. Look at Cassius. His side was doing quite well really, and might have won if he had stuck to his post. Instead he got his orderly to kill him, for fear he might be taken prisoner. My wife's sister's husband he was, so I know all about it. Though I don't know why I should be discussing it now, in this company,' he ended with a frown. He was sleepy, and that had made him forget the dignity proper to a Triumvir.

'Such a great lord as Caesar may well have killed himself rather than admit defeat,' said Agathon humbly. 'Or he may have been drowned on the way back to Italy.'

'But he may turn up smiling tomorrow. We don't know,' said Eunomus.

'That's right. We don't know,' Lepidus agreed hastily. 'We mustn't do anything rash. Well, I think that's all for tonight. Eunomus, see your agent through the picket-line, and make sure he has the promised reward. My good man, I am grateful to you. I hope that in Utica you will prosper.'

'Under your government honest business must prosper, my lord. Please remember me, if you should happen to want a few young dancers to amuse your leisure.' Agathon bowed himself out, and made haste to travel westward with his silver. A lot of history was going to be made round Messana; he could feel it coming. History is always bad for business.

By morning the army of Africa was snugly entrenched. The camp blocked the western road from Messana, but the foremost pickets remained out of range of the walls, and no attempt was made to emplace siege-engines. In this obscure situation the wisest policy was to wait.

The Imperator rode round his forward positions, to give his troops a chance to recognise and cheer their leader; as far as possible he did this every day. Then he returned to his quarters and disarmed. He was tired after the exertion of the forced march, and he needed rest before the council of war arranged for midday.

But Eunomus, full of plans, would not leave his lord in peace. If young Caesar was really out of the game the assets which had made him a great man could be distributed afresh. The legates who rule Italy in his name would be seeking a new lord, and in practice they could choose only between Lepidus and Antonius. Yet three was the proper number for the rulers of the world; two equal colleagues would mean civil war at once, and a single tyrant would be assassinated. If Pompeius were made Triumvir that would bring peace to the west and conciliate the remnant of the Optimates; and he would be junior to Lepidus, who must rise from third place to second. Most important of all, the party was without a leader. The Caesarians had followed that boy because he was heir to the Divine Julius; they must still follow someone. The mob might prefer Antonius the rake, but every man of property and position would think first of Aemilius Lepidus, the mature aristocrat who had been Master of the Horse to the Dictator nearly twenty years ago.

The party had ruled since the crossing of the Rubicon. The leader of the party held more power than the commander of any number of legions; for every legionary, except the pirate-bands who followed Pompeius, was a Caesarian even before he was a soldier. Could Antonius, in his luxurious exile, prevail in an election against the veteran Lepidus, present in the Forum?

Eunomus poured these schemes into the ear of his tired lord. He wanted to send envoys to Pompeius, to bribe Menas to change sides again, to make a truce with Plinius and then break it by a sudden surprise attack. If they could not raise enough ready cash to bribe every commander in the theatre of war, he proposed that they should leave Messana untaken and at once invade Italy. The Forum must be crammed with leaderless Caesarians. They would acclaim the first eminent Caesarian who appeared at the head of a few cohorts and delivered a rousing speech.

As the ascending sun filled the hut with the breathless heat of August Lepidus panted petulantly on his couch. He would not be hurried. He was too tired and too hot to decide anything. His secretary must go right away and not bother him. By midday the Triumvir was asleep, ignorant whether he was now the second greatest man in the world or still merely the third.

When his officers arrived for the council he sat on the edge of his couch, clad only in his nightshirt. He saw smiles, and guessed he had reminded them of the famous occasion when he had paraded in his nightshirt to find that Antonius had stolen an army from under him; but it was too late to send for his armour. With all the dignity he could muster he called the meeting to order, and commanded Gallus to report on the situation.

It was impossible to get a firm opinion out of anybody. Rumours must be already running through the army, and every subordinate would be thinking first of his own career. But nobody wanted to fight, that presently became obvious. Nothing was sure about a battle, except that good Caesarians would be killed; it was not even certain that tomorrow Pompeius would be an enemy. Gallus reported that Plinius lay quiet in his well-fortified camp. The Pompeians also were waiting for the situation to clear.

The council had just decided unanimously against breaking ground for an investment of Messana, when there was a disturbance outside the hut. A sentry challenged, and the guard turned out in alarm; confused scuffling ended in the rhythmic clash of the general salute. The centurion of the guard pushed his head through the door, calling breathlessly: 'Sir, here's a strange officer. He doesn't know the password. But he's all alone. He insists on coming in.' Then another voice shouted: 'Of course I shall come in. Don't you know me? I am Caesar's chief legate.' A young man entered.

He gave a really good salute, as though to prove that he was a professional soldier and not one of those young politicians who put in a year or so of staff-work as a qualification for office. Then he smiled with easy self-confidence, speaking directly to the Imperator.

'Good afternoon, Triumvir. I'm sorry to force your sentry, but this is urgent. I know you will remember me. You do, don't you? Vipsanius Agrippa. We met outside Perusia. I suppose I should have sent a messenger; but there's a war on, and I must talk things over with you.'

'Where on earth have you sprung from?' was all Lepidus could find to answer.

'From Tyndaris, a little harbour to the north. My fleet is inside it; but I haven't much of an army on shore, and it was quite a job to break through the Pompeians. Their cavalry is pretty slack, but I haven't a single horseman of my own. I came here on foot, over the hill. Perhaps you can lend me a mount to ride back.'

He looked round the room, smiling cheerfully.

'I'm in luck, to break in on a council of war. Now I can tell my news to all of you at once. First of all: we've just about won this war. My navy holds a secure base, and we can fetch over from Italy all the troops we need. Cornificius has three legions now, or what's left of them, on the far side of the lava-fields. He will struggle round Etna to link up with you in a day or two. Once Caesar and Lepidus are united, or perhaps I should say Lepidus and Caesar, Pompeius won't bother us for long. Now, Triumvir, can you spare me some baggage-mules, and a detachment of horse; or must I go on carrying all my supplies by boat?'

'What news of Caesar? Is he with you?' Lepidus asked anxiously.

'He's over in Italy now, but I expect him almost immediately. Oh, I see. Those rumours have reached you. Yes, it's true he was missing for a day and a night. He came ashore with Cornificius, and then decided to go back to the mainland. That meant crossing the strait in an open boat, and on the way he was chased by a pirate. But Caesar's Luck, you know. . . . He got safely away. The trouble was he had to jump ashore on a deserted beach, and

227

no one knew what had become of him. He spent the night among the rocks, with only his orderly for company. It's given him a beastly cold in the head, but otherwise he's none the worse. I suppose the pirates boasted that they had killed him. By the way,' he looked round the room again, this time without a smile, 'it's odd that the rumour should have reached you so quickly. Some of your men may be fraternising with the enemy. I should look into it, if I were you.'

'That's splendid news about my colleague,' answered Lepidus before anyone else could speak. This was politics again, not warfare; and in that he could hold his own with any young careerist from nowhere. Of course Eunomus had not been alone in exploring the possibility of a Pompeian alliance; probably half his officers had been negotiating on their own account with their opposite numbers in the Pompeian camp.

'I hope you will stay to dinner,' he went on, 'and afterwards we shall send you back with an escort of Numidian horse, fellows who will impress even soldiers straight from the City. If you like I shall come with you. Take a good look at my camp first, so that you know how much help you can count on. Later I would like to see your men. Muster-rolls do very well for paymasters; we fighting soldiers can plan better after we have seen the men on the ground.'

There were polite murmurs round the table as Agrippa took a stool and a servant hurried in with wine and cakes. Then Gallus shot out a question which had slipped clean out of Lepidus's recollection.

'What about the pirate fleet? I suppose, since your ships are in Tyndaris, the Pompeians are at the bottom of the sea?'

'Not yet,' Agrippa answered cheerfully. 'They are still bobbing about in the harbour of Messana. I dodged across when they weren't looking. But I am ready to fight them the next time they come out. In the end we must win. My crews get more handy every time they fight, and Caesar can build ten ships for every one that's sunk. Sicily by itself can't take on the rest of the civilised world. In the end the pirates will sail away to go plundering somewhere else.'

'I see,' Gallus said curtly. 'But in the meantime we are cut off on this island.'

As the council of war trooped out to dinner Agrippa was surrounded by eager questioners, anxious to hear the latest gossip from Rome.

That afternoon Lepidus the great Triumvir, commander of fourteen war-hardened legions, rode over with the young legate to inspect this chance reinforcement. In his mind nothing was as yet settled. Caesar seemed to be on the way out; himself he could not win a victory, even over the scratch forces of a shady pirate; his young admiral was a careless optimist, who dodged the hostile fleet instead of fighting it. Yet Caesar had enormous resources. The great Popular party served him with devotion, and he ruled all the good recruiting-grounds. A time might come when it would be prudent for Lepidus to break with the ambitious, bloodthirsty, incompetent boy; for the present the alliance might as well continue.

At dusk he rode back to his camp, alone save for the impressive escort of Numidian horse. He was even more undecided than when he set out. Since the campaign opened Agrippa's troops had been soundly trounced every time they met the enemy. They were good soldiers, picked men, sons of the legionaries who had conquered the civilised world; they still appeared brave and willing, though shabby and underfed. But there was something in the way they held themselves, even on a ceremonial parade in the presence of a Triumvir, which showed that they expected to be beaten again the next time they went into battle.

For the present, of course, they were loyal to the magic name of Caesar. But if the boy exposed them to defeat after defeat, and at the hands of a disreputable enemy, they would in time begin to look for a luckier commander. On the spot there was a successful, prudent, victorious and solvent leader, who would welcome them to his Eagles.

He had watched the legate Laronius lead out a detachment, to link up with Cornificius who was supposed to be fighting his way across the lava-fields of Etna. Some men were barefoot when they set out, none were shod to march over lava. Pompeius had only to delay Cornificius, and thirst would drive the remnant of three legions to surrender. Would Caesar's prestige survive yet another disgraceful defeat, especially when you remembered that he had first landed with Cornificius and then fled back to the safety of Italy?

By the time he was in his bath, with hot steam taking the stiffness out of his riding-muscles, Lepidus had made up his mind to postpone the issue. If Cornificius were destroyed he would at once open negotiations with Pompeius; if Laronius brought in the stragglers the Triumvirate might yet survive. In that case he would see Caesar privately, and tell that conceited young man some of the home truths which had been bottled up in his breast ever since that ghastly interview among the butchered corpses of Perusia.

Three days later Laronius marched by the Lepidan camp, escorting the rescued survivors of the journey over the lava-

229

fields. The walls of Messana, and the nearby entrenchments of Plinius, were hung with laurels in gratitude for victory; Agrippa also decorated his camp, and sacrificed in gratitude for the victory granted to him. Puzzled, Lepidus asked Crastinus to find out what had really happened, out there among the petrified streams of lava.

Well supplied with secret-service money, the orderly invited a few veterans from Agrippa's praetorian cohort to an all-night drinking-party. Next morning he reported in good shape, except for foul breath and a bleary eye; what he had been told was still fresh in his mind.

'Both sides claimed a victory, sir, as you may remember; and it seems to me that for once both sides were right. Those three legions were in a very bad way, short of food and sleeping in the open; now the Eagles, and a fair proportion of the men, are safe with the legate Agrippa. That's a victory for Caesar, though not a very glorious one. But those imitation legions of Pompeius, Sicilians and pirates and mongrels all pretending to be Roman soldiers, they also have something to celebrate. They met real Romans, the pick of Caesar's cohorts; and before the day was ended they had seen their backs. That's a bit of a surprise, isn't it, sir? I think the Pompeians were as surprised as anyone. As far as I can make out, this is how it happened.'

He collected his thoughts and began again, scoring the table-top with a thickened thumbnail.

'Cornificius was *here,* by the coast; and the Pompeians were waiting for him *here,* on the far side of the lava. That's a stretch of only eight miles, but it took the Caesarians two days to cross it. They tell me the country is unbelievably rough, and the lava is all sharp edges that cut your feet to ribbons. To make things worse, there's no water. Well, Cornificius set out, and on the first day covered about six miles. By night fall his men were all in, and they had to sleep where they lay; no baggage, no blankets, no firewood to cook a meal. No water, either, of course, except what they carried with them. But they are good men and well trained; they didn't open their bottles until the tribunes gave them permission. On the second day it was hotter than ever, and the going still so rough that they must use their hands. Presently they could see the edge of the lava-field, and beyond it a spring of fresh water. Of course when they saw it they drank all they had left in their bottles. Then five cohorts of Pompeians suddenly took post round the spring. So the three legions, or what was left of them found themselves with empty bottles and a battle to fight before they might drink again. . . .

'You know, sir, how it can go in an army. One minute everyone's slogging along, grumbling, but obeying the last order and not bothering about what the next order will be; then in a flash everyone loses hope, and even the legate can't get himself obeyed. That's what happened when they saw they must fight for their water. Cornificius ordered them to deploy for attack; they just sat down and told him they were too tired and thirsty to go any farther. Tribunes drew their swords and centurions banged about with their cudgels; but the troops wouldn't budge. Cornificus saw there was nothing for it but to surrender. He was briefing envoys to go over and get in touch with the Pompeian commander when suddenly the enemy retreated. So his men scrambled forward and had their drink. Then they formed up again, as right as rain.'

Crastinus paused again, for effect.

'At the last minute that silly Pompeian amateur soldier had thrown away all his advantage. He saw Laronius coming up behind him, and thought he was being encircled in some deep Caesarian trap. Instead of hanging on to the spring to the last man and the last javelin, as any professional officer would have done, he disengaged to a flank, at a fast double. If he had held his ground for an hour he might have gone home with three captured Eagles. As it was, he attacked the Caesarian rearguard when they were safely past him. Cornificius's men broke, shamefully. They would have scattered all over Sicily; but Laronius and his fresh troops stood firm while they rallied. As I see it, the net result is this: Cornificius has saved his three Eagles; but the men who march with them are not worth having in any decent army.'

'Do you think all Caesar's troops are unwilling to fight?'

'Perhaps, sir. It's hard to say. I was drinking with old soldiers, veterans who know that there's nothing more dangerous than to run away in blind panic. They would never break ranks, though if things looked very bad they might kill their officers and go over to the enemy. But Caesar's new recruits are not the stuff they were in my young days. I wouldn't trust them. Anyway, the Caesarian army can't compare with *our* legions. They have been beaten so often that they expect to be beaten next time. If they turned against us we could wipe the floor with them.'

'That's most interesting. Thank you, Crastinus. You understand that these Caesarians are our loyal allies, and that shoulder to shoulder we shall overcome Pompeius? There's no question of war between Caesar and myself. All the same, it's comforting to know that my army is the strongest in these parts.'

Lepidus had planned a quiet day, an inspection of his troops and then a really long bath to keep him fit in this more than

African heat. But by noon a message had been received from Agrippa, and there was another tactical movement to be arranged.

Politically the most important news was that soon Caesar would join his soldiers in Tyndaris. He professed himself eager to meet his fellow-Triumvir; there was much to be discussed between them. Lepidus hastened to send back a polite acceptance, but he did not propose a date for the interview. He was still not sure about the line he would take with this young puppy, whose sole asset was his lucky name; but obviously there would have to be an adjustment of their relative positions. The conqueror of Sicily could not remain the subordinate of a young man who had lost three fleets in two years.

A second dispatch had been composed by Agrippa on his own initiative. Spies had informed him that reinforcements were due to reach the Pompeians in Messana. Titienus, a veteran Optimate who had been lucky enough to escape from Perusit, had levied some irregular cohorts in the south-west of the island; he would try to slip past the blockade to join the main Pompeian army. Agrippa hoped to ambush him in the hills. As he explained, this Optimate band was not of great military importance. But a small tactical success would raise the spirits of his own legions, who had not yet won a single skirmish; and for many years a stake had been waiting in the Forum for the head of Titienus. He enclosed a sketch-map to illustrate his contemplated movement, and trusted the Triumvir would render any assistance necessary.

'He wants to be sure we are still at war with Pompeius,' said Gallus as soon as he had read the dispatch. 'A clumsy way to find out, but then Agrippa is not very bright. Caesar's boyfriend, twenty-five years of age, and they give him supreme command of both army and navy! Love will be the ruin of the service! But we may as well humour him for the present. Our men will enjoy killing Optimates. It will remind them that even this petty war is being fought for liberty. Let me have a look at that map. We ought to send a detachment to save our gallant allies, before Titienus chases them halfway up Etna.'

Unfortunately the map was no help at all. However it was turned it would not fit the broken hill-country in plain view from the camp.

'If it was Antonius I'd say he had sent us the wrong map,' said Gallus pettishly. 'But Agrippa is a painstaking methodical ass. He must believe this thing represents the hills round Messana. I suppose a few scouts fudged it up in the canteen, and persuaded their innocent commander that they had ridden over these imaginary hills and valleys. Well, there it is. Titienus will get through, and Agrippa will lose himself. I suppose we must

232

send out patrols to find him, before all his men fall over a cliff.'

Lepidus was glad to agree. It was heartening to see that his own subordinates estimated the allied army so justly. If, during the coming interview with young Caesar, he was driven to the crudity of uttering threats, the attitude of his men would make those threats convincing. But it was unlikely that things would reach that stage. Caesar had been eight years in politics, and with that experience he would yield to overpowering force before a sword had to be brandished before his eyes.

In the evening Eunomus crept in to talk over the future. Lepidus was feeling cheerful, after a good dinner and a good bath; and at last the weather was breaking, after the hottest summer within living memory. Thick clouds, laced with lightning, promised rain and blessed coolness.

'That ambush out in the hills will get very wet,' said Eunomus with a titter. 'But I suppose all Caesar's men are expert swimmers. They must be, to have survived so many shipwrecks. I shall sleep the sounder for thinking of them splashing about in the mud.'

'It's of no importance, only a small detachment,' answered his patron. 'But I want to go over with you what I shall tell Caesar when we meet. So listen carefully.'

'Now,' he continued, lolling back in his couch and rubbing his hands, 'I want to continue the Triumvirate, if Caesar shows himself reasonable. If I begin making changes at the top all sorts of obscure politicians will harbour absurd ambitions, and before we know where we are there will be another civil war. So Antonius, Caesar, and myself will continue to direct affairs. Antonius is the greatest soldier in the world, and if it came to fighting he would beat me. That's the first stone of my foundation. But the second stone is that Antonius seeks plunder, not power. He can be bought, and I can afford to buy him. The third stone is that I am now more powerful than Caesar. Yet Caesar is still the much-loved head of the Popular party. So Caesar remains my colleague.'

'You might give him Africa, my lord,' sniggered Eunomus.

'He can't stay in Rome, certainly. But I would like to keep Africa as well as Italy. After all I did in Utica they will want me to stay. Caesar can have the barbarous provinces, Gaul and Spain. The Druids of Gaul practise human sacrifice, so they will like to be governed by the hero of Perusia.'

'Ha ha, very witty, my lord. Mind you repeat it in the Senate. We must keep on reminding Rome that young Caesar is a savage. People forget these things very quickly.'

He continued, in a wheedling tone: 'Can you find some little corner in your government for Sextus Pompeius? He is a gallant young man, and the best sailor alive. Before this war began he had been promised a Consulship. If you made him proconsul in Cilicia he would get on very well with the inhabitants, and in Rome the surviving Optimates would be gratified to see the son of their old leader forgiven and prospering.'

'He's not the kind of man I could take for a colleague. He tried to starve his own City. There can never be a place for him in Rome. But there is no blood-feud between us. Let him make his peace with Antonius and live quietly in the east.'

'Is that the best you can offer, my lord? Exile, without even a propraetorship to give him standing among the provincials?'

'That's all, and even then I am being generous. He has spilled too much Roman blood. I know you admire him, but I don't. And in a few days I shall be supreme ruler of the world.'

'Very well, my lord. You are just and merciful, and Sextus Pompeius deserves no more than bare life. I shall not intercede for him again. What will you do with Caesar? Will you order him to resign his command here in the island, or will you take him with you to Rome and get your new government confirmed by the Senate?'

'You've got it in the wrong order, my Eunomus. I shall be more careful. My interview with Caesar must come *before* I crush Pompeius. Then, if Caesar proves awkward, I can combine with Pompeius against him. Even the most conceited young man must give way before that threat.'

'Masterly, my lord! You will be a mighty ruler. When will you hold this interview with your unfortunate colleague?'

'I don't know. Probably in a day or two. They tell me Caesar is about to visit Sicily.'

Lepidus had been misinformed; Caesar was already in the island. He had himself led out the detachment which was to cut off Titienus. Thanks to the inaccurate map he had missed him, and was wandering with his men among the tangled hills. In an urgent message he asked his colleague to join him immediately, to concert further action against Pompeius.

'What's the weather doing?' asked Lepidus, when at last he had been roused. 'If it's still raining I shall wait for the storm to pass. It's five years since Caesar bothered to see me. He can wait a few hours longer.' He turned over and went back to sleep.

By mid-morning the sun shone from the blue sky, and the air was pleasantly fresh. Riding gently through a charming landscape, surrounded by his vivid escort of Numidian horse, Lepidus had to check himself from singing aloud. It was hard to

234

keep a dignified gravity while the mastery of the world fell into his lap.

He found the drenched Caesarians amid the rivulets of a streaming hillside. For lack of dry fuel, they were munching uncooked oatmeal from their haversacks. Their leader, that young coxcomb, affected to share the hardships of his troops as though he were a second Alexander. He sat on a wet boulder under the Capricorn flag which was his personal standard; except this standard and a couple of weary sentries, nothing indicated his headquarters. Even though his name was Caesar, he was just a young man sitting shivering in a bog.

Yet his self-assurance was unimpaired. He sat calmly watching the approach of his colleague, and only at the last moment rose to greet the Pontifex Maximus. Then he slumped down again on his rock, leaving Lepidus to stand until a trooper brought the leather travelling chair that was stamped with Eagles.

At last Caesar spoke. 'I expected you at dawn. You are late, but here you are at last. Now we must plan a joint attack. It's time your army did something. How soon can you mount an assault on the walls, to co-operate with my naval attack on the harbour?'

With a great effort Lepidus controlled his rage, to answer quietly. It would be undignified to quarrel openely in the presence of the troops. 'You abandoned three of your Eagles on Etna. If they were saved it was not by you. My army has conquered nine tenths of Sicily while your men were falling into the sea. But we are fighting for Rome, and must all do our best. If you try again I shall help you, as before. Perhaps this time your sailors will not run away from the pirates.'

It seemed as though Caesar had not heard him. The cold young face remained unmoved.

'Three days hence, on the 3rd of September, my new fleet will challenge the Pompeians to battle. Pompeius must come out and fight, because his men will insist on it. Soon Messana will fall, and they can escape only by sea. They dare not see the straits held by a hostile fleet. This time I think I shall win. Agrippa had to learn, like anyone else; but now he knows. There isn't time to bring my legions to the landward walls of Messana. When we destroy the pirate fleet you must immediately assault the town.'

He hesitated, said 'Excuse me' most politely, and fell over in a faint.

His orderly bustled up with a wine-flask. 'Here, Imperator Caesar, drink this. Rub his hands. Get his head between his knees. There, that's better. Pile on the cloaks and he'll soon be sweating.'

'You see, my lord,' he added to Lepidus, 'our Imperator has such a high fever he hardly knows what he's doing. He's not strong, and last night's storm nearly finished him. There's no shelter on this hillside, and the ground was too wet for him to lie down. He stood right through the night, while we kept the rain off him by holding shields over his head. But he's Caesar. He'll be up again in a minute, and conquering Messana in a few hours.'

'I am sorry to learn he is unwell. This is not the time to bother him with a conference, but of course I did not know that when I set out. Now I shall leave him, to recover at his leisure. As soon as I reach my headquarters I shall send out a litter with my personal physician, and a jar of really good wine.'

As he rode back to camp Lepidus felt more joyful even than in the morning. The heat, the drought, the flies would be back again in a few days, long before the sick man could recover; Sicily was notoriously unhealthy, the grave of many great armies. It seemed unlikely that the butcher of Perusia would ever see Rome again.

His self-confident elation lasted for two whole days, and then things happened so quickly all around him that he felt himself losing control of events. That had always been his weakness. If he had plenty of time he could reach a wise decision; but if people shouted into his ear, beseeching him to give orders at once, he was inclined to lose his head in the flurry.

He was awakened at dawn on the 3rd of September with news that the pirate fleet could be seen putting to sea. The enemy might be planning to land behind his lines, and he prudently ordered his whole army to stand to before he snuggled down again among the pillows. By midday everyone in the camp knew that a desperate sea-battle was being fought to the northward. Look-outs on high ground could see squadrons of ships charging against one another, beak to beak, and single galleys crawling, crippled, out of the *mêlée*. For the last century and more there had been a standard pattern of warship. Though the pirates were said to be faster and lighter, and the Italian vessels more strongly built, at long range no one could tell them apart. If common gossip was to be believed even experienced seamen made mistakes, and a ship was nearly as likely to be rammed by a consort as by an enemy. The most shortsighted soldier could make out that a great battle was being fought; the best eyes in the camp could not tell who was winning.

Two hours after midday the battle still raged. The legions showed themselves a little restive at being under arms for so long, and Lepidus gave orders that alternate cohorts might stand down for dinner, before mustering again to parade while their comrades ate.

All this time damaged pirate ships struggled back into the harbour, and others, hastily repaired, put out to join in the fight. With this perpetual coming and going no landsman could see which side was winning; the sea, right up to the horizon, was filled with charging ships. There seemed to be very little boarding. This was a classic sea-fight, in which the weapons were oars and the ram.

When only two hours of daylight were left the advanced picket sent back word that Plinius was leaving his camp. Lepidus was seated outside his headquarters, with his staff standing or sitting round him; they were all staring out to sea, and most of them had forgotten that there were still eight legions of foes encamped within a mile of them.

'Marching out, is he?' exclaimed Gallus. 'It's much too late in the day to offer battle, unless he is trying a sudden surprise attack. He can't be doing that. If his men are capable of any sort of scouting they must know we have been under arms, waiting for them, for the last eight hours.'

'A prudent precaution, that no sensible commander would neglect,' said Lepidus, nettled at the legate's tone. 'If the men think it an infliction to be kept on parade while a great battle is fought under their eyes, I don't know what the modern soldier is coming to.'

'Never mind the feelings of our men, Imperator,' answered Gallus, too excited to be respectful to his superior. 'It's what Plinius is feeling that interests me. Where's he going, if he isn't coming out to fight? H can't retreat without falling into the sea, and he won't try to give us the slip in broad daylight; though I have been afraid he might try dodging round to the west again. Where else can he go? By Jove, I think I've got it! Pompeius is beat, and the pirates are running for the eastern sea. So Plinius thinks it time to dodge into Messana and negotiate his surrender from the cover of stone walls!'

'That's it,' shouted a tribune. 'Look, I can see his van. He is making for the town. Imperator, now's our chance! Tell the trumpeters to blow "Hot Pursuit". If we catch up with his rearguard we may win a gate before they can shut it, and sack Messana by nightfall.'

'Nothing of the sort. I command here,' said Lepidus decisively. 'We don't want a lot of Romans killed after the war has been won. If the pirates are beaten the town must fall. We shall get just as much plunder if we let them negotiate a peaceful surrender. When Plinius has all his men inside the walls our legions may dismiss. Patrol forward, and pass back any envoys straight to this hut. We ought to be hearing from Agrippa also, if he has really won a victory. Keep a look-out for his messengers. I shall go and bathe before supper.'

The messenger of victory arrived first. By sunset a salt-stained marine was telling his story to a group of interested senior officers. The written message he brought was short, but informative: Agrippa reported that he had sunk twenty-eight pirate ships, and captured no less than 163, for the loss of three Caesarian ships sunk and none captured. The victory was final and overwhelming, though Pompeius himself had escaped into Messana.

'But it's not over yet,' said Eunomus, who was so excited that he had come to rub down his master after the bath as though he were still a slave valet and not a freedman secretary. 'There is still a Pompeian army. Plinius leads eight legions. We don't know Caesar's strength on land, but we do know that his soldiers are most remarkably unsuccessful; they must be feeling discouraged. Pompeius might still attack the camp at Tyndaris and snatch a victory; he might even kill Caesar. Of course, if you combine with Caesar, Pompeius won't have a chance. But if you keep out of the battle you can make what terms you please with the victor.'

'I shall fight if I must, and negotiate if I can,' answered Lepidus. 'That's a good motto for the commander of any army. But Pompeius can never fill Caesar's place. Remember their names, and what they stand for. Of course, as a Greek you can't see that. I think Caesar will beat Pompeius single-handed, but if he is losing I must strike in to help him. The government needs Caesar's name, to keep the troops in order; and thanks to his misadventures on this campaign young Caesar is now definitely below me. He will remain a Triumvir, but second to Aemilius Lepidus.'

'Very well, my lord. I think you are missing a chance. You know I have a weakness for Pompeius, and not only because he used to bribe me. He is a better ruler of Greeks than most other Romans, the Romans who have been educated in Rome. But whichever colleague you choose I shall be secretary to the ruler of the world. I should be a fool if that prospect were not enough to content me.'

'That's so,' Lepidus answered lazily, wriggling with pleasure as his skin tingled from the rubbing. 'Whoever wins at Tyndaris must make his terms with Lepidus. A comforting thought. I wonder what in fact Pompeius will do next?'

238

The whole army wondered, throughout the evening. On normal days the trumpets blew 'Lights Out' an hour after dark, and except for sentries the camp slept. Tonight the men would be too excited to rest, and at any moment they might be called into action. Orders went out that every soldier was to remain fully armed, though the men might dismiss and sit round their cooking-fires.

The senior officers remained at headquarters, lounging and drinking. After such a great sea-battle in the day, surely something would happen tonight? Pompeius was a man of quick decisions adept at snatching victory from defeat. by all the rules he should have been finished when the Divine Julius smashed his army at Munda, ten years ago; and here he was, still the most dangerous adversary of the Triumvirate. He would beat all comers, or combine with one Triumvir against the other. Certainly he would not sit down to endure a hopeless siege of Messana.

They lay on their couches, sipping wine and exchanging conjectures, while Lepidus in the highest place let his thoughts wander to the improvements he would decree when he ruled in the City. About midnight, when Agrippa arrived, he was received with congratulations on his glorious victory. But there was a note of patronage in the felicitation. Agrippa was Caesar's favourite, and that made him a very great man; but his hosts were the favourites of the mighty Lepidus.

Agrippa brought news of Caesar, who seemed to be flitting about the theatre of war more like an unlooker than an commander. Of course the poor young man suffered from deplorably weak health; but it was odd, almost un-Roman, that he was always somewhere else when there was fighting to be done. He was now with the main body of his army at Naulochus. The object of Agrippa's visit was to implore Lepidus not to negotiate with Pompeius until Caesar could join him.

There had been hard fighting in the sea-battle, and a new type of fighting-castle, designed by Agrippa, had worked very well. There was plenty to talk about.

They were still talking about it, or rather listening to Agrippa, when the envoys arrived. The callers were a deputation of Roman citizens resident in Messana, and they came properly dressed in their togas, bearing herald's staffs. It would be more natural for Pompeius to send an officer, if he feared to trust his own person to the conventional immunity of a herald. At sight of these civilians every politician in the room began doing sums in his head.

Agrippa seemed to expect that he would be included in this

delicate negotiation; but Lepidus summoned the chief spokes-man to confer with him privately in his office. There he came bluntly to the point. 'Who sent you? Show your credentials,' said he.

'This document, my lord, bears the common seal of Messana. I come in the name of the town council, fully empowered to negotiate on their behalf. Here, in addition, is a tablet sealed by the legate Plinius; his military tribunes have scratched their initials on it. I speak for the garrison as well as for the citizens.'

'But not for Pompeius?'

'Pompeius has deserted us. Under cover of darkness he sailed away, with seventeen ships only. The sailors had thrown their fighting-castles overboard to go faster. They are out of the war. Pompeius told us he would sail east and make his peace with Antonius. We in Messana are masterless men, who now seek protection from the rulers of Rome.'

'That includes Plinius and his eight legions?'

'They are the most eager for peace, Imperator. If you will send him a safe-conduct Plinius will come to your headquarters at dawn.'

'Then for the moment there is no more to be said. I shall draft an ample safe-conduct, and you will take it back.'

The envoy began to declaim an elaborate plea for mercy to his unfortunate fellow-townsmen, coerced into rebellion despite their overwhelming loyalty to Rome. Lepidus cut him short.

'Don't bother me now. If you leave the written version I shall glance through it at my leisure. I am curious to know the stan-dard of rhetoric you attain in Sicily. What matters tonight is the attitude of the soldiers. Provided they are willing to surrender no one need be hurt.'

'Unless our own garrison sacks the town before your men can enter it. I beg you, Imperator, send a few cohorts to keep order.'

'I can't do that. I won't have my men blundering into a hos-tile fortress in the dark. Someone would start a skirmish, and then I must exterminate eight legions of foot, up and down the alleys of a populous seaport. It would cost more lives than were lost at Cannae. Take your safe-conduct and be off with you.'

That was the way to do it. Short, sharp, and decisive, as was fitting when the ruler of the world conferred with wretched pro-vincials. Besides, Agrippa would be poking his nose in unless the deputation returned to Messana at once.

There was nothing more to be done until dawn. Lepidus sent word to the supper-party that he was turning in for what re-mained of the night. But since pirates were quite capable of mak-ing a surprise attack under cover of negotiations he sent orders

that the troops must remain under arms. That brought Gallus
into his bedroom, to protest that he was working his men too
hard. They were willing to fight, but these incessant parades
while the leaders negotiated made them surly. If they must stay
up all night they would face it more cheerfully if the Imperator
walked down the ranks and perhaps addressed them. Lepidus
replied with severity that grave issues of peace and war hung in
the balance, and that the brain of a Triumvir was a precious
instrument; mere swordsmen, spared the necessity of thinking,
could carry out their orders just as well when feeling drowsy.

As he pulled the coverlet over him he wondered whether he
had been too unsympathetic. But no, it was sensible to begin as
he meant to go on. He was much more important than these
common soldiers, a different sort of man altogether. He must get
it into their heads that he was different, so that they would pass
on to the general public some of the awe with which he inspired
them.

Three hours later he awoke, feeling much worse than if he had
not slept at all. Perhaps it would have been wiser to follow the
example of Antonius to sit up all night drinking with the troops.
But Plinius was waiting for him as promised; the prospect of
gunning eight legions would make any commander feel alert.

Plinius Rufus was a tough, capable, wary veteran, with the
formal manners of the lesser Optimate gentry. These formal
manners were not especially courteous, for the ancestors had been
boorish and proud of it; but an old-fashioned patrician knew
where he was with a man of that stamp. They quickly got down
to business.

First Plinius must make it clear that he was not a deserter.
Pompeius had abandoned his army, giving his subordinates a
free hand to make terms for themselves. Plinius might have surrendered as an individual, leaving his troops to shift for themselves. But he felt a personal responsibility for these men, who
had stuck gallantly to their Eagles even when faced with the
mighty army of Africa. They were good soldiers, who could
march and dig when they were tired; which every veteran admits
to be more difficult than dying gloriously in clean clothes with a
full stomach. It would be a tragedy if such men were to flee into
the hills, to end as crucified brigands.

Lepidus granted all that.

'Therefore, Imperator,' Plinius continued, 'I ask you to send
me back to Messana bearing a message of hope for these brave
soldiers. Permit me to tell them not only that they have been
granted quarter; let me add good news as well. Let me tell them
that there is room for them in the army of Lepidus the Triumvir,

16                                    241

the great army whose strength they withstood so manfully for sixty days. Accept them into your service, as they stand: eight war-hardened legions, grouped in their cohorts, obedient to their officers. If you wish them to surrender their arms they must do so; they cannot resist your might. But such soldiers are worthy of a better fate than captivity. If you permit, by nightfall the piratical trident on their banners will have yielded place to the African lion. They will swear, on the Eagles your mercy has saved from profanation, to live and die faithful followers of Aemilius Lepidus.'

'What did they swear to Sextus Pompeius?'

'The same oath, I grant you. They did not break it. He did. He fled, leaving his soldiers leaderless. They are worthy of a better leader. You will find them worthy of the army of Africa.'

'And I shall have twenty-two legions instead of fourteen. A numerous army, but Rome can support it. By the way, are your men paid up to date, or do you look to me to make up the arrears owed by Pompeius?'

'Their pay is months in arrears, Imperator, as indeed is my own. We are all penniless, and I don't see how we can march until we have a little money. But I don't expect you to pay us out of your own purse. I have thought of a means by which we can be supplied.'

'The pirate treasure? That belongs to the African legions, who have won it in fair fight.'

'It is a great treasure. There will be enough for all. Consider, Imperator. Our faithless leader sailed at a moment's notice, with only a few ships. He cannot have taken all his hoard with him. But there is more than his hoard. For years Sicily has preyed on the rest of the world; every merchant and landowner received his share. As we withdraw before your victorious advance the rich sent their gold and silver to Messana. Every house in the town is stuffed with plate. Let my men mark their return to their true allegiance by the plunder of those rebellious provincials. Then your army will be reinforced by eight legions of contented soldiers.'

'But my fourteen legions will be disappointed. They have already spent the plunder of Messana, sure it must come to them. However, those townsfolk are doomed to be plundered, by one army or another. It serves them right, for getting mixed up in a rebellion. . . . Well, Plinius, I shall trust you. We'll strike a bargain. Before the sack begins your men must throw open all the gates of the town. Then my troops can join them; and I hope you are telling the truth when you say there is enough for all. But this must be done today, as soon as you leave me. Otherwise we shall

242

have Caesar bringing over his army from Naulochus, and no town can make *three* armies rich.'

Plinius looked worried. 'I had forgotten Caesar. I didn't know he was so near. When I have made my peace with you I suppose Caesar will consider me a friend? Does your seal bind him?'

'It will, my worthy legate, even if at this moment it doesn't. Tell your men not to fret about that. When he sees the army of Africa with twenty-two eagles in line Caesar will be most friendly.'

'Of course, Imperator. Whatever you say. Then shall I go back at once to put these terms to my men? They will accept, I know; and when you see the gates thrown open your army may enter and be welcomed.'

'That's right. And don't be greedy. Leave my men a few virgins as well as the silver. Remember, we chased you from Lilybaeum to Messana, and we have fourteen legions to your eight.'

Lepidus was uneasily aware that he had just concluded a really dastardly bargain; it seemed easier to carry it off on a swashbuckling note.

The moment Plinius had left Agrippa bustled in, without asking permission. His manner was barely respectful, as he stood stiffly before the Imperator's desk.

'What's this I hear, sir?' he said, without waiting for leave to speak. 'Is it true that you have granted terms to the pirates? This matter concerns Rome, not Africa. They must surrender to the ruler of Italy. It is not at all certain that Caesar will grant quarter to every man in their ranks. They have among them some dangerous Optimates, who escaped the proscription.'

'Legate, you forget yourself,' answered Lepidus, speaking with all the gravity of a patrician and pontifex. 'Loyalty to your commander has made you insubordinate, and because loyalty is a virtue I pardon your lack of respect. But let me hear no more of this. The civilised world is governed by three equal rulers. Any one of us may decide in the name of the Three. I have granted quarter, and my decision cannot be altered.'

'But, Imperator, Caesar is quite close; at Naulochus, only a day's journey from here. Of course I don't deny your right to do what you have done, and if my manner was disrespectful I apologise. But it's only a delay of one day. When Caesar has arrived you and he together can decide what is to be done with the rebel army.'

The young man was doing no more than his duty. Of course he could not sway the mind of a great Imperator, but a magnanimous reply would be even more crushing than an outburst of temper. Lepidus smiled gently as he spoke,

'Come, Agrippa. Which of us has overthrown the rebel army? Yesterday you destroyed the pirate fleet, and again I congratulate you on your prowess. But when you captured all those ships, did you pause to consult me before dealing with their crews?'

The young man pulled himself together, and spoke respectfully in reply.

'Imperator, whatever may be the form of the Triumvirate enacted by the Senate and People, Rome is ruled by Caesar. You ought to consult with him.'

That was the last straw. Courtesy was wasted on this oaf, too stupid and too ill-bred to recognise political realities unless they were put into plain words.

'Caesar does not rule the whole world. By pure luck he acquired a famous name, to which his blood does not entitle him. Today he may be ruling in Rome. But I rule here in Sicily, and tomorrow I shall rule Rome also.'

'It is hard to foretell the future. . . . ' Agrippa began.'

'But easier for the Pontifex Maximus than for most men,' Lepidus cut in. 'Be off with you, young man, before one of us says something he will regret afterwards. Now that the fighting is finished I expect Caesar will visit your camp. Tell him I shall be delighted to receive him whenever he wishes to call.'

In the afternoon the gates of Messana were thrown open, and the legions of Africa flocked to share in the sack. Lepidus seized the opportunity for a leisurely bath between dinner and supper, to make up for his broken night. Just for the present, he had no troops to look after; during the next few hours any attempt to give orders would mean only the execution of good soldiers for mutinous conduct. The high command must keep out of the way until the men had recovered from their orgy.

Unpleasant sounds were borne on the wind even into the calm of headquarters: the screams of women and the crash of falling buildings. Dozing in his bath, Lepidus refused to hear them. No one was the richer for pushing over a temple, but there was a knack in knocking away the right column, and some of the men enjoyed it. On these occasions girls screamed at what was done to them, and older women at what they saw done to their daughters. But Messana was a legitimate prize of war, and the soldiers were receiving no more than their due. Luckily after the recent rain the place would not burn, and he had forbidden indiscriminate massacre. These Sicilians were really getting off very lightly; they had afforded a safe refuge to the pirates, and he would have been within his rights if he had sold them all as slaves. They should never have submitted to Pompeius in the first place.

While he was dressing for supper he was surprised to notice his orderly strolling outside. 'Hallo, Crastinus,' he called graciously. 'Aren't you missing some fun? The pirate treasure was stored in Messana, and there ought to be plenty for everybody.'

'Well, my lord, I have been your orderly for more than ten years. There are pickings in that. I don't need the plunder.'

'Even so, a sack has its amusing side. Don't you want to chase a few pretty girls?'

'I prefer them willing, my lord. But it isn't only that. I am a soldier by trade, like my father before me. I don't like seeing good soldiers go to pieces. It's one thing to fight your way over a wall, kill some men who are trying to kill you, and then help yourself to their silver and their daughters. That all goes together, if you take my meaning; and anyway at the time you feel like doing it. But marching in through an open gate to rob harmless civilians who have never fought anyone in their lives . . . there's something cold-blooded about that, so cold-blooded that it's disgusting. Our men haven't earned this plunder, and it will make them greedy instead of brave. Money for nothing never improved anyone. I wish I could have told you this before you permitted the sack. We had a very fine army. It will never be the same.'

'Don't be gloomy, Crastinus. Just because you and I are too old for this game, that doesn't mean the youngsters don't enjoy it.'

'Oh, some of them will enjoy it. The trouble is that they will be panting to do it again. Next time they may not wait for permission. You have put it into their heads that soldiers can be robbers, and that will make it easier for some other general to buy them. Plain speaking, my lord. But if you went down into the town you would hear plainer, and plenty of it.'

'No need to go there while I have an orderly. I'm glad you spoke frankly, but I think you are wrong. I came to soldiering late in life, and I've heard it said I'm too strict, an old-fashioned spoil-sport. No one can say that in future. Antonius himself could not have done more for his men.'

As Crastinus wandered off to drink in solitude at the canteen, the only soldier who paid for his wine that day, the orderly sighed. His Imperator aspired to be a freebooter like Antonius; but until he could march and fight like Antonius he ought not to imitate his failings.

By evening of the next day the army was back in camp, reinforced by eight legions of Pompeians. When the praetorians had beheaded two hard cases, and propped their headless bodies against the gate, the rest stopped singing rude songs about their officers and came back willingly. There were hardly any desertions; for it was raining again, and Messana now offered little shelter to a straggler.

In the morning a council of war assembled, to make plans for the future. The augmented army contained more than thirty senior officers; as he prepared to address the group, sitting in rows behind Gallus and Plinius, Lepidus imagined that he was once again making a speech in the Senate.

That was a familiar sensation; familiar also was the knowledge that he had not yet made up his mind what to propose. Oh well, a hasty decision need not be an unwise decision; an experienced politician should think on his feet, picking up pointers from the reactions of his audience.

But how on earth was he to break it to them that they must follow him to Rome and overthrow the government of Caesar? For one thing, they could not start until after months of preparation, probably not until next year. Agrippa's fleet commanded these waters. He must increase his own navy, gather transport and supplies, and collect enough money to give every man in the ranks a good bounty before opening the campaign. He had a sound head for business, and saw exactly what a mighty undertaking this would be. He had never expected to see the rivalry come to breaking-point. He had assumed that Caesar, that wary politician, would sense his own weakness at the first hint; the boy ought to be clever enough to yield gracefully before his supplanter was driven to threaten naked force. Lepidus maundered on, emphasising the need to hold the island securely as a loyal and prosperous base; but he was slow in coming to the point. Granted that they needed a base for their next campaign, who was to be their next enemy?

In the end Gallus drove him to it, interrupting to ask a direct question. 'Those Caesarians in Tyndaris, Imperator,' said he. 'Agrippa is pushing out his patrols all over the place. What happens if his men seek admission to a town garrisoned by us?'

'We refuse admission, and back our refusal by force if necessary,' Lepidus answered shortly. 'Furthermore, this morning I shall send a circular to every town-council in the island, informing them that they must surrender to our army, and that if they admit a Caesarian garrison I shall regard it as an act of war.'

'But my men thought they were surrendering to you and Caesar jointly,' cried Plinius. 'They saw the Caesarians destroy our fleet; that's what decided them to surrender. If they had known that by joining your army they were committed to war against Caesar they might have decided differently.'

'What else could you have done?' asked Gallus contemptu-

246

ously. 'You had to surrender. You were beaten.'

'We could have held Messana for two more days, until Caesar arrived to guarantee our safety. You don't think you could have got in yesterday if we hadn't opened the gates to you?'

'I'll walk through any gate you close, with a centurion's cudgel, not a sword. Your men are not even good enough to be pirates! If Pompeius had thought them worth deck-space he would have taken them with him.'

'Silence, both of you. I am speaking,' said Lepidus. 'We follow the same Eagles, gentlemen, and this is no time for quarrelling. It can't come to open war. When Caesar's men see what they are up against they will force their leader to negotiate. He is no soldier himself; otherwise he would have recognised the situation and sought a parley.'

At that moment envoys from Caesar were announced, come to seek a parley. The council adjourned, and Lepidus offered a prayer of thanks to the genius of the gens Aemilia for getting him out of this impasse so neatly.

The envoy was a messenger, not an ambassador. A mere trumpeter brought a letter proposing an immediate meeting, in the open country between Tyndaris and Messana. The man wanted only a plain answer, Yes or No, and would not discuss anything else. These were high matters, to be decided by Triumvirs; his orders were to deliver a letter and carry back the answer. After a few moments of indecision, Lepidus agreed to go to the meeting.

They met, briefly, that same afternoon; and almost at once Lepidus realised that he was wasting his time. Caesar could not grasp the fact that a new power had arisen in the world, that the army of Africa was stronger than the army of Italy. He began by giving orders, as though to an inferior. When this was countered by the reasonable proposal that he should take as his realm the barbarous west, conquered by his deified father, and leave Rome to the Pontifex Maximus, he answered as though the Pontifex Maximus were still a helpless fugitive outside Perusia. After that Lepidus did not bother to suggest that the two of them should share equally in the government of the City, the alternative which he had ready in case Caesar should show himself prepared to haggle, the bare minimum which a great Imperator might accept to bring the boon of peace to a shattered world. There was nothing for it but open war; if you could call it war when one side had a great army and the other a mere landing-party holding a little harbour.

That evening Lepidus supped with Gallus and Plinius, to begin working out the orders for an immediate attack on Tyndaris. While Agrippa ruled the sea there could be no question of an invasion of Italy; but a sudden assault might capture Caesar, and so end the war at a blow. The two legates were curiously unenthusiastic; they made all sorts of difficulties about boots and supplies, and explained that the troops needed rest after their exertions in Messana. Besides, Caesar might yet give in, when he had passed a few more days counting and recounting the twenty-two Eagles ranged against him. In the end Lepidus agreed to postpone his attack.

He went to bed early; but he could not sleep, for his thoughts were racing. His most faithful officers were reluctant to begin another civil war, and he must find a way of making his army angry with Caesar. That was very like the kind of problem he used to deal with in the old days, before the Divine Julius crossed the Rubicon. He must inflame his supporters until tempers were lost. Let me see, a well-publicised insult can do as much as an injury.

In his dream he was speaking from his bench in the Senate, delivering a more than Ciceronian Philippic at a shrinking culprit who had sometimes the face of Catilina, sometimes the face of young Caesar: when he was roused by Crastinus, urgently shaking his shoulder.

'Wake up, my lord. That Caesar has been making speeches to the Pompeians, and their eight legions are getting ready to desert our camp.'

'Caesar? How can that be? He's in Tyndaris. Never mind. Get my armour immediately. Years ago I addressed the troops in my nightshirt, and I've never heard the last of it. The men will see their Imperator in full dress, if it makes me late for my own funeral.'

'It's not as bad as that, my lord. It's only Plinius and his pirates; we are better without them. Our own army of Africa is thoroughly loyal, and we'll soon show those rascally Pompeians that they have picked the wrong side again.'

'But how did Caesar get in? The camp is at war, with gates barred.'

'Yes, my lord, but this is *Caesar*. No sentry would bar a gate against Caesar.'

'Listen. That little man was born Octavius. He's no more Caesar than you are.'

'My lord, he is Caesar, all the same.'

'What do you mean? I'm just beginning a war against him. Will my men refuse to fight?'

'Oh no, why should they? Fighting is their trade. But he is still Caesar. They won't harm his person.'

'I shall, for one; and so will you, Crastinus, unless you want to lose your head for disobeying a direct order from your Imperator. I am ready now. Take those javelins, and give me a couple.'

The streets of the camp were crowded with armed legionaries; though they milled about at random, since as yet no authority had ordered them on parade. Lepidus pushed his way to the eastern palisade, where the eight Pompeian legions had fortified an adjoining camp of their own. In this stream of disorder he was comforted to find an island of sanity. A century of the praetorian cohort, his own personal bodyguard, was drawn up in perfect order on the parade ground.

With praetorians clearing the way he made better speed to the eastern gate of the camp. Even in the dark he knew when he was approaching it, for great bonfires burned just within the palisade. They lit up the crowd of listening soldiers, and were reflected in the polished corselet of young Caesar.

The young man stood on a pile of ration boxes, alone save for his orderly. He was plodding through a set speech, with the routine gestures of the conscientious orator; though the crowd made such a noise that Lepidus could not hear what he was saying.

'Where's his bodyguard? Surely he didn't venture here alone?' he shouted to Crastinus.

'A few horse came with him as far as the gate, my lord. He left them outside,' was the shouted reply.

When Lepidus looked again he could make out a cluster of horsemen at the far edge of the circle of firelight. He saw also, in the same moment, a Pompeian Eagle lurching above the press, as it was carried from his camp. The sight enraged him. This was the Argenteus over again; no general could suffer his army to be stolen from him twice in a lifetime. He balanced a javelin in his right hand, then hurled it at that shining figure on the platform. As his hand came forward Crastinus also swung, and the two weapons hissed together through the air.

Caesar's orderly saw the flash of them in the firelight, and caught both on his great shield. But the centurion at the head of the praetorians had his wits about him. Seeing the example set by his Imperator he rapped out a command; a whole flight of javelins curved into the light.

Lepidus shuddered with mingled awe and relief. Even he felt it as something horrible that young Caesar, heir to the Divine Julius, should be struck down by the weapons of Roman soldiers. No orderly could protect his officer from such a volley; this act would end the war before it had begun.

Then he saw that an orderly could protect his officer from any danger, if he was willing to do his duty to the utmost. The Caesarian leapt in front of his commander, to receive in his own breast a sheaf of javelins. As he fell one last missile whirred past his head, gashing Caesar in the shoulder before it fluttered out of sight. Caesar clutched at the wound, then stood a moment motionless, staring at his bloody fingers. In a flash he had sprung from the platform, and dodged through the open gate behind him.

'We have shed the blood of Caesar,' someone called with a great bellow of anguish, and the cry was taken up by all that crowd of soldiers. Only the praetorians remembered their duty. A score of them charged through the open gate as the troopers of the escort galloped up to defend their lord.

The handbooks of tactics took it for granted that drilled foot could always withstand a charge of cavalry; but these praetorians were not formed in rank, and there were not enough of them. As the last of their plumed helmets sank out of sight some quick-witted Lepidan closed and barred the gate. As the wooden bar clanged home in its staple Lepidus looked out at the backs of galloping horsemen and felt himself secure, in his own camp, among his own legions.

Now the soldiers round the bonfire were shouting in unison.

'We have shed the blood of Caesar,' the screamed in a frenzy of self-accusation. Someone reopened the gate, and they streamed out after the retreating cavalry. With Crastinus at his side, Lepidus thrust himself into the gateway, trying to stem the tide of hysterical desertion. Looming above the helmets he saw the towering staff of an Eagle, unescorted, clutched precariously by a solitary Aquilifer. To see this sacred image thus desecrated was almost as painful to him as the desertion of his soldiers. As the Eagle came up with him he strove to wrest it from its bearer.

'Out of the way, fatty. All the Eagles of Rome follow Caesar, and shall until the ending of the world,' shouted the Aquilifer, an enormous bearded figure. The coarse hairs of his leopard-skin mantle rasped the Imperator's cheeks, and his lungs were choked with the stink of the half-cured pelt. Then he was sprawling on the ground, clutching with both hands at an agonising pain in his belly. But the Aquilifer, as much in contempt as in mercy, had thrust with the hilt of his sword, not the point; as the Eagle disappeared through the gate he knew that he must still decide for himself whether he should see another sunrise. Leaning on Crastinus, he limped back to his hut.

Three hours later he was still sitting on the edge of his bed, staring at his toes as they wriggled on the floor. As Crastinus entered he looked up, and saw with incurious surprise that the orderly wore full parade armour, with all his decorations.

'I thought you might be wanting me now, Imperator. There are no soldiers left in camp. The Nineteenth were the last to go, because they waited to do the thing in style. They marched out very smartly, with proper garlands on their Eagle and a full escort round it. Gallus led them, after inspecting the parade.'

'Have they all gone, even the cavalry? Those barbarians took oath to me personally, not to Rome. I would have thought them faithful.'

'They left only a moment ago, my lord; but that was because they waited for an answer to their message. They sent to ask Caesar whether they should bring your head with them, but Caesar said No. They were a little disappointed. So now it's all over, and time for us to be up and doing.'

'What do you mean?' asked Lepidus, in genuine puzzlement.

'An awkward thing to put into words, Imperator. I hoped you would be expecting me. Well then, where do you want it? In the throat or in the heart? I shan't hurt you; and if you feel lonely remember I shall be coming after.'

Lepidus struggled to his feet. So this was the end for which all his fifty-four years had been a preparation: a noble death, without whining or flinching, a death worthy of an Aemilius, the true Roman answer to irreparable disaster. It had come to many of the politicians with whom he had debated in the Senate: Cato, Metellus, Brutus, Cassius. Unless you were lucky enough to be killed in battle it was the natural consequence of defeat. And yet. . . .

He paused and hesitated. Finally he answered in a miserable voice.

'Twenty years ago I could have done it with my own sword. Ten years ago I would have bared my breast to you. But now it's too late. I'm fat and comfortable, and I enjoy the world. Sunshine is very pleasant, and soon there will be the laughter of my grandson. I'm getting on; whatever happens I shan't enjoy them much longer. It seems a pity to waste what is still left to me. If I behave humbly, Caesar may show mercy. You need not draw that sword.'

'Beg your pardon, Imperator, but I think you ought to take my advice. I must draw this sword anyway, to use it on myself. Did you ever hear of my uncle? Primipilus of the Tenth he was, senior centurion in the most famous legion that ever followed the Eagles. He took his discharge, but he came back as an unpaid volunteer for the war against Pompeius Maximus. When Caesar rode down the line in the morning of Pharsalus he stopped to chat with my uncle before the whole army. Uncle Crastinus

251

swore he would do something famous that day, even though it killed him. He was killed by a rear-rank Pompeian just as his century pierced the enemy line and the Optimates turned to flee. Caesar put it all down in that book he wrote, and while Caesar is remembered my uncle will not be forgotten. My family isn't noble, but we have our standards. Not one of us has ever surrendered. So you see, if you plan to surrender to young Caesar, it's time for me to leave you; and now it's so late there is only one way out of here.'

He continued, in a cajoling voice as though talking to a child.

'You ought to come with me, Aemilius Lepidus. The world we live in doesn't suit us. I stuck by you because I thought you were trying to change it, but now I see it has been changing you. That proscription, for instance; it wasn't worthy of your ancestors. I know that between us we saved your brother; even so, we shouldn't have been compelled to save him secretly. As for this Sicilian war, the whole thing makes me sick. You were gallant enough at Lilybaeum. As I told the boys, that proves you are more than just a bag of guts. But since then, what's happened? Armies on the march, but never any fighting; legates making rousing speeches while they haggle secretly with the other side; allies rejoicing in the defeat of their allies. I joined the army to protect the City and the provinces. Now all my mates, and the enemy too, think of nothing but sacking a Roman town which has already thrown open its gates. And you yourself, Aemilius Lepidus. You were brave once, but what of it? Who ever heard of a cowardly patrician? It was the least you could do. Since then you've grown so lazy and idle and greedy that all your soldiers have deserted you for a better man; and if it wasn't for my own private honour I would go with them. Young Octavianus isn't much of a warrior, but at least when it rains on his troops he gets wet with them. Your men stay on parade all day, because you can't be bothered to interrupt your bath to give the order to dismiss. The City was rotten before I was born, yet we could respect the army. Now the legions are rotten too, and so is my Imperator. If young Octavianus is the best Roman alive, and he is, it's time I joined the ancestors. Here goes. I always wondered why they made these fancy corselets so thin. Now I know.'

Crastinus whipped out his sword and reversed it, holding it near the point with the hilt towards the floor. As he flung himself forward the blade pierced the flimsy corselet to sink into his heart.

The cold calm figure of Caesar glowed splendidly in splendid armour, twenty-two Eagles grouped before him. He had listened attentively, but without change of expression. No onlooker could forecast what his answer would be.

He looked down at the grovelling creature who tried to clasp his boots.

'Let me remind you of what I said at Perusia,' he said. 'To kill the Pontifex Maximus is to incur bad luck. If you wish it, you may live. I hope you reach old age. Perhaps, as the years go by, you may begin to doubt whether today I have shown myself truly merciful.'

*Before her mirror the lady Clodia plucked out a few grey hairs. As she searched for them she muttered to herself. 'One from three leaves two, and it takes two to make a quarrel. Which will come out on top? Antonius would give more amusing parties, but I shall feel safer under Caesar.'*

# EPILOGUE
## 13 B.C.

The lady Clodia liked to be seen in the company of distinguished elder statesmen. Her notorious great-aunt had run after young aediles until the whole City was scandalised; but that was in the gay vanished days of the Republic. Though the Princeps was a stern guardian of morals, even he could not object if she asked a grey-headed Consular to walk beside her litter. When she ran into Balbinus outside the scent-shop she took him in tow. They were together when the funeral passed.

It was the sort of funeral you saw far too often nowadays. A line of ancestral masks that stretched out of sight, Consuls, Censors, Triumphators; the Vestals and all the priestly colleges; augors and haruspices and a few embarrassed elderly noblemen. But no throng of mourning citizens and no clients. This must be the burial of one of the old, superseded politicians; the government might be displeased if private individuals lent it the support of their presence.

When the bier came into sight Clodia gasped in surprise.

'Consul iterum, Imperator iterum, Triumphator iterum, and something very grand that I don't recognise in the religious line. Who on earth can that be? The Princeps isn't in mourning. I bowed to him half an hour ago. I thought only members of his family were allowed to be as grand as that.'

'Yes, who is it? Ah, that head-dress would tell you, if you knew your ritual as a Roman matron should. At last our beloved ruler can be Pontifex Maximus. I happen to know he's been hankering after the honour for years and years.'

'I see. Wiser not to mention names, in this crowd. The poor old man. . . . Did you ever meet him?'

'Only once, and that was years ago; just after Actium, in the year of my Consulship. They arrested his elder son for treason, and his wife as accomplice to the plot. A clear case, unfortunately; and as Caesar was still in the east I had custody of the prisoners. One day when I came out of court I saw a shabby old man hanging about. He looked like a gentleman, so I spoke to him. It turned out that he had been waiting all day to see me, but since he hadn't any money to bribe the doorkeepers they wouldn't let him in. It was Marcus you-know-who, the man on that bier. He wanted to put up bail for his family.'

'And what did you do?'

'Well, I couldn't resist reminding him that my name had been on his proscription-list, and that if I hadn't escaped to Sextus Pompeius he would be dealing with another Consul. That shook him up a bit. But after rubbing it in I felt I must do what I could for him.'

'Could you help?'

'Not much. We discussed the queer death of Sextus for a bit. I thought he might know the inside story, but he didn't. We agreed that Antonius never ordered the execution, but that whoever killed him when he was in flight from Messana did it thinking to please Antonius. That's as far as anyone will ever get. As regards his son, well, the Princeps ordered him to be sent out east for trial in his presence. They sent his ashes home. I was able to free the mother, though; a gallant old girl with enough dignity to make even a Consul feel small. The old boy himself was quite innocent. The real villain was a Greek freedman, a nasty type. But Eunomus died most amusingly in the arena, and that made everyone feel more lenient to the family. I didn't even ask bail for the mother, for I knew as well as the next man that her husband hadn't two pennies to rub together. By Jove, there she is, Junia, walking behind the body. Now there's a real matron for you. You don't see many of that kind nowadays.'

'No, the old days were better, weren't they, for all their civil wars?'

'Remember this funeral, Clodia. You are seeing the last of a bit of old Rome. Do you realise that when that corpse was a young man he had to persuade the citizens to choose him for office, against the competition of his equals? He began young, and he lived to be old. He must be the last of the true magistrates, the rulers elected by free men. When he was elected praetor there was no government to tell the citizens how they must vote. Only thirty-five years ago, and now it's all gone and forgotten!'

In his emotion, Balbinus forgot the spies of the secret police. He straightened himself, and raised an arm in greeting.

'Farewell, Marcus Aemilius Lepidus, praetor of a free City. That far you got on your own merits. Never mind the false honours that came after. Keep a good seat for me, wherever you are going. I shall join you very soon.'

The lady Clodilla prodded her litter-bearers to make them move on. Really it wasn't safe to be seen in the company of Balbinus. You never knew what he would say next.